JUBA!

More from Walter Dean Myers and HarperCollins*Publishers*

Monster: A Graphic Novel

Darius & Twig

The Get Over
(AVAILABLE AS E-BOOK ONLY)

Tags
(AVAILABLE AS E-BOOK ONLY)

Just Write: Here's How!

All the Right Stuff

We Are America:
A Tribute from the Heart
ILLUSTRATED BY CHRISTOPHER MYERS

Kick
COAUTHORED BY ROSS WORKMAN

Looking for the Easy Life
ILLUSTRATED BY LEE HARPER

Lockdown

Muhammad Ali:
The People's Champion
ILLUSTRATED BY ALIX DELINOIS

Dope Sick

Game

Ida B. Wells:
Let the Truth Be Told
ILLUSTRATED BY BONNIE CHRISTENSEN

The Harlem Hellfighters:
When Pride Met Courage

Street Love

Autobiography of My Dead Brother
ILLUSTRATED BY CHRISTOPHER MYERS

It Ain't All for Nothin'

I've Seen the Promised Land:
The Life of Dr. Martin Luther King, Jr.
ILLUSTRATED BY LEONARD JENKINS

Shooter

The Dream Bearer

Handbook for Boys: A Novel

Crystal

Patrol:
An American Soldier in Vietnam
ILLUSTRATED BY ANN GRIFALCONI

Bad Boy: A Memoir

Malcolm X:
A Fire Burning Brightly
ILLUSTRATED BY LEONARD JENKINS

Monster

Angel to Angel:
A Mother's Gift of Love

Glorious Angels:
A Celebration of Children

The Story of the Three Kingdoms
ILLUSTRATED BY ASHLEY BRYAN

Brown Angels:
An Album of Pictures and Verse

The Righteous Revenge
of Artemis Bonner

Now Is Your Time!: The African-
American Struggle for Freedom

The Mouse Rap

Scorpions

Tales of a Dead King

JUBA!

A NOVEL BY
WALTER
DEAN
MYERS

Amistad
An Imprint of HarperCollinsPublishers

Photo credits:
Pages v, 15, 22, 103, 138, 149, 154, and 166:
Courtesy of the Walter Dean Myers Archives
Page 133: Courtesy of the Harvard Theatre Collection,
Houghton Library, Harvard University
Pages 144 and 161: Courtesy of Library of Congress
Page 151: Courtesy of British Newspaper Archive
Page 195: Courtesy of General Register Office
Page 196: Courtesy of Register of St. Martin's
in the Fields Free Parochial Cemetery in Liverpool

Amistad is an imprint of HarperCollins Publishers.

Juba!

Library of Congress Cataloging-in-Publication Data
Myers, Walter Dean, 1937–2014.
    Juba! / Walter Dean Myers.
        pages   cm
    Summary: A young African American man tries to make it as a dancer in New
York's Five Points district and in England in the 1800s.
    ISBN 978-0-06-211271-2 (hardback)
    1. Lane, William Henry, approximately 1825–1852—Juvenile fiction. [1. Lane,
William Henry, approximately 1825–1852—Fiction.   2. Dancers—Fiction.   3. African
Americans—New York (State)—New York—Fiction.   4. Prejudices—Fiction.
5. Five Points (New York, N.Y.)—History—19th century—Fiction.   6. London
(England)—History—19th century—Fiction.   7. Great Britain—History—Victoria,
1837–1901—Fiction.]   I. Title.
PZ7.M992Jub   2015   2014042527
[Fic]—dc23   CIP
                                                                              AC

Typography by Erin Fitzsimmons
15 16 17 18 19   LP/RRDH   10 9 8 7 6 5 4 3 2 1

First Edition

Portrait of Juba

CHAPTER ONE

"It's not right," Stubby said. "That's all I have to say. It's just not right." Sunday morning, and Stubby Jackson was trailing after me, complaining.

"Stubby, I know it's not right, and you know it's not right, but what can you do about it? You told me they only need nine waiters to work a shift. Isn't that what you said?"

"That's not the point, Juba," Stubby said. "I'm the best waiter they got. And this is Saturday, so they're going to need the best. I should be one of the nine waiters. I was looking forward to working tonight because I need the money. Plus I got the cleanest shirts."

"You want to stop and watch this street party for a while?"

I asked. "It'll calm your nerves."

"Me working will calm my nerves!" Stubby said.

Mott Street was filled with people. There was a little band—an accordion, a drum, and a tuba—playing halfway down the block. Children were running through the crowds like ants, weaving in and out of the people selling meat pies and other foods from small carts. In front of the band some men were putting out chairs in a big square.

"They're probably going to make some speeches or something," Stubby said. "I don't want to hear any speeches. I don't know why people in New York City have to give so many speeches about how they want to change things. This is 1842, and if things haven't changed by now, they're not going to change."

"They're not about no speeches," I said. "Those are Jews, and I think they're going to dance. You ever see Jews dance?"

"I live in New York, don't I?" Stubby was pouting.

Some men in the street were forming lines, nothing too straight, just as if they were walking in rows, very casual. Then the little band started up. First the drum, beating out a rhythm that seemed off at first, but I could feel it was three-eighths time. The men moved toward the center of the chairs as the people around them began clapping along with the drum. Without a signal that I could see, the men took each other's hands and swayed together in a small group—but when they separated, they were in a circle.

"Stubby, you see how they formed that circle?"

"They look out for each other, that's what that circle means." Stubby still had his mad face on. "They all got jobs, I bet."

The men danced together in the circle, first going one way and then reversing. They all knew the steps, when to stop, when to change direction, when to pause and let their hands go. The dance wasn't much in the way of steps, and the rhythm was strange to me, but what made it work was how happy they looked.

"I wonder if something special happened, or is that just the way they always look when they're doing that dance?"

"I don't know anything about Jews," Stubby said. "Except there's a hundred and fifty things they don't eat. You know they won't touch oysters, right?"

"That has nothing to do with us," I said. "Lots of people don't eat oysters. I just like the way they dance."

"Why don't they dance with their women?"

"The women will get into it, after a while," I said. "They don't touch the men, but they dance in circles like the men do. I have never seen any Jewish people dancing and looking mean or sad. Maybe you should go over and dance with them. It'll cheer you up."

"Let's go on home," Stubby said. "I don't want to see any happy people today."

"If you want me to, I'll get a stick and beat myself on the way," I said.

3

Stubby mumbled something about people trying to stop his career and then mumbled some more just to be mumbling. He had his ideas about becoming the most famous cook in the world. All his plans were laid out, and they seemed to be reasonable, too. His big plan was to work at the Broad Street House restaurant and learn how to make all the dishes there, and then he was going to move into another restaurant as an assistant to the chef. The way he had it figured, everything would take him four years to complete, and by the time he was twenty-one, he would be the best cook in New York.

I liked Stubby. I liked anyone with a plan, but I couldn't be sure of my own plans the way he was. Stubby would figure out things in secret and then spring them on people. We both worked for Jack Bishop, our landlord, whenever he needed us, and Stubby had surprised us both one day when he whipped us up a batch of creamed smoked oysters. They were all right to me, but Jack thought they were just the most wonderful food he had tasted and went on about them for almost an hour, until I thought Stubby was going to swell up and explode, he was being so prideful. What I knew was that Jack sold his smoked oysters to rich folks over on the West Side and he knew he could make money selling creamed oysters in pots.

Jack was a good man. He had been married for almost thirty years, and people told me that he almost drank himself to death when his wife died. They didn't have any children, and Jack lived alone on Baxter Street. He said he was just about ready to jump into the river and end it all when Grace—that had been his wife's name—came to him in a dream and gave him a piece of her mind for even thinking about dying.

"She told me to get on with my life," he said. "She said get on with it like you got some sense. And I knew she meant every word of it!"

I think he rented me and Stubby a cheap room just to have somebody to hang around with. His business hadn't been doing that well, but he owned the building we lived in, so he didn't need that much money. Then he came up with the idea of smoking the seafood he bought.

In the mornings he would go down to the fish market and buy whatever looked good to him, and me and Stubby would help him smoke the fish and the oysters for sale. Sometimes, because Stubby kept himself looking so clean and fresh, Jack would take him on his selling trips. He wouldn't take me.

"Stubby doesn't look as black as you," he told me. "You're liable to scare people to death, knocking on their back door."

I didn't care about what Jack had to say, because I knew he was a fair man. Maybe the fairest white man I had ever met. He didn't charge me and Stubby that much for rent, and if we were a little short once in a while, he didn't make a big deal of it. In his heart, though, I knew he thought more of Stubby's plans than he did of mine. Everybody had to eat, and Stubby wanted to be a cook. You couldn't beat that. Me, I wanted to dance. In *my* mind you couldn't beat that, but Jack Bishop didn't see it.

"You're only a kid now," he said. "And hopping around feels good to you. You reach my age and it won't be so much fun."

Me and Stubby got home and he went on in and lay down. In two minutes he was asleep and snoring. I don't know how a man who looked as bright and lively as Stubby could snore so loud and so strong. I had to make a decision. Should I wake him up and listen to him mumbling and grumbling about how the world was treating him or let him sleep and listen to him making noises like a pig? We lived on the third floor, and I decided to go into the hallway and sit on the steps for a while.

It was almost noon, and I was sitting on the stairs waiting for Stubby to sleep off his mad when Margaret Moran came out into the hallway with the boy. Miss Margaret was not young, and not exactly pretty. But she was the kind of woman who put herself forward, and as Jack said, she was as Irish as she was tall.

"Joey, if you didn't want to dance with the group, you should have spoken up a long time ago," Miss Margaret said.

"I want to dance, but I just can't get it right," the boy answered. "You got too many things going on at the same time!"

I looked down through the banister and saw Miss Margaret.

She was wearing a loose green blouse, tied around the waist, and a long green and yellow skirt that came down almost to her short boots. There was an amber necklace around her neck and a lace scarf around her shoulders.

The boy was skinny and pale, with long hair that covered the tops of his ears and a look that said he wanted to be anywhere but in the hallway.

"There are not too many things going on," Miss Margaret said. "You are just too thickheaded and dumb to learn them. You did all right until you got to the cross. Everybody has to do the cross at the same time. You flick that right foot across the ankle—not all the way across the ankle, just halfway across—and then you bring your foot right back to the floor. You don't pick your foot up and swing it across your knee!"

"I didn't mean—"

I guessed he was going to say something about not meaning to swing his leg so high, but Miss Margaret gave him a slap across the top of his head.

"Now do it!" she said. From where I was sitting on the stair, all I could see was the back of her head, but I could tell her nose was right on the boy's nose.

She backed off a bit, turned her head sideways, and started humming a little tune. It was the same Irish tune I had heard coming up the airway to my room. The boy didn't want her on top of him like that, but he was scared to move away. He hunched his shoulders a few times to get the rhythm of what she was humming, and then he started an awkward little dance. It looked a little like a step dance and a little like the boy was a puppet bouncing on a string.

Sure enough, when he got to the part where he was supposed to be crossing his foot, he brought it up across his knee and got another slap for his trouble.

"Joey, it is one week to the recital and you are still getting it wrong!" Miss Margaret said. "Try it again, and this time—are you listening to me, Joey Curran?"

"Yes, ma'am."

"This time don't cross at all!" Miss Margaret said. "When you get to the cross, you just wait a half beat and go on with the dance!"

She stepped back and I could see the boy, his face white, his eyes squinched up tight, and his shoulders moving forward. I thought he was going to run, but when Miss Margaret started humming that song again, I saw him nodding his head along with her. When Miss Margaret got to the cross, the boy just stopped. He froze up and didn't move a muscle.

Whack! She slapped him on the right side of his head, and before he could get his hand up, she had pushed him against the wall with her big bosom and slapped him again as he bounced off.

"You know, Miss Margaret, he's doing it okay," I said. "You

can bring your leg up higher on the cross."

Miss Margaret turned to see who was talking. Only she didn't turn like she was surprised, more like she was mad. She had both hands on her hips and moved slow, like a ship turning in the harbor. Her mouth got tight and she started coming toward me. I knew she was going to let me have it.

"Well, if it isn't Mr. Juba himself. You know, Mr. Juba, I don't need some black fool telling me how to do an Irish step dance!" she said. The words came out with a hiss.

"You need somebody telling you," I said. "Because you don't know how the dance goes. I can see that. All you're doing is bumping that little boy around. That's not dancing. That's just bumping a kid around."

"Why don't you just shut up and crawl back up to your room, sir," Miss Margaret said. "And maybe see to it that it's your own business you're minding on a sunny afternoon!"

"You hum that little tune for me and I'll show you how it's done," I said, standing and coming down to the landing.

Miss Margaret didn't back off. She was nearly as tall as me and maybe had thirty or forty pounds on me.

"I'm not humming anything for no lopsided, ignorant, fish-smelling fool!" she said. "Now, if you don't get away from here, I'm going to get somebody to beat the back side of your head until it gets to be as ugly as the front side. Are you understanding me, bucky?"

I knew it wasn't any use exchanging words with Miss Margaret, so I started clapping my hands in rhythm.

"This is the way the rhythm is supposed to go, lady," I said.

Then I began to dance. It was a simple step dance she was trying to teach the boy, but she had drained all the fun out of it. I moved through some of the introduction, crossed at the ankles like she wanted the boy to cross, and watched her face.

She kept her eyes right on me because she didn't want to let on that she wanted to know how I was taking what she thought was her dance and running with it. I did a turn and moved away so she could see more of my body. She was still mad, but she hadn't stopped watching yet or left the narrow hallway.

That was when I heard Jack Bishop coming up the stairs.

"Juba, come down and help me with this basket!" he called up.

I kept dancing. I moved into a more complicated step, all the time keeping my crossing low. Miss Margaret was shooting daggers at me from her gray eyes, but she still hadn't turned away. Jack came up a few steps and watched through the banister.

"You can't push anybody into dancing," I said. "When you're dancing, you're supposed to be happy. Isn't that right, little man?"

The boy looked over at Miss Margaret, but he didn't dare say anything.

"And if you get really happy, your feet don't want to stay that close to the floor," I went on. "They want to lift themselves up and show how happy they are."

I was crossing higher and higher, and I saw Miss Margaret's eyes flick down at my legs and I knew I had her.

"Come on, boy, dance with me." He was still flat against the wall, but I knew he was ready.

When the boy started out, he was kind of awkward-looking, so I slowed down and kept a steady rhythm that he could follow. When I got to the cross, I clapped my hands twice in the air, something no real Irish dancer would do, but it was enough to get Miss Margaret looking at my hands and not noticing the slowdown. It was just enough to let the boy get that leg higher on the cross and keep on going.

Moving a little closer to Miss Margaret, I gave her a big grin, and she meaned up her face the best she could and got her hands back up on her hips.

"C'mon and dance, lady," I said. Turning sideways, I gave her left hip a little nudge, then brought my foot down, crossed low at the ankle, then nudged her two more times.

Miss Margaret reached out and grabbed the boy's shoulder and rushed past me as she headed toward her apartment. When she reached her door, she pushed it open and shoved the boy in, but not before he could turn and give me a big grin. She slammed the door behind her, and I could hear her running off at the mouth to the boy. But what could she say to him that would wipe away the grin he gave me? Nothing.

"You up here dancing in the hallways again?" Jack's face was red from carrying a basket up the narrow stairs.

"What else I got to do?" I asked him.

"If you're working for me, you got plenty to do," Jack said. "I got three baskets of oysters downstairs that need to be brought up to the roof."

We took the oysters up to the roof, put down some tin on top of the roof, and set up the grate. The wood chips were under a heavy cover against the side walls, and I laid a layer of them on the grate. Jack started the fire, and I put the grill on.

"So the way I see it, you're about ready to pop the question to Miss Margaret," Jack said as we waited for the chips to get burning right. "Every time I come around, you're messing with her."

"She's supposed to be teaching dancing to the kids around here and she can't hardly dance herself," I said. "She hates to see me coming because she knows I can do what she can't."

"If you say so," Jack said. "But I still think you're sweet on her."

"You know I'm sweet on dancing," I said. "And I would like

to get some of her students. I asked her how much she charged them and she wouldn't tell me."

"Why should she? She's got something good going on and she knows it," Jack said. "You go down to the waterfront and there's more Irish coming ashore than there are oysters. Back in the Old Country, every little village had a dancing master— somebody who would teach all the young people how to dance. A girl wasn't considered turned out right if she didn't know how to dance. Now they're coming over here—the ones who survive the trip—and they're wanting to bring a piece of the Old Country with them."

"I can teach them better than she can," I said.

"Most of them have never seen nothing that looks like you!" Jack said. "If you were walking down the street in Kilkenny, where I'm from, and saw a black man walking toward you looking anything at all the way you do, you'd think you'd met the devil himself. They got to get used to black people once they get off the boats, and then they got to get used to you dancing."

I watched as Jack spread the chips around the grate, then put the screen over it. The smoke was coming up good, and he started putting the oysters on the screen.

"They'll get used to me," I said. "They get used to everything else. Or maybe I should go over to—where you say you from? And teach over there."

"Lad, if your brain was as fast as your feet, you'd be able

to think a lot better than you're thinking," Jack said. "If all those people are leaving Ireland, spending their last dollars to get on those floating coffins to make it to New York and Boston, there's got to be a reason. Over there they didn't have nothing to speak of, but at least it was a nothing they knew about. Folks around Kilkenny wouldn't have a penny to spare to put on a dead man's eyes, let alone pay for no dancing lessons."

It took us until late in the afternoon to finish smoking all the oysters and putting them in the pots that Jack would carry them around in. He had a whole list of swells who would buy smoked oysters and pay good money for them, too.

When the oysters had been smoked and put in the little pots that Jack had invested in, I helped him load them on the hand cart, made sure all the pots were covered good, and watched him pull off uptown.

I thought Jack really didn't have to work. He had bought the house on Baxter Street when Andrew Jackson was president, and things were cheaper downtown and expensive uptown. He made enough money renting out rooms to get by since he had given up drinking. He wasn't getting rich, but he wasn't barefoot, as he always said. The tenements in Five Points were mostly beat-up wooden shacks. People said one wooden match would burn down the whole neighborhood in thirty minutes if the wind was right. Jack had some income from renting out two floors.

Street in Five Points, New York City, circa 1861

There wasn't much to the job of helping him. Jack was the kind of man who kept busy all the time. He would be up at first light every morning and down to the docks haggling with the fishermen who were just coming in. What he'd figured out, and he was a figuring man, was that instead of selling fish to everybody, he would just smoke oysters, crabs, and some croakers if they had them for sale, and sell them to the rich people uptown.

It was funny the three of us being together, Jack at least seventy and me and Stubby still in our teens. The black people over on the square used to call Jack my white daddy, which didn't bother me at all. I had a steady income and a decent place to live.

Besides Stubby, the only person I spent a lot of time with was Freddy Flamer. Freddy played fiddle, danced a little, and did a few magic tricks. He got a few jobs playing the fiddle and sometimes made a few coins doing magic tricks uptown around the theaters, but he was getting by mostly by cleaning clothes and tailoring. His mama had taught him how to sew and do some patching up of men's clothing. Jack said Freddy looked like a gentleman.

"You got to look like something that deserves money before people will let it loose from their pockets," Jack said. "Freddy looks like he could be having tea with the Queen of England and she'd be passing him the cakes."

I didn't know about that, but I did like the way Freddy carried himself. There was an elegant style about him, like he knew something about himself that nobody else knew. When we were on the down side, scraping the dregs, so to speak, sometimes we would perform on the corners up near Fourteenth Street. Freddy would start to fiddling and catch people's attention, and then I'd dance. Maybe if they would throw us coins because we were good or maybe because they didn't expect a black man to be dancing Irish jigs. Didn't make any difference to either of us—we would usually get enough money for food.

My name is William Henry Lane, but when I dance, I call myself Master Juba, and people I know just call me Juba. Juba is a dance that black people do in the South. They say it comes from Africa. I don't know about that, but most dancers in Five Points give themselves stage names, so I settled on Juba. It has a nice ring to it.

I live to dance. The first time I saw a good dancer perform, it was old Jim Lowe, who is as old as dirt but moves like he has extra joints in his legs. He saw me watching him and grinned at me and asked me if I could dance. I didn't know if I could or not, but I said yes.

"Show me what you got," Jim said. "Dance for me."

I tried dancing the way I had seen Jim dance, but I couldn't do what he did. When I stopped, he looked at me and said, "Boy, you got something. You really have got something." I've been dancing ever since and loving what I do.

Freddy called himself a dancer, as I did, even though he didn't dance all that well. Stubby didn't dance at all, but he was something special. It was Stubby who said that one day the three of us were going to be rich and famous.

"I'll open up a big restaurant," he said. "Maybe I'll buy Fraunces Tavern and serve nothing but the best food and the best wine. Then you and Freddy can come by and we'll sit at a table near the window and eat clams baked in walnut shells."

"I don't eat clams," Freddy said. "Clams can rotten out your insides. You can ask Jack about that."

I didn't believe him, but I asked Jack anyway.

"You ever look a clam in the eye?" Jack asked me.

"No, I have not," I said.

"If you look a clam in the eye, or at least where its eye is supposed to be, you can see a map of just what's in you," Jack said. "The outside of a clam is the same as the inside of a human being. My grandmother told me that."

I didn't want to say anything bad about Jack's grandmother, but I didn't believe that the outside of a clam was like the inside of a human being. You didn't argue with Jack Bishop, and I thought that was why him, Stubby, Freddy, and me got along. We let Jack tell his stories, and we didn't argue with him about them and he didn't argue with us.

CHAPTER
TWO

Monday. I helped Jack load up his cart and watched as he and Stubby started off. I knew they wouldn't be back until around four, maybe four thirty, and I wouldn't have anything much to do until then, so I went over to Peter Williams's place. Peter was a big black man with a thick neck, slitty eyes, and big lips. He ran Almack's, a club he had gotten from an Englishman who owed him money. All the black men around Five Points said Almack's was the best club in New York City for dancing and meeting up with women who were more or less on the wild side. They served decent food on most days and had as many ways for a man to get into trouble as you would want.

Where Jack Bishop was a straightforward, hardworking man who just got by from day to day, Peter Williams was a schemer, and as cold as the club he ran. The place had three stories. The first story was the Club Room, where people danced and where the food was cooked by Peter's wife, Miss Lilly, and whoever she got to help her. That was also where they kept the whiskey, tobacco, and anything else they had to sell.

The room had chairs and tables all around the walls and a big space in the middle of the floor for dancing. On the far end of the room was a little roped-off part, and that was where Peter had people put on their shows.

The shows Peter put on depended on who was coming in the door. If it was a bunch of sailors from the docks, then it was some skinny girls dancing and showing off as much as they could show without catching their death of pneumonia. The sailors would buy drinks from Quincy, who sat at a table with boxes of whiskey next to him and the open bottles on the table in front of him. Quincy was also the man who kept order in Almack's. It was known that he did not mind putting a rowdy customer to rest and leaving his bruised and battered body in a gutter somewhere in Five Points.

When the sailors had enough drink in them so that the light-skinned girls started looking pretty, they could buy a dance. A dance with one of the girls meant some quick kissing, some slow rubbing, and maybe a trip upstairs to the top floor, where other stuff was going on.

I wasn't interested in any of the girls, or none of the whiskey, but I *was* interested in the occasional shows Peter had. Peter was about selling you whatever he could convince you that you needed. When he saw that some uptown people had come into his club and maybe there were a few loose coins floating around, he would arrange to put on a little show with some real good dancers, like John Diamond, or the Artis sisters, or me.

John Diamond did all kinds of Irish dancing, jigs, step, and clog, you name it. He could move good, but he also moved with style. He was a tall, thin white boy who gave off the impression that he was an upper-crust gentleman just cruising downtown for a night's amusement. The first time I saw him, he was sitting at a table, kind of sideways, so he could put one leg way back so you would notice it, and had a blue silk scarf wrapped around his neck so that it covered the lower part of his face. That man could just sit still and make people watch him. Once in a while, when somebody from the newspapers came over—the *Herald* or even the Newark, New Jersey, paper—Peter would get John to sit out in the audience like he was a regular customer, only he would be wearing a cloak and a top hat. Then Peter would have a few dancers go through their numbers, and just when everyone thought they

*Map of lower Manhattan showing the Five Points area
in Ward 6. New York Herald, 1863.*

were seeing something good, Peter would signal John to take the floor, and that would knock everybody out. That's how good John Diamond was, and he knew it. He was nasty, too. I told Jack about how nasty John Diamond was, and Jack said God gave some talent to nasty people just to keep the rest of us on our toes.

The Artis sisters were good-looking. The big thing about them was that they were fifteen-year-old identical twins and moved together in a fascinating kind of way. I don't know how they learned to slink around a dance floor like that, but they could really do it. Once in a while they would dance behind John Diamond and he would pretend they were his women or something. Other times they would dance with the regular girls, the ones who would dance with whoever came into Almack's. It was something to see the coal-black twins dancing around the yellow-complexioned regular girl dancers. There would be seven or nine light-skinned girls—always an odd number—and the two Artis sisters sliding in and around them.

There were some white girls dancing in Almack's, too. Some could dance pretty well, and some were only fair. But they had to mix with the crowd, so you didn't get any top dancers. Also, most of the dancing wasn't meant to be looked at, it was meant to loosen up the pockets.

Then there was me.

I was born in South County, Rhode Island, and was raised

by my aunt Hattie. She brought me to New York City when I was five, and we lived on Cherry Street until she died in 1838. Since then I'd been more or less on my own. What I had was what most people called a normal life. The only thing that was different was that when I was seven, I had seen Jim Lowe dancing on the Bowery in front of the theater that used to carry three or four small acts besides whoever it was that was the headline star. He was dancing in front of the theater, and the woman with him was inviting people over to see the signs that told about what was going on in the theater that evening.

I loved the way people were watching the man, and I loved even more the way the man was moving and enjoying himself. He thought I could be a dancer and showed me a few things, and I loved it. I started dancing along with him on weekends, and he was all right with that. People were clapping and throwing us pennies, and it was the grandest thing that had ever happened to me.

A lot of the people in Five Points were Irish, and they did the most dancing. It didn't take but two seconds and a tambourine to get the Irish up on their feet. They'd dance in twos or threes or with a whole pack of dancers, according to the situation. But what made it best for me was that the men danced just as good as the women and they wanted to be dancing!

I learned every Irish dance I could by watching their feet and remembering the tunes I heard. Then I would go home and practice until I felt like I had it down. They had lots of dance contests in Five Points. Every time one of the political parties had a candidate for anything, they would have a party in the streets—usually Baxter Street or up near the Paradise Square—and pass out free food and have a singing contest and a dancing contest. The Dead Rabbits, a group of street hustlers from the area, worked for the Republicans and the Independents, and they would keep order and run the contests. That's how I first got noticed. I ran up against John Diamond, who was always broke or near broke and looking for a dollar or four bits, and entering the contests. Most of the contests he entered he won, but one day me and him had a dance-off and I threw out all my best moves. I won the contest and he called me a few choice names and said they just wanted to give the fifty cents first prize to a blackie. I didn't believe that at all. I knew how good I was.

Almack's was nearly empty by the time I got there. Miss Lilly gave me a lemonade and told me how glad she was that the Africans on the *Amistad* had won their case.

"What case?" I asked.

"Juba, baby, you need to bury your head in some books for about two years," Miss Lilly said. "There's more to this world than dancing and entertaining people. You're acting just like this child over there."

I didn't know who the girl was, but she was light-skinned, skinny, and sad-looking as she carried a pail and a mop across the room and started washing the floor down.

"So what are you doing with yourself these days, Mr. Dancing Man?" Miss Lilly went on.

"Trying to keep my backbone in back of me and my navel closed up!" I said.

"Boy, where did you hear that dumb saying?" Miss Lilly asked. "It had to be from that Jack Bishop. That man got more old sayings in him than he got sense or fish. You want some more lemonade?"

"Wouldn't mind," I said.

"Go get it from behind the bar," Miss Lilly said.

I hadn't gone more than two steps when I heard a cry and looked over to see that the girl who was washing the floor had fallen.

"Go get your lemonade!" Miss Lilly called to me. Her voice was kind of sharp.

I got the lemonade and brought it back to the table. The girl was struggling to get up and she was crying hard.

"We need this floor done before the afternoon crowd comes in," Miss Lilly called to her. Her voice was still hard.

I watched the girl dip the mop back in the bucket and start back into washing the floor.

"Who is she?" I asked.

"Just another frail thing who's finding out that life don't come with no lace handkerchiefs. She's sweet in her way, but sweet don't get you very far in Five Points," Miss Lilly said. "Goes by the name of Cissy Daniels, but her real name is Priscilla. She owes Pete money and he wants it."

"That's not a good place to be," I said.

"Then she shouldn't have gone there," Miss Lilly said.

"She don't like to wash floors, I guess."

"She don't mind washing floors." Miss Lilly sipped her lemonade out of a mug and made a face.

"If she don't mind washing floors, why is she crying?"

"I didn't know you did missionary work, Juba." Miss Lilly managed a smile. "Or did you trip over your feet and fall in love?"

"Just wondered," I said.

"Pete don't pay her but thirty-five cents a day to clean up around here," Miss Lilly said. "And since she's not cleaning all day, she's not worth any more than that. But she owes him over twenty dollars, and the way she's paying him a few cents a day, she knows she's going to be working for him for the next hundred years. He told her he'd pay her sixty cents if she danced when the customers came in, but she didn't want to do that."

"She's a dancer?"

"She got two legs and she's not dead, so I guess she can

do something," Miss Lilly said. "Pete wants her to dance with the customers."

"Oh."

I knew what that meant. Dancing with the men who came into Almack's was more about standing up and wrestling with them than anything else. And more than one would want to drag her upstairs to one of the rooms.

Pete came down the stairs. The man walked heavy, banging his way down the wooden stairs like he was falling from one step to the next. He looked around the room, saw the girl washing, and then came over and sat with me and Miss Lilly.

"You ain't giving him none of my good lemonade, are you?" Pete asked Miss Lilly.

"He's drinking the same as I am," Miss Lilly said.

"Juba is nothing but a boy, but he's got so much money he walks lopsided just from the weight of it," Pete said. "Plus, he's got a big job with the fish king. He makes about ten dollars a week from him. Isn't that right?"

"Ten dollars? He pays me fifteen dollars just to keep the fish happy!" I said. "I sing to them at night so they wake up smiling in the morning."

"If he's got that much money, he can help Cissy pay off what she owes you," Miss Lilly said. "She was laying on the floor crying, and it got Juba's heart pounding."

"You didn't let her cry on my floor, did you?" Pete asked, shaking his head from side to side. "She's probably got them salty tears, and you know how salt can mess a good floor up."

"You're a hard man, Mr. Williams," I said.

"Me? Hard? No, sir! I'm the easiest man in the world. Didn't I wink at the judges and let you win that contest against John Diamond?"

"You didn't let me win anything," I said. "I beat down John Diamond fair and square, and those other dancers weren't even close."

"So when you coming to work for me?" Pete asked. "Those contests only come once in a while, and I can guarantee you two dollars a week and fifty percent of all the tips you pick up. And you wouldn't have to go around smelling fishy all day."

That was funny, and I had to laugh. Maybe he could guarantee me two dollars a week, but there was no way I would ever let him take half of the tip money, too.

We watched as Cissy finished mopping the floor and started to leave. Pete told Miss Lilly to call her, and Miss Lilly snapped her fingers and signaled for her to come over.

When Cissy reached us, Miss Lilly asked her if she wanted some lemonade.

"No, ma'am," Cissy said quietly.

"Sit down," Pete said, which she did after pulling a chair over.

29

"If you look at this gal up close, you can see she's not that bad-looking if she could manage to put a smile on her face once in a while," Pete said. "At the rate she's going, she's going to be about thirty or forty before she's going to finish paying me off, though. If she played her cards right, she could pay me off in eight months, maybe even in six. Then she could go out and get herself an easy job taking care of the white folks' babies. That's what you want, isn't it?"

Cissy didn't answer. Pete looked at her kind of mean and then turned away. "You're liable to be dead before you finish paying me my money," he said.

Up close Cissy was good-looking, as Pete had said. She had a thin, heart-shaped face with light brown eyes and a small bow mouth. She could have been a looker if she gained a few pounds. Once, she glanced at me but quickly looked away.

Miss Lilly asked her again if she wanted some lemonade, and another tiny little "no, ma'am" came out. For a few seconds nobody spoke, and then Miss Lilly started talking to Pete about the carpenter.

"What he said was that he could build a small platform like they used to have at that club up near Pearl Street, across from the cigar store," she said. "You could pull it out from the back wall and lay it down where you wanted it. Then when you were finished with it, you could put it back against the wall and lift it up so it would be out of the way."

"How much he want for that?"

"Twelve dollars," Miss Lilly said. "I didn't like the idea that much. We don't have a platform now and nobody is complaining."

"Maybe they would say something if we had one," Pete said. "Then whenever we had something special going on, people could tell because we brought the platform out. What you think?"

The girl was crying again, and truly it touched my heart a little. I hate to see people sad. I felt Pete nudge my hand and realized he was talking to me. I asked him what he wanted, and he asked what I thought of the platform.

"You thinking it would bring in some uptown money?" he asked.

"I don't know," I said.

"Cissy, why don't you go on upstairs," Miss Lilly said.

We watched as Cissy started to leave, then came back for the mop and pail and carried them off with her.

"Miss Lilly likes that girl because she's polite, but she's also hardheaded," Pete said. "She can't figure out that nothing comes for free. Everything you get in life has got some kind of price to it. The only things that are free are air and water, and one day somebody is going to figure out how to get air and water in a bottle and sell that. You're not looking for a wife, are you?"

"No, I'm not," I said.

"Because with you dancing for Pete Williams and her washing floors for Pete Williams, the both of you could become famous," Pete said. "Maybe you could get her out on the dance floor and have her sweeping the floor around you as you danced. Then maybe I'd have that platform built. We'd call it the Master Juba stage.

"You know your boy was here earlier—what's his name, the one walks like he got a stick up his butt?" Pete asked.

"I don't know who you're talking about," I said. "None of my friends carry sticks in that position."

"The one who speaks so proper and wants to be a cook," Miss Lilly said. "He was here when Mr. Reeves was talking about hiring some dancers and singers. I know he told you about that."

"He didn't mention anything to me," I said. "Who is Mr. Reeves?"

"You remember that theater that was closed about eighteen months ago?" Pete asked. "The one over the Playhouse?"

"Something about it not being safe?" I said.

"Well, he's got a chance to get a license to open it up again," Lilly said. "He wants to invite some people here from City Hall and some backers to talk it over. It should be kind of informal, but he wants a nice show. That's why he's holding auditions this weekend. If you're interested, maybe Pete can put in a word for you. You work for Mr. Reeves and a lot of people are going to be seeing you."

"He wants to put on a show *here*?" I asked.

"You got a problem with Almack's?" Pete asked.

"No," I said. "None at all."

My mind was working hard, but I couldn't come up with anything that made sense. There was nothing wrong with Almack's for giving a show, but there were a lot better places. Pete kept talking about how he could put in a good word for me if I signed a contract to work for him for one year. I told him I would think about it.

"Don't think yourself out of a good chance to get ahead in the world," Pete said.

"I'll try not to, Mr. Williams," I answered him. "I'll certainly try not to."

Home, and Stubby wasn't back yet, so I sat out on the stoop to wait for him. I knew he would be rushing back with something to cook for supper. Sure enough, I spied him coming down the street with a package under his arm.

"What's going on?"

"You tell me!" I said. "Pete said you were over to Almack's and they were talking about having auditions for a show. He said they were looking for dancers and singers. Why didn't you tell me?"

"I was going to tell you when I got off work." Stubby was trying to sit down with me, but I got up and faced him. "I was going to tell you, but it slipped my mind when they said I wasn't working today."

"When are they going to have the auditions?"

"Saturday," Stubby said. "Let's go inside, Juba. What's wrong with you?"

"Pete said he'd put in a word for me with Mr. Reeves if I wanted," I said. "This could be the break I was looking for."

"I told Freddy," Stubby said.

"You told Freddy, who is looking to get the same job I'm trying to get, and you didn't tell me?"

"I told him and he said he had already heard about it from Simmy Long, and he wasn't sure how legitimate it was." Stubby had started up the stairs and had his hand on the doorknob.

"Freddy probably told you that so you wouldn't tell me," I said. "He can't dance with me and he can't sing with me, and he knows it."

"No, not Freddy," Stubby said. "Simmy said there was something wrong with the deal. He said Mr. Reeves was going around asking people to come to the auditions, but he wanted them to keep it quiet. Simmy doesn't trust white men who go around telling you to keep things quiet."

"Look, Freddy is a dancer, and Simmy is a dancer," I said.

"We're all out here looking for a place to perform. Neither one of them wants to give me a hand up. You think we should ask Jack about it?"

"Couldn't hurt," Stubby said.

I was getting excited and trying not to get excited at the same time. Having an audition at Almack's, with Pete on my side, sounded like a good deal, even though there was no way under the sun that I wanted to work for Peter Williams. But any time I had a chance to show people how well I danced, it was a good thing. People remember talent. They talk about fiddlers they heard four and five years ago, or singers they went to hear when they were young. If I could show a theater owner what I could do, it had to be a good thing.

There were some beans left over from the night before, and I put them in a pot with some water and a little fatback and started heating them up. Stubby asked me if I wanted him to cook the fish filets he'd brought from the docks, and I told him I didn't mind one way or the other, and he said he wouldn't cook them but I knew he would. He couldn't stay out of a kitchen if his life depended on it.

By the time Jack got home, I had almost changed my mind about telling him about the tryouts or the theater opening again. The truth was I didn't want anything to be wrong with it. Knowing Jack, I knew he would find something bad to say. The man could find fault with a newborn baby.

"You have to have three things to open up a theater," Jack said, washing his hands at the washstand. "You need somebody with money behind you is the first thing. Money is like oil—it gets the machinery going. If this fellow Reeves had any legitimate money, he wouldn't be sneaking around in the dark. So the money he's sniffing out has got to be dirty. Nothing wrong with that, but you got to know it, so I put it on the table.

"The second thing you need is a theater."

"He's got that little place over the Playhouse," I said. "The one that got closed down before."

"He's got that place, but it's closed down. It might as well not exist unless he can bribe somebody in the city to get him a license," Jack said. "So we're back to money again. The third thing you need is a blanket to put over everybody's head so they don't see what's going on."

"You don't know for sure that something shady is going on," I said.

"If Pete Williams is involved, and this Reeves fellow, and they're talking about keeping things quiet, I know there's something shady going on," Jack said. "You can go on and try out for the dancing, but keep your eyes open. Don't let your eyes get bigger than your belly."

Jack was right about me being so excited I didn't want to see anything wrong. But it was hard for a dancer to make a living. The Irish dancers enjoyed themselves, and sometimes, if they were good enough, they were asked to come to parties and celebrations. But they only made a few dollars when they came, unless someone threw them a few coins. Once in a while there would be a contest and the best dancer would get a dollar or two, but that wasn't enough to get excited about.

The real money was in the theater. Any kind of theater where people came and paid their money to see you dance. Sometimes a show would last for months, even years. I had never seen a show with a black dancer in it. There were minstrel shows, where white men put on black face paint and pretended they were colored, but it wasn't the same. They were being paid to clown around and tell jokes, not to dance.

I didn't know much about Mr. Reeves except what I had heard. People said he recognized talent when he saw it but didn't want to pay very much for his acts. That was all right with me. All I needed was someplace where people could see me dancing, and I would let my feet do the rest. When Mr. Reeves's little theater got closed up, he tried renting out other theaters, but he never got anything going that lasted more than a few performances. Once he worked putting on sideshows with Mr. Barnum, but they had a falling-out.

I decided to make the best showing at the audition, so I met up with Fred and asked him to come practice with me.

"You can fiddle while I dance," I said.

"Juba, I don't know how many black dancers they're looking for," Fred said. "But you're a dancer and I'm a dancer, so that's two, and I don't know who else may show up. I'm not going to sit around and fiddle for you when I should be practicing."

In my heart I knew that Fred Flamer couldn't dance anywhere near my level, but I had to give him credit for thinking the thing through. Any dancer I would ask to practice with me would be nosing around to see what was going on and trying to make a place for himself. Then I thought of one dancer who might be willing to give me a hand. It wouldn't be easy.

"I do not like people knocking on my door," Miss Margaret said. "And I especially do not want the likes of you standing here when I'm trying to get my sewing done."

"If I didn't need help, I wouldn't be here," I said. "And if you weren't the only person in the world who could help me, I wouldn't be here. But I do need the help, and the good Lord has done me the favor of putting you here."

"You'd better be having another cup of tea with the Lord and getting some more names, because I don't give money to insolent children," Miss Margaret said. The door slammed inches from my face.

"Thought you could help me with my dancing!" I called through the closed barrier.

No answer. I had started walking away when a flash of light from Miss Margaret's apartment hit the floor in the hallway. I turned and saw her silhouetted in the doorway. "So?"

I explained to Miss Margaret how Mr. Reeves was trying to open up his theater again and was having auditions for both black and white dancers and singers. "If anyone is looking for the best dancer in New York City, they don't have to look any further than me," I went on. "But I just want to be good and ready for this audition, because I got a feeling it's going to work out just fine. Once he sees me dancing, once he sees my style, he's got to hire me."

"Do you get kinks in your neck from patting yourself on the back?" Miss Margaret asked me. "Because I've seen you dancing in the hallway and I'm not writing to the Pope about how wonderful you are. And if you're as good as you think you are and half as good as you *say* you are, then why do you need me?"

"Because I know that practice makes perfect," I said.

"And what's my piece of this pie?" Miss Margaret asked.

"You watch my dancing, and tell me if you see anything off, and I'll . . . give you my first week's pay when I'm working for Mr. Reeves," I said.

"Which is like telling me that I'll get the first bucket of sunshine on a cloudy day," Miss Margaret said. "But I'll take you on, just to see if you really know anything."

CHAPTER THREE

One of the things about Miss Margaret Moran that I liked was that although she wasn't very fond of me, I could tell she was still keeping an eye on my dancing. I knew if she saw anything wrong, she was going to point it out as fast as she could. She told me to show up at two thirty, and that was fine with me, because by then me and Stubby had got Jack's cart loaded up and they were on their way.

"You want to watch me dancing in the hallway?" I asked her. "I can dance up and down this—"

"No, I don't want Miss King poking her nose over the steps and seeing me with you," Miss Moran said. "That woman can take a puff of bad air and blow it up into a hurricane in a heartbeat."

Miss King was about eighty and lived on the first floor with her two dogs. Whenever you came in late at night, you could see her door cracking open and you knew she was peeping at you. And if you were doing anything that she could spread around the neighborhood, she would certainly be spreading it.

Miss Moran's apartment was a surprise. Most of the places Jack rented out had a few pieces of furniture, maybe a bed and a table, a stove, some chairs, and a chest of drawers. The room that opened up onto the hallway in Miss Moran's apartment was large and had a small kitchen area, and chairs she had put around the wall, and two or three rugs she had kind of thrown together to cover most of the floor.

"Can you do a square clog step?" she asked.

"I can do anything," I said.

"So let's see it!"

I started thinking of something to dance to and came up with a tune called "Kerry Strutting," which I figured Miss Moran would know. I hummed a bit of it and started with a basic step for four beats, then doubled it, then back to the basic for just two beats and doubled it again.

"You're off-rhythm!" Miss Moran said.

"You can't count, Miss Moran," I said. "If there's anything I know about, it's rhythm!"

41

"No, you don't," Miss Moran said. "You call me Margaret. I'm not so old you need to call me like I'm your mother. And you wait right here until I get back."

She flicked her fingers like she was snapping them, but it didn't produce any sound. She turned and headed for the door and was out like a shot, leaving me alone.

I liked the way the place looked, and saw that she had a nice white tablecloth with a lacy trim on the table. There were little lady signs all around. A small statue of Jesus was on the mantel next to a wooden house with windows and an open door. There was a tea set on the board near the stove that covered the bathtub and a jar of something I figured to be sugar. I wanted to take a closer look, but then I heard Miss Moran's—Margaret's—voice coming up the stairs.

The door opened and she came in with a skinny fellow carrying a fiddle. He took one look at me and stopped in his tracks.

"I'm not playing no fiddle for the devil!" he said, pointing a bony finger at me. "It takes a woman to beat a devil, not a fiddle!"

"He's not a devil, Rafferty, he's a dancer."

"He looks like a devil!"

"Play a clog dance for me."

"You sure he's not got you befuddled?"

"Play!"

The old man looked me up and down and started to play. I didn't know the tune, but I knew the rhythm and started to dance. He knew how to fiddle and tried to throw me off by playing faster, but I just increased my tempo and stayed with him. All the while, Margaret was doing that thing with her hand, keeping time in the air but not making any sounds. Finally, when the old man finished the chorus, he leaned away from me, bending his back and turning his shoulders so he could see me from a different angle.

"Thanks, Rafferty," Margaret said.

"Watch him close, dearie," the old man said. "Real people don't move like he does. *Devils* move like that."

The old man actually asked me to close my eyes so I couldn't see where he was going, as if a real devil would have trouble finding him.

"You'd think he'd been playing for devils all his life," Margaret said.

"You knowing now that I'm dancing in the right time?" I asked.

"Your feet are dancing in the right time, Booby—"

"Juba!"

"Your feet are dancing in the right time, Juba," Margaret said. "And your hands are moving in the right time, but you're not dancing right for somebody watching you. Oh, sure, they'll look at you and see you can move your skinny little legs around, and some will be impressed by that. But none of them can move their legs around like you."

"That's why they're watching me and I'm not watching them!" I said.

"If you weren't so thickheaded, you'd know they were watching you because they want to enjoy themselves, not marvel at you. You ever go to an Irish dance and see the young people swinging themselves around and kicking up their heels and the old people watching them? The old people are thinking back on a time when they were young and they could do the same thing the young people are doing. But you have to give them something they can do, if only on the floor between their ears, if you get my drift."

"What floor was that?"

"They're thinking about themselves dancing, and you can see their shoulders moving a bit with the music and their heads nodding, and in their minds they're doing things they could never do in real life," Margaret said. "But if you get their heads going in the right direction, they can do anything. You're switching up so fast and doing so many tricks that I can't keep up with you in my mind. If I knew what you were going to do, even if you did it like your pants were on fire, I could keep up with you."

"I don't get it," I said.

"You ever see a dancer who just wasn't that good, but they

were handsome and carried it off?" Margaret asked.

"Yes, I have."

"Look, Juba, start a slow reel," Margaret said. "Come on, you can do a slow reel, can't you?"

She was getting on my nerves, but I started the slow reel. Then she got up and stood next to me, waited for a moment until she had the feel of what I was doing, and began to dance. I hadn't expected it, and I felt a little embarrassed. She could dance, and she knew it. She was showing me something I didn't know about Irish dancing: that even though the dancers didn't touch in many of the dances, there was something going on between them. All right, I liked it.

I looked at Margaret and she was smiling. When I stopped, she put her hands on her hips and gave a nod.

"Now put everything I said in your head and stew on it for a while, and see if you come up with something useful," she said. "I'm doing some washing for people on Fifth Avenue tomorrow, so I'll see you the next day. Just knock on my door."

"You think I'm looking good?" I asked her as she opened the door to let me out.

"You could look better," she said.

Margaret didn't make me feel very good. I didn't think she knew as much as she thought she did. She seemed jealous of me, and I didn't figure to be knocking on her door anymore. What I would do was work out my routine for the auditions in

45

my head, because I knew that whatever my brain could think up, my legs and feet would carry out.

We had two windows, and one had cracked in the winter. Me and Stubby had nailed a piece of wood over it to keep the cold out. That was fine in the winter, but in the summer it made the room dark in the daytime. I went to the good window, the one over Stubby's bed, and looked down into the street. People were already bringing out boxes to sit on to catch whatever cool breeze might be wandering down the street. Across from me a woman was sitting in the window, and next to her a cat was sitting on a pillow.

When I saw Stubby and Jack Bishop coming down the street, I could tell they had had a good day. Stubby was pushing the cart like it was nothing and talking a mile a minute, the way he always did, and Jack was nodding and smiling. I went down and helped Stubby bring in what was left of the pots while Jack chained up the cart.

"You people must have made a fortune today," I said.

"A doctor near Madison Square bought enough oysters to start an oyster war," Stubby said.

"What's an oyster war?"

"I don't know." Stubby was grinning. "But he bought a lot of smoked oysters."

Stubby had also bought some sandwiches from a shop on Delancey Street, and there was one for me, which was good, because I didn't like fish every day.

"Stubby, what do you think of my dancing?" I asked later, before we'd gone to bed.

"You're the best I've ever seen," Stubby said. "I haven't even heard of anybody as good as you except for John Diamond, and I don't think he's got you beat. You can always tell what he's going to do. With you, it's different. Sometimes I think your body doesn't even know what it's going to do until it's doing it. You know what I mean?"

"Like I was possessed by the devil?"

"No, Juba, and you shouldn't even say something like that," Stubby said, a serious look on his face. "Did I ever tell you about a pastry chef I heard of who got possessed by the devil, and every cake he made after that fell flat? His family took him to a doctor in Delaware. . . ."

I must have fallen asleep as Stubby was talking, because I don't remember much else he said about the fellow making cakes. But I did think more about what he was saying about my body not knowing what it was going to do next. Maybe Margaret had something after all.

I practiced two more times with Margaret Moran during the week, once with the old man playing the fiddle and once without him. She was saying that although I was a good dancer, people didn't feel as if they were part of my performance. There was no way I was going to cut myself down to anything simple, but it was something to think about. Did I want people to feel as if they were part of what I was doing?

On the morning of the auditions at Almack's, Stubby said he'd go with me. We told Jack Bishop where we were going; he shrugged and said he'd tag along.

We arrived at nine o'clock, and I was given a number. Other dancers were already there, and one or two people I knew who were fairly decent singers. There were also a lot of fat-legged Irish girls, who I imagined danced together as a group.

"You should be on in an hour or so," a dark-looking man, probably Italian, said. "Just don't forget, the auditions are over at twelve sharp."

I felt confident, as if all I had to do was to show up and people would take notice. No matter how many times I repeated Margaret's warning about getting overconfident, I was itching to get on with it.

I was surprised to see how many people were already there. There were a lot of older people, too, no doubt the parents and friends of the singers and dancers. The place had a good feeling to it, and when I looked over at where Pete Williams was sitting, I could see he was pleased.

Miss Lilly saw me, came and took me by the hand, and walked me over to where Pete sat with two white men and John Diamond.

"Juba, this is Mr. Reeves, who is having the auditions," Lilly said. "Mr. Reeves, Juba is one of our best dancers. You'll like him a lot."

I reached out my hand to Mr. Reeves, but he didn't reach out his hand to me. That was okay. He didn't know me yet, or what I could do on the floor.

I went and sat with Jack Bishop and Stubby and told them that the man next to Pete was Reeves.

"And the other man is a lawyer named Louis Browner," Jack said. "He's involved in the slave trade somehow."

"He don't look like it," Stubby said.

That was a funny thing to say and not a funny thing to say. On the one hand, how was someone involved in the slave trade supposed to look? On the other hand, it just pointed out that anyone could be a slave trader.

"Let's watch this act coming up," Jack Bishop said.

Two young white fellows and two girls came out onto the floor. The fellows wore blouselike white shirts and black pants, and the girls wore white blouses and black and green skirts. They looked good.

Just before they started, I glanced over at where Mr. Reeves and Pete were sitting. I didn't like the idea of John Diamond sitting there. Had they already hired him?

The piano player started in on a lively tune, and the four dancers on the floor began their routine. It was nothing special except for the fact that the expressions on their faces looked as if they were having a great time. Their rhythm was right on cue, but it was simple and their steps were even simpler. They danced for a good three minutes and then went into a nice ending bow. Again, nothing special.

"Number eight!" John Diamond called out.

I looked at my number even though I knew it was twelve, my lucky number.

Number eight was tall and slim. He came out in a step dance but quickly went down into a full split, then a scissors lift to a standing position, back to the step moves, then down on his hands. I thought he was going to push himself up, but he only pushed halfway up, then swung his leg around, got his arms out of the way, and brought his legs full circle. Nice, but the guy wasn't a dancer, he was an acrobat.

For the next minute or so the fellow showed how strong he was and how agile, but when I glanced over at Mr. Reeves, I saw he was already looking away.

"Nine!" John Diamond again.

Nine was a sweet-looking girl, maybe eleven or twelve, with red fringe that came almost down to her eyebrows. She went to the middle of the floor and didn't move, even after the piano player started playing. An older woman, maybe her mother, went out on the floor, nervously patted the girl on the shoulder, and whispered something in her ear. The piano player started up again and the girl still didn't move, but I could see she was breathing hard. The mother started out on the floor again, but then the girl began to dance. She was into a regular jig pattern, then changed it to a clog pattern, then switched it back and forth as gracefully as you pleased. It wasn't sensational, but it was good.

"If she don't have seven babies before she's nineteen, she'll be a good entertainer," Jack whispered to me.

When the girl finished, a few people started clapping, and after Mr. Reeves stood up and gave her a hand, everyone joined in.

"Ten!" Ten was a light-skinned black man with sandy hair. He started doing a reel, with a little too much spinning, and Mr. Reeves stood up and called to the piano player to stop.

"Are you colored, or what?"

"I'm colored," the dancer said.

Mr. Reeves sat back down, and the piano player started again.

"That piano player know what to play for you?" Stubby asked me.

Panic. "Stubby, go tell him to play 'Old Rattler' clog when I dance," I said. "Wait until this fellow is finished."

As soon as the dancer was finished and bowing, Stubby went over to the piano player and whispered in his ear. I looked over to where Mr. Reeves was sitting and talking to

John Diamond. Their heads were just about touching, they were so close together.

The door banged open and four fellows came in. They all had bandanas tied around their legs, so we knew they were from one of the local gangs. They found spots against the far wall and leaned against it.

"Probably from the mayor's office." Jack Bishop chuckled. "Out looking for the dancing voters!"

Fred Flamer was number eleven. When he started out to the middle of the floor, John Diamond stood up.

"Show us your minstrel stuff, Fred!" he shouted. "You're the best!"

John Diamond was running the auditions, and I didn't like that one bit. I had to think he was already hired.

I thought Fred would go for a clog dance, his best move, but instead, the piano player started a step dance. What Fred did surprised me. I sat back in my chair and just watched. Fred wasn't a first-rate dancer, but he was better than the fool I saw on the floor. He came out reeling and staggering around like he was drunk. He looked over toward where Mr. Reeves was sitting and began rolling his eyes. John Diamond started laughing, and so did Mr. Reeves. The more they laughed, the more Fred clowned it up, even falling to his knees and shaking his shoulders as if he were having a fit or something. I felt myself getting madder and madder.

It felt to me like Fred was on the floor longer than any of the others. He lay on his back and started shaking. He smiled with his chin on the floor. He was throwing away his skills. John Diamond roared with laughter, and when Fred had finished and had stood up and taken a deep bow, John began to applaud.

"Twelve!"

Whatever I had in me I was going to put out on the floor. The piano player started in on "Old Rattler," and I hit the rhythm on the first chorus. The song had been a good choice because it let me show off my clog-dancing skills, marking a steady beat on the floor and keeping the momentum moving throughout my body. I had a pattern that I had worked on to get the audience going, and every time I did a stutter step toward the front, people started clapping with me. I knew I had them going, and I wanted to keep them going even higher.

"Coon it up! We want to see some minstrels!" John Diamond yelled out.

I ignored him and kept dancing, but the clapping began to slow down.

"Coon it up, boy—this is a colored dance!" John Diamond again.

I kept dancing, doubling on my steps, beating my hands together, keeping my elbows high.

"Come on, Juba, do you want a job or not?" Pete Williams's

voice boomed through the small hall.

"Thirteen!" John Diamond called the next dancer even though I hadn't finished my routine.

I was beat down, tired, and hurt. I went back over to where Stubby and Jack Bishop were sitting and plopped down in the chair.

"You done good, Juba," Jack said. "You done real good."

Number thirteen was an old man I had seen around the neighborhood. They told me he used to be a dancer. He was smooth, but he was grinning like he had lost his mind; he was "cooning it up," even though he was white.

The auditions over, I sat with Jack and Stubby and watched as the dancers started getting their things together and leaving. The woman who had brought the little girl I liked came over and patted me on the hand. She didn't say anything, just patted me on the hand.

John Diamond, Mr. Reeves, and the man Jack had said was a slave dealer left together.

"Juba, you want to tell us how you're feeling, or should we just look at your face and figure it out?" Jack asked.

"The way I feel? Like everything that is me, the real me, the inside me, is dead," I said. "I don't even know if I feel that or if I just know it."

"So I'm going back to the house and getting some more smoked oysters ready to sell to rich people," Jack said, easing himself up from the table. "You can come help if you want, but take your time. The oysters will always be there."

Jack and Stubby left, and I wanted to go, too, but my legs just didn't seem to have the strength to move on.

"Juba, there are things we can't change in this world." A soft voice spoke to me. "You're old enough to know that by now."

I looked up to see Miss Lilly sitting across from me.

"That's what I used to think, Miss Lilly," I said. "But they just changed all my dreams about dancing and all my hopes to make something of myself. My dancing didn't mean a thing. The only thing they see in a black man is a clown or a slave. How long did it take? Four minutes?"

"You used those minutes well, Juba," Miss Lilly said. "They'll come back again."

I doubted it.

CHAPTER FOUR

Jack Bishop was sick, so me and Stubby went down to the docks to buy fish.

"Tell them the fish are for the old Bishop," Jack said.

It was cold and rainy at four o'clock on Monday morning, and I didn't want to go fish buying, even if it was for Jack. Stubby was all for it, though, saying that buying good food was a big part of cooking.

"If you buy old, tough meat, there's not a lot you can do with it," he was saying. "You got to boil it to death to get it so you can chew it. The same thing with fish. You get old fish and it starts falling apart on you before it's done. Then it's not good for anything."

"You do the talking," I said. "I'm not a cook and I'm not a fish buyer."

"These fellows down here are rough," Stubby said. "They won't go for dancing."

"Stubby, you don't know that," I said. "Maybe I'll invent a new dance just for the docks. I'll call it the octopus and dance like I have seven legs. How many legs does an octopus have?"

"Octopuses have eight arms and no legs," Stubby said. "So they don't dance."

Stubby thought that was the funniest thing in the world, that an octopus didn't have any legs. I thought it was the funniest thing in the world that he knew about octopuses.

My mind was still halfway on the auditions. Jack said my hopes had been too high, which was wrong. My hopes hadn't been too high. They were just where I wanted them to be. I knew I could dance, and anybody who saw me knew it. John Diamond was almost twenty, and he couldn't dance next to me without looking second best, so he decided he was going to take away my chance. Sometimes at night I lay in bed and thought about punching him in the face. "Now *you* coon it up!" I imagined myself saying.

And I didn't want to hear any common sense coming from Miss Lilly or Jack Bishop or anybody else, white or black. They came around telling me they knew how I felt when they

57

didn't know anything about it. It's one thing if you don't have anything going for you and people say they're sorry you're sad. You're sorry, too, but you figure there's a reason for you to be sad and you settle into it. But when you got something going for you, when you have feet people watch and a body that people want to see moving across a stage, nobody can tell you anything, because they're nowhere near where you are.

"He's only done what he knows how to do," Jack said, telling me how I shouldn't be mad at Fred Flamer. "You can't blame a man for that, can you?"

Yes, I could. I could, and it was filling me up inside to a point where I thought either I was going to have to puke it up or it was going to kill me.

We reached the docks, and Stubby went over to one corner where a tall, thin fellow was standing next to a row of baskets.

"Where's the Bishop?" the man asked.

"Home with a cough," Stubby said.

"Weak," the man replied. "Old and weak!"

He had to be as old as Jack, and in the early-morning light he didn't look any healthier. He and Stubby talked for a while about how calm the sea was and what it meant. The fisherman said it meant there was a storm coming up. After a while they agreed on a price, and Stubby wrestled a basket of oysters onto the cart.

"I'm buying three of them," he said.

I loaded the next two as Stubby paid the man. As we pulled off, the oyster man called out to us to tell Jack to rub some warm tallow onto his chest.

Then we went to another fellow and bought two baskets of different kinds of fish. Stubby looked pleased, but it just added to my misery.

"We did good," he said. "Those fish are so fresh, they're still talking to each other."

"Stubby, I don't want to spend the rest of my life selling fish or cooking them," I said. "You're a good man, but I don't see doing what you do."

Stubby didn't answer, and I thought I might have hurt him, which I didn't mean to do.

It was getting lighter by the time we rolled the cart back to Baxter Street. The corner lamp man was walking down the street with his ladder, and I watched him as he leaned the ladder against a pole, climbed up it, and put out the lamp. People had all kinds of jobs, from fishing to lighting lamps at night and putting them out in the morning. There was nothing wrong with any of them, but they just weren't for me.

We took the oysters upstairs to the roof, and I started building a fire to smoke them. Stubby left with the cart to sell what he could. Jack Bishop's dog, John Tyler, came through the roof door and over to where I sat waiting for the chips to start burning evenly. He sniffed at me and sat down, and I shoved him away. The dumb dog just turned and looked at me, then came back and sat down next to me again.

I pushed him away again.

Next to come up to the roof was Margaret. She came over, picked up a stick, and poked through the chips, evening them out on the grill.

"Jack told me you were all beat up inside," she said.

"I don't care what he told you," I said.

"You think you're the only one in the world who ran over a bump in the road?" she asked.

"No, but I'm the only one wearing my skin who's had a hard time," I said.

"I grew up with three sisters and two brothers," Margaret said. She was rubbing the back of John Tyler's head. "Two of the girls and one of the boys died before they were six. That was what it was like. If you got sick, you prayed to Saint Blaise. If he didn't help you, then you died. It wasn't a huge thing for a child to die, but it was hard to get used to."

"Am I supposed to feel bad about that?" I asked.

"Glory, no!" Margaret looked at me sidewise. "You already have a mouthful of sour lemons—how could you fit any more in there? And let me tell you something about life, my black friend: you're just about old enough for your piss to get a little smell to it. There are going to be days when the auditions will look like a Sunday picnic to you!"

She was right, but it didn't help me any. When she went downstairs, John Tyler started to go with her, then turned around and came over to me again. "John Tyler, you are stupid—even for a dog you are stupid!" I said.

By the time the bells in the church on Mott Street rang ten o'clock, I had finished smoking most of the oysters and was ready when Stubby came up to the roof. He asked me how I was doing, and I told him I didn't need him looking out for me.

"I'm looking out for the oysters," Stubby said. "How are you doing with the oysters?"

"Okay," I said, feeling a little stupid for thinking that Stubby had meant me personally and not the oysters.

"You don't need me to tell you who's looking for you, either?" he asked.

"Who's looking for me?"

"That should be 'Who is looking for me, Mr. Jackson?'" Stubby said.

"Jack Bishop?"

"Miss Lilly was in front of the house asking where you live," Stubby said. "She said her husband wanted to see you."

"Forget Pete Williams—I don't have any respect for that man," I said.

"Jack said Pete probably has another scheme up his sleeve, and Margaret said if the devil gives a party, he plays his own tunes, so you'd best be careful."

"Why are you talking about somebody wanting to see me to Jack Bishop and Margaret?"

"I was going to talk to you about it first, but I thought you didn't want anybody looking out for you," Stubby said.

"Stubby, what do you think I should do?" I asked my friend. "You think he's just got another trick up his sleeve?"

"Well, if Miss Lilly came looking for you, there's got to be something bright shining somewhere," Stubby said. "She's a hard woman, but she's not a mean woman."

I didn't want to talk it over with anybody else, because I already knew I had to go and see what Peter Williams wanted. I knew I was going to be mad if Pete said something wrong, but I was already mad, and I would be just as mad not knowing as knowing.

"Can you finish smoking the oysters?"

"You know I can," Stubby said. "And tell Miss Lilly it was me that found you."

"I don't know if Pete is up, but Miss Lilly is in her little study," the cleaning man said when I arrived at Almack's. "She said you might be sliding by."

"Well, I'm here," I said.

"Saw you dancing the other day." The cleaning man leaned on his mop. "You trying to be one of them black Irishmen or something?"

"Dance is dance," I said. "Where is Miss Lilly's study?"

He pointed to a room in the corner, and I made my way to it and knocked on the door. Miss Lilly and Peter Williams sat at a small table. Miss Lilly was usually a pretty imposing woman, but sometimes she could be more imposing than at other times. She was sitting straight up when I entered the room. She was wearing a high-necked beige dress with a little brown and beige jacket.

"How you doing, Juba?"

"Just fine, Miss Lilly," I said.

"Peter wants to talk to you," Miss Lilly said, without looking toward where her husband sat.

"You seemed a little bothered the other day," Pete said. "Did something rub you the wrong way?"

Did something rub me the wrong way?

"Look, Pete, we were both there," I said. "We don't have to pretend we're light-headed or nothing. They were turning the auditions into a minstrel show. You've been around enough to know that."

"That was a business meeting," Pete said. "If you doing business, then you got to bring people what they want or they'll take their business someplace else."

"Jack Bishop said one of the white men there was a slave trader," I said. "That's the business you in now?"

"Look, Juba, I don't have to take no lip from you," Pete said.

"Miss Lilly invited you here because she thought you could talk like you got a brain in your head. I own this place—I don't have to take nothing from nobody! And if you don't understand that, or don't like it, you can just get on up out of here!"

I stood up, ready to go.

"Sit down, Juba," Miss Lilly said. "Peter, if you want to play like you don't have no sense and bully your way around, then it's up to you. You said you wanted something, and that's the only reason I asked Juba to come over here. Now, don't make *me* look like a fool, because I don't have a use for being foolish."

Pete looked at me and then away. He sighed deeply and crossed one leg over the other.

"There was some things I liked about what went on that day and some things I could forget about," he said. "What I liked was that there were people in here who were never in here before. They were looking around and seeing that it wasn't a bad-looking place and seeing that white people—I mean classy white people, not no riffraffers—looked comfortable. I liked that and I know that idea could bring in some money.

"I don't know what everyone did when they left the place. They could have been slave traders, or they could have been slave owners. I don't know. A lot of people living in New York City and running around with their noses in the air got plantations down South. But what I know is that if somebody can get them all coming into Almack's, I can build this business up so it looks respectable, feels respectable, and makes some respectable money. Miss Lilly thinks you're the man who can pull it off for me."

"Juba, you know dancing, and you know a lot of people." Miss Lilly leaned toward me. "What you were doing—your kind of dancing—wasn't what they were expecting, but I could see how you were drawing the people in. They weren't clapping along with anybody else. You've got class, and they know it and I know it and Peter knows it. *Don't* you, Peter?"

"He's all right."

"*Don't* you, Peter?"

"For a young man, he's got a lot of class, Miss Lilly," Pete said. "But what I want is a whole forty-minute show, like they have in the regular theaters. I want some white dancers and some black dancers. I want some singers, some decent food, a forty-minute show, and whatever it takes to let people know this is a top-of-the-line establishment. If I get them in here one time and show them they don't have anything to be afraid of, maybe I can get them in here two times. And if I can get them in here two times, maybe I can keep them coming."

"What do you think, Juba?" Miss Lilly asked.

"You want food, too?"

"Whatever it takes," Miss Lilly said.

"Why didn't you ask John Diamond to do it?" I asked. "You

two seemed to be hitting it off pretty swell."

"Because deep in my heart, I'm a race man!" Pete said. "I don't need any white boy running my business! I'm throwing twenty dollars into this adventure, and I need somebody who has my interest in their heart! Are you the man? That's a very simple question, Juba. Are you the man?"

"I think he is," Miss Lilly said. "I truly do. And maybe he can get Cissy going."

"Cissy?"

"You didn't know she sings?" Miss Lilly asked. "You've got to use her in the show."

She glanced over at her husband, who rolled his eyes away.

"You mean to tell me that Peter Williams, after ruining your audition the other day, had the nerve to ask you to set up a show for him?" Jack Bishop sat up in his bed. "And what did he say when you told him to bugger off?"

"I said I would do it," I said. "I didn't mean to say I would do it, but that's the way it came out."

"Your tongue and your lips were having a fight or something?" Stubby asked. "If you didn't mean to say something, how come you said it?"

"Because he's figured out that there's things you have to do in life because they're the right things to do at the moment," Jack said. "That's the way life is sometimes, with righteous stink on both ends of the stick."

"I said it, but I don't know how I'm going to get it done," I said. "Pete wants it sometime during the next two weeks, and I don't know where to start. I've never thought about getting a forty-minute program together."

"You can have breaks like they have in the regular shows," Stubby said. "Have somebody dance for three minutes, and then have a five-minute break. That's eight minutes gone already. So you have five dances, which is going to add up to fifteen minutes, and then you have five breaks, which will add up to twenty-five minutes. Fifteen and twenty-five make forty. Nothing to it."

"Juba, why are other people's problems so easy to solve?" Jack said. He pulled the blankets around his thin shoulders. "All you needed to do was to call on Stubby and your problems are solved! Of course, you'll have a show with mostly breaks in it and Pete will want to skin you alive, but Stubby will have an answer for that, too."

"You don't owe Peter Williams anything," Stubby said. "You're doing him a favor."

"And he's putting up twenty dollars cash money to pull this thing off," I said. "So if I don't get it right, he's going to want his money back."

"Did he actually make a promise to give you the money, or did he just talk about it?" Jack asked.

When Pete had started talking about money, I had felt the same way Jack Bishop did, that it was going to be all talk. But then Pete had taken out a small leather pouch and put it in the middle of the table. He had asked me if I knew what was in the bag, and although I had heard the clink of coins, I had just shrugged my shoulders.

Pete emptied the bag onto the table and dumped out twenty silver dollars. He made sure that the pouch was empty and started putting the coins back in. Then he pushed the pouch over to me.

I'd already figured that Peter Williams was rich, but I didn't think he was so rich he could just hand out twenty dollars like that. When I looked at him, he was staring at me directly in the eyes. What I figured him to be thinking was that I would be really impressed with the money. I hadn't fainted, but my knees were beginning to feel weak.

I took the pouch from my pocket and put it in front of Jack Bishop.

"Twenty dollars—I counted it four times," I said. "He wants a forty-minute show, with black and white performers, and they've got to be classy. Plus I have to make a meal for about fifteen tables. Pete says he'll sit special guests at the tables and treat them royal, and everybody else will just be in regular seats around the room."

"If you let some of your guests eat off the good plates and

the fine linen, then everybody will think they're being treated like swells," Jack said. "Are you sure Peter isn't English? He sounds sneaky enough."

"You think I can pull it off?" I asked.

"You can if you don't hang all your clothes on one nail," Jack said. "Look around and see who you can call on to help you. You know who can dance and who can sing. You know who's got clean shirts and who don't, too. All you have to do is get them all lined up, see what's in it for each of them, and let their interests take over."

"You can leave the cooking to me," Stubby volunteered. "If they're looking for the top drawer, then I'm your man."

"Give him a shot, Juba," Jack said. "He'll make you proud of him."

What Jack was saying made sense. I did know most of the entertainers in Five Points and some from as far away as Twenty-Third Street. They were all hungry to show off their talents, and most of them would work for nothing if I asked. When I went over what Stubby had said, about only needing five acts, it gave me a way to think about how many people I had to get. Some people could perform twice, so I figured seven should do it. Fourteen performances would be the whole forty minutes with a little over. I would be the main dancer, and I knew I could probably get Simmy Long to dance. I needed one more colored dancer and some white performers. I had an idea of where I was going to get the white performers, but I wasn't sure about the colored dancer. I didn't want to even talk to the one I knew best, but I knew I at least needed to feel him out.

"Juba, I needed to get the job at the auditions," Freddy said. "Look around this place. This is how I'm living. I deserve better than this."

It had been easy for me to find Freddy. I knew he lived on Cherry Street, and I just asked some kids where the colored man who always carried a cane stayed, and they pointed out his place. A round-faced woman sitting on the stoop told me Freddy lived on the second floor and that he had just moved in a little while ago.

The place smelled horrible. It was dark in the middle of the day, with people sleeping in the corners. The sewer ran right under the building, and you could smell the waste.

"I don't even have my own place," Freddy said. "I rent a space here to sleep on the floor. I don't have no decent place to live, and I can barely get up enough money to eat proper. When John Diamond was calling to me to make my act more like a minstrel show, it hurt me. It truly did, because I know I'm better than that. I am not nobody's *nigger*. But look at the way I'm living. You got to see what was pulling on my coattail, Juba."

There was a noise, and I looked to see a pile of rags on the floor move. A woman, rags tied around her legs, was sleeping against the wall with a coat pulled partway over her. The whole place was dreary, dark, and disgusting.

"You're not living well, Freddy," I said. "But to throw yourself away completely didn't make any sense. If you're going to let people put you in whatever place they want, you're never going to have their respect. And when you jumped into that place, grinning and carrying on, you dragged me right in with you."

"Look, I'm sorry, Juba. I truly am, but we can work together on this. Peter talked to me about putting on a show, and I was all for it. He said you and me could pull it off. We could work together."

"He said we could work *together*?"

"Miss Lilly was pulling for you. She didn't think you wanted to work with me," Freddy said. "But I think we could do well together. We could put on a good show. What do you say?"

Freddy held out his hand. I didn't take it.

"When did he talk to you, Freddy?" I asked.

"Right after the auditions," Freddy answered. "We need to put bygones behind us, Juba. You and I are the best entertainers around here. I know we can do it!"

I was getting mad at Pete again for talking to Freddy before he talked to me.

"We can't work together, Freddy," I said. "I'll bring you in on this if you do what I say. If you don't want to do what I tell you, then you got to move away from me."

"I'll do whatever you say, Juba," Freddy said. "Just give me a chance."

I didn't feel right when I left Freddy. What I knew, or thought I knew, was that if the chance came for him to throw his manhood and his talent away to get over, he would do it. Peter Williams didn't care about that. Pete didn't even think of himself as a black man. He thought of himself as a money man. Still, I needed another colored dancer, and Freddy could dance. He could carry himself well, too, when he wanted. But I had to make the show good enough that he would want to be something special.

"Isn't it funny, Stubby, that you got to convince people not to hurt themselves?" I asked my roommate when I got home.

"Freddy is doing what he thinks he can do," Stubby said. "That's not easy sometimes."

"That's not good enough for me," I said. "And I got some words I have picked out for Freddy. I'm just saving them for a special occasion."

From the dancing at the auditions, I thought maybe John Diamond had got the white dancers on board. They were all kinds of good, and I thought about asking John for their names, but he and I were always butting heads about who was the best between us, and I knew he wouldn't do me any favors. We had even danced together at times when some promoter wanted to put on a black and white show, but I could tell he didn't like sharing the stage. Margaret taught mostly young Irish girls, and I wondered if she would help.

In the afternoon Stubby came and asked me if I was going to help him put up the cart and bring the unsold fish upstairs. There wasn't that much fish left, but only half the smoked oysters were gone.

"When Jack is selling, he just kind of mushes his way through a conversation and gets people nodding and smiling, and then they feel too ashamed not to buy something," Stubby said. "When I'm selling, I'm begging them to buy, and they start acting like the fish are moldy and the oysters are rotten."

"So how do you think I should go ask Margaret if she's going to help me get this thing together?" I asked.

"You're not even interested in selling these fish, are you?"

"Stubby, dancing and entertaining people is what I love," I said. "If fish could clap their hands, I'd be dancing for them. So do you think Margaret will help me get a show together?"

"Fish don't have hands," Stubby said. "And Margaret's not going to help you, because she doesn't like you that much. She told me that."

She didn't like me that much, but I had a sneaky feeling she liked dancing enough to think about working with me.

I had been in Margaret's apartment a couple of times, and she had shown me some interesting things about dancing.

She was tough in a way and had a quick tongue on her, but there were things she knew, and it came to me that maybe all the white dancers didn't have to be that good just to put on a show. In fact, the more I thought about it, the clearer I realized they didn't have to be good at all. As long as they didn't fall down on the floor, they could fill up the space between when I was dancing and when Freddy and Simmy were dancing.

The Artis twins were a little weird, but that was part of their act. They were not that good-looking, but they moved together well. Pete told people they were from Africa, but I knew they were from Philadelphia. He had them dress alike in white, gauzy costumes, and sometimes they played castanets as they danced. They were a popular act.

The show was going to be a colored dance performance with some white dancers and singers just around to show it was a mixed group. So when I got to Margaret's place, after washing up to get the fish smell off my hands and clothes, I was feeling pretty good as I explained to her what I had in mind.

"If you think for one hot minute that I'm going to be out rounding up dancers and helping you put on a show just to show off the talents of three colored boys, you have put your hat on the wrong part of your body, Mr. Juba."

"I'm not wearing a hat," I reminded her.

"And you don't have much of a head to put it on if you *were* wearing one," Margaret said. "There are young white people out there who can dance just as well as you can and will put their hearts and souls into it. But they are not as stupid as you seem to think they are, that they're going to just sweep the floor for the coloreds."

"I didn't say they couldn't dance," I said.

"Yes, you did, Juba." Margaret leaned her face toward me. "You were spitting some of the words and swallowing some of them, but you got your teeth together enough to say that they didn't have to be that good, didn't you?"

"Yes, ma'am."

"So go get yourself some bums off the streets and see what they can do for you!"

"Miss Moran, can you help me?" I thought of Stubby trying to sell fish. "If I can get a show together for Pete Williams, it will mean a lot to me. At the auditions they wouldn't let me dance. The man who owned the theater was asking me to 'coon it up'! Do you know what that means?"

"Because you're wearing a scarf doesn't mean you're the only one in the village with a neck, Juba," Margaret said. "It means they wanted you to forget about your dancing and be something that amused them—the same way you want the young white people to forget about their dancing and be something that amuses you. Jack Bishop told me what happened at the auditions. He felt really bad for you, and when he told me, *I* felt really bad for you. But now I see that nobody has to feel anything for you, because you have it all covered by yourself."

"I didn't think of it that way," I said.

"You always think with yourself in the middle of your mind and everybody else floating around on the edges."

"So there's nothing you can do for me?" My voice seemed small.

"If you're ready to get down off your throne, Mr. Juba Almighty, I might lend you a hand," Margaret said.

I had to sit for another ten minutes while Margaret reminded me how stupid I was for thinking she was going to betray the Irish race and then described my dancing as something that wasn't much more than clog dancing in the first place, and said I had stolen everything I knew from the street corners and festivals around Five Points.

"Okay, Margaret, I see where you are right about me not thinking about the white dancers in the same way that John Diamond and Mr. Reeves hadn't thought about the black dancers at the auditions," I said. "I was just so upset about what happened that I was hoping to make up for everything, to make it all right, by turning out a spectacular show.

"You're right that I have learned a lot from clog dancing, and that I've borrowed some of the steps and some of the moves. But where you're wrong is important, too. I bring a lot of rhythms to the dancing, and a lot of moves that make my dancing special. I'm dancing from my heart and using everything I know, and some of it I don't even know where it comes from. But I can tell you this. Whenever I see a person move, my eyes kind of record it, and I can feel that movement in my muscles, and in my legs, and in my arms. When I see somebody running, it's almost like me running.

"Sometimes I watch the little girls jumping rope on Avenue A, across from the school, and if I watch them long enough, I get tired because my body is moving right along with theirs. At the auditions, I saw the white dancers and I watched them and I liked what I saw. I wanted to get out there and take what they were doing and build on it. They were dancing so well that people were watching their feet, the way you say old Irish people always do, but I wanted to dance so good that people would want to see if my feet were still touching the floor. I'm not just trying to make money, or even to entertain people. I love what I do, and I want to do it because I love it. And sometimes all that loving of dancing I have just gets in the way of my thinking straight. I'm always ready to learn something new about dancing, Margaret. Jack Bishop is teaching me a lot about being a good person, and I love to hear Stubby talking about cooking. I'm glad you got my head straight about how I was looking at the Irish dancers. I'm not that big a fellow, but I'm bigger now than when I knocked on your door this afternoon."

"Well, just don't let that tongue of yours tie up knots that it can't get loose."

"So do you think you can help me pull it all together?"

"We'll see," Margaret said. "We'll see."

CHAPTER FIVE

I was lying in bed trying to make myself go to sleep, and Stubby was snoring away across from me, sounding like he was doing it on purpose. First he would give a couple of snorts, then a big noisy snort, and then a little wheezy sound would come out of him. Usually, him snoring didn't bother me, but now everything was working on my nerves. What Margaret had said didn't get under my skin that much, although I did think she got the flame under her kettle a little too high. What did bother me was how many people I was relying on to bring this show together.

Peter Williams said he wanted a forty-minute program, and

that wasn't much to think about when he was saying it, but the doing was something else. The only white dancers I knew up close were John Diamond and his friends. I didn't want any part of John Diamond, because I knew he would sabotage anything I did. As long as he thought of himself as the number one dancer in Five Points, I was going to be a thorn in his side. But when he didn't have his race on his side, as he did at the auditions, we were equals. And when it came to dancing, he was good, but I was still the best, and he knew it.

Food was going to cost money, and I wanted to pay the dancers, too. Artists need to make money for their art so they can see it's worthwhile, even if they love what they're doing. I thought a dollar for each would be right, but when Jack and I worked it out, using seven performers, it was getting shaky.

"So you're talking nearly half your money already," Jack said. "And you haven't actually hired a dancer or singer yet. Remember, you need some money in reserve for emergencies, too. Or costumes. Or musicians."

"You having doubts?" I asked Jack. "You thinking I can't pull it off?"

"No, just concerns," Jack said. "Show business is a lot like stealing hams from a smokehouse. You stick your hand through a hole in the wall and grab a ham, and everybody thinks you're wonderful. If you stick your hand through the hole and the owner is waiting inside with a meat cleaver and chops it off, then you're a chump. You have to decide if the risk is worth it."

It was worth it to me. I hadn't had to deal with that many people before, but I was already thinking that if I did put on the show and it made people happy, that was something I could do someplace else.

I asked Fred Flamer to come to our room and talk it over, just to make sure I wasn't missing anything. I asked Margaret, too, and she said no, that she didn't go into men's rooms.

The meeting didn't go well. Stubby was saying yes to everything I said, and to everything I asked, and he wasn't even thinking about how much it was going to cost.

Fred Flamer was even worse. He kept sitting on the edge of Stubby's bed, nodding his head up and down and smiling, and I knew he was desperate for a chance to perform. I thought about asking him to "coon it up" for us, just to see if he would do it. That was wrong and I knew it, but to see anybody be so desperate was strange to me. Fred was a step away from giving up dancing, and he knew it.

"I'll take fifteen of the forty minutes," I said. "Freddy, you can take seven, and we'll give the white dancers and singers eighteen minutes. What do you think?"

"Sounds good to me," Freddy said. "You know I can fiddle, too."

"We've got to work it out with Margaret, because she's

going to help us line up some good Irish performers," I said. "We're going to have some rehearsals, and *everybody* has to show up. This is a chance to do ourselves some good."

"You think Almack's is thinking about keeping us on for good?" Freddy asked.

Peter Williams hadn't said anything about permanent jobs, and I knew he wasn't going to be throwing around that kind of money every week. He had a greedy little mind, a taste for money, and an eye for where the money was hidden.

"I just think he wants to see what can be done," I answered Freddy. "I've performed for him before, but most of what I was getting was jingle thrown out on the floor, and Pete wants part of that."

When Freddy left, me and Stubby took the cart out to sell fish. Stubby was full of talk about getting real menus printed up, and I told him I didn't want to spend money getting anything printed for just one day. He looked disappointed.

We didn't sell much. Stubby talked to a black cook and asked her if he could borrow some serving plates for a party he was giving. She said he could if he was nice enough to her, and Stubby said he would be as nice as she wanted him to be. I don't think he understood that she was wanting some kissing and hugging. She was twice as big as Stubby, and just about twice as old, so he was going to have to cook up something special for those plates.

Back home, I was so tired. It seemed like every day I was getting more and more tired, and I knew it was because I had too many things to think about. Jack was disappointed that we didn't sell more fish, and he said so.

"You just got your mind on this one night, and you're letting the rest of your life slip away from you!"

That was right. I wasn't as hard up as Freddy, but I was feeling the same cold breeze he was feeling. A good chance only came along once in a while, and you had to jump on it when it came your way. If we didn't put on a good show for Pete Williams, everybody would know about it and it would be hard to get any kind of job dancing or singing.

I fell asleep on the bed and was surprised when I heard a banging on the door. I thought Stubby had left his key someplace. It wasn't Stubby, but Miss Lilly and Priscilla, the girl she called Cissy.

"I told Cissy you didn't bite, so there was no reason for her to be shy about telling you she was ready to sing for you," Miss Lilly said. "Go on, girl, sing."

Now, the thing is that nobody who did any acting or singing could do it just like that. You had to get yourself in the mood, or warm up, or put your lucky charm in your pocket, or whatever it took for you to be somebody else. That was what show business was about. For a few minutes or a few hours, you were somebody else, somebody with a strange kind of magic.

The girl had her head down and didn't move.

"You sing for Juba and then you come back over to Almack's," Miss Lilly said. "You got a peck of work to do, girl."

I watched as Miss Lilly started down the stairs, stopped, sent a mean look toward Priscilla, and continued on down.

"You want some tea?" I asked.

Priscilla shrugged, and I moved aside so she could come in. She stood in the doorway for a minute and looked inside, then stepped in.

I went to the cupboard and took down the tin we kept the tea in. Empty. "You want some water?"

She shrugged again.

"You like working at Almack's?" I asked.

"I owe him a lot of money," she answered. Her voice was soft and a little breathy. "The way I'm working now and paying him a little every week, I'll never get finished."

"That's about how half the people in the world work," I said. "I know people who owe their bosses so much money, they got to borrow their pay every week."

"He wants me to dance with his customers," Priscilla said.

Dancing with the customers at Almack's, when the sailors fell in from the ships or when the workers from the warehouses drifted in with their smells and heavy feet, was a rough and tumble business. Men who most women would not have looked at twice began to think they were something special as they ran their hands over the women or tried to kiss them. All the time, Pete and his staff would be peddling booze and pushing the girls out on the floor if they sat down for more than a minute. It was a scene you didn't want to see.

"You can sing?" I asked.

"Some," she said.

It wasn't the answer I was looking for, but I sat on our one chair and put my palms up. "Let's hear you," I said.

Her voice was weak, and she came near the key some of the time, but most of the tune got away from her. And she looked so sad.

I could see why Pete kept her around the club. She was still young, and she was light-skinned, which was what he was looking for, and most of all, she didn't have any spunk in her. He could push her around and get her to do what he wanted, and that was all that mattered to him. He'd make his money and go to sleep happy. His dealing with a slave trader made sense.

Lilly was another story. She was bringing Priscilla to me to see if I could do something with her. Why any woman would want to be with a man like Peter was a mystery, but I guessed that some women just stuck with who they found themselves with. Lilly had a good heart, and a little bit of influence with Peter, enough to push him in the direction of improving Almack's but not enough to protect the women in the place.

Priscilla finished singing the song, and I told her I would talk with her later.

"I didn't do too good, did I?" she asked me.

"I'll find a place for you in the show," I said.

"You're trying to wear four hats and you've only got one head!" Jack said when I told him about Priscilla. "Be careful you don't find yourself out in the rain getting wet."

"Jack, what does that mean?" I asked.

"You're trying to pull off a show, you're trying to raise this man's club to something it ain't, you're trying to show off your talents, you're trying to save this girl, you're trying to get blacks and whites together on the same program, you're trying to help Stubby set up his catering business, and you're trying to elevate the colored race," Jack said. "What more are you going to do, train some monkeys to knit sweaters?"

"That's more than four things," Stubby said. "First you said he was trying to pull off a show, that's one thing—"

"Stubby, I can count," Jack said. "I'm just trying to say he's doing too many things."

"What kind of business did you say I was in?" Stubby again.

"Catering," Jack said. "That's when you cook for parties or private people and bring the food to them."

Stubby was very interested in the catering business and

was getting Jack to explain it to him. Jack kept looking over at me, but he was being patient with Stubby and explaining how the event could help him, too.

I felt a headache coming on because I knew Jack was right. The pressure was getting to me, and I was reaching in too many directions. Some decisions had to be made, and most of all, the decision about what I was going to be doing in the show. Everybody had their own interests, and I couldn't let them run around me and not let my light shine. I decided to make a list of people who were going to be in the show, and what they wanted. The first thing I needed to do was to see if Margaret was really going to get some Irish dancers or if I would have to go find them.

Margaret had her hair up with strands tied around paper. She looked like pictures of clowns I had seen in books.

"What are you looking at?" she asked me. "You've never seen a woman with her hair up before?"

"Looks fine to me," I said.

"You're a little scared of women, aren't you?" Margaret said. "You don't like to be around us, right?"

"That's not true," I said.

"So what do you want?" she asked.

"You said you could get some Irish dancers, and I just wondered . . ."

"If you tell them what they're going to do, it's easier than just saying come and dance for some black fellow," Margaret said. "And they want to know who they're dancing for. You're black, Peter Williams is black, and other dancers on the program are going to be black. Don't forget that."

"So why is race important?" I asked. "Dancing is dancing!"

"If it goes good, then everybody's happy," Margaret said. "You want some tea? And if it goes bad, then they're dancing for niggers. Don't act with me like you were born yesterday, Juba."

"How can I tell somebody how long they're going to perform if I don't know who's going to show up?" I asked.

"Well, you can have a show where everybody steps up and does their things for a few minutes, or you can have a story," Margaret said. "If you have a story, then it's easy to get people to play a part."

"What kind of story?"

"Can you read?" Margaret got out a notebook and opened it up. On the top it read *Little Red Riding Hood*. The next lines read *Scenes*, and they were numbered.

"I can read, but this is a children's story, right?" I said.

"Everybody's going to know it, including the dancers, and it'll start somewhere and end somewhere," Margaret said. "There's an Irish version of it that all the young dancers will know. And you can make as much out of it as you want to if you know what you're doing. Take it with you and look it over. And don't forget to bring my notebook back."

Margaret's Notes

Little Red Riding Hood

Scene 1—There is a great FOREST (Irish dancers), 3 minutes

Scene 2—Enter LITTLE RED RIDING HOOD Irish dancer through the FOREST, 3 minutes

Scene 3—Enter the BIG BAD WOLF, 1 minute

Scene 4—BIG BAD WOLF and LITTLE RED RIDING HOOD dance, but she is protected by the FOREST, 2 minutes

Scene 5—LITTLE RED RIDING HOOD starts to Grandmother's house, 30 seconds

Scene 6—BIG BAD WOLF starts to Grandmother's house, 30 seconds

Scene 7—LITTLE RED RIDING HOOD stops to play, 1 minute

Scene 8—BIG BAD WOLF sneaking through the FOREST, 30 seconds

Scene 9—Enter the WOODSMAN, 5 minutes

Scene 10— LITTLE RED RIDING HOOD at Grandmother's house, 2½ minutes

Scene 11—BIG BAD WOLF pounces on LITTLE RED RIDING HOOD, 1 minute

Scene 12—A CHIPMUNK (deer?) tells the WOODSMAN, 1½ minutes

Scene 13—The FOREST opens and leads the WOODSMAN to Grandmother's house, 1 minute

Scene 14—Battle between WOODSMAN and BIG BAD WOLF, 3 minutes

Scene 15—LITTLE RED RIDING HOOD *is saved, 2 minutes*

Scene 16—LITTLE RED RIDING HOOD *dances with* WOODSMAN *and then goes home, 3 minutes*

Scene 17—WOODSMAN *dances with* FOREST, *6 minutes*

Scene 18—FOREST *celebrates, 1 minute*

THE END

LITTLE RED RIDING HOOD—*15-year-old Irish girl*

BIG BAD WOLF—*black dancer*

WOODSMAN—*Juba*

FOREST—*Irish troupe*

CHIPMUNK—*black dancer*

NARRATOR—*anybody*

At first it looked a little silly to me, but then it started to make sense. I would be the Woodsman and have the longest role. I could put in Fred Flamer as the Big Bad Wolf and maybe Simmy Long as the Chipmunk. It looked good. I especially liked the battle between the Woodsman and the Big Bad Wolf. My spirits got really high. Margaret had made the day ready, and I was going to save it.

John Diamond and a couple of toughs stopped me on the street.

"Heard about the show you're doing up at Almack's," John said, standing close to me. I could smell liquor on his breath.

"You trying to get fancy with yourself, are you?"

"Is that what I'm trying to do?"

"What's Pete paying you?"

"What's it to you?" I asked.

One of the toughs, a beefy, dark-haired fellow with a broad face, grabbed me by the collar. Two black dustmen who were passing stopped to see what was going on. John's friend took a look at them, saw they were as big as he was, and let my collar go.

"Why don't you hire me to bring some class to your show?" John spoke with a half sneer on his face. "I saw what you did at the auditions for Mr. Reeves, and it wasn't that much. You still don't know what the people want to see."

"If you know so much, why don't you go and dance for Reeves?" I asked. "I thought by now you'd be the top star at his theater."

"He'll get it open soon enough," Diamond said. "I can start the show at Almack's for you, you can perform somewhere in between, and I'll finish the program for you. I heard you're going to have some Irish kid dancers. How many acts you going to have, three or four?"

"I don't need your help, Diamond," I said. "But I'm glad you're hearing good things about the show. Maybe you ought to come and learn something."

He turned and spit on the ground and then started off. The

two fellows with him waited a few seconds and then followed.

It was good that John Diamond had heard about the show. And if he had also heard about the Irish dancers Margaret was getting together, he had probably figured out I had something going. The next news I got about the show was from Stubby. He told me one of the men who hung around Almack's had let him know that Pete wanted to see him. When he went to Almack's, he was told to set up five more tables than we had planned.

"Why didn't he come to me?" I asked. "I'm supposed to be paying you for the food."

"I don't believe he wants to pay any more money," Stubby said. "He just wants more food."

I asked Jack what he thought about it, because I was beginning to worry that Pete was going to mess the program up and then try to blame me for it. Jack said he didn't think five extra tables would mean that much.

"They're only sitting two people at those little tables," Jack said. "So that's fifty meals instead of forty. Stubby's pulling it together, and he's not looking to make a profit on it, so a few extra meals won't be a problem."

He was wrong.

CHAPTER SIX

The dance program was supposed to start at seven in the evening, and the dinner was going to be at six. But by five thirty the place was already filling up. Miss Lilly said all the Irish dancers had invited their friends and family, and some other people from the nearby Roman Catholic churches had come as well. Most of them had never been to Almack's before, and they were looking around the large room with the dance floor and at the black help who were setting up tables. Pete had borrowed four tables from a nearby café to add to the five he had stored away. I could see Stubby beginning to sweat.

"He said he was going to make the girls who dance here do the serving," Stubby said.

"Can you handle that many women?" I asked him.

Stubby smiled and said he would do his best.

I felt myself getting nervous as six o'clock arrived. When I saw Stubby coming out with a tray of bowls, followed by four girls with the same kind of bowls, I was as curious as the other spectators.

"Onion soup," Jack Bishop said to me. "Always a good start."

He handed me a handwritten paper that said *Menu* on top.

Onion Soup

Creamed Smoked Oysters

Veal Tenderloin

Filet of Striped Bass

Potato and Spinach Casserole

String Beans

Peach Pudding

Sweet Buttermilk or Tea

Margaret and her dancers got there halfway through the meal, and many of the Irish people started applauding as soon as they saw them arrive. Margaret called me into the back room that Pete had given us to get ready in and told me how excited all the young dancers were.

"Do you think there's going to be any food left over for them?" she asked.

I told her I'd find out and went looking for Stubby. He was in the kitchen with Miss Lilly, stirring a big pot. I asked him if there was enough food for the dancers, and he shook his head. His eyes were getting bigger every minute, and I thought there was something wrong.

"Juba, they're eating everything!" Stubby said.

"You shouldn't have cooked it so good," Miss Lilly said. "You know most of the people out there aren't used to a menu this fancy."

"I need to grow another pair of hands just to get it all ready to be served," Stubby said.

"And there's two reporters from the *Evening Post* and one from that new paper, the *New-York Daily Tribune*," Miss Lilly said. "If they mention your food in their papers, you going to have to grow another set of legs to go with those hands."

My stomach was jumping, and I could feel my heart beating faster. We were bringing this show together just fine. We were making the whole night a celebration instead of just dancing and singing for the people. The food was loosening the people up, and all the talk about local dancers being part of the program had helped build the excitement.

Pete came into the kitchen grinning, his eyes shiny with anticipation.

"The police just brought in some gentlemen and a lady from the mayor's office," he said. "I might have to hire Juba for the rest of the year!"

Pete was getting to see what we could do, but I had been working like a dog, along with Stubby and Margaret and Jack Bishop, and we weren't going to be working all year for Peter Williams, I thought.

By the time Stubby was down to serving the peach pudding, I was exhausted, and I hadn't been on the floor yet. The crowd was still growing. I looked around to see how many whites and how many blacks were there, and I saw there were more whites than blacks. At the tables I saw some gentlemen who looked overstuffed in their suits and cravats, and I thought they must be from the mayor's office. There was one white man who looked young enough to be not yet twenty, and I was pretty sure he was a man despite the fact that he had long hair. He was writing at his table. I figured him to be a reporter from the *Evening Post*.

Then it was seven o'clock, time for the show to start.

"Wish us luck, Jack," I said.

"With all the work you put into this, you won't be needing luck," Jack answered.

It was different for me. Usually I would be going out on the floor by myself, with maybe a drummer or a fiddler. Now I had to wait until I fit in with Margaret's fairy tale. The little Jewish woman Margaret had got to play the piano went out and sat on the stool. Then she got up and turned the seat so she would be higher. A cold trickle of sweat ran down under my arm. In my mind, I was calling for the woman to get it going, but she just sat in front of the upright piano for a long time. Then she lifted her hands to the keyboard and started playing.

The audience quieted down, and I was holding my breath.

"Little Red Riding Hood!" Margaret called out. "There was once a great forest . . ."

The moment the Irish dancers got onto the floor, straight as arrows with their hands behind their backs, some of the spectators began to applaud. The dancers made a half circle, always facing the tables, where Stubby and some of the girls were just clearing away the last dishes. Then the dancers brought their hands from behind their backs, and they were carrying small paper trees.

More applause. I felt myself relaxing.

They danced their little number, making lines of five and five that were weaving in and out, so that a line would be four strong and another would be six, and then they would reverse to five and five and sometimes three and seven. They danced precisely and in rhythm. I glanced at the older Irish people, and as Margaret had said, they were looking at the dancers' feet.

"Into the wood, on the way to Granny's house, came Little Red Riding Hood!"

The dancer was fifteen, but she looked older and moved smoothly. There was applause that welcomed her onstage as she moved through the other dancers representing the forest. She wasn't that good, and none of her steps were spectacular, but she moved almost as if she were suspended from a string, as if she had no weight. She brought everybody into the story.

When Fred Flamer came on as the Big Bad Wolf, a few people snickered, and I hoped he wasn't going to mess it up. He lost his way through the forest a couple of times, and tried to smooth it out by double-stepping. He wasn't adding anything to the show, but he didn't take away too much, either.

The story of Little Red Riding Hood was simple, and I didn't think it was going to be that effective, but the audience was respectful and quiet. It was high class, just what Peter had wanted.

It seemed forever before I would go on, and I stood in the shadows doing a couple of toe touches to stretch my legs. I watched for a moment as Fred Flamer went sneaking through the forest to Grandma's house, and then I came out just before he went off.

What I started with was the same jig the forest dancers had used, with my arms straight down, my head up. I did it in the same rhythm for ten seconds, then moved faster, increasing the rhythm to double time. Someone started applauding, and then the applause increased.

The kids were moving well, and they were responding to me. They kept the slower rhythm and moved in perfect unison. The crowd loved the way we were dancing together, and I was loving it, too.

When I left the floor, there was more applause.

I was against the wall when the Big Bad Wolf came out again and was actually booed. Fred smiled. I didn't know if he felt embarrassed or if he was pleased, but with his long face he looked sinister.

Maybe Margaret had said something to the forest dancers. When I was going through them again, I saw that the boys were dancing in the same rhythm as the first time I had danced with them, but the girls had picked up the pace. They hadn't done that in rehearsal.

I danced the rhythm the girls used, then took a chance and danced with one leg doing all the work and the other marking time. I heard applause.

A young girl danced near me and increased the pace again. I looked at her and could tell she was having fun. I danced at her pace as I made my way through the forest again.

I slowed down my dance battle with the Big Bad Wolf. There was no use in making Fred Flamer look bad, and I didn't want him doing anything to mess up the story. I just danced with him, cutting him off from going near Little Red Riding Hood, until he slunk off into the shadows.

More applause.

My last dance was with the forest dancers again, and I knew I wanted to make them look good. I could sense that they were pleased with their performance, and so was I. We danced for three minutes, then they moved offstage. I increased the pace of my steps for a frantic thirty seconds and then, turning, beckoned the forest dancers back. They were surprised, but they got themselves together and we danced faster and faster until the pace was too fast for almost all of us, and then I raised my arms, turned to them, and bowed.

I was supposed to finish by myself onstage, but I gave it over to the forest dancers, and they finished with a flourish.

I thought we had been great.

The applause felt good, and when all the dancers and Margaret had gathered in the dressing room, we were all still excited and chatting away.

"You could be Irish if you worked at it!" Little Red Riding Hood said to me.

"Thanks."

Peter Williams came in as the dancers left. He was looking like a crocodile that had just finished its supper, with more teeth showing than I thought could fit into a regular mouth. He shook my hand and Freddy's and everybody else's he could find.

A huge police officer came in and said that if I wasn't

too tired, someone wanted to speak to me. I *was* tired, but I followed him out to one of the tables. It was the white man with long hair who I had thought was a reporter.

"I'm delighted to meet you, sir," the man said. He had a soft face and very small hands.

"Pleased to meet you," I said.

"Please join us." The man, who had stood, gestured toward an empty chair. "I was sitting here, watching you dance, being amazed at how well you danced, really, and wondered who you were."

"William Henry Lane," I said. "When I'm dancing, I'm called Master Juba. Some of my friends just call me Juba. A lot of entertainers take on stage names."

"And writers, too" was the quick reply. "My name is Charles Dickens, but I often write under the name of Boz. I'm touring your country, writing about how remarkable it is in so many ways. We are similar people, the English and you Americans, but so different in so many ways. Have you always lived in New York?"

"I lived in Rhode Island for a while, but most of my life in New York," I said.

"New York, to me, is like London's wilder cousin," Mr. Dickens said. "It has all the better places, and some of the wilder places as well. Americans are so full of life—I think more so than the English, although we like to portray ourselves as being always on the top crust of the pie, so to speak."

"I've never been to England."

"They'd love to see you dance in England," Mr. Dickens said. "I can't imagine that we have anyone who quite fits what you do. When you're dancing, do you—do you mind me asking you questions about your dancing?"

"No, I like talking about what I do."

"Good—so do I," Mr. Dickens said. "Get me talking about writing or about my stories and you've got yourself a problem. But you have a way about you when you dance. Your body seems so free, your movements so absolutely crammed with life, that you make everyone around you want to dance as well."

"Do you dance?"

"Good gracious, no." Mr. Dickens looked away. "But there's a freedom about the way you move that makes me wish I *could* dance. Have you ever had a difficult time in your life?"

"At times, everything seems hard," I said. "I'm not sure what tomorrow is going to be like. I'm just hoping it's something good."

"I imagined—and I know I'm talking too much—that you must have had some difficult times along the way. I think that's the mystery of greatness and of people who achieve wonderful things," Mr. Dickens said. "That somewhere in their lives they have felt the cold winds of despair, but have kept their hearts warm nevertheless."

Engraved portrait of Charles Dickens

"I wish I could remember what you just said, sir," I said. "I'll never get the words just right, but I liked the way you said it."

"Are you going to dance again?" Mr. Dickens asked. "I would love to see you perform one more time before I leave."

"Charles Dickens is one of the most famous writers in the

world," a puffy man next to Mr. Dickens said. "I'm sure you'd like to dance for him."

When somebody admires what you do, and tells you to your face, you really do want to do something to earn his good opinion. I said I'd dance again.

I told Miss Lilly that Mr. Dickens wanted to see me dance again, and she got her husband to clear people off the floor to give me room. The Jewish woman who had been playing piano was going toward the door, and I went and asked her to play one more time.

"I don't know. My husband doesn't like me out too late," she said.

"I'll get someone to walk you home. And there's an extra fifty cents in it for you," I said. "Do you know 'Morrison's Jig'?"

"I sure do," she said.

"Don't play it too slow."

Middle of the floor. I looked over to where Mr. Dickens was sitting and nodded toward him. He smiled and nodded back. I could see all the eyes around the rest of the room focused on me.

The piano player hit a chord, then a second that I knew was a lead-in, and then began to play "Morrison's Jig."

The music swept through the room as I began to dance. I had thought about dancing as well as I could, but suddenly there was no reason to think about dancing at all. I let the music take me over and sweep me across the floor. I spun, I moved across the floor on one leg and back on the other, I double-stepped, slid on one leg as I moved backward, switched to a six-beat clog step. I danced faster than I had ever danced, with more precision than I had ever had before, and with more joy in my heart.

Mr. Dickens had stood and was clapping his hands, and everybody who was still in Almack's followed his lead.

I danced until it seemed I couldn't dance anymore. When the piano player got to the last chorus, I was tired and exhausted, and as happy as I had ever been in my life.

Mr. Dickens came out onto the floor and put his arms around me. I was sweaty and hot, but he didn't seem to mind.

"Thank you," he said. "Thank you, Master Juba."

CHAPTER
SEVEN

"I do not need any smelly-breath Negro standing nose to nose with me spitting fool talk in my face!" Margaret was yelling at me. "If he is your friend, then he is your friend, but you keep his large black face away from my door. Do you understand me, Mr. Juba?"

"No," I said, stepping away from the door.

Stubby had tried to get me up earlier but had given up when I started fighting to keep the covers over my head. I was still exhausted from the day before and certainly wasn't up to slowing down Margaret as she brushed by me.

"This morning Mr. Peter Williams came knocking on my door and offering me a job at Almack's to run regular shows,"

Margaret said. "I told him I didn't run the show, that you did, but he said he couldn't deal with you and offered me five dollars a week to—how did he put it—provide entertainment for the people."

"He offered you five dollars *every* week?" I asked.

"That he did," Margaret said.

That didn't sit too good with me. He hadn't offered me anything, and I wouldn't do it for what he was offering Margaret. I started explaining to Margaret how Peter was trying to get everything for nothing. She said I didn't have to explain anything to her because she hadn't been born the day before.

"Or this morning!" she threw in. "Everybody is walking around talking about how great the show was and when the next one is going to be. One old codger with a Southern accent even asked me if I owned you!"

"Owned me?"

"Do you know how excited my boys and girls were when they were leaving?" Margaret asked. She was relaxing, and I could see she was really pleased with herself. "They were dancing in the streets as happy and as dumb as starlings on a Sunday morning. That's the way life was meant to be, Juba. Happy and as dumb as starlings on a Sunday morning."

"They were great, Margaret," I said. "You had them just perfect."

"Anyway, there's a fellow who wants to talk to you, and

he said he'd been told you lived somewhere in this house," Margaret said. "I told him maybe you did and maybe you didn't. He's a reporter from a newspaper in Newark, New Jersey."

"What does he want to see me for?"

"He wouldn't tell me."

"Where is he now?"

The newspaper reporter was waiting for Margaret on the front steps, so I put on my last clean shirt and went down to meet him. Margaret sat next to me on the steps, took off her apron, and put it over her knees.

"Here he is, mister, the great Juba!" Margaret said.

"Hello, my name is Bains," the man said. "I understand that you are quite a dancer!"

"You want to put that in your paper?" I asked. "That I'm quite a dancer?"

"Well, no. Actually, I'm doing a story on Charles Dickens. I wanted to talk to you about him," the reporter said. "The *Tribune* said you were chatting with him after the main show and that you invented a new dance just for him. Is that true?"

"I talked to some people after the show," I said. "One of them said his name was Dickens."

"You don't know who Charles Dickens is?"

"I know he liked my dancing," I said.

"Charles Dickens is an amazing author—can you read?"

"I can read and write," I said.

"Well, you should read *Nicholas Nickleby* or *The Old Curiosity Shop*," the reporter said. "He publishes monthly in the London papers, and people over there adore him. What did he say to you?"

"He just said he liked my dancing," I said. I felt a little embarrassed. So much was going on around me, and I wasn't keeping up with it at all. Mr. Dickens hadn't come up to me and said he was famous or anything. He had just said he enjoyed what he did, and I'd told him *I* enjoyed what I did. His exact words had slipped my mind.

"It's not often a famous British writer has a conversation with a black man." The reporter was standing and putting away his notebook.

"What's my color got to do with it?" I asked.

He didn't answer, just looked at me, nodded, and went on his way.

Good. There was a lot of excitement going on, and I wasn't sure if I could handle any more than I already had.

Jack and Stubby came out with trays of oysters and fish, and I helped put them on Jack's cart.

"You feeling okay now?" I asked Jack.

"Fair to middling," Jack said. "Margaret said everybody in the world wants a piece of Master Juba today. She said people were knocking on her door as soon as the sun came up."

"Miss Lilly said a lot of people complimented her on the food, too," Stubby said. "She asked me if I wanted to cook at Almack's on weekends."

"Always looking out for themselves," Jack said. "I told Stubby he could probably get a better job if he held out."

"What are you going to do?" I asked Stubby.

"Jack said I needed to think about what went right and what went wrong and figure out how I could have handled the whole thing better," Stubby said. "What went wrong was that nobody knew it was me who did the cooking. Pete's spreading the word that Miss Lilly did the cooking, and she's not walking away from that."

"He sure can't say he did the dancing." Jack grinned.

I went along with Jack and Stubby, selling fish and oysters. It wasn't something I liked to do, and Jack usually didn't want me along, but he was so happy for me and Stubby that he didn't mind. He told everybody he sold fish to that I was the world's greatest dancer.

"And to prove it, he's pushing fish down Ninth Street," a woman with a big bosom said.

Jack started to argue with her that one thing didn't have anything to do with the other, but I wasn't sure. Something good had happened to me and I needed to figure out how to handle it, just as Jack had said something good had happened to Stubby and he needed to step back and think it through.

We sold fish all morning, and Stubby ran his mouth a mile a minute all the time. He reminded me of Mr. Charles Dickens, because he was loving cooking and serving food as much as Mr. Dickens loved writing.

We put the cart up at two o'clock, and Jack said he had to lie down for a while. He didn't look too good and he was coughing, so me and Stubby put everything away. Stubby wanted to go over to Almack's, and I didn't think that was a good idea. If Miss Lilly was saying she did the cooking, it was because Peter Williams put her up to it. Stubby was *eager* smart, and Jack was *old* smart, but Peter Williams was *mean* smart, and I got the notion that maybe mean smart was stronger than what me, Jack, and Stubby had.

"If I'm going to think everything through, like Jack said"— Stubby's shoulders were jerking up and down a little from him being nervous—"I think I should do the thinking over where I did the cooking and serving."

My friend made me smile, but I went over to Almack's with him. When we got there, Peter was talking to Fred Flamer and two dandied-up gentlemen. The gentlemen were young, maybe twenty-eight to pushing thirty. One wore a suit that looked a little tight, like he wasn't comfortable in it. The other one wore a short jacket, pants that didn't quite match, and a silk scarf around his neck. He was the talker.

"When we heard about the show and how you and Mr.

Flamer danced, we knew immediately that you were the fellows we needed for a show we're going to be putting on in Washington," he said after shaking my hand for too long. "We want to start the performance at a theater that is a terrific place in the heart of Washington. We're willing to pay you seven fifty a week apiece for the first month—we need to recoup some of our investment—and after that we'll give the two of you one percent of the total profits along with the seven fifty. But we need to get the whole thing going pretty soon, because the Majestic Theater won't be available for very long."

"We're seeing it as an opportunity we can't pass up," the other fellow said.

"And what they're telling me is that you'll be dancing there four nights a week, and you can come here and work at Almack's for two nights," Peter said. "That's a lot of traveling, but it could work out good. We could bill you up here as performers from the famous theater in the nation's capital."

"Is it really famous?" Freddy asked.

"What we want to do is to make it famous," the gentleman with the scarf said. "And I think we can do that. What do you say?"

"Sounds good to me," Freddy said.

"I'll think about it," I said, remembering what Jack and Stubby had been saying about thinking things through.

The two gentlemen asked me a lot of questions about how

many more dancers I would need to create a show as good as the one at Almack's. I asked them if they had seen the show and they said they hadn't, but that word of mouth was what made show business successful. That if you had enough people talking about you, the money would follow.

Fred was nodding and agreeing with everything they said, but I wasn't sure. What I would have liked to know was what kind of deal they were working out with Peter Williams, and why they were talking about investing money when they hadn't seen me dance. Also, it seemed wrong that they were offering me and Freddy the same deal. I had seen a lot of people calling themselves dancers or singers who got some attention, but they weren't that good.

Still, I felt bad when I didn't sign up with them on the spot the way Freddy did. Something deep inside me said I was being too scared, that I was going to throw a good chance away.

At home, lying across the bed, I watched a cockroach crawl up the wall. Where did it think it was going? Halfway up, it stopped for a second, then started again at an angle. I didn't think it had anywhere special in its mind, if cockroaches have minds, but its legs were moving. I thought maybe that was what I was doing, just moving with no place in mind. I thought about going with Freddy Flamer to that theater job.

Washington was an important city. The White House was there, and the president.

I also thought about Freddy Flamer. He couldn't dance with me for more than ten seconds, but if he got a job in a real, legitimate theater, he would be outdoing me. It wasn't as if I was jealous of him; I just knew that sometimes how good you were didn't matter. Like when we were at the auditions and I saw John Diamond sitting with Mr. Reeves, who wanted to reopen the theater. John Diamond was good, better than most, but he was starting way ahead of everyone else. When he came to me and said he would be part of my show, he was trying keep his name on top, and he knew it. But just being white gave him a head start in life.

When he was yelling for me and Freddy to "coon it up," he was making sure we were staying in our places as black performers. That made me mad, but there wasn't anything I could do about it.

The chance to be in a theater in Washington was jumping around in my head. All the theaters I knew were the ones around Five Points, one over on Bedford Street, and a few of the ones uptown. If Freddy got that job and did well, I would be hurt.

Stubby came in all smelly. He had been out back emptying the slop pot and some had spilled on his pants.

"How did that happen?"

"This girl came out in the backyard to hang up some clothes, and I didn't want her to see me with the slop pot," Stubby said.

"You know the girl?"

"No, but I didn't want her to know I used a slop pot," he said. "Mostly old people use slop pots, and I'm not that old."

When it was cold out, a lot of people used slop pots to do their business in instead of sitting out in the outhouse behind the building. In fact, the outhouse smelled so bad you couldn't stay in it very long before you felt sick. And if you were shy, the way Stubby was shy, you always used a slop pot.

"I'm thinking of taking a job in Washington, D.C.," I said. "Some people are looking for dancers to work in a regular theater down there. Peter Williams said me and Freddy Flamer could work there for a few days every week and then come back to New York to work at his place."

"Freddy's going to work there, too?"

"They offered me and Freddy a job," I answered.

"What kind of act is it?" Stubby asked. "You got to put black paint on your face and paint your lips red?"

"I thought about that," I lied. "What I was thinking was that even if I had to 'black up,' I'd be working in a real, honest-to-God theater, so it might not be so bad."

"That's what you want?"

"No."

"So why are you thinking about doing it?"

"If you had a chance to cook for Delmonico's, to be their top chef, but you had to black up and shuffle around, would you do it?" I asked.

"No, I wouldn't," Stubby said. "Because you just don't have to *do* something good, you have to let people know it's you that's doing it. If I was shuffling around acting like a clown, then people wouldn't give me any credit for doing the cooking. They wouldn't be saying Stubby Jackson is the top chef, they would just be saying I work there. You see how Pete Williams was talking about how the food came from Almack's, and how Miss Lilly was a great cook?"

"I saw that," I said. "Pete's like a snake in the grass."

"And if he gets in the loudest say, then everybody is going to listen to him and not me," Stubby said. "You don't see quiet people at the top. You see noisy people up there."

Stubby was right. I still told him he smelled bad, though.

I let Stubby borrow a pair of my pants, and he hung his out the window. Under his regular pants he was wearing cut-down long drawers in the middle of the summer. I asked him how come he was wearing them and he said those were the only undergarments he had.

"I don't like to go around with no undergarments," he said. "When they get old, I cut the legs down, but I don't want to cut all of them down in case I got to wear them in the winter."

Stubby was a little strange, but I loved him to death.

Jack came by and asked if me and Stubby wanted to go down to the docks and get some crabs.

"We can make smoked crab legs," he said.

I thought Jack would smoke a cross-eyed pigeon if he could catch one.

CHAPTER
EIGHT

What I wanted to do was to figure out my next move. The show was everything I wanted it to be, but it hadn't taken me anyplace. Peter was making me an offer, but I didn't trust him. The men who wanted me and Freddy to work at a theater in Washington had made an offer, but I didn't know what they had in mind, and they didn't think they had to lay it out to me. Freddy was jumping like a grasshopper that landed on a hot stove, but he was coming from a different place than I was.

Me and Stubby started pushing the empty cart down the street, and Jack was going on about how good the springs were in Ireland.

"The fields were so green, and the countryside was just beautiful," he said. "The fog in the morning washed everything down with dew and moistened the ground. Then the fog would lift, but you could see the dew glistening in the morning sun. It would look like a blanket of diamonds. A beautiful sight. A truly beautiful sight.

"When times got hard and we were stealing our own potatoes to eat, we had to figure out whether we had a chance to survive," he went on. "It wasn't about living good, it was just about surviving. People were starving in a land that should have fed us all. That's why so many of us took a chance on coming to America. It wasn't the opportunity to get rich or make it big, it was just a chance to live. Coming to America seemed to be a good thing, and staying behind in Ireland seemed to be a good thing. Some of us were wanting to go, and some of us were content watching the others go. That was a funny feeling right there, watching somebody else taking the chance you wanted to take. But that's how life is at times."

"Jack, that's what you're always saying," Stubby says. "That thing about 'that's how life is at times.' Life can't be about anything that happens."

"Sometimes it can," Jack said.

We got down to the dock and asked around, and the only crabs we found were soft-shelled crabs. That wasn't what Jack wanted. He wanted king crabs with their long legs.

"The smoke goes through the joints and even seeps through the shells," he said, disappointed. "And they're different enough so that people will buy them."

Stubby wanted to buy some soft-shelled crabs to cook, and he got enough to make a supper for the three of us.

"Jack, you thinking I'm scared to take a chance on going to Washington?" I asked as we started back to the house.

"I don't think you're scared, Juba," Jack said. "I think your menu's too long. You can't decide on what you want because it all looks good."

It all looked good and it didn't look good at the same time. I was wary of the offer to go to Washington from men who hadn't said a thing about my dancing and didn't seem to care whether I was really good or not. It was a feeling I had in my stomach rather than a set of thoughts I could lay out and speak on. But it was there.

It didn't stop me from feeling flat-out terrible when Freddy came around to say good-bye to everyone. He was shaking hands and flashing his smile from ear to ear.

Peter Williams said that if Freddy got into the fast life in Washington, he might not even bother coming back to dance in New York again.

Even though I didn't like it, I danced at Almack's over the next few months because I needed the little money that Peter was giving me, and it kept me going. People were still coming up to me and telling me how great the show had been, but it didn't seem to lead to anything. Charley White knew I could dance and sing, so he asked me if I played any banjo, and I told him yes even though I wasn't really that good at it and I really wanted to be dancing. He asked me to sit in with his minstrels, and I did it for the money.

I got a good billing for two nights at the Chatham Theatre and the same at the Bowery Theatre. But what I had to do was dance in between acts of a regular play. Sometimes the people would be talking and drinking as I danced, which I didn't like at all. John Diamond was on the same programs with me and it was billed as a dance contest, but Diamond just clowned around. For the two nights at the Chatham I got five dollars, and for the two nights at the Bowery Theatre I got four dollars a night, which was good money.

I went up to Boston with the Georgia Champions, a black minstrel show, and danced at the Concert Hall, but I only got five dollars for three nights' dancing and two days' travel.

The weeks with me holding my breath and waiting for something wonderful to happen stretched out to months and then started fading away to a memory as a first and then a second year passed. Nothing wonderful happened except that I noticed that life was going on around me the same way it always had. Freddy never came back from Washington, so

I felt he must be getting along. I wondered how I might have done if I had gone with him. Five Points was getting a little grimier, and all the promises of fixing up the waterfront were falling through the cracks.

Stubby was disappointed, too. His hopes of becoming a great chef just didn't happen. He cooked at a number of restaurants for short times, but the owners would almost always put somebody white over Stubby, even if they didn't know as much about cooking as he did. After a while, Stubby gave up the idea of owning his own restaurant and became a cook at the Colored Orphan Asylum.

I didn't give up. But, like Jack Bishop said, I came close.

"Juba, you're like a bird strutting down the avenue," he would say. "You're strutting just fine, but how come you're not flying?"

Jack knew how black people were treated in New York. We were second-class people every day and third-class performers when we tried to exercise our talents outside the black community. What he did was to needle me so I wouldn't give up altogether, and in a way, I appreciated it. In a way, I didn't, though, because sometimes he made me feel that when I accepted a job with a minstrel band or put on blackface, I was betraying my people. To me, putting on blackface was the strangest thing in the world. I was born black, and yet the promoters wanted me to dress up like some kind of strange image of a black person that really wasn't a true Negro. It was as if a lot of white people had a place in their heads for black people, and you had to fit in that place in a certain manner or they didn't want you. They wanted black performers to talk bad, say stupid things, and be like pets. Jack said a lot of white people were afraid of real black people.

"If half the country can convince itself it's okay to make black people slaves," he said, "then you got to figure we don't know who you are. So we make you into something we know by putting you in blackface. That's easy to figure."

It wasn't easy for me to figure, but it made sense in a way. Anyway, Jack was still a good person and we were always close. So when I got my next break, almost six years after the Almack's show, I was glad Jack was with me.

There were some girls playing hopscotch in front of the house. When they saw us coming with the cart, they all stopped playing and shouted down the street. A boy who was walking toward Avenue A turned around and started coming our way. The girls who had been playing hopscotch pointed toward me.

The boy who came up to me was pale, with buck teeth and hair that came down over his ears. His clothing was a shirt tucked into loose pants, shoes that were two big for him, and a hat that he had slapped to one side of his head. He was about twelve or thirteen.

"You the dancing nigger?" he asked me.

"What do you want?" I asked him.

"Let's see you dance!" he said.

"Get away from here," I said, brushing past him.

"I don't think you can dance at all!" the brat insisted.

Jack told me to ignore the kid, but I wasn't as patient with fools as I used to be and really thought about sending a punch toward his jaw.

"Mayor Brady told me to tell you to be down at City Hall in the morning, nine thirty, in room one-oh-three," the brat said. "He wants you to meet with some people. He said I could get a dime off you."

"He was wrong," I said.

"Nigger!"

"Get out of here before I swat you across the face!" Jack said, drawing his hand back.

The kid spit on the ground and took off. He'd be in a gang within a year, if he wasn't in one already.

"The mayor wants to see you?" Jack looked at me, puzzled. "What for?"

"No idea, unless he's thinking of putting together some private party," I said.

"He ever see you perform?"

"Jack, I wouldn't know the mayor of New York if he was standing right here on the stoop," I said.

Jack was feeling poorly. He had a hitch in his walk, and I had the feeling he was in more pain than he let on. I helped him to his door, then went upstairs to my room. Stubby had moved uptown near Seneca Village, where a lot of black people were living, so I had the place to myself.

The next morning I found a clean shirt, put it on, and made the ten-minute walk to City Hall.

Mayor William Brady was a big man, bald on top of his head and kind of rough-looking. He wore a big silver ring on his right hand, which looked a little out of place on a man. When the officer who met me at the door announced my name, Brady pointed to a seat without saying a word to me.

There were two other men in the room, an older one who Brady was sitting next to and a younger man I thought I had seen before. Brady was talking to the older man about getting some wagons over to Pearl Street to move a city office.

"Just get it done today," he said. "You got that?"

The man nodded and followed Brady's lead in standing up. When the man left, Brady turned to me. He wasn't exactly smiling, but he had a grin on his face that could have been a smile with a little practice.

"This is Gilbert Pell. He's a cousin of my wife or some such nonsense, and he tells me he wants to take you to England with the Ethiopian Serenaders so you can pretend to be black," Brady said. "I don't know if you've ever been to England, but I think you've got the black bit down pretty good."

Gilbert Pell spoke slowly and had a soft voice. He was younger than I thought the leader of a group like the Serenaders would be. He seemed shy, not like so many show business people who were ready to tell you what was on their minds and what was on yours as well. There were a few chairs out in the hall, and we sat together while the mayor went on about the city business.

"There are a lot of minstrel groups around the country," Mr. Pell said. "Some do well, and some just manage to lose money slowly. There's a minstrel tradition in this country. A group of white men with blackened faces and woolly wigs dance and sing in imitation of how they think Negroes do. My group, Pell's Ethiopian Serenaders, are good and a little different. We try to present Negro music the way you people sing and play it. We're not so much dealing with comedy."

"You know how we sing and play our music?" I asked.

"My mammy taught me spirituals when I was a child," Mr. Pell said. "I would sit on her lap and she would sing to me and rock me to sleep every night. Sometimes she would take me to the quarters and I played with the black children, as we all did until we got to be about nine or so. Then we were separated. Whites were taught our lessons, blacks were sent to the fields to work. Eventually, I had to learn to look at my mammy differently—Lois was her name—but I could somehow never leave the music."

He drifted away for a moment, lost in thought about something very far off, and I didn't interrupt him. When he came back to the moment, it was with a wave of his hand, as if he were pushing something away from him. I wondered what it was.

"Anyway, we've been to Great Britain before. England, Ireland, and Scotland, and we did well. We even performed before the queen of England. She was a little stiff, I thought, but she was interested in seeing what we did.

"We're going back to England, and I'd like to take you with me," Mr. Pell said. "I saw you at the Bowery, and you were outstanding, even though you weren't onstage very long. I can give you top billing with the other players. Your dancing and your singing will make us unique. And I'm really pleased to see how young you are. What do you think?"

"Well, I'm interested," I said.

He kept on talking about how he thought my dancing and singing would fit into his group and how we would all be equals once we got onstage.

The Serenaders had been around for a while, and I had seen them perform. Some of them were good and some just okay. They didn't get as much publicity as Christy's Minstrels, but they did all right. As Mr. Pell talked, my head was spinning. To me, what the minstrels did most was to prance across a stage making fun of black people. Sometimes they would throw in a few good songs, and both the Serenaders and Christy's Minstrels were better at that than some. The idea of me being part of an act that made fun of my own kind didn't leave a good taste in my mouth.

"Do all your players wear wigs and black grease on their faces?" I asked.

"I'm thinking . . ." Mr. Pell looked away for a moment, then back at me. "I'm thinking of calling the group I'm taking to London this time by a different name. Maybe leave off *Ethiopian* and just be Pell's Serenaders, to make it different from the other groups. If you don't want to black up or wear a wig, then that's fine with me. We can make up the rules as we go along. How does that sound to you?"

It sounded good and bad. Getting together with a well-known group could be a big step, and then it could be nothing, like the show we did at Almack's. I didn't push Mr. Pell on how I would have to look onstage, because I needed to figure out whether I wanted to take the chance before I questioned it.

Before I left, the mayor, who came out of the office for a while, asked me if I had ever been to London before.

"No, sir," I answered. "Have you?"

"I'm waiting for the queen to send me a personal invitation," he said, and let out a big laugh.

Why that was funny got away from me. I looked at Mr. Pell, and he wasn't laughing, either.

Mr. Pell said he had a week to find somebody, so he needed my answer as soon as possible. He gave me an address where I could contact him. It was Butler's Theatre.

I thought about it and thought about it. It was like wrestling with a slippery eel. Soon as I wrapped my mind around "yes," it would slip over to "no." And as soon as I wrapped my mind around "no," I would see something pointing to "yes." One of the things in the back of my mind was how good Fred Flamer was doing, or how good I thought he was doing. He had gone to Washington to that job and had never come back to Five Points.

I ended up with a "yes," and Mr. Pell said he was glad and that he thought I would be glad as well. He set up a time for me to meet the other performers.

Mr. Briggs was the friendly sort. He reached out and grabbed my hand and shook it as if he had known me for a long time.

Mr. Ludlow was young and narrow shouldered but had a lot of quick jokes he could call up in a minute. Mr. Everton acted like his face wasn't made for smiling. Mr. Valentine said he thought I would do all right with him.

"England is different from America," Mr. Valentine said. "They speak two kinds of English over there. The first is the high-class English, and you have to listen really carefully to understand what they're saying. The second is the low-class English, and it doesn't matter how hard you listen, you won't understand them."

CHAPTER NINE

The strangest thing about leaving New York was saying good-bye to people. What I learned about good-bye was that you were telling everyone that you were leaving where you were and going someplace else. But if you didn't know where that someplace was, if it was just a dot on a map, then you didn't have that much to say.

"So what you going to be doing different in London, England?" Miss Lilly asked me.

"I don't know," I said. "But I hope they like what I do."

Miss Lilly patted me on the wrist and told me not to worry, that I would always have a home in Five Points. She wrote down the address Mr. Pell gave me as our English contact and said she would write to me. She had been kind to me whenever she could.

Jack Bishop gave me six dollars to take with me and a small Bible printed in Gaelic. "It's okay if you can't read it," he said. "Just remember that you don't have to go to church to get the Lord's help."

"Think about me when all those English people are clapping for you," Stubby said. "You think about me and I'll feel it, too."

On the *American Eagle,* Mr. Valentine complained all the time about his cabin and how small and cramped it was for him and Mr. Everton. I was the only one with a cabin by myself. I slept on a cot that was fastened to the deck, and the rest of the cabin was piled high with trunks full of our stage gear. When none of us was seasick, we practiced on deck, and people on the ship came and watched us. Briggs was really good, and so was Pell. They could all move and dance and sound as if they were black, and I felt a little uncomfortable with them. When Gil, which is how Mr. Pell wanted me to address him, asked if I was all right, I told him I was getting a little nervous.

"If everyone is showing black people as being stupid and lazy, then it doesn't matter too much what I do," I said.

"It matters if you make it matter," Gil said. "People should

Gilbert Pell headed the Serenaders and performed the role of Bones in blackface, as was the custom for minstrels.

come away from our performances thinking about what they've just seen."

"What does that mean?" I asked. "How do we know what they're thinking?"

"Doesn't matter what *we* know. If they come expecting just a bunch of clowns in blackface and nappy wigs and that's what they see onstage, then they won't think anything as they leave," Gil said. "But if they come expecting dumb Negro acts and they see great dancing and great singing, then they'll think maybe they were wrong about black people. Or at least a few of them will.

"Do you know why minstrel shows are mostly held in the North?" Gil asked. "Because people in the South have seen and heard real Negroes. They're not funny, and their music isn't funny, either."

That was something to think on.

We arrived in London on a cold, rainy Saturday afternoon. Gil arranged for two carriages, and we loaded our trunks and went to where we would be staying. Cheshire Street looked a lot like Five Points. The streets around it were narrow, and there were a lot of people just standing around. Children stared at us as we came out of the carriages, and a few followed us to 110 Cheshire, which was going to be our home in London.

The next day, the entire group met with our London manager, Mr. Campbell, at a steamy restaurant. We were supposed to meet someone from a British newspaper, the *Times* of London, and map out our plans. I didn't know what to order from the menu and was glad when Mr. Campbell ordered something called bangers and mash for all of us.

"The ticket sales have been disappointing, to say the least," Mr. Campbell said.

"They haven't seen us yet," Gil said. "Once the reviews start coming in, the people will follow."

"We've been canceled at Lyceum and I'm looking for a new place to perform" was the quick reply. "I'm even thinking of a theater outside of London."

That didn't sound good. Valentine asked what had happened, and Mr. Campbell said people just didn't have that much money to spend on entertainment.

"London is a great city for entertainment," he said. "People from all over the British Isles come here on holiday and are very supportive of all kinds of shows. But every theater is struggling, and when they struggle, they go to revivals and trot out all the old shows. You can't blame them, but it makes booking hard."

"It was my understanding that we were scheduled to perform at the Lyceum for a month," Gil said.

"The small print said it depended on us selling a certain number of tickets before the first performance," Mr. Campbell said. "And we aren't even close to filling the number of seats the owner wants. He's booked in *The Beggar's Opera*."

The food came, and it turned out to be sausages and potatoes. The waitress brought out tea for everybody and asked me something I didn't understand.

"She wants to know if you're an African," Mr. Campbell said.

"I'm an American," I said.

The answer surprised her, and she stepped back. "You're a slave?"

"No," I said.

She gave me a look that said she didn't believe me and went on about her business. I asked Mr. Campbell if they had many black people in London, and he said no. It had been hard trying to see out of the carriage on the way to Cheshire Street, so I didn't know what kinds of people there were in London.

A quiet came over the group as we ate the sausages, which weren't that bad, and the potatoes, which were kind of strange-tasting. Cancellations were pretty common in show business. We were always scrambling around looking for places to perform and hoping that somehow we would be paid at the end of the week. But Gil acted as if he was really down, and I wondered if I was going to be on a boat headed back to New York in the morning.

Mr. Campbell was telling us about a theater in Birmingham, which was about a day's journey north of London, when the man from the *Times* joined us. The waitress who had asked me if I was a slave came over, took his order, and gave me another funny look. Mr. Campbell introduced Gil and told the reporter about the cancellation and how he was sure we would soon book another theater. The reporter asked for our names, and Gil produced a paper from his pocket with all of our names on it.

"You're Juba!" The man from the *Times* pointed a stubby finger at me. "The one Charles Dickens wrote about?"

"I'm Juba," I said, not sure where he was going.

"Well, you're the anointed one, and all of London will be anxious to see you, sir."

"That's good," I said.

"Half of London has heard about Boz's Juba, and they'll want to see him for themselves," the reporter explained to us. "No doubt about him being the main attraction, is there?"

That made me feel really good.

Gil and Mr. Campbell decided to sit tight and wait to see what happened when the story of me being in London made the papers. They didn't have to wait long. We had an offer to fill a two-week gap at Sadler's Wells starting on the weekend. Mr. Campbell was congratulating the group because the new deal was better than the one that had been canceled.

"And hundreds more people will see and hear us, and the critics will be there, too," Mr. Campbell said.

The reporter from the *Times* didn't refer to my real name, William Henry Lane, at all. To him I was Boz's Juba, and I didn't have a problem with that. Gil went out and bought the paper and we all sat around while Ludlow read it to us.

Advertisement for performances at Royal Vauxhall Gardens,
including the performances by G. W. Pell and Master Juba

Pell's Serenaders have arrived in London and with them they have brought the celebrated African that our own Charles Dickens has anointed as the world's best dancer. We are referring of course to Boz's Juba, the young man that our Author referred to in his well-received book, American Notes. *I have seen the subject dancer and note that he is keen of eye and full of nervous energy, not at all like the slow blackies that sweep the sidewalks at Cecil Court and other places in London. I, for one, am eager to see him educate us with his flying feet. If he is half as good as Boz describes him, he will be a wonder to behold!*

The whole troupe was excited and eager to start. I was the most excited. I thought back on meeting Charles Dickens, and although I liked him, I hadn't made that much of our conversation. I tried to remember what he looked like and could only think of a kind of softness about him.

The idea of people in England wanting to see me dance, even knowing my name, made me feel lighter than air. If they had been told by Charles Dickens that I was something special, then I wanted to be something so special they would never forget me.

The Sadler's Wells Theatre was like something I couldn't even imagine. It was huge, with a stage that was as deep as it was wide. The back of the stage, from the high curtain wall to the back brick wall, was flat. The front twenty feet of the stage declined toward the audience.

There were fifty-four seats across in the first row, and there were twenty-two rows on the first floor. I don't know how many seats the balcony had. There were boxes on both sides, and if you stood exactly center stage, you got the feeling that the whole world could see you. After our first rehearsal, which went very well, I stood center stage and tried to imagine every seat filled with people leaning forward to see Pell's Serenaders. As I stood there, all my fears went away. I could almost hear the music, and I wanted to dance on the spot. I did a few steps across the rough floor.

"How do you like it?" Gil asked.

"It's a little soft," I said. "The audience could miss the rhythm."

"You've got wooden soles, haven't you?"

"I might look for a new pair," I said.

I was hoping my nervousness wasn't showing. Coming to England, I had hoped for the best, a chance to show my skills and to get paid for doing it. The stories in the newspapers had taken me by surprise. I wanted to buy all the newspapers and take them to our rooms with me.

The theater had dressing rooms for the performers, too. No theater I had ever been in had official dressing rooms, but Sadler's Wells did. In the rooms were long tables with mirrors, and lamps that you could move from side to side or up and down on a sliding bar.

"Do you put on your own face paint?" The voice startled me.

I turned and saw a round-faced girl, who looked to be about eighteen or so, standing in the doorway.

"Yes, I do," I said.

"I do sewing for your wardrobe," the girl said. "If you need anything repaired or adjusted, I can do it. I'm really quite good."

"I'm sure you are," I said. "And your name is . . . ?"

"Sarah Felton," she answered. "My father is a tailor. That's where I learned the trade. You're black, aren't you?"

"Yes." I had to smile. "I am very black."

"It must be pretty hard to live in a country where they make slaves of your people," the girl said. "I think it would twist my bonnet something terrible! I can't imagine people walking down the street looking at me as if I were something that could be bought and sold. The very idea of it!"

"It makes me mad, too," I said. "And it hurts me as well."

"I can believe that, sir," she said. "I can truly believe that. Well, if you need anything repaired, or need to know where anything is around the theater, I'm your girl."

"Thank you, ma'am."

"And do you dance as well as they say, Master Juba?"

"I hope so."

* * *

141

It was our first night, and my stomach was jumping around as if I were going to ask it to dance instead of my feet. Looking through the curtain, I saw the theater filling up with people, and I didn't feel as bad about Gil arguing with Mr. Campbell earlier. Mr. Campbell said he had to give the theater a better deal than we thought we were going to get. Gil said we'd just about break even after we paid all our expenses.

For the time being, it didn't matter. The rest of the troupe was putting on blackface in the dressing room, and I was thinking about my lines and the songs I was going to sing. I wanted to sing "Mary Blane," but Valentine got that one, so I was going to sing "Come Back, Stephen."

Huff, which was what everybody called Mr. Everton, had got into an argument with Gil over something, and each had screamed at the other. The thing was that all the players knew they could scream at Gil. He seemed like a good fellow, but every so often he would slip into a mood, and he would go quiet.

We were side stage when the curtain opened, and the audience started their applause as they faced the row of chairs onstage. I came out first, turned to the audience, and made as if I were surprised that they were there. Lots of laughter. Then the rest came out, one by one, with each of us pretending to be unaware that we were in a large theater.

Briggs started playing at a fast tempo. His banjo seemed

almost alive in his hands as he plucked the strings and beat a rhythm on the tight leather skin. The man could really play. Pell started up next on the bones, catching the rhythm that Briggs laid down and tossing his body around as he sat in the chair. The way he was moving, his shoulders going up and down, one at a time, that left leg banging out a rhythm on the floor, was enough to make anyone want to move in their seat!

By the time we got through the first medley, with Briggs setting the pace, Huff playing the violin, Pell on bones, Valentine on lute, Ludlow on low banjo, and me on tambourine, we had the audience just where we wanted them. They were clapping and stomping their feet and were just as much part of the show as we were.

Serenaders sheet music

CHAPTER TEN

The first two parts had seven numbers each, with mostly Ludlow, Gil, and Valentine doing the solos. There was a short break after each of the first two parts for us to run offstage. I saw Gil go into the dressing room after the second part, and he looked a little upset.

"You doing good?" I asked him when he came out.

He smiled and said he was. I smelled whiskey on his breath.

On the break, Sarah was passing out towels for us to wipe the sweat from our foreheads, and she was also touching up the blackface that had begun to run from the heat. I looked over at Valentine, and he had a big, broad smile on his face. He caught me looking at him and pointed a stubby finger at me.

"We got them running through the woods, Juba. Bring 'em home!" he said.

The third part started like the first two, with six songs, including "Come with the Darky Band," a six-eight number that bounced with Valentine's singing and the rest of us backing him up. And then it was the troupe sitting down again and me on the floor by myself. I didn't expect to be jumpy, but I was as I started across the floor. Briggs must have felt me, because he laid his beat down stronger.

"They're going to be watching your feet, Juba," Margaret had said.

So I let them watch my feet and hear the rhythm of my feet and try to figure out where I was going next. There were some people in the audience beginning to keep time with me by clapping, and they made me smile, because I knew they couldn't keep up with me.

Briggs picked up the tempo, and for a while, we exchanged beats. We hadn't rehearsed it like that, but we were rolling through the dance together. Gil was accenting the beat on the bones, and he was standing. At rehearsal he had sat. There was a growing tension in the theater that I could feel swell with the music, and then, as if I had been swept up by the music, I just let go and something magical took over my body.

I couldn't hear the crowd, but I could feel them. Some had

begun to stand up, and soon most of them were standing. They had come to see me dance, and they were seeing the best Juba who had ever moved across the floor!

When the program ended and the audience was giving each of us a round of applause, I bowed and could hardly straighten up. I was exhausted.

"Juba! Juba! Juba!" They called my name. "Juba! Juba! Juba!"

"They want an encore," Mr. Campbell was shouting into my ear. "Can you give them something? Three minutes? Two?"

I was on the stage again. This time I started dancing slowly with my back to the audience—a straight jig with a shuffle step. Then I shifted the beat to my right leg as I turned to face the audience. They were clapping for me, but as I clapped my hands, I changed the beat. Briggs picked me up on the banjo. Something was coming to me, something I had never tried before.

Get it right, Juba. Get it right.

I concentrated on the rhythm, and on Briggs's banjo. I moved the feel of it from my legs to my hips to my waist. And then back down to my right leg, keeping the same rhythm, the same hard beat, as I lifted my left foot away from the floor. I was doing a traditional jig on one leg.

Suddenly there was silence. The audience stopped clapping. Had I missed it?

"Bravo! Bravo!"

A shout from the balcony, and the whole theater exploded in cheers and applause.

I brought my left leg down and held out my hands to the audience as I danced backward into the wings.

"You are a marvel! A marvel!" Gil threw his arms around me and I nearly collapsed into them.

It was the happiest moment of my life.

In the dressing room, we were congratulating each other again. Mr. Campbell showed up with a woman who could have been his daughter and passed out cigars. He told me to take one even if I didn't smoke.

We finally changed into our street clothes and were ready to leave when Sarah came up to me and put her hand on my arm.

"I don't even believe you, Mr. Juba," she said. "I truly don't!"

"Then you think my performance was good enough for this theater?" I asked.

"This and any other theater in the world, I would think," Sarah said. "And you were looking fairly handsome out there for a bit, as well."

"You still in costume?" Huff came by.

"No, I . . ." I started to answer him and realized that he knew I had taken off my dancing clothes. It was just my black face that I hadn't removed.

The reviews of my dancing were great. One or two of the smaller papers used the word *nigger* to describe me, but I

Engraving showing Juba dancing from the
Illustrated London News

shrugged that off. Almost all of the papers connected me to
Charles Dickens, or Boz. I read everything I could by him and
about him, as I had done in the years following our meeting in
Five Points. I particularly liked *A Christmas Carol,* with Tiny

Tim and Scrooge and all the characters who were so easy to remember. Dickens came to our third performance and visited me backstage after the show.

"You surpass everything that I've ever written about you," he said.

"Thank you, sir," I said. I had thought that if he came to the show, I would apologize for not knowing who he was or how good a writer he was when I first met him, but nothing came out.

"I always see people as potential characters in my books," Mr. Dickens said. "I like those characters who are distinct, somewhat bigger than life, but grounded in a reality that I can handle. That is not you, Juba. You are so much bigger than life, your dancing is so much bigger than life, that you are almost otherworldly. It is such a pleasure to meet someone who enjoys his art as much as you do, sir. It is a great pleasure indeed."

We shook hands, and as quickly as he had appeared, he was gone. I had the feeling I had been in contact with a great man.

I thought about writing to Stubby. What would I say? London was busy and twisting and wonderful. I thought I could just walk the streets all day and never stop being amazed. Me, Gil, and Valentine went down to a place called Piccadilly Circus. The stores were swell and the people, some young and some old, dressed in suits and walked about as if

Reviews of Juba's performance

ETHIOPEAN SERENADERS. — The original company of the black faced gentlemen, so many imitators of whom have traversed the country, under the style and title of Ethiopean Serenaders, commenced a series of representations of American negro life and music, in the Free Trade Hall, on Monday night. The present company maintains its superiority to all we have heard. The vocalists are apparently five in number, for "bones" sings little if any, confining himself to manipulation, gesticulation, grimacing, and jokery in abundance. Two of the five, especially have excellent voices. one a true bass, and the other a baritone, of fine quality, and the whole of the voices blend most exquisitely in the various harmonised pieces, and which appeared in the programme. Many of the songs were adapted to popular melodies in well known operas, and we sometimes thought ourselves transported back to the presence of the English opera company, at the Theatre Royal. One of the five is a tolerable violinist, and another an excellent banjo player, and "bones" rattles his rough castinets with an accuracy of time, undisturbed even in most furious *fortes* The company has with it a coloured youth, who has been heralded as " Boz's Juba." and his name has been associated with a passage from Dickens' "American notes." Whether this be the same Juba that Boz there alludes to we know not, but certainly the feats of the present claimant of the name appear to be quite equal to him in extraordinary feats of agility and marvellous flexibility of body. The dances he introduced were distinguished for eccentricity, rapidity of motion, and the accuracy of the time kept. They approximated, in some respects, to those wild dances that may be witnessed sometimes in the remoter parts of the Highlands, including the sword dance, as there known; besides having the same idea of clanking the heels, as pervades the Polka. But it is not the office of the legs alone to do all this; the head, arms, and body generally take full share of duty, and assume such extraordinary positions, that only a being possessed of the power of Proteus could calculate upon taking. He was decidedly the lion of the evening; and though the songs of the vocalists were frequently encored, and the jokes of the two speakers, old as many of them were, heartily laughed at, he has done the most to secure those good houses, which it is not unlikely will be assembled at the nightly entertainments

The Manchester Courier and Lancashire General Advertiser 10/18/1848

LIVERPOOL.—*Theatre Royal.*—The dramatic season terminated on Monday last, the performance being for the benefit of Mr James Brown, the popular comedian, who appeared in two of his favourite parts (in *Road to Ruin* and *Robert Macaire*), the house was respectably attended though far from being full. G. W. Pell and his very clever troop of "darkies," are now attracting excellent houses by their talented performances; but the chief attraction is Juba—Boz's far-famed Juba—whose muscular heel, toe, and joint performances, perfectly amaze the beholder, who is bothered completely and, but for the staring evidence of his optical understandings would deem it an utter impossibility for a two-legged human being to execute one half of Juba's wonderful feats. The many new songs, &c., artistically executed by the Serenaders, have created a very favourable impression upon the numerous patrons of this establishment.

The Era 11/12/1848

they were the most important people in the world. Valentine thought they were funny, but I liked to see people walking like that, looking as if they were special. We also went to see the changing of the guard at Buckingham Palace, and Gil, who was from Virginia, said the horses were acting just like the people. They were special and they knew it.

The expense money we were given was in shillings, and we were supposed to do some mental arithmetic to figure out how much we were spending in dollars. Valentine said he had a foolproof way of doing it.

"You give it over to an English shopkeeper and hope they're honest," he said. "Otherwise, I don't have a clue. Huff thinks we're getting a shady deal, being paid in English money."

"He's got problems," Gil said. "He thinks we'd make more money being like Christy's Minstrels."

"Christy's Minstrels don't know the people they're dealing with," Valentine said. "They might as well be from New York, because they can live around black people all day and not understand them."

"What I would love is for everyone to understand the music and dancing of colored people," Gil said. "If you like colored people or you don't like them, there's something special in their music. If you have ears and eyes, you have to know that's true."

"Mr. Valentine, have you noticed that I am from New York City?" I asked.

"You don't count," Valentine said. "You were born black. So what you know about being that way doesn't really matter. Not in show business, anyway."

I looked at Valentine thinking he would be smiling, but he wasn't.

We stopped at a shoemaker on a small street in Bethnal Green. There was a kettle on a stove, and the steam filled the room and made it feel damp. I asked the store owner if he could make me a shoe with a wooden sole that would still look stylish. He looked at me somewhat suspicious and asked if I would remove my shoes and step up on his "fitting stand." It was a foot high, and he looked at my feet for a while and then went into the back of his shop.

"That's where he keeps his elves," Valentine said. "They really make the shoes."

The man came back a few minutes later carrying a pair of women's shoes with a flat heel.

"Just try these on," he said. "They were meant for display so as not to waste the leather. I can fix them for you, take off some of the lace and what have you."

I tried them on, and they felt pretty good. I was still on the fitting platform, so I tried a few steps to see how they would sound. On the hard wooden floor of the platform they were great.

"You're going to break the sole if I don't put a small sliver of leather over it," he said. "Not a problem there if you want it done."

Two gentlemen watching me came over, and one pointed at my feet. "Those the feet that the Boz brought over?" he asked.

"The very same," Gil said.

"Well, I guess you are worth seeing after all!" he said as they left the shop.

Gil said he should have me dancing up and down Regent Street from noon until five to advertise our performances.

Piccadilly Circus looking up Regent Street, circa 1860

***

When I got back from a full day of running around London, looking at the buildings and the stores and listening to the people on the streets, I was tired and wishing I had someone to talk to like Stubby or even Jack Bishop. Valentine's statement about me being black so it didn't matter what I knew was something to think about.

The truth to it was that I wasn't doing much thinking about anything except me being on the stage. The theater's lights seemed to create a world just for me, and I was floating through it like some crazy baby bird that had just been pushed out of its nest but had learned to fly. To fly, to fly across the stage, to fly across the waves of applause, to fly across the "bravos" and the "hurrahs" of the audience. I kept telling myself to calm down, but I wasn't listening.

We had done ten performances in and around London when Gil and Huff got into it again. Mr. Campbell, our London manager, and Sarah were there, too. Huff was saying we should start changing our act so that we could bring it home.

"You can't bring Juba to Atlanta," he said. "Not the way he dances. You need to put a wig on him and puff his lips up a little so he looks . . . like what they want to see in Atlanta . . . or we won't get any bookings down there."

"Maybe we can teach them how to see something different," Gil said. "And maybe that's why we're called Pell's Serenaders,

155

because I have a vision. And maybe, just maybe, you ought to open your eyes and see something different, too."

Huff walked across the room and put his nose an inch from Gil's. "What I see with my own two eyes is that I'm not going to make no kind of steady living working for a nigger. And that's what I'm doing over here, working behind *Boz's Juba* or whatever it is he's calling himself. In America you make a living working with *white* men, and *for* white men. And I aim to go back to America, back to Mableton, Georgia, and make a living. And if I want any coloreds around me, I'll buy a few!"

Something inside me jumped, and I was on my feet in a second. Huff was a good-sized man, but I had fought men his size before. He saw me coming and turned and tried to tackle me around the waist. I hit him two shots in the head before his momentum knocked me backward into a wooden closet.

The fight was short, with Huff finding out I could do more than dance as I hit him on the side of his head and jaw. He staggered backward and put his hands up as Valentine and Mr. Campbell came between us.

"You can go back to Georgia today, Everton," Gil said, using Huff's real name. "I'll be glad to see you go. You're wrong, and there's no way under God's sky that you don't know it!"

"Juba, you're a good dancer, and I don't have any reason to offend you." Huff was bleeding from the nose, and his eyes were bloodshot. "But I'm not wrong. You can say what you want, Gil, and you can scratch around for a better answer, but your head and your eyes tell you that I'm right. Not you, me! In America, he ain't Boz's Juba, he's just colored, and what that means is going to depend on where he finds his black ass!"

Huff walked out of the dressing room and slammed the door behind him. The room got real still, and one by one, we started to leave. Gil came over and patted me on the wrist. He started to say something, then just shrugged and left.

"You feeling bad?" Sarah asked me.

"No."

"Liar," she said quietly.

"He doesn't mean that much to me," I said.

"Do you know where Edgware Road is?"

"No, where?"

"Where I live," Sarah said. "Come along, I'll show it to you."

CHAPTER
ELEVEN

Sarah lived in a two-room flat on Church Street, off Edgware Road. It was a nice area with lots of small shops and restaurants that sold food I had never seen before.

"Many of the people here are French," she said. "They mind their own business."

She made tea and served some cakes that weren't at all sweet. She talked about what Huff had been saying, and added that Valentine was worried about how much money the group was making.

"Is Gil paying you?" I asked.

"Yes, he pays my salary, but the theater gives him an

allowance for wardrobe upkeep," Sarah answered. "I don't know how good he is with money, though. Mr. Campbell just about manages everything, I think."

Mr. Campbell was a lot stronger than Gilbert Pell. Gil was about my age, maybe a year or two older, but he seemed tired. He was really talented once he got into the performance, but as soon as it was over he would go into a funk, and more than once I thought he was drinking before we went on.

Over the next two weeks, two things happened. The first was that when our production was over, Mr. Campbell booked us into a theater in Kilburn, an Irish neighborhood. We went over big there, and the Irish really loved my dancing. At one performance they were even dancing along with me in the side aisles. That was sweet, and I enjoyed it. I slowed the pace down and did jigs they all would know. But Gil got into a shouting match with Mr. Campbell about money, and he was told that two other companies were now performing minstrel shows in London.

"You tell me," Gil said. "Are they as good as us? Are they nearly as good as us?"

"No, they're not," Mr. Campbell said. "But they don't have to be. When a good act breaks the ice, then everybody jumps into the water. And if somebody sees three minstrel shows playing at the same time, they're going to pick one of them. If the one they pick isn't that good, then they won't go see the others."

"We've got Juba and we've got the connection with Charles Dickens," Gil said. "Nobody else has that."

"You could have a connection with Moses himself and it would only make a slight difference." Mr. Campbell was turning red. "How many people do you think read Dickens? Everybody *says* they read Dickens when his stories come out every month, but how many actually read him and how many are going to take his advice to see Juba? I'm not saying you're not the best in London, because you are. I *am* saying you're not the only game in town."

"I find you very annoying, sir," Gil said.

"Look, do you know how much business you've created for the black circus, that Pablo Fanque deal? People say there's a black show and it's great, then there's a black minstrel show and that's great, but how do you separate them? You tell me that, Pell. How do you separate them?"

Mr. Campbell was walking on the same ground that Huff had walked on. Gil said he was doing his best, but what his best produced was a real mix of places for us to perform, from regular theaters to public houses with little places to perform on the second floor, and once even in a tent at a fair. They would all have been good, except for the money. Another thing that happened was that in some of the places, Mr. Campbell wanted us to perform more like the Christy's Minstrels.

"It was the only way I could sell you," he said.

Poster

And what that meant was that we had to make ourselves look like what they thought black people looked like in America. I remembered John Diamond yelling at me at Almack's to "coon it up."

"I know that hurts," Sarah said. "But maybe it'll only last for a while. If you can get one really long-term contract, then you can just dance the way you want to."

The other thing that was happening was that I was falling in love with Sarah Felton. At first I told myself it wasn't happening, that she was just somebody I could lean on once in a while, who understood what I was going through. But then I found myself thinking about her all the time, and going around London with her on the days the troupe wasn't working.

Sarah was nineteen, kind of pretty, with a round face and dark hair that she wore long so that it lay on her back or sometimes in front of her shoulder. But what drew me to her most was that she always knew what was bothering me. There would be a hitch—somebody missed a cue during the performance, perhaps—and I would have to change my act while I was onstage. Nobody would say anything about it, but Sarah would know, and her mouth would tighten up and her eyes would flash when she talked about it. Sometimes I would say that it didn't really bother me that much, but she knew it did. She always knew.

"What's it like in America?" she asked me once when

we were in Hyde Park. "I imagine cowboys and Indians and covered wagons. That's what we see in the *Illustrated News*. But I imagine New York must be more like London. Is that true?"

"New York doesn't have as much history as London," I said. "In London you talk about things that happened hundreds of years ago. Windsor Castle is older than America. Many of the streets and parks are older than America, too. The biggest difference is that you don't have slavery over here. Just knowing that you can go somewhere in America and see people being used as slaves is scary."

"Not if you're free," Sarah said.

"Even if you're free," I said. "Because you know that the people who are slaves are slaves because they look like you."

"And there's nothing funny about that, is there?"

Sarah's tone surprised me. It gave me the same feeling that I'd had sometimes when I had seen a dancer do a move or make a step that I didn't expect but that was somehow so right for the moment, so accurate, that I would remember it forever and want to put it in my act. When she said there was nothing funny about people being slaves because they looked like me, she was describing everything I wanted to show when I danced. I danced the way the Irish danced, and I danced the way the black people danced, but they were all dances of people I loved. I needed to make my dancing show that—that

I loved the people and I appreciated them.

"Juba, you've grown quiet on me," Sarah said.

"I think you're getting to be very special to me, Sarah," I said. "Does that bother you?"

"Not particularly," she answered. There was just a hint of a smile on her face. "I'm thinking you could do worse than me if you put your mind to it."

It was clear that how Gil went, the troupe went. And more and more, he was falling into a pattern of getting depressed, then drinking too much, then screaming at everybody. I didn't think it was me who should pull him aside, but I did.

"You aren't doing yourself much good," I told him. "We both know that, don't we?"

Gil smiled. "I'm not doing myself a whole lot of good, Mr. Juba," he said. "But then again, I don't know if there's a whole lot of good out there for me to do, either for myself or for anybody else. I'm not even sure if I'm going home after this tour runs out."

"Why?"

"That's the question I asked myself," Gil said. "Why would I not go home, on the one hand, and why *would* I go home, on the other hand? I don't have anybody waiting for me back in the States. You have a sweetheart back in New York?"

"No," I confessed.

"You thinking of taking Sarah back with you?"

"Well, I wasn't thinking of it," I said.

"Don't act surprised," Gil said. "The two of you are closer than peas in a pod. I guess you might be all right in New York, a black dancer and a white woman. It wouldn't do you good to come down to Virginia, though."

I hadn't known that my connection with Sarah was that open. When Gil laid it out like that, I guessed it had to be.

My talk with him didn't do any good. He was still inside himself most of the time, and getting frustrated with our bookings. I asked Valentine if he thought we were doing really bad.

"This is the way we always go," he said. "We make a living most of the time, but nobody's getting rich. On the other hand, we're doing what we want to do. That's something, isn't it?"

When January came, along with the cold weather, we had even fewer bookings. I never did well in the cold weather in England. The dampness seemed to settle in my chest and stay all winter. The new plays and shows had opened in London, and they got all the reviews. No one was mentioning Pell's Serenaders or Boz's Juba.

We did a few performances in Sheffield, one in Brighton, two in Liverpool, and three days in Birmingham. When we had been booked in London again, Campbell asked us to put our earnings into publicity.

Women also formed minstrel groups.

"If we can get the ball rolling, we might be able to gain enough momentum for the reviewers to start taking notice," he said.

Nobody believed it would happen. We worked the entire week, putting everything we had into the shows, even trying some new material, but the seats were mostly empty. Mr. Charles Dickens came one evening and asked to see me. I was thrilled that he had come, of course, and shook his hand enthusiastically.

"I thought you had gone back to America," he said. "The press haven't been too kind to you, have they?"

"I guess they have to do what they have to do," I said. I didn't want to seem as if I was complaining.

"How are things going for you?"

"When things are going good, when I'm onstage and feeling the music, then those are the best of times," I said. "When we're sitting around hoping to get a booking, then those are the worst of times."

"Yes, of course, but isn't that what all true art is about?" Mr. Dickens said. "Taking the everyday flotsam and jetsam of life, the worst of times. And making it into something so special that they become the best of times. That's what the artist does—we make change possible by showing people different ways of looking at things. I think that's true whether one uses paints or dancing or words. Do you agree?"

I wasn't quite sure what he meant, but I nodded as wisely as I could. He nodded, too, so at least he understood my nod.

Mr. Campbell lived on Cecil Court, and we were told to check in with him at least three times a week. It wasn't a good feeling, because I didn't think he was seriously looking to find us anything. The walk from Church Street to Cecil Court took almost an hour, but my funds were running low and I didn't want to spend the money for the public coach. Sarah was being as sweet as she could be and encouraging me to practice as much as possible. I did practice some, but my heart wasn't in it. I had got down a routine in which I could shuffle across the floor without crossing my ankles and still keep a steady rhythm. It was a good step and Sarah liked it, but practice didn't mean as much when there didn't seem to be anything to practice for.

"I think Campbell will come up with something wonderful," Sarah said. "You'll all be together again and burning up the stage!"

"Look, you're taking in sewing and last week you cleaned flats in Hanover Square," I said. "I don't want you to kill yourself while you're waiting for the Serenaders to get back together."

"Juba, is it killing you to do what is necessary for someone you love?"

I turned toward Sarah, who was sitting by the window. She was looking down at the sewing in her lap, her face silhouetted by the afternoon light. Outside, the horses from the palace guard were passing, their feet clip-clopping on the hard road surface. We hadn't talked much about love before. We had mentioned, in passing, some future plan that gave us a picture of the two of us together some weeks, or months, or even years down the road. But we had shied away from being direct, even though we were sharing her small flat. When it came to mind, when I would be walking down the street and feel myself picking up the pace to get home to her, I would attribute it to the convenience of having a woman, or to having a cup of tea when I arrived.

But in my heart I knew I loved Sarah. I knew I wanted to be with her almost as much as I wanted to dance. Dancing was the way I wanted to live; Sarah was the one I wanted to be with.

"You know, Sarah, there are problems with us being together," I said.

"Oh, good, I enjoy solving problems," she answered, her voice light and clear. "Are they interesting problems?"

"To begin with, I'm not British," I said.

"You can tell people you're from Barbados and therefore are a British subject," Sarah said.

"You've thought of everything, haven't you?" I asked. "How about the idea that I'm black and you're very white?"

"It matters to me as much as it matters that you dance and I don't," she said. "It's something I'm willing to live with. Are you?"

The question was simply put.

"Yes," I answered. "Yes, I am."

"Shouldn't you do something dramatic at this point in the conversation?" she asked.

I took a very deep breath, stood up, and began to dance.

It was a happy dance, with me leaning back and kicking my legs high into the air. I spun and did a series of slow glissades while tapping all the time.

Sarah stood and applauded. I wanted to do a thousand more things for her, to dance along the walls and across the ceiling—and I almost felt as if I could. Then I stopped. The troupe wasn't booked into anything, we were all running out of money, and my joy turned instantly to sadness. Sarah came to me and put her arms around me. She knew what I was feeling. Sarah always knew.

As bad as things were that Tuesday morning, they were worse by noon. The weather was bright but still a bit foggy, and as I started out, I wore a scarf that Sarah had found for me. She told me not to walk the entire distance, but I did. I needed to think, to come to some kind of decision about the troupe, and about me and Sarah.

A funny thing. In London, down in the Strand, there were street singers and dancers who dressed in blackface, performed on the corners or in the squares, and then passed the hat around. They called themselves minstrels or serenaders or even niggers. We had had a huge impact on London, but it wasn't doing us very much good.

Campbell was just locking up his place on Cecil Court when I arrived.

"Juba, just the man I wanted to see!" he said. "Do you have time to come to my office?"

I nodded while I searched his face, looking for a clue as to what he was going to tell me. His office was small and messy. There were papers piled on the desk, on a cabinet, and even on the chair behind the desk. I wondered where he sat.

He took the papers off the chair, sat down, and started going through them.

"I'm afraid that Gilbert Pell came in yesterday afternoon, and it wasn't a pretty sight," he said. "He was coughing rather badly, and he reeked of drink."

"He can pull himself together if he has to," I said.

"That I doubt," Mr. Campbell said. "The boy has demons. He said the troupe was free to do whatever you please. You can use his name if you so desire, or any other name. That's not a very good idea, because his is the better-known name connected with your group. Everybody is calling themselves the Serenaders or the Ethiopians, or something similar. Gilbert Pell's brother Richard is mucking about trying to book shows for his own group."

"How's he doing?"

"Not good," Mr. Campbell said. "He's older, less energetic, and quite a lot less talented than Gil. At any rate, Gilbert Pell has taken himself off to Bristol for what he says is a holiday. I think he's going into hiding."

"From whom?"

"From himself," Mr. Campbell said. "But he's left you two letters. One, I know, contains a ticket for you back to America and the money he owes you. I believe it amounts to a little over ten pounds. The other is a letter he received for you from America."

Mr. Campbell handed me the letters. They seemed heavy in my hand, because I knew they might make me act in some way I would regret.

"And you have no other bookings for the troupe?" I asked.

"If you decide to stay in London, there is always the possibility of someone looking for a dancer of your caliber and, quite frankly, with your fame," Mr. Campbell said. "It won't be as much as you earned with Pell, of course. But do leave me an address and check with me frequently and I will see what I can do for you."

"Do you know what the others are doing?"

"Mr. Valentine has left for America, and I think Mr. Briggs is preparing to go," Mr. Campbell said.

I felt crushed. A light rain made the darkening skies even darker as I started home. What we had all known about the tour, that it was over, was now staring me in the face. My life seemed to have so many ups and downs that the ups didn't matter that much anymore. When I got home, Sarah had made a chicken in crust, like a pie, with peas and carrots. I told her what Campbell had said, and she tried to be brave.

"Only one ticket to America?" she finally asked.

"Yes."

"And the other letter?"

I hadn't opened the other letter and got it from my jacket pocket. It was addressed to me, William Henry Lane, and was from New York. I opened it and saw a neat handwriting. It was from Miss Lilly, Pete's wife.

Dear Juba,

I hope this letter finds you in good health. Peter says that you are probably filthy rich by now and may have an English accent. For me that would be funny because I cannot imagine you with an English accent.

We have heard about your success in London and hear that you are well. Things are going good here in New York. Almack's is busy. Peter is thinking about starting his own theater and is talking to some people from the mayor's office to get a license. If you decide to come back to New York, you will always find a good job here.

There is also some bad news. You remember Fred Flamer, who went to Washington to get a job. Peter said that Fred had gone to Washington and you had gone to London and that showed what Negroes could do if they set their minds to it. But word has come that Fred was sold into slavery. He tried to run away and got to a newspaper to tell them of his predicament but then was caught and had the backs of his heels cut so he could not run away again.

Peter said that if you do return, he would appreciate a

letter from you so he could put an advertisement in the
paper that Boz's Juba was going to make an appearance.
Good-bye for now, and please stay in touch.

Yours truly, Lilly Williams

I read Miss Lilly's letter three times, and still it was so shocking that I didn't want to believe it.

"Who is she?" Sarah asked.

"She's the wife of the man who owns a dance club," I said. "He's a bit of a scoundrel, but she's pretty nice."

"The man she's talking about was a slave?"

"He wasn't a slave when he was in New York," I said. "But sometimes men will come to a free state, or just find a free black man, and sell him into slavery."

"But if the man—if he told them he wasn't . . ."

"If people can have slaves in the first place, then why does it matter where they came from?" I said. "If they stole them from Africa or from New York, the thing is that there's a lot of money in slavery. A full-grown man can be sold for hundreds of dollars. And if someone is caught selling free people, or trying to sell a free person, it won't make a difference in a Southern court."

CHAPTER
TWELVE

"Sarah, my life is falling apart," I said.

"You can't go back to America, Juba," Sarah said. She sat next to me at the table and put her head close to mine. "It's too dangerous."

"It's not just the danger. I've learned to live with that," I said. "You have to watch yourself, but you can live with it. Freddy—the man Miss Lilly is writing about—was chasing a dream. I've danced with him. We actually made up a dance story—*Little Red Riding Hood*—and we danced it together. But it seems that my whole life is coming apart."

"It's not your fault that Gilbert Pell has left," Sarah said. "I think he always drank too much and ran around too much. It seemed that he could never sit still."

"Maybe it was because his life had reached the same point as mine has," I said.

"Juba, you have me," Sarah said. "And we have each other."

"But all my life I've dreamed of being a dancer. Not just a dancer, but a great dancer," I said. "I wanted to do something with dancing that nobody else has ever done. But every time I think I've made it, every time I feel I'm just about ready to take off, to fly away from the crowd, I end up with nothing. When Freddy and I danced together—it was over seven years ago—the program was great and people were talking about how much the dancers had done. There were Irish kids dancing, and black dancers, and some I didn't know what their backgrounds were, but they gave it everything they had. And after all the applause had stopped and people took their smiles and handshakes to their daily lives, I was nobody again.

"Freddy let his guard down because he needed to have a dream to hang on to. I came to England as Boz's Juba. I loved meeting Mr. Dickens and talking to him. He made me feel like an artist, and what he said about me, and about my dancing, was more than I expected from such a great man, but it was exactly what I needed. He made me feel like I mattered, Sarah. He made me feel as if I really mattered."

"Oh, you do, Juba." Sarah put her arm around my waist. "You really do."

I felt sorry for myself, and sorry for Sarah that she had to put up with me. We talked more about Gil and about Mr. Campbell, and even a little about Charles Dickens. Sarah said there were probably times when he felt bad about who he was or how his life was going. I didn't think so. He had seen his "worst of times" and had moved on. He was where I wanted to be.

Sarah's father had worked for a tailor in Dudley, some seventy-five miles north of London. Sarah said that the tailor, a Mr. Preece, had said he would always give her a job if she wanted it.

"My father had a room with him, and I think we could take that room now that my father is retired," she said. "Would you like that?"

"I think he'd be surprised to see you coming to Dudley with a black fellow," I said.

"We don't get many surprises in Dudley—it might be good for him."

I didn't really know what to do. I thought of Stubby back in New York, and how his dream of becoming a top chef hadn't worked out. Freddy Flamer stayed on my mind as I wondered how things would have been for him if we had hit it off better.

I could have helped his dancing and maybe . . . maybe things would have worked out differently. As it was, I didn't imagine there was much for me back in Five Points. Working for Peter Williams would lead nowhere. No matter how well I danced, it wouldn't help. I was still black, still someone who could be sold in parts of the country I called home.

Dudley, in a way, would be a new beginning for me, and although I was terrified that we were making a mistake, Sarah's enthusiasm and faith in me gave me courage. We arranged to be married in a small chapel in Marylebone, with a Reverend Cotter looking over his glasses at me and asking Sarah twice if she was sure about the wedding. She said she was. We had rounded up Mr. Campbell and a lady friend of his to witness the ceremony. I explained to him that I had assumed the name of Henry Juba to start my new life with Sarah, and that satisfied him.

Reverend Cotter ended the ceremony with "May you both be blessed with the strength of heaven, the light of the sun and the radiance of the moon, the splendor of fire, the speed of lightning, the swiftness of wind, the depth of the sea, the stability of earth, and the firmness of rock."

As we left the chapel, Sarah held tight to my arm, smiling. I could see her eyes glistening with tears that matched my own. It was a new start for both of us, and I determined to make her life with me really fine. I had more faith in our love than anything I had found in my life.

It took us three days to conclude our business in London. Mr. Campbell went with me to turn in the ticket and managed to scream and turn red when the ticket seller tried to tell me there was a charge and they could only give me half of the money. I finally got it all, and Sarah and I took the train from London to Birmingham and then a coach to Dudley that very night.

Mr. Preece did have a vacant room and didn't much care about who took it as long as we could pay for the first week's lodging. The room was large enough for the two of us, and we had free use of the kitchen. Sarah was used to Dudley, a very small town with its center less than a mile square. The people spoke differently than they did in London, but I could understand most of them.

"What is it that you do, lad?" an old gentleman in Mr. Preece's tailor shop asked me. His wife, almost a head taller than he, clung to his arm and gave me the sharpest look she could muster.

"I'm a dancer," I said.

"A dancing master?" he replied. "You teach dancing? That's not very likely, is it?"

I remembered Jack Bishop telling me that many towns in Ireland had dancing masters who taught the young people. I told him that I did indeed teach dancing, and he cleared his throat several times and sniffed. "Do you have anyone

179

around who can hold a fiddle?" I asked.

He said he could certainly find someone over the next hour if I intended to stay in town. It was nearly two hours later when the man returned with his wife in tow, a man carrying a fiddle, two more women, a clergyman, and a man in uniform. They stood in front of the shop looking for me to provide a bit of entertainment.

"Play," I said to the fiddler.

"Play *what?*"

"Do you know any jigs?"

He frowned, but he put his fiddle to his chin and began to play. I gave him four measures to warm up, and I began to dance.

It was the women who began to clap their hands in rhythm first, and then the man in uniform. The fiddler, a stocky sort with thick, curly hair, leaned into his playing. He was better than I thought he would be.

Within the week I put up a sign in the window of our rented room that read *Dancing Master* and had my first two pupils. They only had a few pence to spare, and it wasn't worth my time to try to lighten the feet of the two girls who came on Tuesdays and Thursdays, but it gave me an air of being respectable. It meant more to Sarah than it did to me.

Sarah, dear, dear Sarah. I hadn't imagined that she would ever mean so much to me. But she was my crutch; she had put her sturdy soul under my arm for the past two years, holding me up in my darkest moments with her cheerfulness. For the first time in the landscape of my memory, something came before dancing. It was Sarah.

When the small crowd in Dudley saw me dance for the first time, they were amazed. A shrewish woman, her face deeply lined with reminders of her age, came over to me after I had ended the dance and poked me. I still remember her amazement that I was real.

"You must be a devil!" she said, craning her neck toward me. "Real people with souls don't move like that!"

For weeks, people would stop me on the street and ask me to dance. "Just a bit," they would say, or "for a moment." A small theater group, dedicated to putting on dramas, asked me if I would dance between the acts.

The people of Dudley were amazed at my dancing, but there was no theater that wanted to book me. As word got out, a few theaters contacted me and offered short engagements. Sarah said it was a start, but I knew better.

"They're offering me up as a novelty," I said. "Something to take the mind away for a few minutes. Nothing more. Charles Dickens said to me that what we did, what he did with his words and me with my dancing, had to transform people. For a long time I didn't know what he meant. But when I think about it, what dancing is and what it needs to be doing, I can see it. I want people to look at me as they first did in Dudley and wonder if I am a man or a devil. I want them to think that a man's body can't move the way mine does, and if mine can move, if I can go across a floor the way I have so many times, then they must think again about everything that is possible. They must be some new person, if only for the minutes they are watching me."

The village people in Dudley were surprised to see me dancing, to see a black man who could perform magic with his body, but they could not support me. Was that always the case with artists? If I ever saw Mr. Dickens again, and if that great man had time, I would ask him: *Did you have moments of despair as you wrote* A Christmas Carol? *When you are alone in the night, the echoes of your readers' praise still ringing in your ears, are you worried that they don't really love you? Do your readers ever think of you as they do of me, that you are a creature who does not need to eat, to be safe with money in the bank and a never-ending supply of wood for your fire? Do they think you are otherworldly, some kind of gifted devil instead of a human being?*

The folks in Dudley grew to like me, to nod when they saw me on the street or tip their hats, but without a theater, I was lost. I even thought of starting my own venture, some small place, like Almack's back in Five Points. Sarah and I rented a hall on Sedgley Road for a weekend, but the seats, like the ones in London, were nearly empty.

London was the only place we knew where I would find steady work, and I made the trip there at the beginning of each week, coming home to Dudley when I could, bringing whatever earnings I had managed to scrape up. I found a job as a waiter's assistant at Mivart's Hotel. It was hard work, on my feet for twelve hours a day, but it brought in some money, and I was able to contribute at least something to our household. Sometimes I would be in London for weeks at a time, living close to the bone and longing for Sarah. In the quiet times, in the cheap lodgings I found, I would try not to ask myself if I had failed. I knew that I had touched some lives with my talents, and had given some people the idea that they could do something different with their own lives, and with their own bodies. I told myself that I had put dancing—no, not dancing, but the ambitions of dancing, the hope for the applause and the headlines—behind me. But then, one raw day, while cleaning up tables at Mivart's, I ran into Mr. Campbell again.

"Juba!" Mr. Campbell's voice caught me by surprise. "Sit down, my boy."

Of course I couldn't sit at his table in a fine restaurant, but he consented to come to the kitchen to see me. We talked. I told him of my circumstances, and he talked of what had happened when I had first arrived in London. He made it seem grander than I had imagined. He told me that Gilbert Pell had fallen on hard times and was no longer performing.

"He'll come back when he's ready," Mr. Campbell said. "How are you doing?"

"I'm doing as good as any other bird strutting along the sidewalk," I said. "It's a hard business."

"That it is. That it is. You know, there's a fellow in Liverpool who is trying to enlarge his theater," Mr. Campbell said. "For the last year or so, he's been doing a few weeks of Shakespeare and putting on some performances of John Gay. It's the Gay piece, *The Beggar's Opera,* that pays his bills. He wants to have a spectacular month-long performance with minstrels, acrobats, and singers for the autumn season. Shall I write to him about you? It would pay reasonably well and might do us both some good. I had a nice business with the Pell brothers and with Christy. Anything American goes over reasonably well, you know."

I tried not to be too excited, but I was. I wanted to sit right down and write Sarah and tell her all about it, but I knew I would be home before she received the letter. Mr. Campbell had asked me to come to his office the following Saturday morning, and I said I would.

Sarah was excited, as I knew she would be, and pressed my shirt so that I would make a good impression on Mr. Campbell.

"If you are you"—Sarah started off slowly as she held my

vest up to the light—"if you are Boz's Juba, then any moment can bring excitement. Just that little idea makes everything worthwhile. Don't you think so?"

"It could be," I said.

Yes, I was bubbling inside. It might be a chance to dance again, to move across a stage and know that hundreds of eyes would be watching my every move. Yes. Yes!

When I got to Mr. Campbell's office on Saturday morning, there were three other performers there. One by one they presented themselves to Mr. Campbell and discussed jobs with him. Some brought flyers, and I was angry with myself for not bringing the flyer advertising me as Boz's Juba. Mr. Campbell would certainly have remembered that billing, but it would have given me more confidence.

What I had done since I had last seen Mr. Campbell was to let my mind do its own dancing. I had built up the engagement at Liverpool to the same size and glory I had lived through at Sadler's Wells. I imagined the crowd roaring their approval and Sarah waiting for me backstage with a pot of tea.

"I did speak to the proprietor in Liverpool, Stephen Powell, and he was quite excited about having you perform there," Mr. Campbell said. "He asked if you had been dancing for the last two years and I told him yes, so you'll have to back me up on that one, Juba. The deal is two weeks of nightly performances and, if things go well, an additional two weeks. He'll check his books after that and decide what he wants to do in the future. But believe me, he is a smart operator, and in my mind, Liverpool is set to become the next London."

"What kind of dancing is he looking for?" I asked. "Does he have a set program?"

"I think he's looking for you to make a contribution there," Campbell said. "Maybe you can negotiate a separate deal with him for the programming. And do you know any minstrels in the Liverpool area?"

"No, but if there are chances to perform, I'll find them," I said.

Two weeks was not the month I had hoped for, and the money being offered was far less than I had dreamed of, but it was dancing and it was money, and it was yet another chance to show the world what I could do.

"You shouldn't go until the weekend," Sarah said. "Your cough sounds awful!"

"I need to go to see the stage, and the theater," I said. "I want to be ready when I meet the people in Liverpool."

It was a day's journey to Liverpool by a crowded coach. I took the cheapest seat I could get, on top of the coach, and knew it was a mistake as soon as we started. My whole body was shaking with the cold, and as Sarah had said, my cough was getting worse. I tried to pass the time thinking about possible programs. Gil Pell had not been very imaginative in his shows. He would have us sit in chairs, tell a few jokes, play the songs and sing, and then I would dance. It worked in a warm hall, and the dancing performances were always the highlights.

I thought about the performance at Almack's, when we did *Little Red Riding Hood.* The audience had loved the performance, and as Margaret had said, knowing what to expect was a big help.

It was dark when the carriage reached Liverpool, and much colder than it had been in Dudley. The carriage had stopped at an inn, but I headed toward the waterfront, where I knew I would find cheaper lodgings. I found the dock area easily enough, by just asking everyone I saw on the street and following their directions.

I looked for a pub, someplace where men gathered to drink, and found one. Once inside, I asked a woman if she knew of somewhere I could find a bed for the night.

"Are you wanting to pay for one or are you looking to chat one up?" she asked, amused at her own joke.

I told her I would be willing to pay a reasonable price, and she directed me down the street to a wooden building that looked for all the world as if it might fall over at any moment. I knocked on the door and found myself talking to a rough-looking tattooed man in his trousers and no shirt.

There were no private rooms to be had, but there was a

large room on the second floor with four cots, and one was empty.

"You're in luck," said the man, who I presumed was the owner. "Usually they're all full by this time of night."

I put my case under the cot as quickly as possible after taking out the crackers and sardines Sarah had packed for me. I ate them quietly on the bed and then stretched out. The rough blanket on the bed didn't do much to warm me up, but I fell asleep soon enough.

In the morning I woke up with my head reeling.

Mr. Campbell had given me the address in Liverpool, and I checked it several times as I was putting my clothes on. I was slightly dizzy, I guess from exhaustion and the cold that I couldn't seem to get rid of. The question in my mind was whether I would take my case from under the bed and carry it around with me. I wasn't feeling well and didn't want the extra burden of the case, but I didn't want to leave it behind for someone to take, either. On the ground floor there were men sitting and having tea. I was startled and stopped in the doorway. Suddenly I felt a hundred times better and crossed the floor to where one of the men sat.

"Stubby! It's me, Juba! When did you get to England?"

"You talking at me, chap?"

"You're Stubby Jackson, from Five Points, right?" I pulled over a chair and sat down.

"No, I'm not" came the quick answer. The man before me leaned back and squinted. "And I don't know who you are, either."

Now the face that had looked so clear a moment before looked less clear. It wasn't Stubby; it was a white man, perhaps Italian, and much older than I imagined my friend must be by now.

I apologized and quickly retreated.

The theater, on a side street, was disappointing. The building was badly in need of paint, and the sign above the main entrance seemed sad, rather than the bright sign I would have liked to see. I knocked on the front door, remembered how early it was, and was about to leave when a voice called out, asking who was there.

"Juba!" I said. "Boz's Juba!"

Some words from within that I couldn't catch, and then the door opened.

"You must have been caught in the morning rain," the man said. "You're soaking wet. I gather you're the dancer Campbell was crowing about. He said you presented a neat package. Come in."

I stepped into the dimly lit room, just noticing that I *was* wet. I hadn't got caught in the rain, but the exertion of carrying my case around had brought on a sweat even in the cold air.

Stephen Powell was nicely built and carried himself well. As we sat in chairs in the lobby, he told me of his plans. More or less, he confirmed what Mr. Campbell had already laid out for me.

"I want to open in February," he said. "High-class material. *King Lear* to start, then perhaps *Romeo and Juliet*, and then *Othello*. All good plays. Dramatic stuff. In between the turnarounds, when one play ends and the next begins, I want to do minstrel and variety shows. But it has to be good stuff as well. If you're half as talented as Campbell says, then you're the man for the job. I can help you round up some minstrels here in Liverpool, and you can direct them any way you choose. You fit for the job?"

"I am," I said.

"Good. Right now I'm getting the first production together. It's a light two-act piece called *Aggravating Sam*. Then *Lear* and the rest."

I was feeling faint and wanted to leave immediately.

"You contact me next Monday, and we'll work out the details and all that. That's five days from now," Mr. Powell said. "Just bang on the door, and either I'll be home or the wife will let you in to wait for me."

"Yes, sir."

Going home was not possible right away. I felt so weak, I was nearly staggering when I left the theater. I went back to where I had secured a cot for the night and arranged for another night's stay.

To spend a day on the carriage to Dudley and then another

coming back seemed senseless. I would just stick it out for a few days and pull my resources together. I slept most of the day and woke in the middle of the night. My pillow was damp from sweat, and I knew I needed rest. But I had only enough money for two or three days. Five days would not be possible unless I found some money to at least fill my belly.

The docks. Nothing is drearier, little can be harder. I went down and begged for work.

"You don't look like you can lift your head, fellow," a dark, shoulder-heavy man said. "Let alone a crate."

Still, he gave me a job. I was to work with a gang to unload coffee from the Philippines. The sacks were heavy, and the pace was killing.

As I walked down the narrow gangway from the ship to the dock, I thought of Stubby again. How could I have mistaken the man drinking tea for my friend? But as I carried the bags, I thought I saw him again. This time he was half in the shadows and half colored by the light from a streetlamp. I put the sack of coffee I was carrying on the cart and walked near the dark figure. Again, it wasn't Stubby.

Panic. Breathing was getting harder in the cold, wet air of Liverpool. Someone was yelling at me to speed it up. To speed it up.

Was I falling? Was I home again? Did I make it through the night? Had I been paid?

I found myself stirring and started to reach for my pockets. Where was my money? I sat up for a moment; then the room began to spin and I fell back again.

"Hey, the black boy is coming around!" someone was saying.

I pushed myself to one elbow and looked around me. There were faces, all white, staring at me. Where was I?

"Where is this place?" I asked.

"Liverpool workhouse," a woman answered. "We thought you'd be dead for sure by now. They were poking you yesterday to see if you were alive. I bet you'd be dead for sure by this morning, but look at you, still halfway living, aren't you?"

The workhouse. Only the poorest wound up in these places. Those who were about to die or go to prison.

"I don't belong here," I announced.

"You don't belong anyplace, but if you want, they'll take you to the edge of Liverpool and dump you," a woman said. "You've been here almost a week, coughing and sweating and talking out of your mind. One of the men thought you might have had Saint Vitus' dance, the way your legs were jerking around. Anyway, you might as well stay here. You'll get a crust of bread in the morning and a bowl of soup."

I closed my eyes again. No, I didn't belong here. I asked around to see what day it was, and it was past the time I was to see Mr. Powell. The moment had come and gone, and I lay on a pallet in the workhouse.

Visions. Visions that I did not chase, or stumble across the floor to touch or greet. Stubby came to mind; I hadn't realized how much he was within me. Once I dreamed of Mr. Dickens, not like the last time I saw him, but the first, at Almack's, with his soft face and long hair. Visions of Miss Lilly and of Peter Williams, grinning, his sly eyes peeking from that round, dark face.

But the vision I had most was of the one who would save me. It was a vision of Sarah. My Sarah.

I sat down and wrote a letter. I asked the woman who had spoken to me if she would post it for me. She said she would, and I gave her tuppence. I read it once again to make sure it was right.

My darling Sarah,

Things have not gone well here in Liverpool. I am ill, no, sick as I can be. When you get this letter you must not fret. Only come to Liverpool to rescue me. Please don't take the cheapest seat. The ride is very hard and very long. There is to be a minstrel show here and Mr. Powell has asked me to perform in it. I think he will be annoyed that I did not show up when he requested, but when you come and nurse me back to health and he sees what I can do, he will be glad to have me on board. Sarah, all I need is a chance to show what is in my soul and in my body. Life will take care of me after that, and I will bring my art to the world after all. When this engagement is over, perhaps we should go to New York. You will be delighted to see the huge city, and New York will be delighted to see my precious Sarah.

Oh, yes, there is a family here in the workhouse. The man looks very bad, and the two children, a boy and a girl, are forlorn. I asked the boy if he could dance, and he said he knew a few steps. Sarah, I showed him how to do a slide using the rhythm of a jig. When he got it down, he smiled. It was a beautiful smile.

I cannot wait to see you again. You will be like an angel sent from God to revive me. In my heart I know we will be all right. I love you,

Your Juba

EPILOGUE

It is not known if Juba's letter was actually mailed, or if it ever reached Sarah. It is only known that William Henry Lane, known to the world as Master Juba, the world's greatest dancer, died in the workhouse in Liverpool. The cause of his death was given as fever.

CERTIFIED COPY OF AN ENTRY OF DEATH — GIVEN AT THE GENERAL REGISTER OFFICE

Application Number 5227707-2

REGISTRATION DISTRICT   LIVERPOOL

1854 DEATH in the Sub-district of Mount Pleasant Liverpool   in the County of Lancaster

Columns:	1	2	3	4	5	6	7	8	9
No.	When and where died	Name and surname	Sex	Age	Occupation	Cause of death	Signature, description and residence of informant	When registered	Signature of registrar
237	Third February 1854 workhouse Brownlow Hill	Bois Juba	Male	30 years	Musician	Debris certified	Jh Ayrton M.D. In attendance Workhouse Liverpool	Fourth February 1854	Joseph Bolm Registrar

CERTIFIED to be a true copy of an entry in the certified copy of a Register of Deaths in the District above mentioned.

Given at the GENERAL REGISTER OFFICE, under the Seal of the said Office, the   22nd   day of   October   2013

DYD 590364

See note overleaf

CAUTION: THERE ARE OFFENCES RELATING TO FALSIFYING OR ALTERING A CERTIFICATE AND USING OR POSSESSING A FALSE CERTIFICATE ©CROWN COPYRIGHT

WARNING: A CERTIFICATE IS NOT EVIDENCE OF IDENTITY.

Registered death certificate for Bois [Boz's] Juba, musician, age 30

Register of BURIALS at the Free Parochial Cemetery of St. Martin's-in-the-Fields, in Liverpool, in the County of Lancaster, in the Year One Thousand Eight Hundred and Fifty-four

Name.	Abode.	When Buried.	Age.	By whom the Ceremony was performed.
Rachel Morgan No.1065	20th Richmond Street	February 6th	3 yrs	Henry Brooks Curate
John Eaton No.1066	N. Infirmary	6th	42 yrs	Henry Brooks Curate
Bois Juba No.1067	Workhouse	6th	30 yrs	Henry Brooks Curate
Archibald Mc Kellar No.1068	Workhouse	6th	42 yrs	Henry Brooks Curate
Sarah Mills No.1069	Workhouse	6th	63 yrs	Henry Brooks Curate
Margaret Wright No.1070	Workhouse	6th	2 yrs	Henry Brooks Curate
Margaret Pellow No.1071	Workhouse	6th	4 mons	Henry Brooks Curate
Mary Ann Kennedy	Workhouse	6th	9	Henry Brooks Curate

Third entry lists Bois [Boz's] Juba,
from the workhouse, age 30, February 6, 1854.

TIMELINE

Circa 1825—Born in Providence, Rhode Island

1842*—Charles Dickens visits Five Points; reviews Master Juba in *American Notes*

1844—Juba vs. Master Diamond at John Tryon's Amphitheatre

Circa 1844—Juba tours New England

1845—Juba given top billing imitating famous dancers

1846—Juba joins Charley White's Serenaders

1848—Joins Gilbert Pell's Serenaders

August 5, 1848*—Vauxhall Garden Performance, London

1848*—Tours England with Gilbert Pell

1849—Tours England with Richard Pell

1850*—Tours solo (accompanied by Thomas F. Briggs)

1851*—Resides in Dudley, England, with wife, Sarah, per census

September 14, 1851*—Appears in Dublin

January 21, 1854*—Admitted to workhouse in Liverpool

February 3, 1854*—Dies of fever in workhouse

February 6, 1854*—Buried in Parochial Cemetery of St. Martin in the Fields in Liverpool

*Documented

A NOTE ABOUT THE BOOK

The story of William Henry Lane, known as Master Juba, was told early on by Marian Hannah Winter in *Dance Index*, February 1947. The original sources she cites are mostly descriptions, advertising flyers, and reviews of his performances, the first of which was the description by Charles Dickens in his *American Notes* in 1842. Juba was at that time seventeen or eighteen years old. His early life is not documented, but most sources say he was freeborn in Providence, Rhode Island, and moved to New York City in his midteens.

The task of telling his story appealed to Walter for a good few years. Here was a very young man born into a time when people of his race were held in slavery. Although New York freed all slaves in 1827, life for a person without many resources was extremely hard whatever his or her race. Poor immigrants and blacks struggled to survive in the area known as Five Points in New York City. Juba was able to become an accomplished performer under these conditions. He traveled to London and was a great success. Information about the times and places that were important in telling the story was easily found, but what happened at the end of Master Juba's life was not recorded. Many of his performances were documented in reviews, as well as in announcements of future appearances in local papers throughout the British Isles. It is clear that Master Juba performed on a grueling schedule for the first years in England. After that, there is no contemporary record of what happened to him. Walter wanted to tell the story, but he felt that some information about what became of Juba was needed to complete the tale.

While in London, Walter researched family history records. Finally, in the 1851 census, an entry was found in the town of Dudley. It shows a couple living as lodgers in the home of John Preece, a tailor. Here we see Henry Juba and his wife, Sarah. Juba is listed as a professor of dance, twenty-six, from Barbados. The English census does not indicate the race of those enumerated. If Juba had listed himself as American, he would have been considered an alien, but as a person from Barbados, he was a British subject.

A researcher, Dr. Stephen W. Taylor, was hired to search for some further information about Juba. He was able to find the documents that tell of the final days of Master Juba. In the records of the workhouse of Liverpool, there is an entry for Boz's Juba. He died February 3, 1854, in the workhouse, Brownlow Hill (Liverpool), listed as a musician who died of febris, or fever. Finally, a burial entry for Juba, age thirty, was found in the Free Parochial Cemetery of St. Martin in the Fields, Silvester Street, Liverpool.

With the final days of William Henry Lane—Master

Juba—now known, Walter was able to craft this story. He had researched the Five Points area extensively for *Riot,* his book on the draft riot of 1863, and London of the mid-1800s for his book on Sarah Forbes Bonetta, *At Her Majesty's Request.* Annie Sieg, an Irish dancer, read the manuscript and contributed many suggestions on dance techniques and some of the feelings of a performer.

Walter included the following historical characters:

Charles Dickens—who wrote about his visit to Almack's in 1842

Peter Williams—the owner of Almack's

Lilly, Peter's wife—mentioned by Dickens (referred to as the landlady, but not by name)

Master John Diamond—a famed dancer

Jim Lowe—an older dancer said to mentor Juba

Gilbert W. Pell—leader of the Serenaders

Mr. Briggs, Mr. Ludlow, Mr. Everton, and Mr. Valentine—the rest of the Serenaders

Sarah Felton—Juba's wife, named in the census of 1851, but her maiden name not given.

Walter added the rest of the cast of characters, surrounding Juba with friends and associates. Stubby, Freddy, Jack Bishop, and Margaret Moran were Juba's principal supporters. Although they were fictional, Walter had photographs of these characters chosen from his photograph collection, which he posted on the wall in front of his computer. They lived in his mind as much as any real character did as he wrote the story of William Henry Lane, known as Master Juba.

—Constance Myers

THE

THE BEAST TAKES POSSESSION

INDWELLING

TIM LaHAYE
JERRY B. JENKINS

Tyndale House Publishers, Inc.
WHEATON, ILLINOIS

Visit Tyndale's exciting Web site at www.tyndale.com

Discover the latest about the Left Behind series at www.leftbehind.com

Left Behind series designed by Catherine Bergstrom
Cover photo illustration by Julie Chen
Designed by Julie Chen

Published in association with the literary agency of Alive Communications, Inc., 1465 Kelly Johnson Blvd., Suite 320, Colorado Springs, CO 80920

Library of Congress Cataloging-in-Publication Data

LaHaye, Tim F.
   The indwelling : the beast takes possession / Tim LaHaye, Jerry B. Jenkins.
      p. cm.
   ISBN 0-8423-2928-5 — ISBN 0-8423-2929-3 (pbk.)
      1. Steele, Rayford (fictitious character)—Fiction.   2. Rapture (Christian eschatology)—
   Fiction.   I. Jenkins, Jerry B.   II. Title.

   PS3562.A315 I54 2000
   813'.54—dc21   00-020562

Printed in the United States of America

06   05   04   03   02   01   00
7   6   5   4   3   2   1

To our agent, Rick Christian,
who recognized the value of the idea and
the potential of the partnership
and introduced us to each other

FORTY-TWO MONTHS
INTO THE TRIBULATION

The Believers

Rayford Steele, mid-forties; former 747 captain for Pan-Continental; lost wife and son in the Rapture; former pilot for Global Community Potentate Nicolae Carpathia; original member of the Tribulation Force; an international fugitive in exile; fleeing Israel, site of the assassination of Carpathia

Cameron ("Buck") Williams, early thirties; former senior writer for *Global Weekly;* former publisher of *Global Community Weekly* for Carpathia; original member of the Trib Force; editor of cybermagazine *The Truth;* fugitive in exile on assignment in Israel

Chloe Steele Williams, early twenties; former student, Stanford University; lost mother and brother in the Rapture; daughter of Rayford; wife of Buck; mother of fourteen-month-old Kenny Bruce; CEO of the International Commodity Co-op, an underground network of believers; original Trib Force member; fugitive in exile, safe house, Mount Prospect, Illinois

Tsion Ben-Judah, late forties; former rabbinical scholar and Israeli statesman; revealed belief in Jesus as the Messiah on international TV—wife and two teenagers subsequently murdered; escaped to U.S.; spiritual leader and teacher of Trib Force; cyberaudience of more than a billion daily; fugitive in exile at safe house

Mac McCullum, late fifties; pilot for Carpathia; New Babylon

David Hassid, mid-twenties; high-level director for the GC; New Babylon

Annie Christopher, early twenties; Global Community corporal, Phoenix 216 cargo chief; in love with David Hassid; New Babylon

Leah Rose, late thirties; former head nurse, Arthur Young Memorial Hospital, Palatine, Illinois; on assignment in Brussels from safe house

Tyrola ("T") Mark Delanty, late thirties; owner/director, Palwaukee Airport, Wheeling, Illinois

Mr. and Mrs. Lukas ("Laslos") Miklos, mid-fifties; lignite mining magnates; Greece

Abdullah Smith, early thirties; former Jordanian fighter pilot; first officer, Phoenix 216; New Babylon

The Enemies

Nicolae Jetty Carpathia, mid-thirties; former president of Romania; former secretary-general, United Nations; self-appointed Global Community potentate; assassinated in Jerusalem; lying in state at GC palace complex, New Babylon

Leon Fortunato, early fifties; Carpathia's right hand and assumed successor; GC supreme commander; New Babylon

The Undecided

Hattie Durham, early thirties; former Pan-Continental flight attendant; former personal assistant to Carpathia; imprisoned in Belgium

Dr. Chaim Rosenzweig, late sixties; Israeli botanist and statesman; discoverer of a formula that made Israeli deserts bloom; former *Global Weekly* Man of the Year; apparent stroke victim; Jerusalem

PROLOGUE

From *Assassins*

BUCK had ducked under a scaffold at the sound of the gun. A tidal wave of humanity swept past him on both sides, and he saw glee on some faces. Converts from the Wailing Wall who had seen Carpathia murder their heroes?

By the time Buck looked to the stage, the potentates were leaping off, the drapery was flying into the distance, and Chaim appeared catatonic, his head rigid.

Carpathia lay on the platform, blood running from his eyes, nose, and mouth, and—it appeared to Buck—from the top of his head. His lapel mike was still hot, and because Buck was directly under a speaker tower, he heard Nicolae's liquid, guttural murmur, "But I thought . . . I thought . . . I did everything you asked."

Fortunato draped his stocky body over Carpathia's chest, reached beneath him, and cradled him. Sitting on the stage, he rocked his potentate, wailing.

"Don't die, Excellency!" Fortunato bawled. "We need you! The world needs you! *I* need you!"

Security forces surrounded them, brandishing Uzis. Buck had experienced enough trauma for one day. He stood transfixed, with a clear view of the back of Carpathia's blood-matted skull.

The wound was unmistakably fatal. And from where Buck stood, it was obvious what had caused it.

———————

"I did not expect a gunshot," Tsion said, staring at the television as GC Security cleared the stage and whisked Carpathia away.

Two hours later GC CNN confirmed the death and played over and over the grieving pronouncement of Supreme Commander Leon Fortunato. "We shall carry on in the courageous spirit of our founder and moral anchor, Potentate Nicolae Carpathia. The cause of death will remain confidential until the investigation is complete. But you may rest assured the guilty party will be brought to justice."

The news media reported that the slain potentate's body would lie in state in the New Babylon palace before entombment there on Sunday.

"Don't leave the TV, Chloe," Tsion said. "You have to assume the resurrection will be caught on camera."

But when Friday became Saturday in Mount Prospect and Saturday night approached, even Tsion began to wonder. The Scriptures had not foretold of death by projectile. Antichrist was to die from a specific wound to the head and then come back to life. Carpathia still lay in state.

By dawn Sunday, as Tsion gloomily watched mourners

pass the glass bier in the sun-drenched courtyard of the GC palace, he had begun to doubt himself.

Had he been wrong all along?

———————

Two hours before the burial, David Hassid was called in to Leon Fortunato's office. Leon and his directors of Intelligence and Security huddled before a TV monitor. Leon's face revealed abject grief and the promise of vengeance. "Once His Excellency is in the tomb," he said, his voice thick, "the world can approach closure. Prosecuting his murderer can only help. Watch with us, David. The primary angles were blocked, but look at this collateral view. Tell me if you see what we see."

David watched.

Oh, no! he thought. *It couldn't be!*

"Well?" Leon said, peering at him. "Is there any doubt?"

David stalled, but that only made the other two glance at him.

"The camera doesn't lie," Leon said. "We have our assassin, don't we?"

Much as he wanted to come up with some other explanation for what was clear, David would jeopardize his position if he proved illogical. He nodded. "We sure do."

———————

"The second woe is past. Behold, the third woe is coming quickly."

Revelation 11:14

Monday of Gala Week

LEAH Rose prided herself on thinking under pressure. She'd been chief administrative nurse in a large hospital for a decade and had also been one of few believers there the last three and a half years. She had survived by her wits and eluded Global Community Peacekeeping Forces until finally having to flee and join the Tribulation Force.

But on the Monday of the week that would see the assassinations of the two witnesses and the Antichrist, Leah had no clue what to do. In disguise and under her alias, Donna Clendenon, she believed she had fooled authorities at the Belgium Facility for Female Rehabilitation (BFFR, or Buffer). She had passed herself off as Hattie Durham's aunt.

A squinting guard, whose nameplate read CROIX and whose accent was unmistakably French, asked, "And what makes you think your niece is incarcerated here?"

"You think I'd come all the way from California if I

1

had any doubt?" Leah said. "Everybody knows Hattie is here, and I know her alias: Mae Willie."

The guard cocked his head. "And your message can be delivered only in person?"

"A death in the family."

"I'm sorry."

Leah pursed her lips, aware of her artificially protruding teeth. *I'll bet,* she thought.

Croix stood and riffled through pages on his clipboard. "Buffer is a maximum security facility without standard visiting privileges. Ms. Durham has been separated from the prison population. I would have to get clearance for you to see her. I could give her the message myself."

"All I want is five minutes," Leah said.

"You can imagine how short staffed we are."

Leah didn't respond. Millions had disappeared in the Rapture. Half the remaining population had died since. Everybody was short staffed. Merely existing anymore was a full-time job. Croix asked her to wait in a holding area, but he did not tell her she would see no personnel, no inmates, or even any other visitors for more than two hours. A glass cubicle, where it appeared a clerical person had once sat, was empty. No one was there whom Leah could ask how long this might take, and when she rose to look for someone else, she found she was locked in. Were they onto her? Was she now a prisoner too?

Just before Leah resorted to banging on the door and screaming for help, Croix returned. Without apology, and—she noticed—avoiding eye contact, he said, "My superiors are considering your request and will call your hotel tomorrow."

Leah fought a smile. *As if I want you to know where I'm staying.*

"How about I call you?" Leah said.

"Suit yourself," Croix said with a shrug. *"Merci."* Then, as if catching himself: "Thank you."

Relieved to be outside, Leah drove around to be sure she wasn't being followed. With puzzling instructions from Rayford not to call him until Friday, she phoned Buck and brought him up to date. "I don't know whether to bolt or play it out," she said.

That night in her hotel room, Leah felt a loneliness only slightly less acute than when she had first been left behind. She thanked God for the Tribulation Force and how they had welcomed her. All but Rayford, of course. She couldn't figure him. Here was a brilliant, accomplished man with clear leadership skills, someone she had admired until the day she moved into the safe house. They hadn't clicked, but everyone else seemed frustrated with him too.

In the morning Leah showered and dressed and found something to eat, planning to see Hattie as soon as she had permission. She was going to call Buffer from her untraceable cell phone, but she got caught up watching on television as Carpathia taunted Moishe and Eli before the eyes of the world.

She sat, mouth agape, as Carpathia murdered the two witnesses with a powerful handgun. Leah remembered when TV cameras would have been averted in the face of such violence. Then came the earthquake that left a tenth of Jerusalem in rubble.

The GC global network showed quake scenes interspersed with footage of the silent witnesses badgered by the smirking Carpathia before their ignominious ends. The slow-motion pictures were broadcast over and over, and repulsed as she was, Leah could not turn away.

She had known this was coming; they all had—any students of Tsion Ben-Judah. But to see it played out shocked and saddened her, and Leah's eyes swam. She knew how it was to turn out, too, that they would be resurrected and that Carpathia would get his. Leah prayed for her new friends, some of whom were in Jerusalem. But she didn't want to sit there blubbering when she had work to do too. Things would get a lot worse than this, and Leah needed the training of performing under pressure to prepare herself and to convince herself she was up to it.

The phone at Buffer rang and rang, and Leah was at least warmed to know that the world government suffered just like the rank and file with the loss of half the population. Finally a woman picked up, but Leah couldn't get her even to acknowledge an employee named Croix.

"A French guard?" Leah tried.

"Ah, I know who you mean. Hold on."

Finally a man picked up. "Who are you holding for, please?" he said, in a hurry.

"Guard Croix," she said, "about six feet—"

"Croix!" the man hollered. "Phone!"

But he never came to the phone. Leah finally hung up and drove to the prison, leaving her phone in the car for safety.

At long last Croix ushered her into yet another private room. This one had a large window that Leah thought might be a two-way mirror. Again she feared her cover might have already been blown.

"I thought you were going to call," the guard said, pointing to a chair, ubiquitous clipboard in hand.

"I tried," she said. "This place is poorly run."

"Understaffed," he said.

"Can we get on with it?" Leah said. "I need to see my niece."

"No."

"No?"

Croix stared at her, apparently unwilling to repeat himself.

"I'm listening," she said.

"I'm not at liberty to—"

"Don't give me that," Leah said. "If I can't see her, I can't see her, but I have the right to know she's healthy, that she's alive."

"She is both."

"Then why can't I see her?"

Croix pressed his lips together. "She's been transferred, ma'am."

"Since yesterday?"

"I'm not at liberty to—"

"How long has she been gone? Where is she?"

He shook his head. "I'm telling you what I was told. If you'd like to get a message to—"

"I want to see her. I want to know she's all right."

"To the best of my knowledge, she's fi—"

"The best of your knowledge! Have you an inkling how limited your knowledge is?"

"Insulting me will not—"

"I don't mean to insult you, sir! I'm merely asking to see my niece and—"

"That's enough, Officer Croix," came a female voice from behind the glass. "You may go."

Croix left without a word or a look. Leah detected an Asian accent in the woman. She stood and stepped to the mirror. "So, what's next, ma'am? Am I to leave too, or will I get some word about my niece?"

Silence.

"Have I now become a prisoner too? Guilt by relation?"

Leah felt conspicuous and wondered whether anyone was behind the glass after all. Finally she marched to the door but was not surprised to find herself locked in again. "Terrific," she said, heading back toward the mirror. "What are the magic words that get me out of here? C'mon, lady! I know you're back there!"

"You will be free to go when we say you are free to go."

The same woman. Leah pictured her older, matronly, and clearly Asian. She raised her palms in surrender and plopped into a chair. She started and looked up when she heard a buzz in the door latch. "You may go."

Leah shot a double take at the mirror. "I may?"

"She who hesitates . . ."

"Oh, I'm going," she said, rising. "Could I at least see *you* on my way out? Please? I just want to know—"

"You're trying my patience, Mrs. Clendenon. You have received all the information you will get here."

Leah stopped with her hand on the doorknob, shaking her head, hoping to weasel something from the disembodied voice.

"Go, ma'am!" the woman said. "While you have the option."

Leah had given her best. She wasn't willing to go to prison for this caper. For another effort, maybe, another assignment. She would sacrifice her freedom for Dr. Ben-Judah. But for Hattie? Hattie's own doctor had died treating her, and she seemed barely grateful.

Leah moved briskly through the echoing corridors. She heard a door behind her and, hoping to catch a glimpse of the woman, turned quickly. A small, trim, pale, dark-haired woman in uniform turned and headed the other way. Could that have been her?

Leah headed for the main entrance but turned at the last instant and stepped behind a bank of phones. At least it looked like a bank of phones. She wanted to pretend to be talking on one while anyone who might follow her rushed out the door, but every phone was in shambles, wires hanging.

She was about to abandon her plan when she heard quick footsteps and saw a young Asian woman hurry out the front door, car keys jangling. Leah was convinced this was the same woman who had ducked away when she turned around. Now Leah was following *her.*

She hesitated inside the glass doors, watching as the woman trotted to the visitor parking lot and scanned the area. Apparently frustrated, she turned and walked slowly back toward the entrance. Leah nonchalantly exited, hoping to get a straight-on look at the woman. If she could get her to speak, she would know whether she had been the one behind the glass.

An employee of the GC and she's worse at this than I am, Leah thought, as the woman noticed her, appeared startled, then fought to act normal. As they neared one another, Leah asked where a washroom was, but the woman tugged her tiny uniform cap tighter onto her head and turned away to cough as she passed, not hearing or pretending not to.

Leah pulled out of the unattended lot and waited at a stop sign a quarter mile away, where she could see the prison entrance in her rearview mirror. The woman hurried out and hopped into a compact four-door. Determined to lose her, Leah raced off and got lost trying to find her hotel via side streets.

She called Rayford again and again. No way this could wait until Friday. When he didn't answer she worried that his phone might have fallen into the wrong hands. She left a cryptic message: "Our bird has flown the cage. Now what?"

She drove into the country, convinced no one was following her, and found her way back to the hotel at dusk.

She had been in her room less than half an hour when the phone rang.

"This is Donna," she said.

"You have a visitor," the clerk said. "May I send her back?"

"No! Who is it?"

"'A friend' is all she'll say."

"I'll come there," Leah said.

She stuffed her belongings into a bag and slipped out to her car. She tried to peer into the lobby through the plate glass, but she couldn't see who was there. As she started the car, someone drove behind her and stopped. Leah was pinned in. She locked her doors as the driver emerged from the other vehicle.

As Leah's eyes adjusted to the light, she could see it was the same car the woman had driven from the prison. A knock made her jump. The woman, still in uniform, signaled her to lower her window. Leah lowered it an inch, her heart thudding.

"I need to make a show of this," the woman whispered. "Play your part."

My part? "What do you want?" Leah said.

"Come with me."

"Not on your life! Unless you want your car in pieces, get it out of my way."

The woman leaned forward. "Excellent. Now step out and let me cuff you and—"

"Are you out of your mind? I have no intention of—"

"Perhaps you cannot see my forehead in the darkness," the woman said. "But trust me—"

"Why should I—?"

And then Leah saw it. The woman had the mark. She was a believer.

The woman pointed to the lock as she removed handcuffs from a holster on her belt. Leah unlocked the door. "How did you find me?" she said.

"Checked your alias at several hotels. Didn't take long."

"Alias?" Leah said as she alighted and turned so the woman could cuff her.

"I'm Ming Toy," she said, leading Leah to the backseat of her car. "A believer comes all the way to Brussels to see Hattie Durham and uses her own name? I don't think so."

"I'm supposed to be her aunt," Leah said as Ming pulled out of the parking lot.

"Well, that worked on everybody else," she said. "But they didn't see what I saw. So, who are you and what are you doing here?"

"Would you mind if I double-checked your mark, Miss Toy?"

"*Mrs.* I'm a widow."

"Me too."

"But call me Ming."

"I'll tell you what you can call me as soon as I can check your mark."

"In a minute."

Ming pulled into a GC Peacekeeping station. "I need an interrogation room," she barked at the man behind the desk, still holding tight to Leah's left biceps.

"Commander," the man said with a nod, sliding a key across the counter. "Last door on the left."

"Private, no viewing, no bugs."

"That's the secure one, ma'am."

Ming locked the door, angled the lamp shade toward them, and released Leah from her cuffs. "Check me out," she said, sitting and cocking her head.

Leah gently held the back of Ming's head, knowing already that anyone who would let her do that had to be genuine. She licked her thumb and ran it firmly across the mark on Ming's forehead. Leah slumped into a chair across from Ming and reached for both her hands. "I can't wait to get to know you," she said.

"Likewise," Ming said. "Let's pray first."

Leah couldn't keep from welling up as this brand-new friend thanked God for their propitious meeting and asked that he allow them to somehow work together.

"First I'll tell you where Hattie Durham is," Ming said. "Then we'll trade stories, and I'll take you back to your hotel, tell my associates that you check out as Hattie's aunt, and let them think that you believe Hattie was transferred but that you don't know where."

"She wasn't transferred?"

Ming shook her head.

"Is she alive?"

"Temporarily."

"Healthy?"

"Healthier than when we got her. In fact, she's in quite good shape. Strong enough to assassinate a potentate."

Leah furrowed her brow and shook her head. "I'm not following you."

"They let her go."

"Why?"

"All she talked about was killing Carpathia. Finally they told her that as it was clear she had lost his baby, she was no longer a threat and was free to go, with a tidy settlement for her trouble. Roughly one hundred thousand Nicks in cash."

Leah shook her head. "They don't consider her a threat? She wants to kill him for real."

"They know that," Ming said. "In my opinion, they think she's dumber than she looks."

"Sometimes she is," Leah said.

"But not dumb enough to lead them straight to the rest of the Tribulation Force," Ming said. "The simplistic plan is that they follow her to the Gala in Jerusalem and to some sort of a rendezvous with one of you Judah-ites."

"I love that title. I'm a believer first, but also proudly a Judah-ite."

"Me too," Ming said. "And I'll bet you know Ben-Judah personally."

"I do."

"Wow."

"But, Ming, the GC is wrong about Hattie. She's crazy enough to go and try to kill Nicolae, but she has no interest in contacting any of us."

"You might be surprised."

"How so?"

"She didn't go to Jerusalem like they hoped. We've tracked her to North America. I think she's onto the GC and wants to get back to safety as soon as she can."

"That's worse!" Leah said. "She'll lead them to the safe house."

"Maybe that's why God sent you here," Ming said. "I didn't know what I was going to do to protect you people. Whom was I supposed to tell? You're the answer to my prayer."

"But what can I do? I'll never be able to catch her before she gets there."

"You can at least warn them, right?"

Leah nodded. "My phone's in my bag in my car."

"And my phones are all traceable."

They traded stories on the way back. Ming was twenty-two years old, a native of China. Her husband of two months had been killed a few minutes after the disappearances when the commuter train he was on crashed when the brakeman and several controllers vanished. She had joined the GC in a paroxysm of patriotism shortly after the treaty was signed between the United Nations and Israel. She had been assigned to the reconstruction administration in what used to be the Philippines, but there she had become a believer through the letters of her brother at home, now seventeen. "Chang's friends had led him to faith," she said. "He has not yet told my parents, who are very old school and very pro-Carpathia, especially my father. I worry about Chang."

Ming had applied for work in the peacekeeping forces, hoping for just this sort of opportunity to aid fellow believers. "I don't know how much longer I can remain inside undercover."

"How did you get to a position of authority over so many guards?"

"It's not so big a deal as it sounds. The population decimation didn't hurt."

"C'mon! You're in management."

"Well, in all humility, a stratospheric IQ doesn't hurt. That and wrestling," she added, seeming to fight a smile. "Two out of three falls."

"You're not serious."

"They know Greco-Roman. I know martial arts." Ming pulled into the hotel parking lot. "Call your friends right away," she said. "And stay away from Buffer. I'll cover for you."

"Thank God for you, Ming," Leah said, again overcome. They traded phone numbers. "The day will come when you need a safe place too. Keep in touch." They embraced, and Leah hurried to get her bag and get back into her room.

There was no answer at the safe house, and Leah worried it had already been compromised. Had it already been overrun? And what of her new friends? She tried Rayford's number, then the safe house, again and again.

Unable to reach anyone, Leah knew she had a better chance of helping the Trib Force in North America than from a Brussels hotel room. She found a flight and headed home that very night. All the way back she tried the safe house phone, to no avail.

ONE

BUCK braced himself with his elbow crooked around a scaffolding pole. Thousands of panicked people fleeing the scene had, like him, started and involuntarily turned away from the deafening gunshot. It had come from perhaps a hundred feet to Buck's right and was so loud he would not have been surprised if even those at the back of the throng of some two million had heard it plainly.

He was no expert, but to Buck it had sounded like a high-powered rifle. The only weapon smaller that had emitted such a report was the ugly handgun Carpathia had used to destroy the skulls of Moishe and Eli three days before. Actually, the sounds were eerily similar. Had Carpathia's own weapon been fired? Might someone on his own staff have targeted him?

The lectern had shattered loudly as well, like a tree

branch split by lightning. And that gigantic backdrop sailing into the distance . . .

Buck wanted to bolt with the rest of the crowd, but he worried about Chaim. Had he been hit? And where was Jacov? Just ten minutes before, Jacov had waited below stage left where Buck could see him. No way Chaim's friend and aide would abandon him during a crisis.

As people stampeded by, some went under the scaffold, most went around it, and some jostled both Buck and the support poles, making the structure sway. Buck held tight and looked to where giant speakers three stories up leaned this way and that, threatening their flimsy plywood supports.

Buck could choose his poison: step into the surging crowd and risk being trampled or step up a few feet on the angled crossbar. He stepped up and immediately felt the fluidity of the structure. It bounced and seemed to want to spin as Buck looked toward the platform over the tops of a thousand streaking heads. He had heard Carpathia's lament and Fortunato's keening, but suddenly the sound—at least in the speakers above him—went dead.

Buck glanced up just in time to see a ten-foot-square speaker box tumble from the top. "Look out!" he shrieked to the crowd, but no one heard or noticed. He looked up again to be sure he was out of the way. The box snapped its umbilicals like string, which redirected its path some fifteen feet away from the tower. Buck watched in horror as a woman was crushed beneath it and several other men and women were staggered. A man tried to drag the victim from beneath the speaker, but the crowd behind him never slowed. Suddenly the running mass became a cauldron of humanity, trampling each other in their desperation to get free of the carnage.

Buck could not help. The entire scaffolding was pivoting, and he felt himself swing left. He hung on, not daring to drop into the torrent of screaming bodies. He caught sight of Jacov at last, trying to make his way up the side steps to the platform where Carpathia's security detail brandished Uzis.

A helicopter attempted to land near the stage but had to wait until the crowd cleared. Chaim sat motionless in his chair, facing to Buck's right, away from Carpathia and Fortunato. He appeared stiff, his head cocked and rigid, as if unable to move. If he had not been shot, Buck wondered if he'd had another stroke, or worse, a heart attack. He knew if Jacov could get to him, he would protect Chaim and get him somewhere safe.

Buck tried to keep an eye on Jacov while Fortunato waved at the helicopters, pleading with one to land and get Carpathia out of there. Jacov finally broke free and sprinted up the steps, only to be dealt a blow from the butt end of an Uzi that knocked him off his feet and into the crowd.

The impact snapped Jacov's head back so violently that Buck was certain he was unconscious and unable to protect himself from trampling. Buck leaped off the scaffold and into the fray, fighting his way toward Jacov. He moved around the fallen speaker box and felt the sticky blood underfoot.

As Buck neared where he thought Jacov should be he

took one more look at the platform before the angle would obscure his view. Chaim's chair was moving! He was headed full speed toward the back of the platform. Had he leaned against the joystick? Was he out of control? If he didn't stop or turn, he would pitch twelve feet to the pavement and certain death. His head was still cocked, his body stiff.

Buck reached Jacov, who lay splayed, his head awkwardly flopped to one side, eyes staring, limbs limp. A sob worked its way to Buck's throat as he elbowed stragglers out of the way and knelt to put a thumb and forefinger to Jacov's throat. No pulse.

Buck wanted to drag the body from the scene but feared he would be recognized despite his extensive facial scars. There was nothing he could do for Jacov. But what about Chaim?

Buck sprinted left around the platform and skidded to a stop at the back corner, from where he could see Chaim's wheelchair crumpled on the ground, backstage center. The heavy batteries had broken open and lay twenty feet from the chair, which had one wheel bent almost in half, seat pad missing, and a footrest broken off. Was Buck about to find another friend dead?

He loped to the mangled chair and searched the area, including under the platform. Besides splinters from what he was sure had been the lectern, he found nothing. How could Chaim have survived this? Many of the world rulers had scrambled off the back of the stage, certainly having to turn and hang from the edge first to avoid serious injury. Even then, many would have had to have suffered sprained or broken ankles. But an elderly stroke victim riding in a metal chair twelve feet to concrete? Buck feared Chaim could not have survived. But who would have carried him off?

A chopper landed on the other side of the platform, and medical personnel rushed the stage. The security detail fanned out and began descending the stairs to clear the area.

Four emergency medical technicians crowded around Carpathia and Fortunato while others attended the trampled and the crushed, including the woman beneath the speaker box. Jacov was lifted into a body bag. Buck nearly wept at having to leave his brother that way, yet he knew Jacov was in heaven. He ran to catch up with the crowd now spilling into the streets.

Buck knew Jacov was dead. From the wound at the back of Carpathia's head, he assumed Nicolae was dead or soon would be. And he had to assume Chaim was dead too.

Buck longed for the end of all this and the glorious appearing of Christ. But that was still another three and a half years off.

Rayford felt a fool, running with the crowd, the hem of his robe in his hands to keep from tripping. He had dropped the Saber and its box and wanted to use his arms for more speed. But he had to run like a woman in a long skirt. Adrenaline carried him, because he felt fast as ever, regardless. Rayford really wanted to shed the robe and turban, but the last thing he needed just then was to look like a Westerner.

Had he murdered Carpathia? He had tried to, intended to, but couldn't pull the trigger. Then, when he was bumped and the gun went off, he couldn't imagine he'd been lucky enough to find his target. Could the bullet have ricocheted off the lectern and into Carpathia? Could it also have passed through him and taken out the backdrop? It didn't seem possible.

If he had killed the potentate, there was certainly no satisfaction in it, no relief or sense of accomplishment. As he hurried along, the screams and moans of Carpathia's faithful all around him, Rayford felt he was running from a prison of his own making.

He was sucking wind by the time the crowd thinned and began to disperse, and when he stopped to bend at the waist, hands on his hips, to catch his breath, a couple hurrying past said, "Isn't it awful? They think he's dead!"

"It's awful," Rayford gasped, not looking at them.

Assuming TV cameras had caught everything, especially him with the gun raised, it wouldn't be long before he would be sought. As soon as he was away from the busy streets, he shed the garb and stuffed it in a trash barrel. He found his car, eager to get to Tel Aviv and out of Israel before it became impossible.

———

Mac stood near the back of the throng, far enough from the gun that the report didn't reach his ears until after the massive crowd began to move. While others near him shrieked and gasped and pleaded to know what was going on, he kept his eyes on the stage, relief washing over him. So, he would not have to sacrifice himself and Abdullah to be sure Carpathia was dead. From the commotion down front and from his view of the platform via jumbo screens nearby, it was clear to Mac that Nicolae had suffered the massive head wound believers knew was coming.

Ever the professional, Mac knew what would be expected of him. He slid his cell phone from his jacket and dialed the Tel Aviv tower. "You got a jockey certified to shuttle the 216 to Jerusalem?"

"Already looking, sir. This is a tragedy."

"Yeah."

Mac dialed Abdullah. From the limited noise in the background, he could tell his first officer was not at the Gala. "You hear, Ab?"

"I heard. Shall I go get the Phoenix?"

"Hang loose; they're trying to get it here. I saw you leave the hotel. Where are you?"

"Doctor Pita's. I suppose I'll look suspicious finishing my meal when the big boss is dying and everyone else has run into the streets looking for a TV."

"Stick it in your pocket, and if you don't hear from me, meet me at Jerusalem Airport in an hour."

Mac made his way to the front of the plaza as the place emptied in a frenzy. He flashed his ID when necessary, and by the time he reached the platform, it was clear Carpathia was in the final throes of life. His wrists were drawn up under his chin, eyes shut tight and bleeding, blood trickling also from his ears and mouth, and his legs shook violently, toes pointed, knees locked.

"Oh, he's gone! He's gone!" Leon wailed. "Someone do something."

The four emergency medical technicians, portable monitors beeping, knelt over Carpathia. They cleared his mouth so they could administer oxygen, studied a blood pressure gauge, pumped his chest, cradled his head, and tried to stanch the flow from a wound that left them kneeling in more blood than it seemed a body could hold.

Mac peeked past the panicky Fortunato to see Carpathia's normally tanned hands and face already pale. No one could survive this, and Mac wondered if the bodily movements were merely posthumous reflexes.

"There is a hospital nearby, Commander," one of the EMTs said, which threw Fortunato into a rage. He had just made eye contact with Mac and seemed about to say something when he turned on the EMT.

"Are you crazy? These—these *people* are not qualified! We must get him to New Babylon."

He turned to Mac. "Is the 216 ready?"

"On its way from Tel Aviv. Should be able to lift off in an hour."

"An hour?! Should we helicopter him straight to Tel Aviv?"

"Jerusalem Airport will be faster," Mac said.

"There's no room to stabilize him in a chopper, sir," the EMT said.

"We have no choice!" Fortunato said. "An ambulance would be too slow."

"But an ambulance has equipment that might—"

"Just get him into the chopper!" Fortunato said.

But as the EMT turned away looking disgusted, a female colleague looked up at him. Carpathia was still. "No vitals," she said. "He's flat lined."

"No!" Leon bellowed, bullying his way between them and kneeling in Nicolae's blood. Again he leaned over the body, but rather than holding Carpathia to him, he buried his face in the lifeless chest and sobbed aloud.

Security Chief Walter Moon dismissed the EMTs with a nod, and as they gathered up their equipment and went for the gurney, he gently pulled Leon away from Carpathia. "Don't drape the body," he said. "Let's load 'im up now. Say nothing about his condition until we're back home."

"Who did this, Walter?" Fortunato whined. "Did we catch him?"

Moon shrugged and shook his head.

Buck ran toward the hostel. He dialed Chaim's number again, as he had all along the way. Still busy. The people in Chaim's house—Stefan the valet, Jacov's wife, Hannelore, and Hannelore's mother—had to have been watching on TV and were likely calling anyone they knew for news of their loved ones.

Finally, Hannelore answered. "Jacov!" she shouted.

"No, Hannelore, this is Greg North."

"Buck!" she wailed. "What happened? Where—"

"Hannelore!" Buck said. "Your phone is not secure!"

"I don't care anymore, Buck! If we die, we die! Where is Jacov? What happened to Chaim?"

"I need to meet you somewhere, Hannelore. If Chaim shows up there—"

"Chaim is all right?"

"I don't know. I didn't see him after—"

"Did you see Jacov?"

"Meet me, Hannelore. Call me from another phone and—"

"Buck, you tell me right now! Did you see him?"

"I saw him."

"Is he alive?"

"Hannelore—"

"Buck, is he dead?"

"I'm sorry. Yes."

She began to wail, and in the background Buck heard a scream. Hannelore's mother? Had she deduced the news?

"Buck, they're here!"

"What? Who?"

He heard a door smashing, a yell, another scream.

"GC!" she whispered fiercely. And the phone went dead.

———

Onboard the Phoenix 216, Nicolae Carpathia's personal physician examined him and pronounced him dead.

"Where were you?" Leon demanded. "You could have done something."

"Where I was supposed to be, Commander," the doctor said, "in the auxiliary trailer a hundred yards behind the platform. Security would not let me out, fearing more gunfire."

As the 216 taxied toward the runway, Leon came to the cockpit and told Abdullah, "Patch me through to Director Hassid at the palace, secure line."

Abdullah nodded and glanced at Mac as Fortunato backed out. The first officer made the connection and informed Leon over the intercom. With creative switch flipping, Abdullah allowed Mac to listen in, while muting the input button to keep out noise from the cockpit.

"You're aware of the awful news, David?" Leon said.

"I heard, yes, sir," David said. "How is the potentate?"

"He's dead, David . . ."

"Oh."

". . . but this is top secret by order of Chief Moon until further notice."

"I understand."

"Oh, David, what will we do?"

"We'll look to you, sir."

"Well, thank you for those kind words at such a time, but I need something from you."

"Yes, sir."

"Scramble the satellites to make it impossible for those who did this to communicate with each other by phone. Can you do that?"

A long pause. "Scrambling the satellites" was not the exact terminology, but David could produce Fortunato's desired result. "Yes," he said slowly. "It's possible, of course. You realize the ramifications . . ."

Mac whispered to Abdullah. "Call Buck, call Rayford, call the safe house. Leon's going to shut down communications. If they need to talk to each other, it has to be now."

"Tell me," Leon said.

"We're all served by the same system," David said. "It's the reason we've never been able to shut down the Judah-ites' Internet transmissions."

"So if they're shut down, we're shut down?"

"Exactly."

"Do it anyway. The landlines in New Babylon would still be operable, would they not?"

"They would, and this would not affect television transmission, but your long distance is all satellite dependent."

"So those of us in New Babylon would be able to communicate only with each other."

"Right."

"We'll get by. I'll let you know when to unscramble."

Two minutes later Leon called David again. "How long does this take?" he said. "I should not be able to reach you!"

"Three minutes," David said.

"I'll check back in four."

"You'll not reach me, sir."

"I should hope not!"

But four minutes later Leon was preoccupied with the doctor. "I want an autopsy," he said, "but zero leaks about cause of death." Through the reverse intercom bug, Mac heard Leon's voice catch. "And I want this man prepared for viewing and for burial by the finest mortuary technician in the world. Is that understood?"

"Of course, Commander. As you wish."

"I don't want the staff butcher in the palace, so whom would you suggest?"

"One who could use the business, frankly."

"How crass! This would be a service to the Global Community!"

"But surely you're prepared to reimburse—"

"Of course, but not if money is the primary concern. . . ."

"It's not, Commander. I simply know that Dr. Eikenberry's mortuary has been decimated. She's lost more than half her staff and has had to reorganize her business."

"And she's local?"

"Baghdad."

"I do not want Nicolae shipped to Baghdad. Can she come to the palace morgue?"

"I'm sure she'd be more than happy . . ."

"Happy?"

"Willing, sir."

"I hope she can work miracles."

"Fortunately his face was not affected."

"Still," Leon said, his voice husky again, "how do you hide the, the . . . awful injury?"

"I'm sure it can be done."

"He must look perfect, dignified. The whole world will mourn him."

"I'll call her now."

"Yes, please try. I'd like to know whether you're able to get through."

But he was not able. Global telephone communications were off the air. And Abdullah too had failed to reach anyone.

Mac was about to shut off the intercom bug when he heard Leon take a huge breath and let it out. "Doctor?" he said. "Can your mortician, ah—"

"Dr. Eikenberry."

"Right. Can she do a cast of the potentate's body?"

"A cast?"

"You know, some sort of plaster or plastic or something that would preserve his exact dimensions and features?"

The doctor hesitated. "Well," he said finally, "death masks are nothing new. A whole corpse would be quite an undertaking, pardon the expression."

"But it could be done?"

Another pause. "I should think the body would have to be dipped. The palace morgue has a large enough tank."

"It could be done then?"

"Anything can be done, Excellency. I'm sorry, I mean Commander."

Fortunato cleared his throat. "Yes, please, Doctor. Don't call me Excellency. At least not yet. And do arrange for a cast of the potentate's body."

T W O

BESIDE the desk in her hangar office, David stood facing Annie and holding both her hands.

"You're trembling," she said.

"I thought *you* were," he said. "You're not as scared as I am?"

"At least," she said. "What's going on?"

He sighed. "I just got a call from a mortician in Baghdad. Says she was told to go through me for large purchases. She wants several liters of some sort of a plastic amalgam delivered to the palace morgue as soon as possible."

"For?"

"I can only imagine. This stuff is used to make casts of faces, body parts, tire tracks, that kind of thing. But she wants enough to fill a tub the size of a whirlpool bath."

"She's going to make a cast of Carpathia's whole body?"

He shrugged. "That's my guess."

"Whatever for?"

"She didn't sound too sure herself. She kept asking how much water would have to be added to how much solution and if that would fill the stainless steel container. She also wanted to know how long I thought it would take that much solution to harden, how long it would remain pliable before drying, all that."

Annie slipped her hands around David's waist and laid her head on his chest. "Someone's put her up to it. Maybe to make a replica of the body so they can make him look better lying in state?"

He pondered that. "I just wonder if they've heard about the prophecy of his resurrecting and want to keep the real body somewhere convenient, just in case."

"They don't believe the prophecies, do they?"

"How could anyone not by this time?"

She looked up at him and shook her head. "What's going to happen around here when, you know . . ."

"It happens?"

"Yeah."

"It's not going to be pretty. I can't wait to see what Dr. Ben-Judah has to say about you-know-who when he's no longer really himself."

"You think there'll be any of the man left of him?"

David cocked his head. "His body, sure. Maybe he'll sound like himself and have the same mannerisms, but he's supposed to be indwelt, and indwelt means indwelt. When I was promoted, I moved into the quarters of that director who was reassigned to Australia, remember?"

"Yeah."

"It's the same place. Same walls, same bed, same lav, everything. It looks the same, but it's not. I'm the new dweller."

She held him tighter. "I don't want to know the new dweller of the potentate."

"Well, it'll be no more Mr. Nice Guy."

"Not funny," she said.

"They should be here any minute, babe."

"I know. My ears are tuned to the '16. I know how long it takes to get the hangar doors open and to position the forklift and winch. I hope security keeps its distance. Did you see all of 'em out there? Have you heard all the rules?"

"Have I! You'd think you were off-loading the body of the king of the world."

She snorted. "Tell you the truth, I'd like to drop the box and run over the whole thing with the forklift. Let's see *that* come back to life."

David tugged her toward the door. "What if he comes back to life while you're transporting the body?"

She stopped and closed her eyes. "Like I wasn't freaked out enough. You'd have to find me in heaven." A hum vibrated the office window. "You'd better go. They're about three minutes away."

———

Rayford could not believe his luck at Tel Aviv. He hurried past the busy counters and out a side exit toward the small-craft hangars. The Gulfstream sat gleaming in Hangar 3.

An armed guard doing double duty as manifest coordinator checked Marv Berry off his list and said, "Wait a minute, there's something else I'm s'posed to ask. Ah, yeah, flight plan reported to tower?"

"You bet," Rayford said, "but they weren't happy with how slow the small craft were being cleared, so I'd better keep you out of trouble by getting out of here quick."

"I 'preciate that," the guard said, clearly more comfortable with a gun than a pen. "They expect lots of passengers on the big birds tonight and want to get the little ones out of the way."

"Understandable," Rayford said. "I'll do my part."

"Wish I'd a been in Jerusalem tonight," the guard said as Rayford circled the Gulfstream, doing a quick preflight.

"Yeah?"

"I'd a killed somebody, guilty or not."

"That so?"

"Dang straight. Somebody'd pay for that. Who'd wanna go and kill our only hope?"

"I can't imagine."

"You're American, right, Mr. Berry?"

"You could tell?"

"Sure, me too."

"You don't say."

"Colorado," the young man said. "Fort Collins. You?"

"What're you doing here?"

"Wanted Gala duty. This is as close as I got. Hoped for potentate bodyguard, but I guess that's all political."

"Like everything else," Rayford said, pulling open the Gulfstream's door and steps.

"Need some help there, Mr. Berry?"

"Got it, thanks."

"Where'd you say you were from?"

I didn't, Rayford thought. "Kalamazoo," he said, mounting the steps and tossing in his bag.

"That's what, Midwest?"

Rayford hated the small talk, not to mention the delay, only slightly less than the prospect of being detained and put to death. "Michigan!" he called out, pulling the door.

"Hang on a second, sir," the guard said. "Squawk box is for me."

"I gotta go," Rayford said. "Nice talking to you."

"Just a minute, please," the young man said with a smile. "Another minute won't kill you, will it?"

It just might. "I've really got to go, son."

"Wyatt."

"Why?"

"Wyatt. That's my name."

"Well, thanks, Wyatt, and good-bye."

"Mr. Berry!"

"Yes, Wyatt."

"I'm not gonna be able to hear the box here if you fire up. Can't you give me a second?"

From the radio on Wyatt's makeshift desk in the middle

of the hangar: "Officer 423, do you copy? Initiate code red screening effective immediately."

"This is Wyatt. You mean those thorough checks on everybody, even small craft?"

"Where are you, 423?"

"Small-craft Hangar 3, sir."

"Then that is what I mean, yes!"

Rayford quickly closed the door, but before he could settle into the cockpit, Wyatt came running. "Mr. Berry, sir! I'm going to have to ask you to step out of the craft!"

Rayford initiated the starting sequence, which only caused Wyatt to rush in front of the Gulfstream, waving, rifle dangling. He didn't appear alarmed or even suspicious. It was clear he simply thought Rayford couldn't hear him.

He motioned for Rayford to open the door. Rayford considered simply starting up as soon as Wyatt was clear of the front, hoping the GC was thin staffed enough and busy enough that they would ignore him. But he couldn't risk an air pursuit or gung ho Wyatt from Fort Collins shooting at him on the runway.

He moved to the door and opened it three inches. "What is it, Wyatt?"

"I've been instructed, sir, to do a thorough check and search of even small craft before departure tonight, due to what happened in Jerusalem."

"Even me, Wyatt? A small-town guy like you? An American?"

"Got to, sir. Sorry."

"Wyatt, you know the Gulfstream, don't you?"

"The Gulfstream, sir?"

"This aircraft."

"No sir, I don't. I'm not an aviation man. I'm a soldier."

Rayford peeked through the slivered opening. "If you knew this plane, Wyatt, you'd know that if the door opens all the way, I have to start the whole ignition sequence over."

"You do?"

"Yeah, some kind of a safety mechanism that keeps the engines from starting until the door is closed."

"Well, I'm sorry, but I have to—"

"I'm sorry, too, Wyatt, because the tower guys were complaining about you, and I was trying to keep you out of trouble, make you look good, by getting away quickly."

"But my commanding officer just told me—"

"Wyatt! Listen to me! You think I shot Carpathia?"

"'Course not. I—"

"I'd need you to teach me about weapons, for one thing."

"I could sure teach you, but—"

"I'll bet you could. And I could teach you to fly—"

"I have to—"

"Wyatt, I just heard on the radio that two wide-bodies are in landing sequence right now, with another waiting to take off. Now my perimeter flange is going to overheat if I don't get going, and you don't want a fire in here. Tell your boss I was already on my way out when you got the order, then we're both covered. You look quick, you avoid a fire, and you're still following orders."

Rayford kept a careful eye on Wyatt's hands and

flinched when the young man moved his right. If he leveled that rifle at him, Rayford would have to comply. But Wyatt saluted and pointed at Rayford. "Good thinkin', sir. Carry on."

Rayford fired up the engines and maneuvered onto the tarmac. He couldn't wait to tell Mac about this one. He heard about other planes on a radio that wasn't on yet? Perimeter flange? Fire? Tsion taught that part of the population decimation might be God's way of removing his most incorrigible enemies in anticipation of the coming epic battle. Wyatt was living proof that the inept had survived. Rayford knew he wouldn't always enjoy such fortune.

"Ben Gurion Tower to Gulfstream!"

Rayford leaned forward and looked as far as he could in both directions, both on the runway and in the sky.

"Gurion Tower to Gulfstream, do you copy?"

He was clear.

"Gulfstream, you are not cleared! Remain stationary."

"Gulfstream to Tower," Rayford said. "Proceeding, thank you."

"Repeat, Gulfstream, you are *not* cleared!"

"Cleared by Officer 423, Tower."

"Repeat?"

". . . been . . . leared . . . two-three . . . wer."

"You're breaking up, Gulfstream! You are not cleared for takeoff. Repeat, not cleared!"

". . . nection . . . wer, thank y—"

"Do we have your flight plan, Gulfstream?"

". . . o copy, tow—"

"Flight plan?"

". . . icer fo—, two, thr—"

"If you can hear any of this, Gulfstream, be aware that satellite coordinates have been scrambled and there is only manual positioning. Copy?"

Rayford depressed and released the talk button rapidly, then held it halfway down, creating static on the other end. *No satellite capability?* For once he would be glad for that. He needn't worry about pursuit. If he was flying blind, so would the GC. Did that mean the phones were out too? He tried the safe house, then Laslos. Nothing. He only hoped he could connect with the Greek believers before he put down there. It made no sense to try to make it back to America. If Leah's message meant what he thought and Hattie was no longer in Belgium, she could have long since led the GC to the safe house. He only hoped his message had gotten to David's computer before the satellites went down.

Buck had been angry with his father-in-law before, but never like this. No contact? Nothing? What was he supposed to do, collect Leah from Brussels, and it was every man for himself? Now the phones didn't seem to be working.

Did he dare try to make it to Chaim's house and see what was going on? Why would the GC storm the place and force their way in? Were they too looking for Chaim? And why? Buck knew somebody already had to have the old man. Someone had spirited him, or his body, from the Gala site. No way a wheelchair-bound stroke victim could have made his own way out of that place with his contrivance in pieces on the ground.

Buck took a cab to the small place he had once used as an Israeli safe house. No one he recognized was living there. He walked several miles in the darkness through rubble, never far from the cacophony of sirens and the flashing light shows of emergency vehicles. When he finally arrived at Chaim's, the place was deserted and dark. Had everyone been taken away? Emergency personnel were stretched, of course, but if they expected Chaim, wouldn't someone be left to guard the place?

Buck crept to the back, suddenly aware of his fatigue. Grief and trauma did that to a person, he told himself. He had not gotten to know Jacov well, but how he had thrilled to the young man's coming to belief in Christ! They had kept up some, not as much as either had liked, due to the risk of discovery. And though he knew he would see Jacov at the Glorious Appearing—if not before—he dreaded having to break the news to Jacov's friend and coworker, Stefan.

Buck had the advantage of knowing, really knowing, this house. He feared he might be walking into a trap. He didn't think the GC knew he was in Israel, but one could never be sure. Maybe they lay in wait for Chaim or even Jacov. It was possible Jacov's death had not made the GC databases yet, though that was unlikely. But where was everyone else?

Buck found the back door unlocked, and he slipped in. A rechargeable flashlight was usually plugged into a socket near the floor, behind the food preparers' table. Buck felt for it and found it, but he didn't want to test it until he was confident no one was waiting to ambush him. He took it into the pantry and waited until he shut the door to turn it on. Then he felt foolish, reckless. He'd never been comfortable with the role he had been thrust into, still part journalist but also freedom fighter, raconteur. What kind of a swashbuckling Trib Force veteran backs himself into a closet with nothing more to defend himself with than a cheap flashlight?

He tried the light switch on the pantry wall. Nothing. So the power had been cut. Buck flipped the flashlight on, then off quickly. Something in his peripheral vision froze him. Did he dare shine the light that way? He let out a quavery breath. Who would lie in wait in a pantry?

Buck aimed the light that direction and turned it on. Just an unusual arrangement of boxes and cans. He doused the light and moved quietly to the door. Creeping through the kitchen into the dining room, the parlor, and then the front room, Buck held the flashlight in front of him as if it were on, but it served more like a blind man's cane. As his eyes began adjusting to the darkness, he became aware of pinpoints of light from the street, and he still heard sirens in the distance.

Later Buck would wonder whether he had smelled the blood before he heard it. Yes, heard it. He knew something was wrong as soon as he reached the front room. It was in the air. Heat? A presence? Someone. He stopped and tried to make out shapes. He felt his own heart, but something reached his ears more insistently even than that thumping. Dripping. *Drip, drip,* pause, *drip-drip, drip.* From two sources? Part of him didn't want to know, to see. He turned his back to windows at the front, pointed the flashlight toward the sounds, and braced himself, ready to defend himself with bare hands and the flashlight, if necessary.

He turned on the light but immediately shut his eyes to the horror. He dropped to his knees, the wind gushing from him. "Oh, God," he prayed. "No! Please!" Was there no end to the carnage? He would rather die than find his friends, his comrades (someday his own family?) like this. In the split second he had allowed himself to take in the scene, it became clear that two victims sat side by side in wood chairs, Hannelore on the left, her mother on the right. They were bound and gagged, heads tilted back, blood dripping into pools on the floor.

Buck did not want to reveal himself to anyone outside. Plainly, this scene was created to "welcome" someone home; certainly the perpetrators had no idea *he* would stumble upon it. Buck knelt before the chairs, repulsed by the sound of the drips. He knew if either of the women had survived, their respiration would have been noisy with their heads in that position. Still, he had to make sure. He lodged the flashlight between his knees, angled it toward the women, and turned it on. As he reached to check for Hannelore's pulse, the flashlight slipped and illumined her ankles, tied securely to the front legs of the chair. As he angled the light up again and tightened his knees to support it, he noticed her wrists tied behind her. A smallish woman, Hannelore's torso was stretched to allow her hands to go around the back of the chair. Great gushes of air rushed past Buck's gritted teeth.

He grabbed the flashlight and moved behind the chair to feel her wrist, but that put his arm in line with the blood dripping from her head. And though her wrist was warm, as he feared, there was no pulse.

Hannelore's mother, less than a foot away, was bound in the same position. A squat, heavy woman, her arms had been yanked into contorted positions to allow her wrists to be tied. She too was dead.

Who could have done this? And wouldn't Stefan, his Middle East maleness coming to the fore, have fought to the death to prevent it? Where could he be? Buck wanted to pan the light back and forth along the floor toward the front, but that might have been suicidal, he would be so obvious from the street. It was all he could do to keep from calling Stefan's name.

Chaim had not been home when Buck had talked with Hannelore on the phone. Did this massacre mean Chaim had arrived, or that he hadn't? Had Chaim himself been forced to witness this? Buck's first task was to locate Stefan, his second to check the entirety of the huge house for Chaim. If Chaim had not returned and this was all meant as a warning for him, could the place be staked out, surrounded? Perhaps it was.

Buck feared he would find not just Stefan's body, but also Chaim's. But how would Chaim have gotten there? Who might have caught him, rescued him, or helped him off that platform? And what was the purpose of murdering these innocents? Had they been tortured for information and eliminated once they provided it, or because they had not? Or was this simply vengeance? Chaim had been vitriolic in his revulsion of GC Peacekeepers, of the breaking of the covenant between the GC and Israel. Though he had never been a religious Jew, he expressed horror over the intrusion of the world government into the very affairs of the temple. First the Jews had been allowed to rebuild; then they were not allowed to conduct themselves the way they wished in the new temple.

But do you extinguish the household of a statesman, a national treasure, for such an offense? And what of the man himself? Buck's head throbbed, his chest felt tight, and he was short of breath. He was desperate to be with Chloe and Kenny and felt as if he could hold them tight for three and a half years. He knew the odds. Each had only a one in four chance of surviving until the Glorious Appearing. But even if he, or they, had to go to heaven before that, he didn't want it to be this way. No one deserved this. No one but Carpathia.

It had been a long time since David had suffered such carping. On the way to his office from the palace hangar, past a full-dress color guard of pallbearers and a heavily armed ring of security personnel, his beeper had signaled a top-level emergency message. The call could have originated only locally, of course, but this sort of a code was reserved for life-and-death situations. He did not recognize the callback number but knew it was located in the palace proper.

Normally he would have called back immediately, fearing danger to Annie or himself, but he took a moment to trace the number against the personnel list and found that the call came from the Arts and Sciences wing. He had been there only once, knew virtually no one there, and had been so repulsed by what was considered artistic that he recalled rushing back to his quarters feeling soiled.

Wanting at least one more clue before replying, David called his own voice mail, only to be met by the foul, nasty rantings of a sassy *artiste*. David had not heard such profanity and gutter language since high school. The gist of the message: "Where are you? Where could you be at a time like this? It's the middle of the night! Do you even know of the murder? Call me! It's an emergency!"

David's beeper vibrated again—same number. He waited ninety seconds and called his voice mail again. "Do you know who I am? Guy Blod?!" The man pronounced *Guy* as *Gee* with a hard *G,* the French way, and *Blod* to rhyme with *cod,* as if Scandinavian. David had seen him scurrying around a few times but had never spoken with him. His reputation preceded him. He was the temperamental but lauded painter and sculptor, Carpathia's own choice for minister of the creative arts. Not only had he painted several of the so-called masterpieces that graced the great hall and the palace, but he had also sculpted many of the statues of world heroes in the courtyard and supervised the decorating of all GC buildings in New Babylon. He was considered a genius, but David—though admittedly no expert—considered his work laughably gaudy and decidedly profane. "The more shocking and anti-God the better" had to have been Blod's premise.

Part of David wanted Guy Blod to have to wait for a callback, but this was the wrong time to start puffing his anti-GC chest. He would take no guff from Guy Blod, but he had to remain above suspicion and ingratiated to Fortunato. He dialed Blod as he settled behind his computer and began to program it to record directly from the morgue on a sound-activated basis.

As Blod answered, David noticed a list of messages on his computer. "This is Guy," he announced, "and you had better be David Hassid." He put the emphasis on the first syllable.

"It's *hah-SEED*," David said.

"That should be easy enough to remember, Mr. Hay-seed. Now where have you been?"

"Excuse me?"

"I've been trying to call you!"

"That's why I called you, sir."

"Don't get smart with me. Don't you know what's happened?"

"Nobody tells me anything, Mr. Blod." David chuckled. "Of course I know what's happened. Did it occur to you that that might have been why I was difficult to reach?"

"Well, I need stuff and I need it right now!"

"What do you need, sir?"

"Can you get it for me?"

"Depends on what it is, Blod."

"That's Mr. Blod to you, sweetie. I was told you could get anything."

"Well, almost."

"I have nowhere else to turn."

"I'll do my best."

"You'd better. Now come to my office."

"Excuse me?"

"Is this a bad connection? I said, come . . . to . . . my . . ."

"I heard you, sir, but I have many things on my plate tonight, as you can imagine, and I can't just—"

"You can do as you're told. Now get your tail over here, and I mean right now." *Click*.

David hung up and checked his messages. Most alarming was one from Rayford: "Our botanist reports the bird has flown. May need new real estate soonest. Signed, Geo. Logic"

David squinted at the screen for several seconds, wishing he could call someone at the safe house, or Rayford. He was tempted to put the satellites back in operation just long enough to do it, but he knew someone would discover that and he would have to answer for it. So Hattie was gone and the safe house was in jeopardy. He deleted the message and hacked his way into the mainframe database of abandoned, condemned, destroyed, and/or radioactive buildings in the Midwest. He looked at his watch when the phone rang. Six minutes had passed.

"What are you doing?"

"I'm sorry?"

"Is this David Hayseed?"

"This is Director Hassid, yes."

"Do you know who this is?"

"Yes! It sounds like Minister Blood. Haven't talked to you in ages. Good to hear from you again—"

"That's Blod, and did I or did I not tell you to get over here?"

"Is this multiple choice? I believe you did."

"Then why are you not here?"

"Let me guess. Because I'm here?"

"Agh! Listen here, you! Get over here this instant or—"

"Or what? You're going to tell my mom? I don't recall being subordinate to you, sir. Now if you have something you need me to procure for you, and you have clearance from the Supreme Commander—"

"A purchasing agent is not subordinate to a cabinet minister? Are you from Mars?"

"Actually Israel, sir."

"Would you stop calling me *sir?*"

"I thought *you* called *me,* sir."

"I mean quit calling me that!"

"What? *Sir?* I'm sorry, I thought you were male."

"You stay right where you are, Director. I'll be right over."

"That wasn't so hard, was it, Guy? I mean, it's you who wants to talk with me, not the other way 'round."

Click.

THREE

ROCKETING over the Mediterranean in the middle of the night, Rayford had about a two-hour flight to Greece. For the first fifteen minutes he monitored the radio to be sure he was not being pursued or triangulated. But the radio was full of merely repetitious requests for more aircraft to help evacuate Jerusalem in light of the earthquake and the assassination. There were also countless calls for planes available to cart the mourning faithful to New Babylon for what was expected to become the largest viewing and funeral in history.

When the Gulfstream was far enough out over the water, local tower radio signals faded without satellite aid. Rayford tested that by trying to call his compatriots, to no avail. He switched off phone and radio, which left him in virtual silence at thirty-one thousand feet in a smooth-as-silk jet, most of the noise of the craft behind him.

Rayford suddenly felt the weight of life. Had it really been a mere three and a half years ago that he had enjoyed the prestige, the ease, and the material comfort of the life of a 747 captain for a major airline? He'd been no prize, he knew, as a husband and father, but the cliché was true: You never know what you've got till it's gone.

Life since the Rapture, or what most of the world called the disappearances, had been different as night and day from before—and not just spiritually. Rayford likened it to a death in the family. Not a day passed when he didn't awaken under the burden of the present, facing the cold fact that though he had now made his peace with God, he had been left behind.

It was as if the whole nation, indeed the whole world, lived in suspended mourning and grief. Everyone had lost someone, and not a second could pass when one was able to forget that. It was the fear of missing the school bus, losing your homework, forgetting your gym clothes, knowing you'd been caught cheating on a test, being called to the principal's office, being fired, going bankrupt, cheating on your wife—all rolled into one.

There had been snatches of joy, sure. Rayford lived for his daughter and was pleased with her choice of a husband. Having a grandchild, sobering though it was at this most awful time of history, fulfilled him in a way he hadn't known was possible. But even thinking about Chloe and Buck and little Kenny forced reality into Rayford's consciousness, and it stabbed.

With the Gulfstream on autopilot nearly six miles

above the earth, Rayford stared into the cosmos. For an instant he felt disembodied, disconnected from the myriad events of the past forty-two months. Was it possible he'd, in essence, lived half a lifetime in that short span? He had experienced more emotion, fear, anger, frustration, and grief that day alone than in a year of his previous life. He wondered how much a man could take; literally, how much could a human body and mind endure?

How he longed to talk with Tsion! No one else had his trust and respect like the rabbi, only a few years older than he. Rayford couldn't confide in Chloe or Buck. He felt a kinship with T Delanty at the Palwaukee Airport, and they might become true friends. T was the kind of a man Rayford would listen to, even when T felt the need to rebuke him. But Tsion was the man of God. Tsion was one who loved and admired and respected Rayford unconditionally. Or did he? What would Tsion think if he knew what Rayford had done, starting with abandoning both Leah and Buck, but worse, wanting, intending, trying to murder the Antichrist, then perhaps doing so by accident?

Something about the altitude, the coolness he allowed in the cockpit, the tension he could postpone until over-flying Greece, the comfort of the seat, and the artificial respite he enjoyed from his role as international fugitive, somehow conspired to awaken Rayford to what had become of him.

At first he resisted the intrusion of reality. Whatever comfort he had found in the buffering quality of life on the edge was stripped away when he allowed raw truth to invade. He told himself to stay with the program, to keep himself as well as his plane on autopilot, to let his emotions rule. What had happened to the scientific, logical Rayford, the one who had been left behind primarily due to that inability to accede to his intuitive side?

When he heard himself speaking aloud, he knew it was time to face the old Rayford—not the pre-Rapture man, but the new believer. He had wondered more than once during the past few months whether he was insane. Now talking to himself in the middle of the night in the middle of nowhere? Much as he hated the prospect, introspection was called for. How long had it been since he had indulged, at least honestly? He had questioned his sanity the past few months, but he seldom dwelt on it long enough to come to any conclusions. He had been driven by rage, by vengeance. He had grown irresponsible, unlike himself.

As Rayford allowed that to rattle in his brain, he realized that if he pursued this, turned it over in his mind like the marshmallows he had tried browning evenly as a child, it would not be himself he would face in the end. It would be God.

Rayford wasn't sure he wanted the blinding light of God in his mental mirror. In fact, he was fairly certain he didn't. But the hound of heaven was pursuing him, and Rayford would have to be thoroughly deluded or dishonest to turn and run now. He could cover his ears and hum as he did as a child when his mother tried to scold him. Or he could turn on the radio, pretending to see if the satellites had been realigned, or try the phone to test the global system. Maybe he could take the plane off autopilot and busy himself navigating the craft through trackless skies.

Down deep he could never live with himself if he resorted to those evasive tactics, so Rayford endured a shudder of fear. He was going to face this, to square his shoulders to God and take the heat. "All right," he said aloud. "What?"

———————

Buck straightened to relieve the aching in his joints from kneeling to check the lifeless women. Standing in the darkness of his old friend's sepulchral home, he knew he had never been cut out to be a hero. Brave he was not. This horror had brought a sob to his throat he could not subdue. Rayford was the hero; he was the one who had first come to the truth, then led the way for the rest of them. He was the one who had been rocked only temporarily by the loss of their first spiritual mentor but stood strong to lead.

What might Rayford have done in this same situation? Buck had no idea. He was still upset with the man, still puzzled over his mysterious self-assigned task that had left Buck and Leah on their own. Buck believed it would all be explained one day, that there would be some sort of rationale. It shouldn't have been so surprising that Rayford had grown testy and self-absorbed. Look what he had lost. Buck stubbornly left him on the pedestal of his mind as the leader of the Tribulation Force and as one who would act honorably in this situation.

And what would that entail? Finding Stefan, of course. Then challenging whoever was watching this house of death, fighting them, subduing them, or at least eluding them. Eluding didn't sound so heroic, but that was all Buck was inclined to do. Meanwhile, the most heroic he would get would be to finish the task inside—finding Stefan and Chaim, if they were there—and then running for his life.

The running part was the rub. It would be just like the GC—even decimated by population reduction, busy with the Gala, pressed into extraordinary service by the earthquake, and left in a shambles by the assassination—to dedicate an inordinate number of troops to this very house. It would not have surprised Buck an iota if the place was surrounded and they had all seen him enter, watched him find what he found, and now waited to capture him upon his departure.

On the other hand, perhaps they had come and pillaged and slaughtered and left the place a memorial husk.

Feeling ashamed, as if his wife and son could see him feeling his way in the dark, fighting a whimper like a little boy rather than tramping shoulders-wide through the place, Buck stepped on flesh. He half expected the victim to yelp or recoil. Buck knelt and felt a lifeless arm, tight and muscular. Was it possible the GC had suffered a casualty? They would not likely have left one of their own behind, not even a dead one.

Buck turned his back to the windows and switched on the flashlight again. The mess the enemy had left of Stefan made Buck's old nature surge to the fore. It was all he could do to keep from screaming obscenities at the GC and hoping any one of them was within earshot. Revolting as it was, Buck had to look one more time to believe what he saw. Stefan lay there, his face a mask of tranquility, eyes and mouth closed as if he were asleep. His arms and legs were in place, hands at his sides, but all four limbs had been severed, the legs at the hips, the arms at the shoulders. Clearly this had been done after he was dead, for there was no sign of struggle.

Buck dropped the light, and it rolled to a stop, luckily pointing away from the windows. His knees banged painfully on the floor, and when he threw his palms before him to break his fall, they splashed in thick, sticky blood. He knelt there on hands and knees, gasping, his belly tightening and releasing with his sobs and gasps. What kind of a weapon would it have taken and how long must the enemy have worked to saw through the tissue of a dead man until he was dismembered? And why? What was the message in that?

How would he ever tell Chaim? Or would his dear old friend be his next discovery?

———

At four o'clock in the afternoon Friday in Illinois, Tsion sat near the TV, trying to sort his emotions. He was still able to enjoy, if that was an appropriate word anymore, the ceaseless curiosity and antics of a one-year-old boy. Kenny cooed and talked and made noises as he explored, climbing, grabbing, touching, looking to his mother and to "Unca Zone" to see if he would get a smile or a no, depending on what he was doing.

But Kenny was Chloe's responsibility, and Tsion didn't want to miss a second of the constant coverage of the assassination. He expected news of Carpathia's resurrection and allowed himself only brief absences from the screen. He had moved his laptop to the living room, and his phone was close by. But his main interest was in Israel and New Babylon. It would not have surprised him if Carpathia was loaded onto his plane dead in Jerusalem and worshiped as he walked off under his own power in New Babylon.

Tsion was most upset at hearing nothing from other members of the Trib Force, and he and Chloe traded off trying to raise them, each of them, by phone. The last word they had heard from overseas was that Leah had not seen Hattie in Brussels, that she had told Buck Hattie was gone, and that she had not been able to communicate with Rayford. Since then, nothing.

Worried about the ramifications, Tsion and Chloe left most of the lights off, and they double-checked the phony chest freezer that actually served as an entrance to the underground shelter. Tsion normally left strategy and intrigue to the others and concentrated on his expertise, but he had an opinion on the security of the safe house. Maybe he was naïve, he told Chloe, but he believed that if Hattie were to give them away, it would be by accident. "She'll more likely be followed to us than send someone for us."

"Like she did with Ernie and Bo."

Tsion nodded.

"And who knows whom *they* might have told before they died?"

He shrugged. "If she was to give us up just by telling someone, she would have done it before she was imprisoned."

"If she *was* imprisoned," Chloe said. And suddenly she was fighting tears.

"What is it, Chloe?" Tsion asked. "Worried about Cameron, of course?"

She nodded, then shook her head. "Not only that," she said. "Tsion, can I talk with you?"

"Need you ask?"

"But, I mean, I know you don't want to miss anything on TV."

"I won't. Talk to me."

Tsion was alarmed at how much it took for Chloe to articulate her thoughts. They had always been able to talk, but she had never been extremely self-revelatory. "You know I will keep your confidences," he said. "Consider it clergy-parishioner privilege."

Even that did not elicit a smile. But she managed to shock him. "Maybe I've been watching too much TV," she said.

"Such as?"

"Those staged rallies, where everyone worships Carpathia."

"I know. They're disgusting. They refer to him as 'Your Worship' and the like."

"It's worse than that, Tsion," she said. "Have you

seen the clips where the children are brought to him? I mean, we all know there's not a child among them older than three and a half, but they're paraded before him in their little GC outfits, saluting over their hearts with every step, singing praise songs to him. It's awful!"

Tsion agreed. Day care workers and parents dressed the kids alike, and cute little boys and girls brought flowers and were taught to bow and wave and salute and sing to Carpathia. "Did you see the worst of it?" he asked.

Chloe nodded miserably. "The prayer, you mean?"

"That's what I mean. I was afraid of lightning."

Tsion shuddered, remembering the knockoff of the Lord's Prayer taught to groups of children barely old enough to speak. It had begun, "Our Father in New Babylon, Carpathia be your name. Your kingdom come, your will be done. . . ." Tsion had been so disgusted that he turned it off. Chloe, apparently, had watched the whole debacle.

"I've been studying," she said.

"Good," Tsion said. "I hope so. We can never know enough—"

"Not the way you think," she said. "I've been studying death."

Tsion narrowed his eyes. "I'm listening."

"I will not allow myself or my baby to fall into the hands of the enemy."

"What are you saying?"

"I'm saying just what you're afraid I'm saying, Tsion."

"Have you told Cameron?"

"You promised you would keep my confidence!"

"And I will. I'm asking, have *you* told him your plans?"

"I have no plans. I'm just studying."

"But you will soon have a plan, because it is clear you have made up your mind. You said, 'I will not . . . ,' and that evidences a course of action. You're saying that if we should be found out, if the GC should capture us—"

"I will not allow Kenny or me to fall into their hands."

"And how will you ensure this?"

"I would rather we were dead."

"You would kill yourself."

"I would. And I would commit infanticide."

She said this with such chilling conviction that Tsion hesitated, praying silently for wisdom. "Is this a sign of faith, or lack of faith?" he said finally.

"I don't know, but I can't imagine God would want me or my baby in that situation."

"You think he wants you in *this* situation? He is not willing that any should perish. He would that you would have been ready to go the first time. He—"

"I know, Tsion. I know, all right? I'm just saying—"

"Forgive me for interrupting, but I know what you're saying. I just don't believe you are being honest with yourself."

"I couldn't be *more* honest! I would kill myself and commit inf—"

"There you go again."

"What?"

"Buffering your conviction with easy words. You're no better than the abortionists who refer to their unborn babies as embryos or fetuses or pregnancies so they can 'eliminate' them or 'terminate' them rather than kill them."

"What? I said I would com—"

"Yes, that's what you said. You didn't say what you mean. Tell me."

"I told you, Tsion! Why are you doing this?"

"Tell me, Chloe. Tell me what you are going to do to—" He hesitated, not wanting to alert Kenny they were talking about him. "Tell me what you're going to do to this little one, because obviously, you have to do it to him first if it's going to get done. Because if you kill yourself, none of the rest of us will do this job for you."

"I told you what I would do to him."

"Say it in plain words."

"That I will kill him before I let the GC have him? I will."

"Will what?"

"Kill him."

"Put it in a sentence."

"I will. I will . . . kill . . . my own baby."

"Baby!" Kenny exulted, running to her. She reached for him, sobbing.

Quietly, Tsion said, "How will you do this?"

"That's what I'm studying," she managed over Kenny's shoulders. He hugged her tight and scampered away.

"And then you will kill yourself, why?"

"Because I cannot live without him."

"Then it follows that Cameron would be justified in killing himself."

She bit her lip and shook her head. "The world needs him."

"The world needs you, Chloe. Think of the co-op, the international—"

"I can't think anymore," she said. "I want done with this! I want it over! I don't know what we were thinking, bringing a child into this world. . . ."

"That child has brought so much joy to this house—" Tsion began.

"—that I could not do him the disservice of letting him fall into GC hands."

Tsion sat back, glancing at the TV. "So the GC comes, you kill the baby, kill yourself, Cameron and your father kill themselves . . . when does it end?"

"They wouldn't. They couldn't."

"You can't. And you won't."

"I thought I could talk to you, Tsion."

"You expected what, that I would condone this?"

"That you would be sympathetic, at least."

"I am that, at the very least," he said. "Neither do I want to live without you and the little one. You know what comes next."

"Oh, Tsion, you would not deprive your global church of yourself."

He sat back and put his hands on his knees. "Yet you would deprive *me* of *your*self. You must not care for me as much as I care for you, or as much as I thought you did."

Chloe sighed and looked to the ceiling. "You're not helping," she said in mock exasperation.

"I'm trying," he said.

"I know. And I appreciate it."

Tsion asked her to pray with him for their loved ones. She knelt on the floor next to the couch, holding his hand, and soon after they began, Tsion peeked at a sound and saw Kenny kneeling next to his mother, hands folded, fingers entwined, eyes closed.

David found Guy Blod more outrageous and flamboyant in person. He showed up with a small entourage of similarly huffy and put-out men in their late thirties. Despite their differences in nationality, they could have been quints from the way they dressed and acted. David offered only Guy a chair across from his desk.

"This is what you call hospitality?" Guy said. "There are six of us, hello."

"My apologies," David said. "I was under the impression it was the responsibility of the *guest* to inform the *host* when uninvited people were coming."

Guy waved him off, and his sycophants glumly stood behind him with arms crossed. "The Supreme Commander has commissioned me to do a sort of bronzy iron thingie of Nicolae. And I have to do it fast, so can you get me the materials?"

They were interrupted by an urgent knock on the door. A woman in her late sixties, blue-haired, short, and stocky, poked her head in. "Miss Ivins," David said. "May I help you?"

"Excuse me," Guy said, "but we're in conference here."

David stood. "It's all right, Miss Ivins. You know Guy."

"Of course," she said, nodding sadly.

"And Guy, you know Vivian is—"

"Yes, the potentate's only living relative. I'm sorry for your loss, ma'am, but we—"

"How may I help you, ma'am?" David said.

"I'm looking for crowd control volunteers," she said. "The masses are already showing up from all over the world, and—"

"It's after midnight!" Guy said. "Don't they know the funeral isn't for at least two days? What are we supposed to do with them all?"

"Commander Fortunato is asking for any personnel below director level to—"

"That leaves me out, Vivian!" Guy said. "And Hayseed here too, unfortunately."

"How about your assistants, Guy?" David suggested.

"I need every last one of them for this project! Viv, surely you don't expect—"

"I'm aware of your assignment, Guy," Viv Ivins said, but she pronounced his name in the Western style, and he quickly corrected her. She ignored him. "I'm on assignment too. If either of you gentlemen could spread the word among your people, the administration would be grateful."

David returned to his seat and tapped out the notice to be broadcast to his workers' E-mail addresses as Miss Ivins backed out and shut the door.

"Aren't we efficient?" Guy said.

"We try," David said.

"I know what her assignment is," Guy said. "Have you heard?"

"I have enough trouble keeping up with my own."

David had acted uninterested enough that Guy turned to his own people and whispered, "That regional numbering thing." David was dying of curiosity but unwilling to admit it. Guy spun in his chair to face David. "Now, where were we?"

"I was about to check my catalog file for bronze and iron thingie suppliers, and you were going to be a bit more specific."

"OK, I'm gonna need a computer program that allows me to figure out how to do this. I'm going to be supplied by the coroner with a life-size cast of Carpathia's body—how ghastly—and I need to quadruple that in size. That means four times."

"Yeah, I recall arithmetic, Guy."

"I'm just trying to help. Truce?"

"Truce?"

"Start over, no hassles?"

"Whatever, Guy."

"Be nice."

"I'm trying."

"Anyhoo, I wanna make this like twenty-four-foot replica of Carpathia out of pretty much bronze, I think, but I want it to come out in a sort of ebony finish with a texture of iron. Ebony is black."

"I remember crayons too, Guy."

"Sor-*ry,* David! You don't want *any* help!"

"I'm going to need it if I'm to find you this material quickly. What do you think you need and how fast do you need it?"

Guy leaned forward. "Now we're getting somewhere. I want the thing to be hollow with about a quarter-inch to three-eighths-inch shell, but it has to be strong enough and balanced enough to stand straight without support, just like Nicolae would if he were that tall."

David shrugged. "So you make him to scale and cheat on the shoes if you have to, since an inanimate object won't make the unconscious balancing maneuvers to stay standing."

"Shoes!?"

"What, your statue will be barefoot?"

Guy giggled and shared the mirth with his clones. "Oh, David," he said, lifting his feet and spinning in his chair. "My statue will be *au naturel.*"

David made a face. "Please tell me you're joking!"

"Not on your life. Did you think the mortician was going to make a body cast of him in his suit?"

"Why not?"

Guy fluttered the air with his fingers and said, "Forget it, forget it, you wouldn't understand. You obviously have some hang-up about the human form and can't appreciate the beauty. You just—"

"Guy, I'm assuming this statue is to maintain a promi-nent place within the palace—"

"Within the palace? Dear boy! This will be THE *objet d'art* of history, my *pièce de résistance*. It shall stand in the palace courtyard not thirty feet from where the potentate lies in state."

"So the whole world will see it."

"In all its glory."

"And it's *your* masterpiece."

Guy nodded, appearing unable to contain his glee.

"So if I took a picture of something and then traced it, I could be an artist too?"

Guy looked disgusted. "You're about as far from an artist as I am from—"

"But what of this reproduction of a dead man's bare body is your work?"

"Are you just insulting me, or is that a sincere question?"

"Call it sincere. I really want to know."

"The concept! I con*ceived* it, David! I will supervise the construction. I will do the finish work on the face, leaving the eyes hollow. I was asked to create a huge statue to represent the greatest man who ever lived, and this came to me as if from God himself."

"You're on speaking terms with God?"

"It's just an expression, Hayseed. It's from my muse. Who can explain it? It's what I blame my genius on, the one thing that keeps me from unbearable ego. Can you imagine how embarrassing it is to be lauded for every-thing your hands create? I mean, I'm not complaining, but the attention becomes overwhelming. The muse is my foil.

I am as overwhelmed at my gift—the gift from the muse, you see—as anyone else. I enjoy it as the masses do."

"You do."

"Yes, I do. And I can't wait to get to this one. I'm assuming I would have access to the GC foundry, as we won't have time to have this done off-site."

David shut one eye. "The foundry is on three shifts, seven days a week. We could have this more cheaply done in Asia, where—"

"Help me stay civil here, David, as it is clearly my fault for not clarifying. Supreme Commander Fortunato—who, in case you couldn't figure this out on your own, will likely be the new potentate once Carpathia is entombed—wants this monument in place no later than at dawn Sunday."

Guy stared at David, as if to let that sink in. It almost didn't. David looked at his watch. It was crowding 1:00 A.M. Saturday, Carpathia Standard Time. "I don't see it," he said, "but I don't imagine you can be dissuaded."

"Why, I believe we have begun to connect!"

Anything but that, David thought.

"Zhizaki," Guy said, "if you please."

With a flourish, an Asian with two-inch green nails produced a computer-generated schedule. It called for the procuring of materials and determining the manufac-turing site by noon Saturday, concurrent with computer design by the artist and cast making by the mortician. By midnight Saturday, the foundry was to create a cast to the artist's specifications, produce the shell, and deliver it to the back of the palace courtyard. There Guy and his staff would do the finish work until the product was ready for positioning in view of the mourners just before dawn Sunday.

"That's more than ambitious, Guy," David said. "It's audacious."

"Audacious," Guy said with a faraway look. "Now there's an epitaph."

"You'll have to work with materials already on hand," David said.

"I assumed that. But we'll need you to override current projects, get this at the top of the list, and let me in there to make sure the consistency and the color are right."

"You'll have to wear protective clothing and a hard hat," David said.

Guy looked at his mates. "I love new clothes."

FOUR

It was to Rayford's advantage that the Global Community had rendered the whole of Greece virtually invisible. In realigning the world into ten regions with sub-potentates—which Tsion Ben-Judah insisted were "kingdoms with kings"—the United Holy Land States had appropriated Greece. Her potentate had lobbied for independence, as most countries' leaders had, then pleaded for membership as one of the United European States.

Carpathia himself had mollified the Greeks with a personal visit and several appearances, during which he took full responsibility for their inclusion in "his" region. Lukas (Laslos) Miklos had once regaled Rayford with a dead-on imitation of the potentate's Eastern-flavored Greek as he flattered the nation into compliance.

"You are a deeply religious people," Carpathia had told them, "with a rich place in the histories of many cherished belief systems. You are nearly as close to the cradle of civilization as you are to the United European States, so I personally argued for your inclusion as a Holy Land state. My own origins are not that far north of you. The line of demarcation that puts both my home-land and my current residence in the same region natu-rally includes Greece as well. I welcome you to 'my' region and trust you will enjoy the benefits from this area's housing the new world capital."

That had won over the majority of Greeks. One huge benefit to tribulation saints was that Greece seemed above suspicion as a spring of rebellion. The exploding church there went underground immediately, worried that it might otherwise draw the attention of the GC. Dr. Ben-Judah corresponded with nearly a thousand Greek evangelists he had identified as likely part of the proph-esied 144,000 witnesses. These were Messianic Jews, many of whom had attended the great conference of wit-nesses in Israel and had returned to their homeland to win tens of thousands of converts to Christ.

Mr. and Mrs. Miklos's own local body of under-ground believers had mushroomed so that the original assembly had split many times and now met as more than a hundred "small groups" that weren't really so small. The new corporate church was too large to ever meet together without jeopardizing its clandestine iden-tity. The witness-leaders of each faction met monthly for training and mutual encouragement, and of course the entire body counted itself part of the new worldwide band of believers, with Tsion Ben-Judah as its *de facto* cyberspace pastor-teacher.

The covert nature of the Greek church, while clearly not impeding its evangelistic efforts, served to keep from waving a red flag before the GC. Buck Williams's private investigations for his cybermagazine, *The Truth,* found—with the help of ultimate hacker David Hassid—that Greece was all but ignored by GC counterintelligence, security, and peacekeeping forces. The country was low maintenance. Most of the forces assigned there had been redeployed into Israel for the Gala and New Babylon for its aftermath.

Thus it was not a surprise to Rayford to find that the tiny airport in Ptolemaïs was not only closed and unmanned but also dark. He had neither the light power nor the confidence to land on an unlit runway with a plane as powerful and tricky as the Gulfstream. He overflew the airfield a few times, not wanting to draw attention to himself, then headed south about twenty-five miles to Kozani and its larger airport. It too was closed, but one runway remained lit for emergencies and private cargo carriers. Rayford watched a wide-body international delivery craft put down, waited until it had taxied toward the colossal commercial hangars, then set his instruments for landing.

He didn't know how he would get hold of Laslos or find a ride to Ptolemaïs. Perhaps he would be close enough to use his phone without relying on satellite technology. He hated to bother the Mikloses at this hour, but he'd done it before. They always understood. In fact, it seemed they loved the intrigue of the underground, Mrs. Miklos as much as Lukas.

Rayford was strangely calm as he descended into Kozani. He believed he had made intimate contact with God during the flight, had communicated more directly, and felt more personally connected to heaven than he had in ages. This had come when Rayford finally heeded the Scripture "Be still, and know that I am God." After months of rationalizing, self-defense, and taking matters into his own hands, he had finally given up and sought God.

His first overwhelming emotion was shame. God had entrusted him, a brand-new believer, with a scope of leadership. God had used the gifts he had bestowed on Rayford to direct the little band of believers that had become known as the Tribulation Force.

Smarter people were in the Force, Rayford knew, including his own daughter and son-in-law. And where on earth was a more brilliant mind than that of Tsion Ben-Judah? And yet they all naturally looked to Rayford for leadership. He had not sought it, nor did he hoard it. But he had been willing. And as the Force grew, so did his responsibility. But though his capacity could have expanded with the scope of his charge, the illogical had invaded. The man who had prided himself on his pragmatism found himself living by his emotions.

At first, becoming attuned to his emotions had been revelatory. It had allowed him to care deeply for his daughter, to really grieve over the loss of his wife and son, and to understand how much he had loved them. It had allowed him to see himself for who he was, to understand his need for forgiveness, to come to Christ.

But, understandably, Rayford had found it difficult to balance his emotion and his intellect. No one could argue that he had been through more than his share of loss and trauma in three and a half years. But the emotion necessary to round him out as a new believer somehow overrode the levelheaded temperament that made him a natural leader. Never one for psychobabble, when Rayford opened himself to God that night, in his spirit he saw his failure for what it was: sin.

He had become selfish, angry, vengeful. He had tried to take God's place as defender and protector of the Tribulation Force. In the process, he had left them more vulnerable than ever to danger. As Rayford dared peek at himself in that spiritual mirror, he hated what he saw. Here was a man who had been wholly grateful to God for his forgiveness and love and salvation, now living as a maverick. He still called himself a believer. But what had happened to his dependence upon God, upon the counsel of his friends and relatives and spiritual mentors? What had happened to his love for the Bible and prayer, and for the guidance he had once found there?

As God seemed to shine the light of truth into his soul, Rayford pleaded for forgiveness, for restoration. Had his rage been sin? No, that didn't compute. The Scriptures counseled, "Be angry, and do not sin," so the anger itself was not wrong. What he did as a result of it clearly was. He had become consumed by rage and had allowed it to interfere with his relationship to God and to those he loved.

Rayford had become isolated, living out his private ambitions. He had fought to see through his tears as God showed him his very self in its rawest state. "I'll understand," he prayed, "if I have disqualified myself from any role with the Trib Force," but God did not seem to confirm that. All Rayford felt was an overwhelming hunger and thirst for the Bible and for instruction. He wanted to pray like this from now on, to constantly be in touch with God as he had been when he first became a believer. What that meant to his role as head of the Tribulation Force, he didn't know. More important was getting back to the basics, getting back to God.

Rayford found the cargo plane crew busy with their own work as he taxied a quarter of a mile north to park the Gulfstream. They barely looked up as he hurried past on foot, his bag slung over his shoulder as if he were headed somewhere specific. As soon as he emerged from the airfield's gated entrance and found a dark spot between road lamps, he phoned the Mikloses' home. Mrs. Miklos answered on the first ring.

"This is your friend from America," he said, and she immediately switched from Greek to her very limited English.

"Say code so I know," she said.

Code? He didn't remember any code. Maybe that was something among the local believers. "Jesus is the Christ, the Messiah," he said.

"That not code," she said, "but I know voice. Saw on television."

"You did? Me?"

"Yes. Did you shoot Carpathia?"

Rayford's mouth went dry. So the cameras had caught him. "No!" he said. "At least I don't think so. I didn't mean to. What are they saying?"

"Fingerprints," she said. "On gun."

Rayford shook his head. He had been so certain that if he shot Carpathia he would be immediately captured or killed that he had not even worried about fingerprints. He hadn't considered escaping. Some criminal *he* was! Why didn't he think to wipe the handle on his robe before dropping the weapon?

"Are they showing my face?" he asked.

"Yes."

He told her where he was and asked if Laslos was there.

"No. With our shepherd. Praying for you."

"I don't want to compromise you," he said. "I'll just fly on to America."

"Don't know *compromise*," she said.

"Ah, sorry. Give you away. Get you in trouble. Be seen with you."

"Laslos would not leave you alone," she said. "I tell him. He call you."

Rayford hated the idea of jeopardizing Greek believers, but Laslos's English was better than his wife's, so perhaps Rayford would have an easier time dissuading him from becoming involved. He gave her the number and settled in to wait for the call in the shadows of the shrubbery off the makeshift road that led north out of the airport.

Upstairs in Rosenzweig's massive house, Buck used the flashlight sparingly as he searched for any sign of Chaim. From outside he heard noises in the underbrush that paralyzed him. He held his breath and crept to the window, peering down while desperate to stay out of sight. Someone signaled a few others, and their shapes moved about in the darkness. He couldn't imagine a scenario that would allow him to escape until it played out before his eyes.

Suddenly all GC Peacekeeping Forces were rallied for one purpose—to find a fugitive. And when the multilanguage announcement came over rolling bullhorns, it was clear whom they were looking for.

"Attention, citizens and all Global Community personnel!" came the announcements. "Be on the lookout for American Rayford Steele, former GC employee wanted in connection with the conspiracy to assassinate Potentate Nicolae Carpathia. May be in disguise. May be armed. Considered dangerous. Qualified pilot. Any information about his whereabouts . . ."

Rayford? Conspiracy? Now the GC was grasping at straws.

From below, the GC Peacekeepers appeared to be arguing whether one or more should stay. Finally their leader barked at them and waved that they should follow. Buck waited a few minutes, then checked every window, staring into the night and listening for any enemy. He saw and heard nothing, but he knew time was his greatest adversary now.

He saved Chaim's workshop till last. It had no windows, so when he threw open the door, he didn't hesitate to shine the flashlight all about. It was empty, but it also looked different from when last he'd seen it. Chaim had shown him his handiwork, but now there was no evidence of that. The place was spotless. Even the vises had been unfastened from the workbenches and stored. The floor was clean, tools hung, counters spotless. It almost looked the way it would if someone were moving or had another function in mind for the room.

Buck backed out and closed the door. Something niggled at his mind, despite the taste of fear and revulsion in his throat. He tucked the flashlight into his pocket and carefully made his way to the front door. The casing had been shattered. Though he was sure the GC had done this and abandoned the place, Buck felt safer leaving the way he had come. As he moved toward the back door, he wondered who had cleaned Chaim's workshop for him. Had he done it himself before the stroke, or had the staff done it after it became clear he would be unable to engage in his hobby?

Buck felt his way through the sparse landscaping in the back and stopped frequently to listen for footsteps or breathing over the sirens and announcements from blocks away. He stayed out of the light and in the middle of earthquake rubble as much as he could until he found an area where the streetlamps were out.

He had to know for sure about Chaim before he could even think about trying to rendezvous with Rayford or Leah. But where should he start? Not that long ago, Buck would have tried to find him through Jacov, Hannelore, her mother, or Stefan. As he broke into a jog, heading for who knew where, tears dripped from his face.

———————

Late Friday afternoon in Illinois, Chloe had been feeding Kenny in the other room when Rayford's photo—the one from his former GC ID—came on television. Tsion blanched and bolted for the set to turn it down and listen from up close. Tsion had been praying for Rayford, worried about him. When Rayford and Leah and Buck had left, Tsion thought he knew their various assignments and missions, and he feared playing mere shuttle pilot would not be enough for Rayford. He had been in the middle of so much action but was now, even more than the rest, merely a fugitive, having to stay out of sight.

Now what would he do? The news implied he had fired the weapon that may have killed Carpathia. How could one do that in such a crowd and escape? Never had Tsion so wanted to talk to Rayford, and never had he felt such a burden to pray for a man.

That compulsion was nothing new. It struck Tsion that he had spent more time in concerted prayer for Rayford than for any other individual. It was obvious why Rayford needed prayer now, of course, but when Tsion closed his eyes and covered them with a hand, he felt uncomfortable. He knew he would have to tell Chloe soon that her father was a suspect in the assassination— or the conspiracy, as the TV anchors called it—but that

was not what made him fidgety. It seemed he was not in
the proper posture to pray, and all he could make of that
was that perhaps Rayford needed real intercession.

Tsion had studied the discipline of intercession, largely
a Protestant tradition from the fundamentalist and the
Pentecostal cultures. Those steeped in it went beyond
mere praying for someone as an act of interceding for
them; they believed true intercession involved deep
empathy and that a person thus praying must not enter
into the practice unless willing to literally trade places
with the needy person.

Tsion mentally examined his own willingness to truly
intercede for Rayford. It was mere exercise. He could not
trade places with Rayford and become a suspect in the
murder of the Antichrist. But he could affect that posture
in his mind; he could express his willingness to God to
take that burden, literally possible or not.

Yet even that did not assuage Tsion's discomfort. He
tried dropping to one knee, bowing his head lower, then
slipping to both knees, then turning to lay his arms on
the seat of the couch and rest his head on his hands. He
worried that Chloe would not understand if she saw him
this way, suddenly not watching TV obsessively as he
had since the assassination, but in a posture of total con-
trition—something foreign to his nature. He often prayed
this way in private, of course, but Chloe would see this
"showing" of humility so aberrational that she would
likely feel obligated to ask if he was all right.

But these concerns were quickly overridden by Tsion's
spiritual longings. He felt such deep compassion and pity

for Rayford that he moaned involuntarily and felt himself sliding from the couch until his palms were flat on the floor.

His head now pressing against the front of the couch, his body facing away from the near silent TV, he groaned and wept as he prayed silently for Rayford. Having not come from a tradition comfortable with unusual manifestations, Tsion was startled by a sudden lack of equilibrium. In his mind's eye his focus had suddenly shifted from Rayford and his troubles to the majesty of God himself. Tsion at once felt unworthy and ashamed and impure, as if in the very presence of the Lord.

Tsion knew that praying was figuratively boldly approaching the throne, but he had never felt such a physical proximity to the creator God. Knees sliding back, palms forward, he lay prostrate, his forehead pressing into the musty carpet, nose mashed flat.

But even that did not alleviate his light-headedness. Tsion felt disembodied, as if the present were giving way. He was only vaguely aware of where he was, of the quiet drone of the television, of Chloe cooing and Kenny giggling as she urged him to eat.

"Tsion?"

He did not respond, not immediately aware he was even conscious. Was this a dream?

"Tsion?"

The voice was feminine.

"Should I try the phone again?"

He opened his eyes, suddenly aware of the smell of the old carpet and the sting of tears.

"Hm?" he managed, throat constricted, voice thick.

Footsteps. "I was wondering, should I try calling—Tsion! Are you all right?"

He slowly pulled himself up. "I'm fine, dear. Very tired all of a sudden."

"You have a right to be! Get some rest. Take a nap. I'll wake you if anything breaks. I won't let you miss anything."

Tsion sat on the edge of the couch, shoulders slumped, hands entwined between his knees. "I would be grateful," he said. He nodded toward the other room. "Is he all right for a minute?"

She nodded.

"You'd better sit down," he said.

Chloe looked stricken. "Was there news? Is Buck all right?"

"Nothing from Buck or Leah," he said, and she seemed to finally exhale. "But you need to know about your father. . . ."

David tried e-mailing Viv Ivins a list of those in his department who might be available for double duty over the next few days, but the message bounced back undeliverable. He would go past her office on the way to the hangar anyway, so he printed out the message and took it with him.

On the way he received a call from the foundry foreman. "You know what you're asking, don't you?" the man said.

"Of course, Hans," David said. "You have to know this didn't originate with me."

"Unless it's from Fortunato himself, I don't see how we can be expected—"

"It is."

"—to comply. I mean, this is way too—it is?"

"It is."

"'nough said."

David slipped the printout into the slot on Viv Ivins's door, but it was not shut all the way and swung open. The small, dark office immediately brightened as the motion-sensitive light came on. The gossip around the palace was that on occasion, Carpathia's alleged aunt on his mother's side dozed for so long at her desk that her office went dark. If something woke her or caused her to move in her sleep, the lights came back on, and she resumed working as if nothing were awry.

David made sure she wasn't in there dozing, then reached to shut the door. But something on her desk caught his eye. She had laid out a map of the world, boundaries between the ten regions clearly marked. It was nothing he hadn't seen before, except that this was an old map, one drawn when the ten regions were members of the newly expanded United Nations Security Council. When Carpathia had renamed the one-world government the Global Community, he had also slightly renamed the ten regions. For instance, the United States of North America became the United North American States. Viv Ivins had not only handwritten these adjustments, but she had also added numbers in parentheses after each name.

David felt conspicuous and nosy, but who knew what significance this might hold for the Trib Force, the Judah-ites, tribulation saints around the world? He concocted his alibi as he moved toward the desk. If Viv were to return and catch him studying her map, he would simply tell the truth about the door tripping the light and the map catching his eye. How he would explain his scribbling the numbers, he did not know.

With one last look out her office window, David grabbed a business card from his wallet and wrote furiously in tiny script as he bent over Viv's map.

The United Holy Land States* (216)
The United Russian States (72)
The United Indian States (42)
The United Asian States (30)
The United Pacific States (18)
The United North American States (-6)
The United South American States (0)
The United Great Britain States (2)
The United European States (6)
The United African States (7)

David traced the asterisk after "The United Holy Land States" to the bottom of the map, where Viv, or someone, had noted in faint, tiny pencil marks "aka The United Carpathian States."

That was a new one. David had never heard another moniker for the Holy Land States. As he was straightening to leave he saw more pencil writing that appeared to have been erased. He bent close and squinted but needed more light. Dare he turn on Viv's desk lamp?

No. Rather, he held the whole map up to the ceiling light, knowing he would simply have to confess to pathological curiosity, if necessary. He only hoped that Viv, like nearly everyone else in the compound, was watching Carpathia's body being transported from the Phoenix 216 to the morgue. He was glad to miss that, knowing that most would hold hands or hats over their hearts, and he wasn't prepared to do that even as a ruse.

With the overhead light shining brightly through the map, David was barely able to make out the erasures. It appeared someone had written "Only caveat: H. L. highest, N. A. lowest."

David shook his head as he carefully replaced the map and headed out.

Viv Ivins was coming toward him. "Oh, David," she said, "I wish you could have seen the spontaneous outpouring of emotion . . ."

"I'm sure there'll be a lot of that over the next few days."

"But to see the workers, the soldiers, everybody . . . ah, it was moving. The salutes, the tears. Oh! Did I leave my light on?"

David explained the door tripping the motion sensor.

"And your list is in the door?"

He nodded and his phone rang, startling him so that he nearly left his feet.

"Carry on," Viv said.

It was Mac. David talked as he walked. "Half thought

you'd be here to greet us," Mac said. "Corporal Christopher waited on the evidence until the pallbearers got the
body out of here."

"The evidence?"

"I don't think I've ever seen pallbearers in dress unies
carrying a big ol' wood crate like it was a polished
mahogany casket. Where were you?"

"On my way, but what'd you say about evidence?"

"Annie's off-loading it now. Couple of huge plastic
trash bags full of pieces of the lectern. And another crate
with apparently the whole fabric backdrop off the stage.
Moon wouldn't let us leave Jerusalem without it. You
heard about the weapon, right?"

"'Course. And our friend."

"Funny thing, though, David."

"Yeah?"

"I'd better save this for in person."

————————————

"Rayford here."

"Mr. Steele!" came the easily recognized voice of
Lukas Miklos. "Where are you?"

Rayford told him.

"Stay in the shadows but walk three kilometers north.
We will pick you up north of the three-kilometer marker.
When you see a white four-door slow and leave the road,
run to us. If there is any traffic, we may pass and come
back, but when we pull off, do not hesitate."

"We?"

"Our undershepherd and me."

"Laslos, I don't want you two to risk—"

"Nonsense! Do you have an alias and appropriate papers?"

"I do."

"Good. How fast can you walk?"

"How's the terrain?"

"Not the best, but don't get near the road until we get there."

"I'm starting now."

"Mr. Steele, we feel just like the prayer-meeting people from the New Testament, praying for Peter while he knocked on their door."

"Yeah," Rayford said. "Only he was coming *from* prison."

———

Exhausted, Buck sat behind a concrete wall, built decades before to protect Israel from shrapnel and mortar from nearby enemies. He was several blocks from the main drag, but close enough to hear the ever-present sirens and see the emergency lights bouncing off the low-riding clouds in the wee hours.

Think, think, think, he told himself. He didn't want to leave Israel without knowing where Chaim was. Buck knew of no other people Chaim might flee to or with if he had somehow survived. If Chaim had defied the odds, he would be looking for Buck as fervently as Buck was looking for him. They could not meet at the obvious places: Buck's hostel, Chaim's house, Jacov's apartment, Stefan's place. What would make sense to both of them?

Buck had never believed in extrasensory perception, but he sure wished there was something to it now. He wished he could sense whether the old man was all right, and if so, that he was trying to somehow communicate with Buck right then. As a believer, Buck was certain that clairvoyance was hogwash. But he had heard credible stories of people, particularly Christians, who somehow knew things supernaturally. Surely it wasn't beyond God's ability to perform such miracles, especially now.

Buck needed a miracle, but his faith was weak. He knew it shouldn't be. He had seen enough from God in three and a half years that he should never again doubt for an instant. What held him up now was that he was dead sure he didn't deserve a miracle. Weren't there bigger, more important things for God to worry about? People were dying, injured, lost. And there was the great supernatural battle between good and evil that Tsion wrote so much about, the conflict of the ages that had spilled out of heaven and now plagued the earth.

"I'm sorry to even ask," Buck prayed, "but at least calm me down, give me a clear mind just long enough to figure this. If Chaim is alive, let us run into each other or both think of a meeting place that makes sense."

Buck felt foolish, stupid, petty. Finding Chaim was noble, but involving God in such a trivial matter seemed, well, rude. He stood and felt the aches. He clenched his fists and grimaced. *Relax! Get hold of yourself! Think!*

But somehow he knew that was no way to open the

mind. He had to really relax, and berating himself for being frantic would have the opposite effect. But how could he calm himself at a time like this, when it was all he could do to catch his breath and will his pulse to decelerate?

Maybe *that* was an appropriate request of God, a miracle enough in itself.

Buck sat back down, confident he was hidden and alone. He breathed deeply and exhaled slowly, shaking out his hands and stretching his legs. He laid his head back and felt the concrete wall against his hair and scalp. He let his head roll from side to side. His breathing became slower and more even; his pulse began to subside ever so slowly. He tucked his chin to his chest and tried to clear his mind.

The only way to do that was to pray for his comrades one by one, starting with his own wife and son, his father-in-law, and all the rest of the brothers and sisters who came to mind. He thanked God for friends now in heaven, including those whose bodies he had just discovered.

And almost before he knew it, he had calmed as much as a man could in that situation. *Thank you, Lord. Now what location would make sense? Where have Chaim and I been together that we would both think of?*

He pictured them at Teddy Kolleck Stadium, but that was too public, too open. Neither could risk it.

And then it came to him.

FIVE

CHLOE fell silent at the news. Tsion might have predicted tears, disbelief, railing against someone other than her father. She just sat, shaking her head.

Difficult as it had been to inform her, Tsion was oddly still reeling from what to him had felt almost like an out-of-body experience while praying. He had heard of those and pooh-poohed them as fabrications or drug-induced hallucinations on deathbeds. But this sensation, so real and dramatic that it had temporarily derailed his empathy and intercession on Rayford's behalf, was something else again. He had long advocated checking experience against Scripture and not the other way around. He would, he realized, have to remind himself of that frequently until the glow—which seemed too positive a word for the disturbing residue of the incident—receded into memory. A verse from the Old Testament teased his consciousness, and his mind wandered from the troubled young woman before him.

As Chloe had not yet responded, Tsion said, "Excuse me a moment, please," and brought his whole Bible text up onto his laptop screen. A few seconds later he clicked on Joel 2. He silently read verses 28 through 32, finding that he had been led to a passage that both illuminated his experience and might provide some balm to her as well.

> *I will pour out My Spirit on all flesh;*
> *Your sons and your daughters shall prophesy,*
> *Your old men shall dream dreams,*
> *Your young men shall see visions.*
> *And also on My menservants and on My maid-*
> *   servants I will pour out My Spirit in those days.*
> *And I will show wonders in the heavens and in the*
> *   earth: blood and fire and pillars of smoke.*
> *The sun shall be turned into darkness,*
> *And the moon into blood,*
> *Before the coming of the great and awesome day*
> *   of the Lord.*
> *And it shall come to pass*
> *That whoever calls on the name of the Lord*
> *Shall be saved.*
> *For in Mount Zion and in Jerusalem there shall*
> *   be deliverance,*
> *As the Lord has said,*
> *Among the remnant whom the Lord calls.*

Tsion looked up with a start when Chloe spoke at last. He detected no trauma in her voice, nothing that would have given away that she had just learned that her father was the most wanted fugitive in the world—except for her words themselves. "I should have seen it coming," she said. "He tried to divert me to Hattie, which wasn't hard. She never had any qualms about saying she wanted to kill Carpathia."

Tsion cleared his throat. "Why would he do it, knowing the death wound is only temporary anyway? Is your father capable of such an act?"

Chloe stood and peeked into the other room, where she was apparently satisfied with whatever Kenny was doing with his food. "I wouldn't have thought so until recently," she said. "He changed so much. Almost as dramatically as the difference in him before and after the Rapture. It was as if he had reverted into something worse than he had been before he became a believer."

Tsion cocked his head and sneaked a glance at the television. Nothing new. "I was aware of tension in the house," he said. "But I missed what you're talking about."

"The rage? You missed the rage?"

Tsion shrugged. "I *share* some of that. I still fight it when I think of my family—" His voice caught.

"I know, Tsion. But you have been a man of the Scriptures your whole life. This is new to Daddy. I can't imagine him actually standing there and doing it, but I'm sure he wanted to. If he did, it sure answers a lot of questions about where he's been and what he's been doing. Oh, Tsion! How will he get away? That they say he's at large makes me wonder if it's not just a lie, a smear campaign to make him and you and us look bad? Maybe he's a scapegoat."

"We can only hope."

She dropped into a chair. "What if he's guilty? What if he's a murderer? There's no exception to God's law if the victim is the Antichrist, is there?"

Tsion shook his head. "None that I know of."

"Then mustn't he turn himself in? Suffer the consequences?"

"Slow down, Chloe. We know too little."

"But if he *is* guilty."

"My answer may surprise you."

"Surprise me."

"Off the top of the head, I believe we are at war. In the heat of battle, killing the enemy has never been considered murder."

"But . . ."

"I told you I might surprise you. I personally would harbor your father from the GC if he shot Carpathia dead, even while urging him to seek God about himself."

"You're right," Chloe said. "You surprised me."

———

David watched Annie work from the corner of the hangar where Mac and Abdullah met him. "What's that smell?" he said.

"Yeah," Mac said, looking at Abdullah. "What *is* that?"

Abdullah shrugged, then held up an index finger. "Oh, I remember now, Captain," he said. "Your idea."

"I'm listening," Mac said.

Abdullah pulled a pungent pita sandwich from his pocket. "Hungry, anyone?" he said.

"Here's hoping I'll never be that hungry," David said, pointing to a trash barrel twenty feet away. Abdullah hit it with a hook shot, and somehow the thing didn't fly apart in the air.

Mac shook his head. "Next you're going to tell me you were an Olympic basketball player."

"Missed the trials," Abdullah said. "Active duty."

David caught Mac's what'd-I-tell-ya look.

"So, Ab," Mac said, "are you 'pout' because you never finished your dinner?"

Abdullah looked away, as if knowing he was being teased but not catching the whole drift. "If I am pout," he said, "it is because I am exhausted and want to go to bed. Is anyone sleeping around here? It seems everyone is about."

"Go," David said. "Don't make it obvious, but go to bed. I'm going to be good for nothing if I don't crash sometime soon too."

Abdullah slipped away. "You look whipped too, Mac," David said.

Mac nodded for David to follow him to his office, across the hall from Annie's. "They're making a big deal about finding Rayford's fingerprints on a Saber," Mac said as he settled into the chair behind his desk. "But who knows if he was even there?"

"I'll find out by listening in."

"I think I already did. The print trace, at least what

they said about it on the plane, sounded legit. Israeli-based Peacekeepers found the weapon, bagged it, and immediately lifted prints and started comparing it against the global database. The only reason it took as long as it did was because they tested it against criminals first and against the former GC employee list last. But the funny thing is that nobody's talking about Rayford as the perpetrator."

David flinched. "When they've got him dead to rights?"

Mac showed both palms. "They must know something we don't know."

"Such as?"

"Well, Neon Leon has a bee in his bonnet for the three disloyal regional potentates. He keeps talking about a conspiracy. I mean, everybody hears a gunshot and heads for the hills. People jump off the stage. Carpathia is down and dying. The suspected weapon is found with a disgruntled former employee's prints all over it, and all Leon can talk about is a conspiracy. What does that tell you?"

David frowned and furrowed his brow. "That the shooter missed?"

Mac expelled a resigned breath through his nose. "That's my theory. If it was so cut-and-dried, why don't they just call Rayford the shooter?"

"In public they do."

"But in private they're still looking. David, something stinks here."

David heard Annie's office door and looked out

through the blinds. She was doing the same, and he invited her over with a wave. She held up a finger and motioned that she had to make a call first. When she finally joined them, they brought her up to date.

"You still planning on listening in to the autopsy?" she said.

David nodded.

"Maybe you ought to patch in to the evidence room too."

"Didn't know we had one."

"We do now. They've cordoned off a section under the amphitheater. Lots of room, lots of light."

"Are you sure? That's next to where they've got Guy Blod fashioning a twenty-four-foot Carpathia statue."

"That's where I delivered the evidence. Two plastic bags, one wood crate. Hickman's got a crew of forensic experts scheduled for ten this morning."

David looked at his watch. "It *is* tomorrow already, isn't it? Well, looks like everything happens then, autopsy and all. Guess both sides need sleep first."

"I heard they're trying to start the viewing at dawn Sunday," Annie said. "That's tomorrow!"

"Bedtime, kids," David said.

———————

Rayford felt grimy and groggy. Despite his fear and the knowledge that his life as a fugitive had escalated a thousand times over, he was buoyed by his eagerness to pray and to get back into the Bible. Maybe it was naïve to think he could elude the GC for long. His recklessness had probably cost him his hope for surviving until the Glorious Appearing. Even forgiven sin, he had learned, has its consequences. He just hoped he hadn't jeopardized the entire Tribulation Force, or worse, saints worldwide.

As he sat praying in the dust fifty yards off the road, the night air dried the sweat on his head and neck and chilled him. In his fatigue and misery he still felt closer to God than he had for months.

His phone chirped, and Rayford hoped against hope it would be someone from the Trib Force, ideally Chloe or Buck. It was Laslos. "Are you in place?"

"Affirmative."

"And you are . . . ?"

"Marvin Berry," Rayford said.

"Check," Laslos said. "We were at a spot about two kilometers back where we could see the entire stretch of road before us. There appears to be no other traffic. You should hear us inside thirty seconds and see our lights soon. Start moving toward the road as soon as you hear us. We will open the back door as we stop, and as soon as you are in and it is shut, we will turn around quickly and head north again."

"Gotcha."

"Repeat?"

"Um, OK!"

Eager to be in the presence of a friend and fellow believer, Rayford was almost giddy under the circumstances. He slapped his phone shut, then opened it again to try one more time to reach anyone long distance. When it was obvious he still could not, he rang off and realized he heard a vehicle. He began jogging toward the road, but something was wrong. Unless he was turned around, it sounded as if the car was coming from the south. Should he dial Laslos back and see if he had misunderstood? But how could he have? Ptolemaïs was north. The church had to be north. Surely Laslos had said he would be heading south.

The engine sounded much bigger than a small car's. Rayford skidded to a stop in the loose dirt, realizing he had nowhere to hide if a vehicle came upon him from the south. And it was becoming obvious that one was. It was loud and it was big and it was coming fast, but he saw lights only on the northern horizon. That had to be Laslos.

The bigger vehicle from the south would reach him first. Regardless who it was, they would likely stop to check out a walking stranger. Rayford spun, frantically looking for somewhere to hide. His shirt was light colored and might be detectable in the darkness. As the sound rushed toward him, Rayford dove face first to the ground, pulling his dark bag atop his back as he lay there. With his free hand he popped open his phone to warn Laslos to abort and keep going, but when he hit Redial, he got the long distance attempt again and realized he didn't even have Laslos's cell number.

He prayed Laslos would see the oncoming vehicle in time to keep from slowing and pulling off the road.

Rayford's phone rang.

"Yeah!"

"What is coming from the south with no lights?"

"I don't know, Laslos! I'm on the ground! Keep going, just in case!"

The vehicle flew past, and Rayford felt the rush of wind. He tried to get a look at the car but could determine only that it was Jeep-like. "That could have been GC!" he said into the phone.

"It was," Laslos said. "Stay right where you are! It doesn't appear they saw you. They will be able to see us behind them for miles, so don't move. We will come back when we feel it is safe."

"I'd feel safer back in the foliage," Rayford said.

"Better wait. They might be able to see movement. We will see if other GC vehicles are coming."

"Why are they speeding around without lights?"

"We have no idea," Laslos said.

———————

Buck couldn't remember the name of the place, but it was one spot he and Chaim had been to together where no one would expect to see either of them. It took an hour to find an empty cab, and he was informed that any ride, regardless of distance, would cost one hundred Nicks.

Buck described the place to the driver and told him the general area. The man nodded slowly, as if it was coming to him. "I think I know place, or some like it. All work same when you want get, how do the Westerners say, medicated."

"That's what I want," Buck said. "But I have to find the right place."

"We try," the driver said. "Many closed, but some still open."

They rolled over curbs, around crumbled buildings, through dark traffic lights, and past accident scenes. The cabbie stopped at two bars that seemed to be doing land office business, considering, but Buck recognized neither. "It's about the same size as this one, big neon sign in the window, narrow door. That's all I remember."

"I know place," the man said. "Closed. Want these, or other place?"

"I want the other one. Take me there."

"I know is closed. Closed weeks." He held up both hands as if Buck didn't understand. "Nobody there. Dark. Bye-bye."

"That's where I want to go," Buck said.

"Why you want to go where is closed?"

"I'm meeting someone."

"She won't be at closed place," he said, but he drove off anyway. "See?" he said, slowing at midblock nearby. "Is closed."

Buck paid him and hung around the street until the cab left, the driver shaking his head. He soon realized he was in sheer darkness, trees blotting out the clouds and far enough from the emergency action that no lights were visible. The cab lights had shown that the earthquake had leveled several buildings on the street. It was clear now that the power was out in the area.

Would Chaim have come here? *Could* he have? They

had come here looking for Jacov the night he had become a believer, Chaim convinced he would be at his favorite bar, drunk as usual. They had found him there all right, and most assumed he *was* drunk. He was on a tabletop, preaching to his old friends and drinking buddies.

Buck was fast losing faith. If Chaim was alive, if he had been able to find someone to cart him around, how long would he have stayed on a deserted, dark, destroyed street? And was there really any hope that they might both have thought of this obscure establishment?

Buck pulled the flashlight from his pocket and looked around before it occurred to him that Chaim would not likely be in sight, at least until he was certain that it was Buck with the light. And how would Chaim know that? Buck stood in front of the closed bar and shined the light on his own face. Almost immediately he heard a rustle in the branch of a tree across the street and the clearing of a throat.

He quickly aimed the beam at the tree, prepared to retreat. Incongruously hanging out from under one of the leafy branches was a pajama leg, completed by a stockinged and slippered foot. Buck kept the faint beam on the bewildering scene, but as he moved slowly across the street, the foot lifted out of sight. The lower branch bent with the weight of the tree dweller, and suddenly down he came, agile as a cat. Standing there before Buck in slippers, socks, pajamas, and robe was a most robust Chaim Rosenzweig.

"Cameron, Cameron," he said, his voice strong and

clear. "This is almost enough to make a believer out of me. I knew you'd come."

———————

Another unlit GC vehicle raced past while Rayford lay in the dirt. All he could think of was the Prodigal Son, realizing what he had left and eager to get back to his father.

When the predawn grew quiet again, Rayford forsook caution and dashed for the underbrush. He was filthy and tried to brush himself off. Laslos and his pastor had to have seen the other GC vehicle and were playing it safe. Forty minutes later—which seemed like forever to Rayford—a small white four-door slid to a stop in the gravel. Rayford hesitated. Why had they not called? He looked at his phone. He had shut it off, and apparently the battery was too low to power the wake-up feature.

The back door opened. Laslos called, "Mr. Berry!" and Rayford ran toward the car. As soon as the door was shut, Laslos spun a U-turn and headed south. "I don't know where the GC is going, but I'll go the other way for now. Demetrius has a friend in the country nearby."

"A brother?"

"Of course."

"Demetrius?" Rayford said, extending his hand to the passenger. "Rayford Steele. Call me Ray."

The younger man had a fierce grip and pulled Rayford until he could reach to embrace him. "Demetrius Demeter," he said. "Call me Demetrius or brother."

Tsion was moved and took comfort in the verse that reminded him that during this period of cosmic history, God would pour out his Spirit and that "your sons and your daughters shall prophesy, your old men shall dream dreams, your young men shall see visions." The question was whether he was an old man or a young man. He decided on the former and attributed what he had felt on the floor to his drowsiness. He had apparently lost consciousness while praying and nearly slipped into a dream. If the dream was from God, he prayed he would return to it. If it was merely some sleep-deprived fancy, Tsion prayed he would have the discernment to know that too.

That the passage had gone on to reference the heavenly wonders and blood, fire, and smoke the world had already experienced also warmed Tsion. He had been an eyewitness when the sun had been turned into darkness and the moon into blood. He read the passage to Chloe and reminded her, "This is 'before the coming of the great and awesome day of the Lord.' I believe that refers to the second half of the Tribulation, the Great Tribulation. Which starts now."

Chloe looked at him expectantly. "Uh-huh, but—"

"Oh, dear one, the best is yet to come. I don't believe it was coincidence that the Lord led me to this passage. Think of your father and our compatriots overseas when you hear this: 'And it shall come to pass that whoever calls on the name of the Lord shall be saved. For in Mount Zion and in Jerusalem there shall be deliverance, as the Lord has said, among the remnant whom the Lord calls.' You know who the remnant is, don't you, Chloe?"

"The Jews?"

"Yes! And in Zion, which is Israel, and Jerusalem, where we know some of our own were, if they call upon the Lord, they will be delivered. Chloe, I don't know how many of us or *if* any of us will survive until the Glorious Appearing. But I am claiming the promise of this passage, because God prompted me to find it, that our beloved will all return safely to us this time."

"In spite of everything?"

"In spite of everything."

"Is there anything in there that says when the phones will start working again?"

Leah Rose had landed in Baltimore and pondered her next moves. Finding Hattie Durham in North America was like pawing through the proverbial haystack for a needle someone else had already found. The GC was on Hattie's trail and clearly hoped she would lead them to the lair of the Judah-ites.

If Leah could get her phone to work, she would call T at Palwaukee and see if that Super J plane she had heard so much about was still at the airport and ready for use. On the other hand, if she could get through to T, she could have gotten through to the safe house and sent them running. Did she dare fly commercially to Illinois and rent a car under her alias?

She had no other choice. Unable to communicate except locally, her only hope was to beat Hattie to Mount Prospect. Finding the woman and persuading her to mislead the GC was just too much to hope for.

"How close can you get me to Gary, Indiana?" Leah asked at the counter, after waiting nearly a half hour for the one airline clerk.

"Hammond is the best I can do. And that would be very late tonight."

Having misled the young man about her destination, she switched gears. "How about Chicago? O'Hare and Meigs still closed?"

"And Midway," the clerk said. "Kankakee any help?"

"Perfect," she said. "When?"

"If we're lucky, you'll be on the ground by midnight."

"If we're lucky," Leah said, "that'll mean the plane landed and didn't crash."

The man did not smile. And Leah remembered: *We don't do luck.*

———

David lay in bed with his laptop, knowing he would soon nod off, but perusing again the abandoned buildings and areas in northern Illinois that might provide a new safe house for the stateside Trib Force. The whole of downtown Chicago had been cordoned off, mostly bombed out, and evacuated. It was a ghost town, nothing living within forty miles. David rolled up onto his elbows and studied the list. How had that happened?

Hadn't the earliest reports said the attack on Illinois had been everything but nuclear?

He searched archives, finally pinpointing the day when the GC ruled the city and surrounding areas uninhabitable. Dozens had died from what looked and acted like radiation poisoning, and the Centers for Disease Control and Prevention in Atlanta had urged the ruling. Bodies lay decaying in the streets as the living cleared out.

Remote probes were dropped into the region to test radiation levels, but their inconclusive reports were attributed to faulty equipment. Soon no one dared go near the place. Some radical journalists, Buck Williams wanna-bes, averred on the Internet that the abandoning of Chicago was the biggest foul-up in history, that the deadly diseases were not a result of nuclear radiation, and that the place was inhabitable. *What if?* David wondered.

He followed the cybertrails until he was studying the radiation probe results. Hundreds had been attempted. Not one had registered radiation. But once the scare snare was set, the hook had sunk deep. Who would risk being wrong on a matter like that?

I might, David thought. *With a little more research.*

He had just studied the skyline of Chicago and become intrigued by the skyscraper that had been built by the late Thomas Strong, who had made his fortune in insurance. The place was a mere five years old, a magnificent eighty-story tower that had housed Strong's entire international headquarters. Pictures of the aftermath of the bombing showed the top twenty-six stories of the structure twisting grotesquely away from the rest of the building. The story-high red letters STRONG had slid on an angle and were still visible during the daytime, making the place look like a stubborn tree trunk that refused to cave in to the storms that leveled most of the rest of the city.

David was about to hack into the blueprints and other records that might show if any of the rest of the structure had been left with any integrity when his laptop beeped, announcing a news bulletin from Global Community headquarters.

His eyes were dancing as it was, so he bookmarked where he had been and determined to go to sleep after checking the bulletin. It read:

"A spokesman for Global Community Supreme Commander Leon Fortunato in New Babylon has just announced that satellite communications have been restored. He asks that citizens employ restraint so as not to overload the system and to limit themselves to only emergency calls for the next twelve hours.

"The spokesman also has announced the decision, reportedly made by Fortunato alone, to rename the United Holy Land States. The new name of the region shall be the United Carpathian States, in honor of the slain leader. Fortunato has not announced a successor to his own role as potentate of the region, but such a move is expected under the likelihood that the Supreme Commander be drafted into service as the new Global Community potentate."

David wondered why he had been asked to interfere with telephone capability and someone else had been asked to reverse it.

SIX

RAYFORD fought to stay awake in the warm backseat of Laslos's small car. Pastor Demetrius Demeter pointed the way to the rustic cabin in the woods, some twenty kilometers south of Kozani. Laslos avoided any talk of Rayford's guilt or innocence but took it upon himself to cheerfully bring Rayford up to date on the growth of the underground church in northern Greece.

Rayford apologized when a snore woke him.

"Don't give it another thought, brother," Laslos told him. "You need your rest, regardless of what you decide."

Suddenly the car was off the highway and onto an unpaved road. "You can imagine what a great getaway is this cottage," Demetrius said. "The day will come when we, or it, will be found out, and it will be lost to us."

Rayford had gotten only a brief glimpse of the young

man when the car door was open. Thin and willowy, it appeared he might be as tall as Rayford. He would have guessed Pastor Demeter at about thirty, with a thick shock of dark hair, deep olive skin, and shining black eyes. He was articulate in English with a heavy Greek accent.

The cottage was so remote that one either came there on purpose or found it while hopelessly lost. Laslos parked in the back where they also entered, using a key Demetrius pulled from under a board near the door. He grabbed Rayford's bag from the car, over his protests. "There's nothing I need from there until I get back home, thanks," Rayford said.

"You must spend at least one night here, sir," Demetrius said.

"Oh, imposs—"

"You look so tired! And you have to be!"

"But I must get back. The stateside people need the plane, and I need them."

Laslos and Demetrius wore heavy sweaters under thick jackets, but Rayford didn't warm up until Laslos had a fire roaring. Laslos then busied himself in the kitchen, from which Rayford soon smelled strong tea and looked forward to it as he would have a desert spring.

Meanwhile, in a small, woodsy room illuminated only by the fire, Rayford sat in a deep, ancient chair that seemed to envelop him. The young pastor sat across from him, half his face in the dancing light, the other half disappearing into the darkness.

"We were praying for you, Mr. Steele, at the very

moment you called Lukas's wife. We thought you might need asylum. Forgive my impudence, sir, as you are clearly my elder—"

"Is it that obvious?"

Demetrius seemed to allow himself only the briefest polite smile. "I would love to have you tell me all about Tsion Ben-Judah, but we don't have time for socializing. You may stay here as long as you wish, but I also want to offer you my services."

"Your services?" Rayford was taken aback, but he couldn't shake the feeling that he and Demetrius had immediately connected.

"At the risk of sounding forward or self-possessed," Demetrius said, intertwining his fingers in his lap, "God has blessed and gifted me. My superiors tell me this is not unusual for those of us who are likely part of the 144,000. I have loved the Scriptures since long before I was aware that Jesus fit all the prophecies of the Coming One. It seemed all my energies were invested in learning the things of God. I had been merely bemused by the idea that the Gentiles, specifically Christians, thought they had a corner on our theology. Then the Rapture occurred, and I was not only forced to study Jesus in a different light, but I was also irresistibly drawn to him."

Pastor Demeter shifted in his chair and turned to gaze at the fire. The fatigue that had racked Rayford, which he now realized would force him to at least nap before trying to return to the States, seemed a nuisance he would deal with later. Demetrius seemed so earnest, so genuine, that Rayford had to hear him out. Laslos came in with steaming mugs of tea, then returned to the kitchen to sit with his, though both men invited him to stay. It was as if he knew Rayford needed this time alone with the man of God.

"My primary gift is evangelism," Demetrius said. "I say that without ego, for when I use the word *gift,* I mean just that. My gift before becoming a believer was probably sarcasm or condescension or pride in intellect. I realize now, of course, that the intellect was also a gift, a gift I did not know how to exercise to its fullest until I had a reason."

Rayford was grateful he could just sit and listen for a while, but he was also amazed he was able to stay awake. The fire, the chair, the situation, the hour, the week he had had all conspired to leave him in a ball of unconsciousness. But unlike in the car, he was not even aware of the temptation to nod off.

"What we who have been called find fascinating," Demetrius continued, "is that God has seemed to stream-line everything now. I'm sure you've found this in your own life. For me the sense of adventure in learning of God was magnified so that my every waking moment was happily spent studying his Word. And when I was then thrust into a place of service, giftings that might have taken decades to develop before were now bestowed as if overnight. I had had my nose in the Scrip-tures and commentaries for so long, there was no way I could have honed the skills the Lord seemed to pour out upon me. And I have found this true of my colleagues as well. None of us dare take an iota of credit, because these are clearly gifts from God. We can do nothing less than gleefully exercise them."

"Such as?" Rayford said.

"Primarily evangelism, as I said. It seems most everyone we talk with personally is persuaded that Jesus is the Christ. And under our preaching, thousands have come to faith. I trust you understand I say this solely to give glory to Jehovah God."

Rayford quickly waved him off. "Of course."

"We have also been given unusual teaching and pastoring skills. It is as if God has given us the Midas touch, and not just us Greeks."

Rayford was lost in thought and nearly missed the humor. He just wanted to hear more.

"But most fascinating to me, Mr. Steele, is a helpful, useful gift I would not have thought to ask for, let alone imagine was either necessary or available. It is discernment, not to be confused with a gift of knowledge—something I have witnessed in some colleagues but do not have myself. Frankly, I am not envious. The specific things God tells them about the people under their charge would weigh on me and wear me down. But discernment . . . now, that has proven most helpful to me and to those I counsel."

"I'm not sure I follow."

Demetrius leaned forward and set his mug on the floor. He rested elbows on knees and stared into Rayford's face. "I don't want to alarm you or make you think this is some kind of a parlor trick. I am not guessing, and I am not claiming that any of this is a skill I have honed or mastered. God has merely given me the ability to discern the needs of people and the extent of their sincerity in facing up to them."

Rayford felt as if the man could look right through him, and he was tempted to ask questions no one could answer unless God told them. But this was no game.

"I can tell you, without fear of contradiction, that you are a man who at this very moment is broken before God. Despite the news, I have no idea whether you shot Nicolae Carpathia or tried to. I don't know if you were there or had the weapon in question or if the Global Community is framing you because they know your allegiances. But I discern your brokenness, and it is because you have sinned."

Rayford nodded, deeply moved, unable to speak.

"We are all sinners, of course, battling our old natures every day. But yours was a sin of pride and selfishness. It was not a sin of omission but of willful commission. It was not a onetime occurrence but a pattern of behavior, of rebellion. It was an attitude that resulted in actions you regret, actions you acknowledge as sin, practices you have confessed to God and have repented of."

Rayford's jaw was tight, his neck stiff. He could not even nod.

"I am not here to chastise you or to test you to see if what I discern is correct, because in these last days God has poured out his gifts and eliminated the need for patience with us frail humans. In essence, he has forsaken requiring desert experiences for us and simply works through us to do his will.

"I sense a need to tell you that your deep feelings of having returned to him are accurate. He would have you not wallow in regret but rejoice in his forgiveness. He wants you to know and believe beyond doubt that your sins and iniquities he will remember no more. He has separated you from the guilt of your sins as far as the east is from the west. Go and sin no more. Go and do his bidding in the short season left to you."

As if knowing what was coming, Demetrius reached for Rayford's cup, allowing Rayford to leave the comfort of his chair and kneel on the wood floor. Great sobs burst from him, and he sensed he was in the presence of God, as he had been in the plane when it seemed the Lord had finally gotten his attention. But to add this gift of forgiveness, expressed by a chosen agent, was beyond what Rayford could have dreamed for.

Fear melted away. Fatigue was put in abeyance. Unrest about the future, about his role, about what to do—all gone. "Thank you, God" was all he could say, and he said it over and over.

When finally he rose, Rayford turned to embrace a man who an hour before had been a stranger and now seemed a messenger of God. He might never see him again, but he felt a kinship that could only be explained by God.

Lukas still waited in the tiny kitchen as Rayford spilled to Demetrius the whole story of how his anger had blossomed into a murderous rage that took him to the brink of murder and may have even given him a hand in it.

Demetrius nodded and seemed to shift and treat

Rayford as a colleague rather than a parishioner. "And what is God telling you to do now?"

"Rest and go," Rayford said, feeling rightly decisive for the first time in months. For once he didn't feel the need to talk himself into decisions and then continue to sell himself on them, carefully avoiding seeking God's will. "I need to sleep until dawn and then get back in the game. As soon as I can get through by phone, I need to be sure Buck and Leah are safe and go get them, if necessary."

Laslos joined them and said, "Give me that information. I will stand watch until dawn, and I can try the phones every half hour while you are sleeping."

Demetrius interrupted Rayford's thanks by pointing him to a thick fabric couch and a scratchy blanket. "It is all we have to offer," he said. "Kick your shoes off and get out of that shirt."

When Rayford sat on the couch in only undershirt and trousers, Demetrius motioned that he should lie down. The pastor covered him with the blanket and prayed, "Father, we need a physical miracle. Give this man a double portion of rest for the hours available, and may this meager bed be transformed into a healing agent."

Without so much as a pillow, Rayford felt himself drifting from consciousness. He was warm, the couch was soft but supportive, the stiff blanket like a downy comforter. As his breathing became rhythmic and deep, his last conscious thought was different from what it had been for so long. Rather than the dread fear that came with life as an international fugitive, he rested in the knowledge that he was a child of the King, a saved, forgiven, precious, beloved son safe in the hollow of his Father's hand.

―――――――――

Buck and Chaim sat in an abandoned, earthquake-ravaged dwelling in the middle of a formerly happening Israeli neighborhood where crowded bars and nightclubs once rocked till dawn. With no power or water or even shelter safe enough for vagrants, the area now hosted only an enterprising journalist and a national hero.

"Please douse that light, Cameron," Chaim said.

"Who will see us?"

"No one, but it's irritating. I've had a long day."

"I imagine you have," Buck said. "But I want to see this walking, breathing miracle. You look healthier than I've ever seen you."

They sat on a crumbling concrete wall with remnants of a shattered beam protruding from it. Buck didn't know how the old man felt, but he himself had to keep moving for a modicum of comfort.

"I am the healthiest I have been in years," Chaim exulted, his accent thick as ever. "I have been working out every day."

"While your house staff feared you were near death."

"If they only knew what I was doing in my workshop before dawn."

"I think I know, Chaim."

"Thinking and knowing are different things. Had you looked deep into the closet, you would have seen the ancient stationary bicycle and the dumbbells that put me in the fighting trim I am in today. I laboriously moved my chair through the house so they could hear the whine of it if they happened to be up that early. Then I locked myself in there for at least ninety minutes. Jumping jacks and push-ups to warm up, the dumbbells for toning, the bike for a hard workout. Then it was back inside the blanket, into the chair, and back to my quarters for a shower. They thought I was remarkably self-reliant for an old man suffering from a debilitating stroke."

Buck was not amused when Chaim stiffened his arm, turned one side of his mouth down, and faked impaired speech with guttural rasping.

"I fooled even you, did I not?"

"Even me," Buck said, looking away.

"Are you offended?"

"Of course I am. Why would you feel the need to do that to your staff and to me?"

"Oh, Cameron, I could not involve you in my scheme."

"I'm involved, Chaim. I saw what killed Carpathia."

"Oh, you did, did you? Well, I didn't. All that commotion, that trauma. I couldn't move. I heard the gunshot, saw the man fall, the lectern shatter, the backdrop sail away. I froze with fear, unable to propel my chair. My back was to the disturbance, and no one was coming to my aid. I shall have to chastise Jacov for his failure to do his duty. I was counting on him to come to me. My other clothes were in the back of the van, and I had a reservation at a small inn under an alias. We can still use it if you can get me there."

"In your pajamas?"

"I have a blanket in the tree. I wrapped it around myself, even my head, as I ran to the taxis. I had not expected to have to do that, Cameron, but I was prepared for all exigencies."

"Not all."

"What are you saying?"

"I'll try to get you to your hotel, Chaim, and I may even have to hide out there with you myself for a while. But I have bad news that I will tell you only when we are there. And only after you tell me everything about what happened on the platform."

Chaim stood and reached for the flashlight, using it to find his way to a man-size hole in the wall. He leaned against the opening and switched off the light.

"I will never tell anyone what happened," he said. "I am in this alone."

"I didn't see it happen, Chaim, but I saw the wound and what caused it. You know I couldn't have been the only one."

Chaim sighed wearily. "The eye is not trustworthy, my young friend. You don't know what you saw. You can't tell me how far away you were or how what you saw fits into the whole picture. The gunshot was a surprise to me. That your comrade was even there was also a shock, and him as a suspect now!"

"I find none of this amusing, Chaim, and soon enough you won't either."

Buck heard the old man settle to the ground. "I did not expect that much chaos. I hoped, of course. That was my only chance of getting away from there with everyone else. When Jacov did not arrive—because of the panic caused by the gunshot, I assume—I leaned on that control stick and headed for the back of the platform, clutching my blanket like a cape. I rolled out of the chair at the last instant, and it went flying. I wish it had landed on one of the regional potentates, who were by then limping away. I tossed my blanket over the side, then rolled onto my belly and threw my feet over, locking them around the support beam. I shinnied down that structure like a youngster, Cameron, and I won't even try to hide my pride. I have scrapes on my inner thighs that may take some time to heal, but it was worth it."

"Was it?"

"It was, Cameron. It was. Fooling so many, including my own staff. Doctors, nurses, aides. Well, actually, I didn't fool every aide. As Jacov and a young nurse's aide were lifting me into the van after my last visit to the hospital, she stalled, locking my wheels and straightening my blanket while Jacov went to get behind the wheel. Just before she closed the door, she leaned close and whispered, 'I don't know who you are or what your game is, old man. But you might want to remember which side was affected when you came in here.'"

Chaim chuckled, which Buck found astounding under the circumstances. "I just hope she was telling the truth, Cameron, that she didn't know who I was. Celebrity is my curse, but some of the younger ones, they don't pay so much attention. I looked desperately at her as she shut the door, hoping she would wonder if it were she who had forgotten. I stayed in character, but if my face flushed it was from embarrassment and not frustration over my lack of ability to speak or walk. She was right! I had stiffened my right arm and curled my right hand under! What an old fool!"

"You took the words right out of my mouth, Chaim. Get your blanket, and let's find a cab."

Without a word, Chaim switched on the flashlight, hurried to the tree, tossed the light back to Buck, and leaped, grabbing the low branch and pulling himself up far enough to grab the blanket. He wrapped it around his head and over his shoulder, then affected a limp and leaned on Buck, chuckling again.

Buck moved away from him. "Don't start that until you need to," Buck said.

Leah Rose awoke with a start and looked out the window. Cities were rarely illuminated in the night anymore, so she had no idea where she was. She tried looking at her watch, but couldn't focus. Something had awakened her, and suddenly she heard it again. Her phone. Could it be?

The one lone flight attendant and the rest of the dozen or so passengers seemed asleep. Leah dug in her bag for the phone and pressed the caller ID button. She didn't recognize the number, but her comrades had assured her the phone was secure. She would not jeopardize them if she answered, even if her number had fallen into the wrong hands.

Leah opened the phone and tucked her head behind the back of the seat in front of her. She spoke softly but directly. "This is Donna Clendenon."

A brief silence alarmed her. She heard a male inhale. "I'm sorry," he began with a Greek accent. "I am calling on behalf of, ah, Mr. Marvin Berry?"

"Yes! Is this Mr. Miklos?"

"Yes!"

"And are you calling from Greece?"

"I am. And Mr. Steele is here. And what is it that those filled with demons cannot say?"

Leah smiled in spite of herself. "Jesus is the Christ, the Messiah, and he will return in the flesh."

"Amen! Rayford is sleeping but needs to know you are safe and how to find y—"

"I'm sorry, Mr. Miklos, but if the phones are working, I have an emergency call to make. Just tell Rayford that I am nearly home so not to worry about me, but that he needs to locate Buck."

———

Tsion experimented with five-minute catnaps every few minutes, fearing he would otherwise sleep through the resurrection of the Antichrist. With Chloe and the baby asleep elsewhere in the safe house, the experiment was not working well. He found himself popping awake every fifteen or twenty minutes, desperate to be sure he had missed nothing. There had been no repeat of his dreamlike state while praying for Rayford, and he began to wonder if it had been more related to praying than sleeping. He also began to wonder how long Carpathia was supposed to remain dead. Was it possible he had been wrong all along? Was someone else the Antichrist, yet to be murdered and resurrected?

Tsion couldn't imagine it. Many sincere believers had questioned his teaching that Antichrist would actually die from a wound to the head. Some said the Scriptures indicated that it would be merely a wound that made him appear dead. He tried to assure them that his best interpretation of the original Greek led him to believe that the man would actually die and then be indwelt by Satan himself upon coming back to life.

Given that, he hoped he had been right about Carpathia. There would be no doubt of the death and resurrection if the body had begun to decay, was autopsied, embalmed, and prepared to lie in state. If Carpathia were dead even close to twenty-four hours, few could charge him with faking his demise. Too many eyewitnesses had seen the man expire, and though the cause of death had not yet been announced, that was forthcoming. The world, including Tsion, had to believe the gunshot provided the kill.

The TV carried yet another airing of an earlier pronouncement of grief and promised vengeance from Leon Fortunato. Tsion found himself nodding and dozing until the phone woke him.

"Leah! It's so good to hear your voice. We have been unable to reach—"

She interrupted and filled him in on Hattie and the danger posed to the safe house. Tsion stood and began pacing as he listened. "We have nowhere else to go, Leah," he said. "But at the very least we had better get underground."

They agreed that she would call if she got near the safe house and was sure no one was casing the place. Otherwise, Leah would keep her distance and try to find Hattie. How, she said, she had no idea.

Despite his weariness, Tsion was suddenly energized. He was responsible for Chloe and Kenny, and though the macho stuff was usually left to Rayford or Buck, he had to act. He trotted up the stairs and grabbed a few clothes from his closet and a stack of books. He returned to the first floor and piled these near the old chest freezer that stood next to the refrigerator.

Tsion added his laptop and the TV to the pile, then outed every light in the place except the single bulb hanging from the ceiling in the hall bath. He carefully pushed open the door to Buck and Chloe's bedroom, knocking softly. He did not hear Chloe stir, and he could not see her in the darkness. He knocked again and whispered her name.

When he heard a quick motion from the crib on the far wall, Tsion fell silent, holding his breath. He had hoped not to wake the baby. Clearly, Kenny was pulling himself up to stand. The crib rocked, and Tsion imagined the little guy with his hands on the railing, rocking, making the crib squeak. "Mowning! Ga'mowning, Mama!"

"It's not morning, Kenny," he whispered.

"Unca Zone!" Kenny squealed, rocking vigorously.

And with that, Chloe awoke with a start.

"It's just me, dear," Tsion said quickly.

Twenty minutes later the three of them were relocated underground, having lifted aside the rack of smelly, spoiled food in the freezer that led to the stairs. Kenny, beaming from his playpen, had loved seeing his mother and Tsion reappear downstairs every few minutes with more stuff. He was not so happy when they muscled his crib down there and he had to make the switch.

Fortunately the underground was large enough that Tsion could set up the TV in a spot where the light and sound did not reach Chloe and Kenny's sleeping quarters. He monitored the doings from New Babylon, but every time he had need to venture into the other part of the shelter, he heard Chloe groggily trying to talk Kenny into going back to sleep.

He poked his head through the curtain. "How about he watches TV with me until he falls asleep again, hmm?"

"Oh, Tsion, that would be wonderful."

"Unca Zone!"

"TV?" Tsion said as he lifted the boy from the crib.

Kenny kicked and laughed. "TV, Unca Zone! Video!"

"We'll watch my show," Tsion whispered as he carried him to his chair.

"You show!" Kenny said, holding Tsion's face in his

hands. Tsion was transported to when his teenagers had been toddlers and sat in his lap as he read or watched television. Kenny was quickly bored with the repetitious news, but he quit asking for a video and concentrated on tracing the contours of Tsion's ears, squeezing his nose, and rubbing his palm back and forth on Tsion's stubble. Eventually he began to blink slowly, tucked a thumb in his mouth, and turned to settle into the crook of Tsion's elbow. When his head lolled over, Tsion gently carried him back to bed.

As he tucked a blanket around Kenny he heard Chloe turn and whisper, "Thank you, Unca Zone."

"Thank you," he said.

"Why didn't you just go straight to the hotel?" Buck asked Chaim as he tried to flag down a cab.

"I was lucky enough the cabbie didn't recognize me. How was I going to fool a desk clerk? I was counting on Jacov to get me in. Now I'm counting on you. Anyway, how would we have found each other?"

"How *did* we find each other?" Buck said.

"I couldn't think of any other place you might look, except at my home, and I didn't expect you to risk that. I don't think anybody is there anyway. I haven't been able to raise anybody."

Buck was struck by that unfortunate choice of words.

"They're there, Chaim."

"You *did* go there? Why don't they answer? Did Jacov make it back? I expected he would call me."

Buck spotted a cab sitting a couple of blocks off a busy thoroughfare. Grateful he didn't have to answer Chaim directly yet, he said, "Wait here, and keep that blanket over your face."

"You workin'?" he asked the cabbie.

"Hundred and fifty Nicks, only in the city."

"A hundred, and my father is contagious."

"No contagious."

"OK, a hundred and fifty. We're only going to the Night Visitors. You know it?"

"I know. You keep old man in back, and don't breathe on me."

Buck signaled to Chaim, who shuffled over, hidden in the blanket. "Don't try to talk, Father," he said, helping him into the backseat. "And don't cough on this nice young man."

As if on cue, Chaim covered his mouth with the blanket and both hands and produced a juicy, wheezing cough that made the driver look quickly into the rearview mirror.

The Night Visitors was dark, not even an outside light on. "Are they closed?" Buck said.

"Only for now," the driver said. "Probably open again at dawn. One-fifty. I gotta go."

"Wait until I see if I can rouse anybody," Buck said, getting out.

"Don't leave him in here! I gotta go. Money now!"

"You'll get your money when we get a room."

The driver slammed the car into Park and turned it off, folding his arms across his chest.

S E V E N

BUCK'S phone rang as he was trying to peer through the front window of the Night Visitors. "Laslos!" he said, stepping around the corner of the building and into the shadows. The cabbie honked, and Buck signaled him to wait a minute.

"Get this man out of my cab!"

"Five minutes!" Buck said.

"Fifty more Nicks!"

"He's there with you, Lukas?" Buck said. "How am I supposed to—does he know he's wanted here—he does? . . . Is Leah with him? . . . Oh, that's good. We need a way out of here, and there's no way he can risk coming back. Never mind. I'll handle that. Listen, does he have to see anyone before he takes off? . . . You can't be sure airport personnel won't be on alert. His face is on international TV every few minutes. Do you know anyone who can give him a new look? . . . He'll need new papers too. Thanks, Laslos! I have to call my wife."

Buck dialed Chloe, but her phone rang and rang.

When he returned to the cab, the driver was out and screaming. "Now! Go! No more this man in my car!"

Buck paid him and helped Chaim out, pushing him into an alley while he banged on the windows and door and tried to rouse the manager.

Tsion heard something upstairs and ran to the utility box to shut down the power. If the GC searched the place, it would be clear someone had been living there recently, as food in the refrigerator would still be fresh and lots of personal belongings remained. But if they found power meters still spinning, they would know someone was still there somewhere.

Tsion held his breath in the darkness. It was a phone! Had Chloe forgotten to bring hers down? He rushed to the stairs, pushed the plywood away from the bottom of the freezer, pushed up the smelly rack, and lifted himself out. He felt his way to Chloe's room and followed the sound to her phone. Just as he reached it, it stopped ringing. The caller ID showed Buck's code. Tsion hit the callback button, but Buck's phone was busy.

While continuing to bang with one hand, Buck speed-dialed David Hassid with the other. He got only David's machine. When he hung up, his call button was illuminated. His caller ID showed he had received a call from Chloe's phone. He was about to call her back when a light came on in the Night Visitors, followed by slamming, stomping, and cursing.

"We have a reservation!" Buck shouted.

"You'll have a bullet if you don't shut up!" came the voice from inside. "We closed at midnight and we open again at six!"

"You're up now, so give us our room!"

"You lost your room when you didn't show up! Who are you, Tangvald or Goldman?"

Buck whispered desperately to Chaim, "Who are we?"

"Do I look like a Tangvald?"

"Goldman, and my father is sick. Let us in!"

"We're full!"

"You're lying! You held two rooms till you went to bed and then gave them both away?"

"Leave me alone!"

"I'll knock until you let us in!"

"I'll shoot you if you knock once more!"

The light went out. Buck put his phone in his pocket and banged on the door with both fists.

"You're a dead man!"

"Just open up and give us a room!"

More swearing, then the light, then the door opened an inch. The man stuck his fingers out. "Five hundred Nicks cash."

"Let me see the key."

The man dangled it at the end of a six-inch block of

wood. Buck produced the cash, and the key came flying out. "Around back, third floor. If I didn't need the money, I'd have shot you."

"You're welcome," Buck said.

The room was a hole. A single bed, one straight-back chair, and a toilet and sink. Buck pulled out his phone and sat in the chair, pointing Chaim to the bed. As Buck tried Chloe's phone, Chaim kicked off his slippers and stretched out on the bed, atop the ratty spread and under his own blanket.

"Tsion!" Buck said. "No, don't wake her. . . . Underground? That's probably good for now. Just tell her I'm all right. I need to get hold of T. May need him to get Chaim and me out of here. . . ."

"I'm not going anywhere," Chaim mumbled from the bed. "I'm a dead man."

"Yeah," Buck said to Tsion, "just like you and me. . . . Kenny OK? . . . We'll keep in touch."

Buck couldn't get an answer at Palwaukee Airport or on T's cell phone. He put his phone away and took a deep breath, kicking his bag under the chair. "Chaim, we have to talk," he said. But Chaim was asleep.

———

Rayford awoke with a start just after dawn, feeling refreshed. He grabbed his bag and padded past a dozing Demetrius to the bathroom, smelling breakfast from the kitchen. While in the tiny bathroom, however, he heard tires on the gravel and pulled the curtain back an inch. A small pickup pulled into view.

Rayford leaned out the door and called to Laslos. "Company," he whispered. "You expecting anyone?"

"It's all right," Laslos said, setting a pan of food on the table and wiping his hands on an apron. "Get a shower and join us for breakfast as soon as you can."

Rayford tried to run hot water in the sink. It was lukewarm. Laslos interrupted with a knock. "Don't shave, Mr. Steele."

"Oh, Laslos, I really need to. I've got several days of growth and—"

"I'll explain later. But don't."

Rayford shrugged and squinted at himself in the mirror. He was due for a haircut, more and more gray appearing at his temples and in the back. His beard was salt-and-pepper, which alarmed him. Not that he cared so much about gray in his mid-forties. It was just that it had seemed to happen almost overnight. Until this morning, he had felt every one of his forty-plus years. Now he felt great.

The shower, a trickle from a rusty pipe, was also lukewarm. It made him hurry, but by the time he scrubbed himself dry with a small, thin towel and dressed, he was ravenous. And curious. He emerged eager to get going, but also intrigued by yet another guest at the table, a pudgy man a few years older than he with slick, curly black hair and wire-rimmed glasses.

Rayford leaned past Laslos and Demetrius and shook the man's hand. The mark of the believer was on his forehead, so Rayford used his own name.

The man looked at Laslos and shyly back at Rayford.

"This is Adon, Mr. Steele," Laslos said. "He speaks no English, but as you can see, he is a brother."

As they ate, Laslos told Rayford about Adon. "He is an artist, a skilled craftsman. And he has brought with him contraband items that could get him locked away for the rest of his life."

Adon followed the conversation with blank eyes, except when Laslos or Demetrius broke in to translate. Then he shyly looked away, nodding.

As Laslos cleared the table, Demetrius helped Adon bring in his equipment, which included a computer, printer, laminator, digital camera, dyes, hair clippers, even a cloth backdrop. Rayford was positioned in a chair under the light and near the window, where the early sun shone in. Adon draped a sheet around him and pinned it behind his neck. He said something to Laslos, who translated for Rayford.

"He wants to know if it is OK to make you bald."

"If you all think it's necessary. If we could get by with very short, I'd appreciate it."

Laslos informed Adon, whose shyness and hesitance apparently did not extend to his barbering. In a few swipes, he left Rayford's hair in clumps on the floor, leaving him with a quarter inch of dark residue such as Rayford had not seen since high school. "Mm-hmm," Rayford said.

Then came the dye that made what was left of the hair on his head look like the lightest of the gray in the long stubble on his chin.

Adon spoke to Laslos, who asked Rayford if he wore glasses.

"Contacts," Rayford said.

"Not anymore," Laslos said, and Adon produced a pair that completed the look.

Adon asked for Rayford's documents, shot a few pictures, and got to work on the computer. While he transformed Rayford's papers with the new photograph, Rayford stole away to the bathroom for a peek. The shorter, grayer hair and the gray stubble added ten years. In the glasses, he hardly recognized himself.

The technology allowed Adon to produce old-looking new documents in less than an hour. Rayford was eager to get going. "What do I owe you?" he said, but neither Laslos nor Demetrius would translate that.

"We'll be sure Adon is taken care of," Laslos said. "Now, Pastor is going to ride back to Ptolemaïs with him, and I will drop you at Kozani. I called ahead to have your fuel tanks topped off."

David sat bleary-eyed before his computer in New Babylon, his phone turned off. He had programmed the autopsy to be recorded on his own hard drive and anything from the evidence room to go onto Mac's computer. Meanwhile he continued to study the Chicago skyscraper he felt had potential as a new safe house. If he was right, it could accommodate hundreds of exiles, if necessary.

The Strong Building was a technical marvel, wholly solar powered. Giant reflectors stored enough energy every day to run the tower's power plant for weeks. So even a several-day stretch without bright sunlight never negatively impacted the building.

It was clear to David that neither the foundation nor at least the first thirty-five or so stories had been compromised by the damage above. The building appeared to have suffered a direct hit, but the impact had knocked the top half of the floors away from the rest of the structure rather than sending them crashing through those below. The question was what had happened to the solar panels and whether there was any way people could live in the unaffected portion of the structure without being detected.

It took David more than two hours of hacking through a morass of classified layers of information before he was able to turn his code-breaking software loose on the gateways that led to the mainframe that controlled the Strong Building. Reaching that point gave him a thrill he couldn't describe, though he would try to describe it later to Annie.

David was amazed that satellite phone technology got him as far as it did, and he had to wonder how much untapped energy was still operative in the condemned city. The longer everyone else remained convinced the place was radioactively contaminated, the better for him and the Tribulation Force. At every cybergateway along the path, he planted warnings of high radioactive levels. And while he was at it, he launched a robotic search engine that found all the original probe readouts and changed more than half of them to positive results. Civilian and GC planes were automatically rerouted so they couldn't fly over Chicago, even at more than thirty thousand feet.

David had to feather his way through the Strong Building mainframe by trial and error, seeing if he could remotely control the heating and cooling system, the lights, phones, sanitation system, elevators, and security cameras. The best video game in history would not have been more addictive.

The state-of-the-art monitoring system clearly reflected how much of the building was malfunctioning. More than half the elevators were off-line due to incomplete circuits. David clicked on More Information and found "Undetermined error has broken circuits between floors 40 and 80." He checked two dozen elevators that serviced the first thirty-nine floors and found that most appeared in running order.

By the time he had played with the system for another forty-five minutes, David had determined which security cameras worked, how to turn on lights on various floors, then the cameras, to show him whether the elevators would run, open, and shut. From nine time zones away, he was running what was left of a skyscraper in a city that had been abandoned for months.

Recording his keystrokes in a secure file, David fired up the camera on the highest floor he could find, the west end of the thirty-ninth. It showed water on the floor, but the mainframe indicated that it was being successfully redirected to keep it from flooding the floors below. He maneuvered the camera to show the ceiling and blinked. There was no ceiling, only a three-sided shell of the building that rose maybe another ten stories and revealed the inky sky, moon shining, stars twinkling.

So the Strong Building had been designed to withstand the worst nature could offer and had largely survived even what man threw at it. David stayed with his search until he found cameras that gave him a good view of what now served as the roof of the tower. By the time he had saved most of the information, he had an idea what the place looked like. In essence, it was a modular tower that appeared mortally wounded but had a lot to offer. Unusual in a modern skyscraper, the blueprints showed an inner core of offices hidden from outside view, surrounding the elevators on every floor. Here was unlimited floor space, water, plumbing, power, light—all undetectable by anyone who dared venture into an area that had been officially condemned and rendered off limits anyway.

The open top appeared large enough to accommodate a helicopter, but David couldn't determine remotely whether the new roof by proxy, which at first appeared to be the ceiling of the thirty-ninth floor, would support significant weight. He found parking underneath the tower, though debris from the top floors blocked two of the main garage entrances. It was a long shot, but David believed that if he could get the stateside Trib Force to the place, they could find ways in and out of that underground carport.

And that gave him another idea. The last rain of bombs to hit Chicago had come with little warning. Employees and residents of tall buildings fled to the streets, but no one would have been allowed below ground with buildings falling. Underground garages would have been automatically sealed off with the city so gridlocked. How many vehicles might still be in that garage? David clicked away until he found the underground security cameras and the emergency lighting system. Once he had the lights on in the lowest level, he panned one of the security cameras until the vehicles came into view. Six levels below the street, he found more than a dozen cars. The problem, of course, was that drivers would have had the keys.

David kept trying cameras at different levels, looking for valet parking. He struck pay dirt near the elevators on the first level below the street. Nearly fifty late-model and mostly expensive cars, at least one of them a Hummer and several others sport-utility vehicles, were parked in the vicinity of a glassed-in shack clearly labeled Valet Parking. David manipulated the closest camera until he could make out a wall next to the cash register, replete with sets of keys. It was as if this place was made for the Trib Force, and he couldn't wait to send someone in to investigate. David wondered how soon he and Annie might be living there.

A call startled him. It was the director of the Global Community Academy of Television Arts and Sciences, an Indonesian named Bakar. "I need your help," the man said.

What else was new?

"Fire away," David said, shutting down his computer with everything saved and hidden.

"Moon is all over me about why we didn't bring back the videodiscs from the Gala. I thought we had. Anyway, we have them secured now, and I had arranged to have them flown here commercially. Walter tells me now that he'll have my job if those discs are out of GC hands for one second."

"Who's got 'em, Bakar?"

"One of our guys."

"Can't he just bring them?"

"Yeah, but he'd have to fly commercially."

"So? He's still not letting the discs out of his sight."

"Commercial flights are full coming here, and Moon doesn't want to wait."

"So you want us to send a plane for one guy?"

"Exactly."

"Do you know the cost of that?"

"That's why I'm begging."

"How did I get so popular all of a sudden?"

"What?"

"Nothing. Be at the hangar by ten this morning."

"Me?"

"Who else?"

"I don't want to go, Director. I want our guy picked up."

"I'm not going to have our sleep-deprived first officer fly a multimillion-dollar, er, Nick, fighter to Israel *and* have to find your guy, Bakar. You're going to ride along so Mr. Smith doesn't have to leave the cockpit. And I won't charge you the thousands for fuel."

"I appreciate it, Director. But couldn't I just have my guy be at a certain place and—"

"Earth to Bakar! This is a seller's, or I should say giver's, market, sir. You make Smith go alone and I'll charge you depreciation on the jet, fuel, *and* his time. And his time is not cheap."

"I'll be there."

"I thought you would."

David called Abdullah.

"I was up anyway," Abdullah said. "I was hoping something would take me away from here today."

"You know how to work a disc-copying machine?"

"I don't know, boss. Is it more complicated than a fighter-bomber? Of course."

"I'm sending one with you. When Bakar finds his guy, you take the discs into the cockpit and tell them regulations say you have to personally log all cargo. Copy them, tag them as logged, and give them back to the TV boys."

"And bring you the copies."

"We're on the same page, Smitty."

David was next to giddy about the Trib Force all being in touch with each other via phone. He would feel better when he knew Buck was out of Israel and that Rayford was also on his way home, but David was unaware he had a message to call Buck.

———

Rayford shook Laslos's hand with both of his, got his promise to again personally thank Pastor Demeter and

Adon, then loped into the airport and to the hangar. His head felt cool with so little insulation, but he didn't want to keep running his hand over it for fear of making it obvious that it was new to him.

A tower official met him at the Gulfstream. "You must be Mr. Berry."

"Yes, sir."

"Here's your fuel bill. Your papers?"

Rayford dug them out and paid his bill in cash.

"Lot of currency to have on your person, Mr. Berry," the man said, shuffling through Rayford's documents.

"A risk I'm willing to take to keep from going bankrupt again."

"Credit cards do you in, did they, sir?"

"Hate 'em."

"Wow, this picture looks like it was taken today."

Rayford froze, then forced himself to breathe. "Yeah?"

"Yes, look here. Karl! Come look at this!"

A mechanic in coveralls wandered over, looking peeved that he had been interrupted.

The official held Rayford's ID photo next to Rayford's face. "Look at this. He got this, let me see here, eight, nine months ago, but his hair's the same length and, if I'm not mistaken, he's wearing the same shirt."

"Sure enough," the mechanic said, leaving as quickly as he had come. Rayford watched to make sure he wasn't going to call someone, but he just moseyed back to the engine he'd been working on.

"Yes, that's something," the man said. "Did you notice that?"

"Nope," Rayford said. "Lemme see that. Well, I'll be dogged. I *had* just got a haircut when this was taken, but 'course the hair doesn't grow much anymore, anyway. And that probably *is* the same shirt. I don't have that many."

"Your own plane and not that many shirts? There's priorities for you."

"My own plane, I wish. I just drive 'em for the company."

"And what company's that, sir?" The man handed back his documents.

"Palwaukee Global," Rayford said.

"What do you transport?"

"Just the plane today. They had too many this side of the ocean."

"That so? You could pick up some business running from Jerusalem to New Babylon this week, you know."

"I heard. Wish I had the time."

"Safe flight."

"Thank you, sir." And thank you, Lord.

———

At ten in the morning in New Babylon, David strolled past the makeshift evidence room, pretending to be checking progress on the nearby Carpathia statue. He knew if he appeared to be snooping on the evidence, Intelligence Director Jim Hickman would shoo him. But Hickman also liked to impress, and allowing a colleague an inside look seemed to make him feel special.

David slowed as he walked by, hoping to run into Jim. Not seeing him, he knocked at the door. An armed guard opened it, and David spotted Jim across the room with a technician on his knees in the middle of a fifteen-by-one-hundred-foot drapery. "Don't want to bother anybody," David said. "Just want to make sure Director Hickman and his team have everything they need. I'll call him in his office."

"I'm in here, David!" Hickman called.

"Oh! So you are!"

"Let 'im in, Corporal! Come over here, David. Slip your shoes off. I wanna show you something."

"I don't want to intrude."

"Come on!"

"If you insist. This is fascinating."

"You haven't seen anything yet."

But David had. Three techies in the corner were hunched over the remains of the wood lectern. They had magnifying lamps and large tweezers, similar to what the technician had in the middle of the drape. He wore a helmet with a light on it and hand held his magnifier.

"Look at this, David," Hickman said, motioning to him. "Got your shoes off?"

"I can come right out there where you are?"

"If I say you can, and I do! Now come on, time's a-wastin'."

David got to within about ten feet of Hickman and the techie when Jim said, "Stop and look down. Whoever was shootin' at this thing had to know what he was doin'. Looks like it went right through the middle. I mean, I never even knew Steele was a shooter, but to get a round, one round, to go through that pulpit dealie and then through the center of this curtain, well . . ."

"What am I looking at here, Jim?" David said, staring at a strange configuration about ten feet in diameter.

Hickman rose and limped over, joining David at the edge of the pattern. "Gettin' old," he said, grunting. "Now look here. The bullet coming from a weapon like that creates a mini tornado. If a real Kansas twister had the same relative strength, it would mix Florida and Maine with California and Washington. This one popped an eight-inch hole through the curtain there—you can see it from here."

"Uh-huh."

"But what you see at your feet is the effect it had on fibers this far from the center."

The force of the spinning disk had ripped the individual threads out of place and yanked them uniformly to create the huge twisted image.

"Now, c'mere and look at this."

Hickman led David to the top of the curtain, where brass eyeholes were set six inches apart along the whole one-hundred-foot edge. "Hooks went through these holes to suspend the whole thing from the iron piping."

"Wow," David said, astounded at the damage. The eight holes on either side of the center had been ripped clean, brass casings and all. The next several dozen were split apart, then more on each side had mangled hooks still attached, all the way to the ends, where the eyeholes were intact but the hooks were missing.

"Just ripped this thing away and sent it flying into the distance."

"Director!" the techie called.

Hickman started toward the middle again, but David hung back until Hickman motioned him to follow.

"Bullet residue," the techie said, holding a tiny shard of lead between slender forceps.

"Bag that up. Ten'll get you twenty we can trace it to the Saber we found."

The technician began dropping pieces into a plastic bag. "I hate to say it, sir, but fragments like this will be almost impossible to positively match with—"

"Come on now, Junior. We've got eyewitnesses who say a guy in a raghead getup took the shot. We found the gun, got a match on the prints, and we know who the guy is. We found his disguise in a trash can a few blocks away. The fragments'll match all right, even if the lab work is inconclusive. This guy's definitely part of the conspiracy."

"Conspiracy?" David said, as they moved to the corner where the lectern pieces lay.

"We think the gunshot was diversionary," Hickman whispered.

"But this Steele guy is being accused—"

"Is a suspect, sure. But we're not sure the bullet even came close to Carpathia."

"What? But—"

"Carpathia didn't die from a gunshot wound, David. At least not solely."

"What then?"

"Autopsy's going on right now. We ought to know soon. But let me tell you somethin' just between you, me, and the whatever: Fortunato's no dummy."

David could have argued. "Yeah?"

"If it turns out the kill wound came from the platform, wouldn't that be highly embarrassing?"

"If one of his—our own did it, you mean."

"'xactly. But the public doesn't know that. The only video that's been shown so far only shows the victim hittin' the deck. People think he got shot. Leon sees that we blame this on the disgruntled former employee, and then he has us deal with the insurrection privately. And by dealin' with it, well, you get my drift."

The technicians digging through the remains of the lectern produced several bullet fragments, some big as a fingernail.

"This sure is fascinating stuff, Jim."

"Well," Hickman said, slowly running his hand through his hair, "it helps if you're a trained observer."

"You're nothing if not that."

"Right as rain, Hassid."

EIGHT

Leah sat fitfully at what was left of the tiny airport in Kankakee. When her phone rang and Rayford identified himself, she was speechless. "I have so much to talk to you about," he said, "so much to apologize for."

"I'll look forward to that," she said flatly. In truth she was more eager to get to the safe house and see Tsion than she was to talk to Rayford. "Thanks for leaving me stranded, but I guess I can see why. Did you kill Carpathia?"

"I just got a call from David Hassid, who seems pretty sure I didn't. I wanted to. Planned to. But then I couldn't do it."

"So what about the gun with your prints? You weren't the shooter?"

"I was, but it was an accident. I was bumped."

"Be glad I'm not on your jury."

"Leah, where are you?"

She told him and filled him in on her plan to fly to Palwaukee and perhaps get a ride with T to near the safe house, where they would try to determine if anyone was casing it. "Problem is, nothing is going that way tonight, and in the morning it's exorbitant. I may hitchhike."

"See if T will come get you. If it's too far to drive, he can fly."

"I hardly know him, Rayford. When will you be here?"

"I should hit Palwaukee about nine in the morning."

"I'll wait for you then, I guess."

"That would be nice."

Leah sighed. "Don't get pleasant on me all of a sudden. I can't pretend I'm not irritated with you. And getting yourself in even deeper trouble with the GC, what was that all about?"

"I wish I knew," he said. "But I *would* like the chance to talk to everyone face-to-face."

"Thanks to you, that's looking more and more remote. You know Tsion and Chloe and the baby are underground now?"

"I heard."

"And nobody knows where Hattie is."

"But someone told you she was in the States?"

"It's a big place, Rayford."

"Yeah, but I still can't see her giving us up."

"You have more faith than I."

"I agree we need to be careful."

"Careful? If I do get T to take me to Mount Prospect,

or if I wait for you, who knows we're not walking into a trap at the safe house? It's a miracle it wasn't found out long before I joined you."

Rayford ignored that, and Leah felt mean. She meant every word, but why couldn't she cut him some slack?

———————

David checked in with Annie—who said she was headed back to bed—then invited Mac to join him in his office to see what was happening in the morgue. They settled close to the computer, and David started by listening live. Dr. Eikenberry was into a routine of announcing for the record the height and weight of the body and her plans for embalming and repair.

"There was some kind of a hassle right at the start," Mac said. "People say she was yelling, demanding the doctor. Can you go back without messing up the recording you're doing now?"

David pinpointed when the microphones in the morgue first detected sound. The time showed just after eight o'clock in the morning, and the recording began with a key in the door and the door opening. It was clear the mortician had two assistants with her, a man and a woman, and both sounded young. She called the young man Pietr and the young woman Kiersten.

The first spoken words were Dr. Eikenberry's. She was swearing. Then, "What is this? They leave the crate in here? Get someone to get it out of here. I'm going to work on this table and I want room. I'm assuming there are no more bodies in storage?"

"I'm here with you, Doc," Pietr said. "I wouldn't know."

"Check, would you? Kiersten, call someone to get rid of the crate."

In the background Kiersten could be heard talking tentatively to the palace switchboard operator. In the foreground, Pietr could be heard slamming a door. "You're not gonna be happy, ma'am."

"What?"

"There are *no* bodies in here."

"None?"

"None."

"You're telling me Carpathia is not in there either?"

"None means none, ma'am."

She swore again. "Kiersten! Get somebody in here with a crowbar. They left the body in this crate all night? I'll be surprised if he doesn't stink."

After several minutes of muttering, a male voice: "You asked for a crowbar, ma'am?"

"Yes, and someone who knows how to use it."

"I can do it."

"You're a guard!"

"Crowbars are nothing. You want the box opened?"

"Put your weapon down, soldier. Why do they send *you* to do this?"

"Security. They don't want anybody in here but you and your staff."

"Well, I appreciate that, but . . ."

David and Mac heard the crate being torn open.

"No casket?" the doctor said. "Get him into the fridge."

"In the bag or out?" Pietr said.

"In," she said. "I don't even want to think how much blood he's lost in there. I'm not starting till ten, per instructions, but let's get ready."

Several minutes passed with minimal conversation, much of it related to their finding the plastic amalgam and her instructing her assistants how and where and when to have it ready. "You think this winch can handle a man his size?"

"Never saw a portable one before," Pietr said. "We'll make it work."

David fast-forwarded until he heard conversation and stopped only when it seemed meaningful. Finally he was at the ten o'clock point, and the cooler was opened again. Dr. Eikenberry switched on a recorder and spoke into a microphone David had seen hanging from the ceiling when he helped deliver her supplies.

"This is Madeline Eikenberry, M.D. and forensic pathologist, here in the morgue at Global Community Palace in New Babylon with assistants Pietr Berger and Kiersten Scholten. They are bringing to the table the body of Nicolae Jetty Carpathia, age thirty-six. We will remove the corpse from the body bag into which it was placed following his death approximately fourteen hours ago in Jerusalem, cause to be determined."

David and Mac heard the transfer of the bag from gurney to examining table. "I don't like the sound of that," Dr. Eikenberry muttered. "It feels as if he may have nearly bled out."

"Yuck," Kiersten said.

"Could you spell that for the transcriptionist, dear?" the doctor said. Then, "Oh, no! Oh, my! Agh! Keep it off the floor! Pietr, make sure it drains through the table. What a botch! OK, transcriptionist, you know what to leave out. Pick up here. The body was not properly prepared for transfer or storage, and several liters of blood have collected in the bag. The body remains dressed in suit and tie and shoes, but a massive wound about the posterior head and neck, which will be examined once the deceased is disrobed, appears to be the exit area for the blood."

It sounded to David as if Carpathia's clothes were being cut off. "No apparent anterior wounds," Dr. Eikenberry said, as the sound of spraying water came through. "Let's turn him over. Oh! Be careful of that!" She swore again and again. "Get his doctor in here now! And I mean now! What in the world is this? I was told nothing of this!"

The footsteps must have been Kiersten's running to the door to have someone look for the doctor, because Pietr could be heard as clearly as the doctor. "I thought you were to look for a bullet entry wound."

"So did I! Is someone trying to kill us?"

More spraying, grumbling, and mumbling. Finally the door opened again. Hurried footsteps. "Doctor," Eikenberry began, "why wasn't I told of this?"

"Well, I, we—"

"Turning over a man with this kind of a weapon still in him is ten times more dangerous than a cop sticking his bare hands in a perp's pocket without checking for needles or blades first!"

"I'm sorry, I—"

"You're *sorry?* You want to help pull this out? Ah, never mind. Just tell me if there's anything else I should have known."

The doctor sounded thoroughly intimidated. "Well, to tell you the truth—"

"Oh, please, at *least* do that. I think it's about time, don't you?"

"Uh-huh, well, you know you're to look for bullet—"

"Damage, wounds, yes. What?"

"The fact is, the EMTs are of the opinion—"

"The same ones who prepared, or I should say left unprepared, a body like this?"

"That wasn't their fault, ma'am. I understand the supreme commander was pushing everyone to get the body out of there."

"Go on."

"The EMTs believe you will find no bullet wounds."

A pregnant silence.

"Frankly, Doctor, I don't care what we find. I'll give you my expert opinion, and if there are also bullet holes, I'll include that. But can you answer me one thing? Why does everybody think there was a shooter, and why is that former employee pretty much being charged in the media? Because his prints were found on a weapon that *didn't* shoot Carpathia? I don't get it."

"As *you* said, ma'am, if you'll pardon me, it isn't your place to care about the cause of death, but only to assess it."

"Well, I'd say about an, oh, say, fifteen- to eighteen-inch, ah, what would you call this, Doctor, a big knife or a small sword?"

"A handled blade, certainly."

"Certainly. I'd hazard a guess that this whatever-it-is entering about two inches below the nape of the neck and exiting about half an inch through the crown of the skull, that certainly didn't enhance the victim's health, did it?"

"No, ma'am."

"Doctor, do you really not know why I wasn't informed of this major, likely lethal wound?"

"I know we didn't want to prejudice you."

She laughed. "Well, you certainly succeeded there! As for nearly slicing open my assistants and me, what do you say to that?"

"I guess I thought you'd see the, ah, sword."

"Doctor, the man was swimming in his own blood! He was on his back! We transferred him the same way, disrobed him, hosed him down, saw no entry or exit wounds on the anterior and, naturally, flipped him to examine the posterior wounds. What do you think I was expecting? I saw the news. I heard the gunshot and saw the people running and the victim fall. I had heard the scuttlebutt that there may have been a conspiracy, that one of the regional potentates may have had a concealed weapon. But I would have appreciated knowing that the man would look like a cocktail wiener with a sword poking through him."

"I understand."

"Do you see the damage this weapon did to significant tissue?"

"Not entirely."

"Well, unless we find bullets in the brain or somewhere else above the neck, it alone killed him."

Water was spraying again. "I see no bullet holes, do you?"

"No, ma'am."

"Pietr?"

"No."

"Kiersten?"

"Nope."

"Doctor?"

"I said no."

"But this blade, and I'll be able to tell you for sure when I get in there, appears to have gone through vertebrae, perhaps spinal cord, the membrane, the brain stem, the brain itself, the membrane again, and then come out the top of the skull, all none the worse for wear."

"That would be my observation too, ma'am."

"It would?"

"Yes."

"Your expert opinion."

"I'm no patholog—"

"But you know enough about the anatomy to know that I should not be surprised if I have guessed the internal damage fairly accurately?"

"Right."

"But more important, that this weapon appears as lethal now as it must have before it was thrust?"

"I'm afraid so."

"You see what I'm driving at?"

"I think so."

"You think so. One of us unsuspecting pathologists so much as brushes a finger against that blade, and we're sliced."

"I'm sorry—"

"And while the victim may be one of the most respected men in the history of the world, we don't know yet, do we, what might be in his blood? Or what might have been on the hands of the perpetrator. Do we?"

"We don't."

"Do you notice anything unusual about the blade, sir?"

"I don't know. I've never seen one quite like it, if that's what you m—"

"Simpler than that, Doctor. The cutting edge is facing out."

"You're sure there's only one cutting edge?"

"Yes, and do you know how I know? Because I was fortunate enough to catch my finger there when we turned over the body. Look here, at the top of his head. As we turned him, my hand went behind the head, and hidden there in the hair was the half-inch protrusion of the blade. As soon as it came in contact with my gloved index finger, I flinched and pulled away. Had I done that on the other edge, I dare say it would have cut my finger off."

"I see."

"You see. Do you also see our challenge in removing the weapon?"

A pause. "Actually, if it is as strong and sharp as you say, removal should be fairly simple. You just pull it back out the way it entered, and—"

"Doctor, may I remind you that the cutting edge is facing away from the body."

"I know."

"Then unless we are precise to a millimeter, the blade could cut its way out vertically. Cardinal rule of forensic pathology: Do as little damage to the body as possible so it is easier to determine how much trauma was actually inflicted from without."

"Ah, Madeline, if I could have a word."

"Please."

"Privately."

"Excuse us," she said, obviously looking at her assistants. Footsteps.

"Madeline, I apologize for any part I played in this dangerous situation. But we have been friends a long time. I sold the supreme commander on you because I wanted you to have the honor and the income. I resent being berated in front of your subordinates and—"

"Point well taken. I'll say nice things about you when you're gone. And I do appreciate the assignment. I don't know what the benefits are to a mortician asked to evaluate the most famous victim in history, but I do owe you thanks for that."

"You're welcome," he said flatly, and David heard him leave.

Pietr and Kiersten returned. "Wow," Pietr said.

"Wow is right," Dr. Eikenberry said. "That man?"

"Yes."

"That doctor who just left?" she clarified.

"Yes."

"I must tell you, he is a complete idiot."

The mortician told the transcriptionist to please disregard everything since the turning of the body and to pick up at that point. She explained how she had irrigated the entire wound area and found "just the one entry and one exit wound, with weapon still in place. The entry wound is considerably larger than the exit, and nearly all the blood flow came from the neck, though understandably there is evidence of blood exiting through eyes, nose, mouth, and ears as well. That the entry wound is clearly larger, while the blade itself is not that much wider there, indicates that the weapon was dug and twisted aggressively. The skull would have held the top of the weapon in place, but the bottom appears to have been flexible enough to inflict severe trauma."

David looked at Mac and exhaled. "Rayford's in the clear. I mean, he might get busted for shooting *at* Carpathia, but he couldn't have killed him."

Mac shook his head. "Sounds to me like Carpathia was murdered by one of his own people."

"It sure does," David said. "There was talk of one of

the potentates with something in his coat, but I want to see the videodiscs."

Buck awoke late morning, stiff and sore. The sun blinded, but Chaim remained asleep. Buck took a closer look at Chaim's ratty blanket. The inside was blood encrusted, and he wondered how the old man could stand it. He also worried that some of the blood might be Chaim's own.

Buck carefully tugged at the blanket to see if any blood stained Chaim's pajamas. But Chaim held tight and turned over, exposing his back. No wounds or stains that Buck could see.

"You awake?" the old man mumbled, still facing away from Buck.

"Yes. We have to talk."

"Later."

"Now."

"Why don't you go find me some clothes? I need to get home, and I can't go like this."

"You don't think the GC is waiting for you there?"

Chaim rolled over to face Buck, squinting against the sunlight. "And why would they be? Where's my phone? I want to call the house, talk to Jacov."

"Don't."

"Why not?"

"Don't, Chaim. I know the truth. I know what happened."

"You saw nothing! No one saw anything!"

"You can't admit to me what I know already? What kind of a friend are you?"

Chaim got up and relieved himself, then returned to sit wearily on the bed. His white hair pointed everywhere. "You should be happy," he said.

"Happy?"

"Of course! What do you care how the deed was done, so long as it was done?"

"I care because *you* did it!"

"You don't know that. And what if I did?"

"You'll die for it, that's what! You think I want that?"

Chaim cocked his head and shrugged. "You're a better friend than I, Cameron."

"I'm beginning to think so."

Chaim chuckled. "I can't cheer you, eh?"

"Tell me how you did it, Chaim."

"The less you know, the less you have to answer for."

"Oh, don't be naïve! You've been around too long for that. I have to answer for everything. I have to be grateful for facial lacerations, because if I had not suffered them, I would have had to change my appearance anyway. Telling me you murdered Carpathia won't add much to my plate. They have enough on me, manufactured and otherwise, to put me away on sight. So, tell me."

"I'm telling no one. This is mine alone."

"But you know you can't go home."

"I can tell my people where I am, that I am all right."

"You must come to the States with me."

"I can't leave my country, my staff."

"Chaim, listen to me. Your staff is dead. They were tortured and massacred last night by the GC, probably trying to get to you."

Chaim looked up slowly, his hair casting wild shadows on the far wall. "Don't talk crazy," he said warily. "That is not amusing."

"I wouldn't joke about that, Chaim. Jacov was killed by a blow to the chin that broke his neck. A guard hit him with the butt end of an Uzi when he tried to rush to you."

Chaim put a hand over his mouth and sucked in a noisy breath. "Don't," he said, his words muffled. "Don't do this to me."

"I didn't do it, Chaim. You did it."

"He's dead? You know for certain he's dead?"

"I checked his pulse myself."

"What have I done?"

"Hannelore and her mother and Stefan are gone too."

Chaim stood and moved toward the door as if wanting to leave but knowing he had nowhere to go. "No!" he wailed. "Why?"

"Someone had to know, Chaim. Someone had to have seen you. Surely you didn't expect to get away with it."

Chaim's knees gave way and he hit the floor hard, a high-pitched cry in his throat. "You checked the pulses at my home too?"

Buck nodded.

"That was not smart. You could have been killed too."

"And *my* death would have been your fault too, Chaim. Look what's happened!"

Chaim turned and leaned over the bed, still kneeling. He buried his face in his hands. "I was willing to die," he managed. "I didn't care about myself. The sword was perfect and fit into the tubing of my chair just so. No one knew. Not even Jacov. Oh, Jacov! Jacov! What have I done to you? Cameron! You must kill me! You must avenge those deaths!" He stood quickly and opened the window. "If I lose my nerve, you must push me! Please, I cannot bear this!"

"Shut the window, Chaim. I'm not going to kill you, and I won't let you kill yourself."

"I'll not turn myself in to those swine. I wouldn't give them the satisfaction! Oh, I *will* kill myself, Cameron. You know I will!"

"You'll have to try without me present. I love you too much, Chaim. I will die before you do to keep you from going to hell."

"Hell? If God would send me to hell for murdering such a monster, I will go happily. But he *should* send me to hell for what I did to my people! Oh, Cameron!" He collapsed onto the bed, rolling into a fetal position and groaning as if about to burst. Suddenly he sat up, seeming eager to relive the deed.

"I was going to leap from my chair at just the right moment, weapon in hand. He is so much taller, I had been practicing my jumping. I was going to leap as high as I could and, with both hands on the handle, drive the blade down through the top of his head. The whole world would see and know.

"There were all those shenanigans on the stage, people

standing, sitting, moving, laughing. I joined in, measuring the distance, seeing where I could maneuver the chair. When he came to greet me and lift my hand, I came close to reaching across my body to lift out the sword and plunge it into his heart. But my angle was wrong. I would not have had the leverage to get the blade out, let alone to thrust it where I needed to.

"I was rolling toward him finally as he moved my way. My plan was to turn quickly at the last minute and trip him. Then I would leap from the chair and kill him. But just as he got near me, the gun went off. At first I thought I had been detected and that his security guards had shot me. But he lurched my way, away from the sound of the gun and the shattering lectern.

"I could see that he was about to tumble into my lap, so I quickly withdrew the blade. I didn't have time even to orient it in my hands. I pointed it straight up and held steady as he fell back onto it. I held firm and tried to scrape the brain from his evil head. He jerked, and I let go. He rolled to my feet. It was chaos. People came running. I steered away and, for an instant, I thought I had gotten away with it. The timing! The shot! I could tell it came from the crowd, and as I ran away I wondered if it might be mistaken for a two-person crime.

"I had plotted an unlikely escape just on a lark. And here I am. Who would have believed it?"

Buck sat shaking his head. Chaim rolled back over, moaning. "You're right," he whispered. "It's all on me. I did this to them. Oh, no, no, no . . ."

Buck heard voices below the window. Three vagrants

sat sharing a bottle. "Which of you would like a fifty-Nick note?" he called down.

Two waved him off, but a young drunk stood quickly. "What I gotta do?"

"Buy me some clothes and shoes with this twenty, and when you bring 'em back, keep the change and get another fifty."

The other two laughed and tried to sing. The young drunk squinted and let his head fall back. "How do you know I won't run off with your twenty?"

"My risk," Buck said. "Your loss. You want twenty or fifty?"

"Gimme," the man said, reaching. Buck let the bill flutter down, which brought the other two to their feet to compete for it. The younger shoved them away and got it easily. Buck felt better about his chances when the man turned back to him and said, "What size?"

———————

"No deal," Abdullah said on the phone.

"What's the problem?" David said.

"The guy had the fear of God in him. Wouldn't let those discs out of his sight. I didn't even get the machine out of my bag. He said he'd stand there and watch while I logged them in, if I had to."

"I just hope they're not bringing them here to destroy them. They're the only hope of exonerating Rayford."

"Exonerating? What's that mean?"

"Getting him off the hook."

"No, sir," Abdullah said. "He didn't even have to pull the trigger to be guilty. He drew down on Carpathia. What more do they need? He needs to stay as far away from here as he can."

NINE

Seven Hours Later

DAVID hated getting so little time with Annie, but he knew their exile was fast approaching. Then, if they could pull it off, they would be together as much as they wanted—and probably a long, long way from New Babylon.

What an incredibly beautiful city New Babylon would have been under other circumstances. Carpathia had employed the best architects and landscapers and designers and decorators. And except for the absence of any God-honoring works of art, the place looked magnificent, particularly at night. Great colored spotlights accented the massive, crystalline buildings. Only since the recent decimation of another huge percentage of the population and the resulting personnel shortages had the place begun to evidence the lack. It took longer for refuse removal or for lights to be repaired. Yet still the skyline was stunning, a man-made marvel.

As dusk crept over the horizon, David sat listening to Fortunato, Hickman, and Moon through the bug in Carpathia's office. He couldn't tell whether Leon was actually in Nicolae's chair, but it sure sounded like it. They were watching the videos that had been brought back from the Gala. David sat with his head in his hands, using earphones to be sure to catch every detail. He wished he could see the videos, but that was not his call.

They played and replayed and replayed clips that included the gunshot. "See?" Moon said. "He's right down there, stage right, about three or four deep, there! See? Pause!"

"I see it, Walter," Leon said. "Good thing we've got fingerprints. I would not have been able to tell who that was in a million years."

"Good getup," Hickman said. "The gray hair stickin' out of the turban. Nice touch. Robes. I woulda thought he was an Arab."

"Some kinda raghead anyway."

They all chuckled.

"Rayford Steele," Leon said softly. "Who'd have believed that? Wouldn't murder be against his religion?"

Laughter. Silence. Then, "I don't know." It was Hickman. "Maybe he convinces himself it's a holy war. Then I guess everything goes."

"Fact is," Moon said, "he missed."

"You look close," Hickman said, "and he had a better

shot earlier. He fires then, he's our guy. But I don't think he even meant to shoot when he did."

"What're you talking about?"

"Look. Slow motion, well, back it up a second first. Look! Right there! Somebody bumps him. A little person. A woman? Can you zoom?"

"I don't know how to run these crazy machines," Leon said. "We oughta get Hassid in here."

"You want me to call him?"

"Maybe. Just a minute. Here, OK. Slow and zoomed. What do you see?"

"There!" Hickman said again. "She trips, loses her balance or somethin'. Ha! Who's that look like? Wally, who's that remind you of?"

"Nah."

"No? Come on! Who am I thinkin' of?"

"I know who you're thinking of, but we've got her eyeballed in North America. Probably trying to get to her sister's funeral. She doesn't know it was a month ago."

They chuckled again, and David picked up the phone. "Rayford," he said, "maybe Hattie's *not* on her way to the safe house yet. GC's tracked her out west, trying to make her sister's funeral."

"That's a relief. Maybe we're OK for a while."

"Don't get overconfident. I uploaded a whole bunch of stuff to Chloe's computer so you can see your new digs, if you need 'em. Where are you?"

"Well, I was about to put down at Palwaukee when I heard from Leah. I'd been having trouble reaching T to see if he could go get her in Kankakee, southeast of here.

She never got him either, so I'm on my way to get her. We'll come back here and use Buck's car to see if we can get to the safe house."

"Call Tsion first. Last time I talked to him he said he thought he heard car noises."

"That's not good."

"Tell me about it," David said. "Hey, Leah might need a new alias."

"Yeah? Why?"

"She's been asking around about Hattie using that Clendenon name. They might try to follow her to Hattie."

"They're already onto Hattie. They don't need Leah."

"Whatever you say, Rayford. Just a thought."

"I appreciate it."

"You'd better be careful. They're going to try to pin this on you." David told him of the autopsy and evidence investigation.

"So I missed, just like you thought?"

"Looks pretty sure at this point."

"Then how can they pin it on me?"

"What, they're obligated to the truth? If you didn't do it, someone on the platform did."

"My money's on one of the three insurgent kings," Rayford said. "Probably Litwala."

"Even if you're right, you're a less embarrassing assassin than somebody behind Nicolae. I'll bet you're the scapegoat."

———————

Buck had sat with the morose Chaim Rosenzweig the whole day. The old man had alternately slept and wept, threatening suicide. Buck wanted to go out and find them something to eat, but he didn't dare leave Chaim. The drunk came back to toss a bundle of used clothes up to the window, but he wasn't interested in more money to find food. Once he had his fifty, he was gone.

Buck called the desk. "Anybody down there that could bring us some food for a fee?"

"What, you think we got room service?"

"Just tell me if you know anybody who wants to make a few Nicks."

"Yeah, OK. When the concierge gets off his break, I'll send 'im up. You'll recognize him by his tuxedo."

Amazingly, ten minutes later someone knocked tentatively. Buck wished he had a gun. "Who is it?"

"I'll get you food," a man said. "How much?"

"Ten."

"Deal."

Buck sent him out for local fare. It was all he could do to get Chaim to eat a few bites. Presently, David called.

"Is it true?" he asked. "About Chaim?"

Buck was stunned. "What about him?"

"That he's dead, burned up at his home along with his whole staff?"

"You know that's not true, David. Hasn't anyone told you I'm with him?"

"I'm just telling you what's on television."

"So that's how they're going to spin it? Hero

statesman dies in a fire. That keeps him out of the conspiracy?"

"They're convinced one of the three insurgents did it," David said, "but that would be bad for morale. What's Chaim's theory? He was right there."

"We need to talk about this later, David. I need to get him out of here."

"How?"

"I finally got hold of T. He's bringing the Super J. I directed him to a blocked-off road. We have to be there when he puts down so he can be in the air again before anyone's the wiser. We'll have to stop in Greece for fuel, though—wouldn't want to risk it over here."

Tsion was alarmed. Chloe was proposing madness. "Can I trust you with Kenny," she said, "that you won't fall asleep?"

"I would give my life for that child, you know that. But you must not go. This is foolishness."

"Tsion, I can't sit here doing nothing. I have informed everybody in the co-op generally what's going on, but there's little I can do until the buying-selling restrictions are sanctioned. Don't keep me from doing something worthwhile."

"I am not your superior, Chloe. I could not deprive you of anything. I'm just urging you to think this through. Why must you go? And why must it be now?

Cameron's car is at the airport. If you take the Suburban, you leave me with no vehicle."

"You have nowhere to go, Tsion. You can't outrun the GC anyway. Your best bet is to stay right here, listen for them, turn the power off if you hear them, and become invisible."

Tsion threw up his arms. "I cannot dissuade you, so do what you are going to do. But don't be long."

"Thank you. And promise me you will do anything but let Kenny fall into GC hands."

"I would die first."

"I want *him* to die first."

"That I will not do."

"You would let them take him."

"Over my body."

"But don't you see, Tsion? That's how it will be! You'll be a martyr, but you will still have lost Kenny to the enemy."

"You're right. You'd better stay here."

"Nice try."

"This is not a smart thing to do in broad daylight."

"I'll be careful."

"Too late. You're already being reckless."

"Good-bye, Tsion."

"What do you make of this?" Hickman was saying as David listened in.

"Ramblings," Leon said. "Hallucinations. Gibberish. Not uncommon in such a situation."

"But first he said that about thinking he had done all you asked. What was that about?"

"Nicolae was not addressing me! I have never, would never, could never ask him to do anything! Anyway, if he was talking to me, it would indicate that he thought I had attacked him."

"But then what is his obsession with the—what does he call it?"

"The veil? Or the vale? What?"

"Listen. Listen to what he says."

David pressed both earphones close and listened carefully. After Carpathia's first lament, which echoed through the sound system, the PA system appeared to have failed, but his next words were picked up through the videodisc machine mike. "The veil," Carpathia rasped. "Was it rent in twain from the top to the bottom?" Carpathia struggled to make himself understood. "Father," he managed. "Father, forgive them, for they know not what they do."

David shuddered.

The exchange reminded him of something he and Mac had heard from the morgue. He called Mac. "What was it Dr. Eikenberry said about reports of Nicolae's last words?"

"Just that it would have been impossible."

"That's what I thought. Once she got in there and saw the damage, she said he wouldn't have been able to speak, right?"

"Exactly."

David re-cued the recording and found it.

"Well," Dr. Eikenberry said, "this gives the lie to the 'last words' business, doesn't it?"

"It sure does," Pietr said. "Unless he could speak supernaturally."

He and the doctor and Kiersten laughed. "This man could not have said a word," Dr. Eikenberry concluded. "Maybe they want to invent something for posterity, but no one had better ask me if it was possible."

———

A few minutes after nine in the morning, Central Standard Time, Rayford put the Gulfstream down in Kankakee. He had told Leah to watch for a smallish jet and to be ready to board quickly. But as he taxied by the terminal, he saw her sleeping in a chair by the window.

He left the jet whining on the tarmac, knowing how conspicuous that would look to ground control, and sprinted into the terminal. "Donna!" he said, as he approached. "Donna Clendenon!"

She jumped and squinted at him. "Do I know you?" she said, clearly terrified.

"Marv Berry," he said, grabbing her bag. "We've got to go."

"Hi, Marv," she whispered. "You've got to tell a girl when you get a makeover."

Rayford heard some kind of warning through the PA system, and a couple of orange-vested officials started his way. He ignored them and was airborne quickly, certain that Kankakee had no GC pursuit craft and little interest in a small jet flyer who had boorishly violated their protocols.

He told Leah, "All I get out of Palwaukee is a tower guy who says T is not there and won't be back until tomorrow, and that he's not at liberty to say where he went."

"I got the same. What do you make of it?"

"I don't know. Wish there was someone in his church I could ask. But T and I have never needed to communicate through third parties. He's usually reachable by cell. He's always wanted to be in on the action, and I need someone to go and ferry Buck and Chaim over here. I'm tempted to call Albie and see if he can find someone."

"Now there's a name I haven't heard," Leah said.

"Albie? Long story. Good guy."

"So tell me."

"Not until you and I clear up a few things."

"Until you do, you mean," she said.

Rayford told her what had happened to him in Israel, on the flight to Greece, and in Greece. "I know that sounds a little too convenient," he said, "and I wouldn't blame you if you thought I just made it up to—"

"Made it up?" she said, obviously emotional. "If you made that up, you'd burn in hell."

"So, will you be the first to forgive me?"

"Of course. And I need to apologize too. I—"

"You've done nothing close to what I did," Rayford said. "Forget it."

"Don't brush me off, Rayford. I feel awful about how I've responded to you."

"Fair enough. We're even."

"Don't be flippant."

"I'm not. You can imagine how I feel about—"

"I'm not saying I was as terrible as you," she said wryly.

———

David responded to an announcement that all GC management personnel from director level and above were to report immediately to the small theater in the education wing. What now?

As dozens crowded into the room, Fortunato stood at the lectern like a professor. "Quickly now, quickly please, find your seats. I've been informed that more than a million people are in New Babylon already with probably at least two million more to come. Our social services are being taxed to their limits, and these people have no outlet for their grief. I want to know if there is any reason we cannot put the body of the potentate in position even this evening and begin the procession past the bier. We're estimating that not half the mourners will stay for the burial, which may have to be postponed as well. Do we have adequate lighting?"

Someone shouted yes.

"And concessions? Stations with water, food, medical services?"

"Could be in place within an hour!" someone said.

"Good. The bier itself and its pedestal?"

"Pedestal is finished and waiting."

"Bier is finished! Per specifications."

"Really?" Fortunato said. "I was told there was some question whether it could be vacuum sealed—"

"Solved, with a little help. Once the body is, ah, placed inside, the air can be quickly removed and the hole secured. The stopper is a hard rubber compound that will be screwed into the Plexiglas—"

"Thank you, we can skip the details. The entire container is transparent?"

"Yes, sir. And on the pedestal it will sit nearly fifteen feet off the ground."

"Yet the mourners will have access . . . ?"

"Via stairs leading up one side and down the other. They will, of course, be unable to touch the glass, as they will be separated from it by approximately five feet with velvet ropes and, um, armed security."

"Thank you," Fortunato said. "Now there are certain details I would like us all to hear, except those of you who need to supervise construction of the restoring stations. You may be excused now, and let's shoot for an 8:00 P.M. start time. Let's get the word out to the people so they can begin assembling. Yes, Mr. Blod."

Guy had been waving and now stood.

"I'm afraid my statue will not be ready until dawn, as originally planned. We're making progress, and I believe it will be stunning, but even the initial goal was nearly impossible."

"No problem. You may go now too, and we'll all look forward to your handiwork."

As Guy rushed from the room, Leon called upon Dr.

Eikenberry to come to the microphone. "It has been her difficult duty to prepare for burial the body of our beloved leader. As she is a loyal citizen of the Global Community and was a great admirer of the potentate, you can imagine what an emotional task this was. I have asked her to report on her findings and summarize the challenges she faced to allow the mourners to have one last encounter with His Excellency in as dignified and memorable a manner as possible, under the circumstances."

Dr. Eikenberry had lost the severe look David had seen when he first met her. Her white coat was gone, and she seemed to have applied fresh makeup and had her hairdo softened. He wondered when she had had time for that.

"Thank you, Supreme Commander," she began. "This has indeed been a most difficult and emotional day for me and my assistants, Pietr Berger and Kiersten Scholten. We treated the body of Nicolae Carpathia with utmost reverence and respect. As expected, the cause of death was severe brain trauma caused by a single bullet from a Saber handgun. The projectile entered the potentate's body just below the nape of his neck in the posteri—in the back and exited through the top of the crani— through the top of his head. The particularly devastating power of this type of projectile destroyed two vertebrae, severed the spinal cord, obliterated the brain stem and posterior of the brain, and left residual damage to the carotid artery and much of the soft tissue in the throat.

"Because of the spinning bullet, the back of the neck and head were laid open, causing the greatest challenge for repair and reconstruction. Without getting into the details, the gaping wound has been stapled and stitched, camouflaged with wax and putty and coloring and a minimum of artificial hair. If the result contributes to an appropriate farewell to the greatest leader the world has ever known, I am grateful and consider it a privilege to have served the Global Community this way."

Amid tears and sustained applause, Dr. Eikenberry began to leave, then returned to the podium with an index finger raised. "If I may add one thing," she said. "There is recorded evidence that His Excellency's last words were an expression of forgiveness to the perpetrator of this heinous crime. Forgiveness has long been ascribed to the divine, and as a medical professional, I must tell you why I concur with this assessment. Besides the *sentiment* of those last words, I can tell you that there is no human explanation for the potentate's ability to speak at all, given the physical damage. Truly this was a righteous man. Truly this was the son of god."

———————

At Palwaukee Rayford tried in person to get more information out of the tower fill-in. "I'm sorry, sir," the man said. "But not only am I not at liberty to tell you, I couldn't if I wanted to. He didn't tell me where he was going but only when he expected to return."

"Do you know who I am?"

"No, sir."

"You haven't seen me around here, don't know I'm a friend of T's?"

The man squinted at Rayford, and Leah cleared her throat. "He, ah, may not recognize you."

Rayford couldn't believe his own stupidity. "Listen, son, I have permission to take an associate's vehicle, but he neglected to leave the keys with me. I need to know you won't feel obligated to phone any authorities if I were to hot-wire the car."

The man's look was not as reassuring as his words. "I won't even be looking your direction."

"He doesn't trust you," Leah said as they strode to the Land Rover.

"Why should he? I wouldn't either. See? Even forgiven sin has its consequences."

"Do we have to spiritualize everything?" Leah said, but Rayford could tell she was bemused. Once they were on the road, she said, "We're not going straight to the safe house in broad daylight, are we?"

"Of course not. We have a stop first."

He drove to Des Plaines and the one-pump gas station run by Zeke and Zeke Jr. Zeke emerged quickly but hesitated when he saw Rayford. He looked past him to Leah. "I recognize the vehicle," he said. "But not the occupants."

"It's me, Zeke. And this is Leah."

"That wasn't Z's handiwork, was it?"

"Hers was."

"Humph. Not bad. Yours either. Need auto work?"

"Yup."

Zeke ignored the pump and opened the ancient garage door. Rayford pulled in, and he and Leah got out so Zeke could raise the car on the rack. Then the three of them took a hidden staircase to the basement, where Zeke Jr. looked up expectantly. "'sup?" he said.

"You know me?" Rayford said.

"Not till you spoke, but I woulda got it. Wha'dya need?"

"New ID for her."

Zeke Jr. stood, rolls of fat jiggling under his black vest and shirt. "Gerri Seaver," he said.

"Excuse me?"

"How's Gerri Seaver sound?"

"How does she look?" Leah said.

Zeke grabbed a file. "Like this."

"You're a genius," she said. The blonde was roughly her age, height, and weight. "I don't know how you do it."

"Lots more to choose from these days," he said shyly. He directed her to a sink and gave her the chemicals necessary to make her a blonde. She and Rayford drove off two hours later with foodstuffs, a full tank, and Leah in a scarf over wet, freshly bleached hair. Her dental appliance had been changed, as had the color of her contacts. In her purse was a wallet with documents to match.

"I'm going to take the northern route," Rayford said. "That'll give us a good look at any other traffic."

"Unless they're hidden."

"Not too many places to do that," he said. "Shall we wait till dark too?"

"You're asking me?"

"We both live or die by the decision," he said.

"That helps."

He phoned the safe house. Tsion answered. "She's where? . . . Tell me she's not! . . . Oh, Tsion! What about the radiation, the—"

Tsion told him what David had told them about the radiation. Rayford pulled over and covered the mouthpiece. "We're waiting till dark," he said, popping a U-turn.

"Where to till then?"

"Chicago, and watch our backs in case you were right about tower boy."

Rayford phoned Chloe and eschewed any pleasantries. "Where are you?" he said.

"Palos area," she said. "I'm guessing, where the Tri-state used to intersect Harlem."

"Ninety-fifth Street?"

"Uh-huh."

"What now? You going the rest of the way on foot?"

"I may have to."

"That'll take hours!"

"What else have I got to do, Dad?"

"At least wait for us. You're more likely to give us away than Hattie is. We've got both vehicles out in the daytime. On foot you'll stick out like a sore thumb. We're as exposed as we've ever been."

"Just tell her what to do, Rayford," Leah said. "You're back in charge, remember?"

"What?" Chloe said.

Rayford covered the phone. "She's a married adult, Leah, not my little girl anymore."

"But she's subordinate to you in the Trib Force. Do what you have to do."

"Chloe?"

"Yes."

"Stay put until we can find you. We're not doing this thing until after dark."

TEN

BUCK was having a crisis of conscience. It would have been one thing to be harboring Carpathia's assassin, had it been Rayford or another misguided believer for whom the deed could have at least been rationalized as an act of war. But Chaim?

He professed no faith, no acrimony toward Carpathia from a spiritual standpoint. The man had committed first-degree murder, and regardless of what Buck thought about the victim, it was a crime.

"So, what are you going to do?" Chaim pressed him as they languished at the Night Visitors hotel in Jerusalem. "Turn me in? Abandon me? Your conscience can't take what I did to your worst enemy. I cannot abide what I have done to my dearest friends. They died for me."

"Greater love hath no man . . ."

"You've quoted that before, Cameron, and I know where you want to go with it. But they had no choice. Perhaps they would have died for me voluntarily, but this was my doing. I forced their deaths."

"Would you have done the same for them? Would you have died for them?"

"I'd like to think I would. I should now."

"Stop talking like that."

"You think I am not sincere? The only things standing in the way are you and my cowardice."

"Cowardice? You planned the assassination for months, virtually told me you were going to do it by showing me your blade making—I don't know where my head was—and you pulled it off according to plan. Right or wrong, it was hardly evidence of cowardice."

"Ach!" Chaim waved him off. "I am a fool and a coward, and the blood of my people is on my hands."

Buck paced. "Because the GC are already announcing that you're dead, they can kill you without explanation."

"Let them. I deserve it. I'm a murderer."

Buck turned the chair backward and straddled it. "What happens when your victim comes back to life? Then what is your crime? Attempted murder? What if there is no evidence of the wound you inflicted?"

"You're talking crazy now, Cameron."

"It's going to happen, Chaim."

"I know you say that, and Tsion says that. But come now. The man was in my lap when I thrust the blade into his brain. For all practical purposes, he was dead before he hit the floor. He could not have survived it. You can't really believe he is coming back to life."

"What if he does?"

Chaim waved him off again.

"Don't do that. You're an intellectual, a lifelong student and teacher and scientist. Humor the debate. What if Carpathia comes back to life?"

Chaim rolled on the bed and turned his back to Buck. "Then I guess you'll all be right; I'll be wrong. You'll win."

"You're not pretending that it has actually happened."

"You said yourself I have a thinking man's brain. I find it impossible to consider impossibilities."

"That's why we've never gotten through to you? All our arguing and pleading . . . ?"

"You've gotten through more than you know, Cameron. I have come from atheism to agnosticism and finally to belief in God."

"You believe?"

"In God, yes. I told you that. Too many things have happened that can be explained no other way."

"Then why not Carpathia's resurrection?"

"You can't tell me that you yourself actually believe this," Chaim said.

"Oh, yes, I can. And I do. You forget I was there when Eli and Moishe came back to life after three days in the hot sun."

"You believe what you want to believe."

Buck looked at his watch. "I wish it would get dark. I want out of here."

"You should leave me, young friend. Distance yourself from me. Pretend you never met me."

Buck shook his head, though Chaim was still turned away from him. "Can't do that," he said. "We go back way too far."

"I was merely the subject of an article. We didn't have to become friends."

"But we did. And now I love you and can't let you go. You think you have nothing else to live for—"

"True enough."

"But you do. You do! You know what I fear for you, Chaim?"

"You're afraid I will die in unbelief and go to hell."

"There's something more frightening. What if you wait too long to change your mind and God hardens your heart?"

"Meaning?" Chaim rolled over to face him.

"Meaning that you finally decide it's true and want to give yourself to Christ, but you had already pushed God past where he would allow you to come back."

"Explain to me how that fits with your view of a loving God who is not willing that any should perish."

"I don't understand it myself, Chaim. I'm new at this. But Dr. Ben-Judah teaches that the Bible warns about just that during the end times. Be careful that you don't go too far, that you ignore too many warnings and signs."

"God would do that?"

"I believe so."

"To me?"

"Why not?"

Chaim let his head rest on the mattress, then covered his face with his arms.

"Ready to engage in the debate?" Buck pressed.

"I'm tired, Cameron."

"You slept well."

"I slept. Not well. How could I?"

"I can't imagine. But this is too important for you to brush aside."

"You have pleaded with me before! I have heard every argument from you and from Tsion. I could make your case for you!"

"Then think about what may happen to you. Say I get cold feet and abandon you. Even if you are a coward and unable to take your own life, someone is going to take it for you. Then what?"

"I like to believe death is the end."

"It's not," Buck said.

"Listen to the new believer, full of knowledge. You can't know."

"Chaim. If all this stuff that has amazed you and made you believe God is real, why shouldn't heaven and hell be real? If there's a God, why would he want you to die and disappear into nothingness? It makes no sense."

"You're repeating yourself."

"You're holding out, Chaim. You're like the faint-hearted who want one more sign. I just don't want you to wait past the point of no return."

"Ach!"

"Just think about it, will you? What it would mean if

the prophecy were fulfilled, Nicolae was the Antichrist, and he resurrected from the dead."

"I don't want to think about it. I want to die."

"You wouldn't if you believed what I believe."

"That, I agree with."

"You do?"

"Of course. Who would want to go to hell?"

"You don't have to, Chaim! God has—"

"I know! All right? I know! Stop talking."

"I will, but just consider—"

"Please!"

"—how you would feel if Nicolae—"

"For the love of—"

"I'll shut up now, Chaim. But—"

Buck's phone rang.

"Maybe there is a God," Chaim said. "The patron saint of phones has saved me."

"This is Buck."

"Buck, is it really you?"

"Hattie!" Buck stood so quickly his chair bounced away. "Where are you?"

"Colorado," she said.

"You're on a secure phone?"

"One thing I absconded with, one of those from your friend on the inside."

"I'm listening."

"The GC think I'm dumber than I am. They released me from prison, gave me money, and then followed me here. I know they were disappointed I didn't go to Israel, but I wanted to see if any of my family was left."

"And?"

Her voice caught. "No. Not for a while. But you know where they hope I'll go now."

"Exactly where I hope you won't go."

"Buck, I have nowhere else to turn."

He ran a hand through his hair. "I'd love to help you, Hattie, but I—"

"I understand. I had my chance."

"That's not it. I—"

"It's all right, Buck. You owe me nothing."

"It has nothing to do with owing you anything, Hattie. I'm in the middle of a situation myself, and until you can shake the GC, I can't advise that you head back to the safe house. Everybody's welfare is at stake."

"I know," she said, and he heard the terror in her voice. "Would you please tell everyone that I never told anyone where they were?"

"Hattie. You as much as put Bo and Ernie on our doorstep."

"They couldn't have found their way back there. Anyway, they're both dead, and if they had told anyone, you'd have been raided by now."

"What will you do, Hattie?"

"I don't know," she said wearily. "Maybe I'll just run these goons on a wild-goose chase until they get tired of me. Heaven knows they gave me enough money."

"They're not going to let you out of their sight. And don't think they couldn't patch in even to this call."

"They're watching my car. They think I'm eating."

"Good time to slip away?"

"Too open. I've got to get them to somewhere more densely populated. Maybe Denver."

"Be careful."

"Thanks for nothing."

"Hattie, I'm sorry. I—"

"I didn't mean that, Buck. I was trying to be funny. Nothing's funny anymore, is it?"

"If you shake them and are sure, try me again. We may not be at the same place, but if we can accommodate you . . ."

"You would, wouldn't you?"

"Of course we would. You know us."

"Yes, I do. You all were better than I deserved. I'd better get off."

"Yeah. I s'pose you've heard they're trying to pin the assassination on Rayford."

"I heard. Has to be a frame-up. He probably wasn't even there."

"He was there, but he didn't do it."

"You don't have to convince me. Rayford kill somebody? Not in a million years. I know him better than that. Listen, just tell everybody I'm safe and so are they and thanks for everything I didn't deserve."

"Hattie, we all love you and are praying for you."

"I know you are, Buck."

———

David, stunned at the difference between Dr. Eikenberry's public pronouncements and the autopsy, frantically

searched his database for a meeting between her and
Fortunato prior to the meeting with management. He had
to know what approach Leon had used, in case Leon tried
the same with him. Via his hard drive, he bounced all over
the compound but had no luck. He did, however, come
upon a private meeting between Leon and an unidentified
male in a conference room near Carpathia's office.

". . . and how long have you been working for us, sir?"

"Almost from the beginning, Mr. For—Supreme Commander."

"And you're from?"

"Greenland."

"You enjoy your work?"

"Until the assassination, yes."

"The shooting?"

"Well, I meant the stabbing. The assassination of those
two guys at the Temple Mount, that was exciting. I
mean, to see His Excellency put them in their place . . ."

"But you didn't enjoy your job so much when you saw
the potentate himself murdered."

"No, sir. I kept the camera right on him, but it was the
hardest thing I've ever done."

"You know the autopsy is finished, and it was the
gunshot that killed the potentate."

David could not decipher the response, but it sounded
like a snort.

"But there was only one gunshot, Commander—"

"There was only one needed, son. It was a weapon
identical to the one His Excellency used on the trouble-
makers at the Wailing Wall."

"I understand that, but from where I sat, above stage left, I saw the wood speaker's thing—"

"The lectern."

"Yeah, that. I saw that get hit and the curtain go flying. No way that bullet also hit the potentate. He was closer to me."

"Nevertheless, it has been determined that—"

"Excuse me, Commander, but the real murder happened right below me, and I saw it happen."

"And you have reviewed this?"

"Watched it over and over. Couldn't believe it."

"And you discussed it with whom?"

"Just my boss."

"That would be Mr. Bakar?"

"Yes, sir."

Footsteps. A door opening. More faintly: "Margaret, would you have Mr. Bakar join us, please? Thank you."

The door shut and David heard Leon's chair. "Look into my eyes, son. There, yes. You trust me, do you not?"

"Of course."

"When your superior gets here, I am going to tell you both what you saw and what you will remember."

"Excuse me?"

"I am going to tell you what you saw and what you will remember."

"But, sir, I know what I—"

"You understand that I will soon become the new potentate, don't you?"

"I assumed that, yes, sir."

"You did?"

"I think most people assume that."

"Do they?"

No response.

"Do they?" Leon repeated. "Don't just nod. Tell me."

The young man's voice sounded hollow. "Yes."

"You understand that my new title will be Supreme Potentate and that I must also be addressed as Excellency?"

"Yes, Commander."

"You may try out the new title now."

"Yes, Excellency."

"And you realize that I will not only be worthy of worship, but also that worship of me will be mandatory."

"Yes, Excellency."

"Call me Potentate. Supreme Potentate."

"Yes, Supreme Potentate."

"Would you like to kneel before me?"

Silence. Then a knock and a loud sigh from Leon. The door opening. "Excuse me, Commander, but Mr. Bakar is currently engaged in—"

"Margaret!" Leon hissed fiercely. "Do not interrupt me again!"

"I'm, sorry, sir, I—"

"I don't want apologies and I don't want to hear that my subordinates have more important things to do! The next person through this door had better be Mr. Bakar, and for your sake, it had better be within ninety seconds."

"Right away, sir."

The door. The chair. "Now then, son, where were we?"

"I was worshiping you, Supreme Potentate." Another chair.

"That's it. Yes, kneel before me and kiss my ring."

"I see no ring, sir."

"Kiss my finger where the ring will soon be."

A quick knock and the door opening. Bakar's voice: "Forgive me, Commander, I—what the devil is going on?"

"Sit, Director."

"What's he doing on the floor?"

"He was just about to tell me what was on the videodisc you brought back from Jerusalem."

"You've seen it, haven't you, Supreme Commander?"

"Of course, but it seems there's a discrepancy between what he and I saw and what you apparently saw."

"Oh?"

"Yes," Fortunato said. "Return to your chair and tell your boss what you saw."

"I heard the gunshot and saw the potentate's head snap back."

"I get it," Bakar said. "A joke. Now the gun killed him? We all know that's not true."

"It's true," the cameraman said.

"Yeah, I was born yesterday and went blind today."

"Did you go blind, Bakar?" Leon said soothingly.

"Wha—?"

"Lean across the table here and let me see your eyes."

"My eyes are fine, Le—er, Commander. I—"

"Bakar, are you listening to me?"

"Of course, but—"

"Are you listening?"

"Yes!"

"Are you listening? Really listening?"

Silence.

"I have your attention now, don't I, Bakar?"

"You do, sir."

"Bakar, you understand that I will soon become the new potentate, don't you?"

David could stand to listen no more and clicked away from the feed. He stood, dizzy and sick to his stomach. He called Annie and apologized for waking her.

"What is it, David?" she said.

"I need you," he said. "Meet me soon, before I get called in to see Fortunato."

Rayford and Leah agreed to meet Chloe in a mostly destroyed banquet hall that had been turned into a dimly lit, dingy bar. They were ignored, sitting in a dark corner, huddled against wind that gusted through huge gaps in the wall.

Rayford and Chloe embraced, but he wasted little time chastising her. "This is more dangerous than staying put, even if Hattie leads the GC right to the safe house. There's a chance they won't find the underground."

"We need the new place, Dad," she said. "And I'm tired of doing nothing."

"Granted, but let's not get crazy."

Leah's phone chirped. "This is, um, Gerri Seaver."

"Oh, I'm—I'm sorry, I—" *Click.*

"Oh, no!" Leah said. "That was Ming, I'm sure of it."

"Hit Callback," Rayford said.

———

Any doubts Buck had about Chaim's physical condition were erased when they finally left the Night Visitors. Chaim knew exactly where they were headed. He had ripped from one clean corner of his blanket a piece large enough to fit under his hat and extend down the back of his neck and both sides of his face. His nondescript shirt and blowsy pants made him look like any other Israeli day laborer, and he had replaced his slippers with boots.

Buck had a tough time keeping up with him. He jogged as Chaim walked quickly, and though the man was a foot shorter and more than thirty years older, he wore Buck out.

"We get to America and what, I'm holed up with Tsion and you? I won't need to kill myself. You'll both talk me to death."

"There's nothing we could say that you haven't heard already," Buck said, gasping and grateful that that comment had made Chaim stop briefly.

"Now there's the truest thing I've heard all day."

"That's not so," Buck said, slow to start moving again when Chaim took off.

"What?" Chaim said, a step and a half ahead.

"The truest thing you heard today was that you are lost!"

Again Chaim stopped and turned. "I'm lost?"

"Yes!"

In the dim light in the middle of the ravaged City of God, Buck saw the pain in his friend's face.

"You don't think I know I'm lost?" Chaim said, incredulously. "If there's one thing I do know, one thing I am certain of, it is that I am lost. Why do you think I would sacrifice myself to murder the greatest enemy my country has ever had? I did not expect to survive! I was ready to go! Why? Because I am lost! Nothing to live for! Nothing! My farewell act was to be of some benefit to Israel. Now the deed is done and I am here and yes, I am lost!"

Buck was desperate that Chaim not give them away with his ranting. But that was only one reason he approached his dear friend, arms outstretched, and embraced him.

"You don't need to be lost, Chaim. You don't need to be."

And the old man sobbed in Buck's arms.

ELEVEN

"DON'T hang up. It's Leah." She had moved out to the Land Rover to make the call.

"It sounded like you," came the voice Leah never felt fit the delicate Ming Toy. "But who is Gerri something?"

"We international fugitives have to keep changing identities, Ming. If it weren't for the intrigue, what would be the appeal?"

"I don't know how you keep your sense of humor. This is too dangerous, too frightening for me."

"You handle it well, Ming."

"I called with a question. Your friend, Williams?"

"Buck, yes."

"No, not Buck. Longer name."

"Cameron?"

"Yes! Where's his family?"

"West somewhere, why? I think only his father and brother are still around."

"I don't think they're around either. There was lots of talk at Buffer today about what happened to Dr. Rosenzweig's house and his people. They don't know where he is, but they're making it look like everybody died in the fire."

"Yes?"

"They're saying the same thing will happen to Cameron Williams's people if they don't give him up."

"His relatives don't know where he is!" Leah said. "He's smarter than to give them that kind of information."

"Leah, they may already be dead. This was supposed to happen right away."

"What was?"

"Torture. Dismemberment. They tell or they are killed. Then comes the fire to cover it up."

"I don't know what to do."

"Just have your friend check on them. Maybe he can warn them in time."

"I will, Ming. How are you doing? Ready to come see us? Whoops! Hang on." Leah slid down in the seat as two uniformed GC officers strolled by. They stopped right next to the Rover, chatting and smoking. "Ming," Leah whispered, "can you still hear me?"

"Barely. What's going on?"

"I've got company. If I don't say anything, you'll know why."

"If you need to hang up—"

"I'd rather stay on with you. Let me give you Rayford Steele's number in case I get caught. He'll answer to Marvin Berry."

"Got it."

Leah felt the vehicle rock. "They're leaning against the car," she said. "Luckily all the windows are tinted except the windshield."

"Where are you?"

"Illinois."

"I mean in the car."

"Floor of the front seat. Wish I were daintier. The gearshift is killing me."

"They don't see you?"

"Don't think so. I can hear them plain as day."

"What?"

Leah didn't want to speak louder. The Peacekeepers were trading wild party stories. She wanted to say, "Yeah, and I'm the Easter bunny," but she lay still.

"This hunk of junk looks like it's been through a war," one said.

"It has, stupid. It's old enough to have been through the war and the earthquake."

"Tough make."

"Not as tough as the Land Cruiser."

"No? Same company?"

"Toyota."

"Really?"

"Expensive."

"More than this?"

"Quite a bit more."

"No kiddin'? This thing's loaded. I think it's got a GPS."

"This rig? Nah."

"Betcha."

"How much?"

"Ten-spot."

"You're on."

"Oh, no," Leah whispered, "they're coming to the front."

"You need me to call Rayford?"

But Leah didn't answer. She tucked the phone between the seats and pretended to sleep.

"See, isn't that the positioning system right there. Hey! She all right?"

"Who? Oh, man! Door's unlocked. Ask her."

A rap on the window. "Hey, lady!"

Leah ignored it, but moved slightly so they wouldn't think she was dead. When one opened the passenger door, she sat up, trying to look groggy. "Hey, what's the deal?" she said. "You want me to call a Peacekeeper?"

"We are Peacekeepers, ma'am."

"There a law against a girl getting some shut-eye?"

"No, but what're you doin' on the floor? Backseat's wide open."

"Trying to stay out of the sun."

She sat up in the seat, desperate to remember her new address and hometown. Zeke Jr. had reminded her more than once to memorize it as soon as possible. She hated being so new at this part of the game.

"This your vehicle?"

"Borrowing it."

"From?"

"Guy named Russell."

"That a first or last name?"

"Russell Staub."

"He know you're borrowing it?"

"'Course! What're you driving at?"

"Run a check on it," one told the other, who immediately got on his phone. "Where's he from, ma'am?"

"Mount Prospect."

"What're you doing all the way down here?"

She shrugged. "S'posed to meet some friends."

"We're gonna find this Rover registered to a Staub in Mount Prospect, right?"

She nodded. "I don't do his paperwork for him, but that's whose it is and that's where it's from."

"You got any ID, ma'am?"

"Yeah, why?"

"I'd like to see it."

"You've come a long way from wondering if I was all right to accusing me of stealing a car."

"I didn't accuse you of anything, lady. You feeling guilty about something?"

"Should I be?"

"Let me see your ID."

Leah made a show of digging through her purse even after she had located the new documents so she could take a last peek at the new information.

"This your current address, Miss, ah, Seaver?"

"If it says Park Ridge, it is."

"You're a long way from home too."

"Only because there are hardly any roads anymore."

"That's the truth."

"Staub, Mount Prospect," the other officer said. "No outstandings and no reports."

Leah raised her eyebrows, her pulse racing. "Satisfied?"

He handed back her ID. "Don't be out and about without something to do, ma'am. Why don't you get this vehicle back to the owner and get on home."

"Can't I get a drink first, in case my friends show up?"

"Don't be long."

"Thank you." She pushed open the car door and saw Rayford and Chloe on their way out, concern on their faces. "Oh, there they are now! Thanks again, officers!"

———————

Annie had hurried to David's office. They pretended it was a normal superior/subordinate meeting, and he quickly told her what he had heard.

She paled. "That sounds like what Buck Williams went through with Carpathia at the UN."

"But who knew Fortunato could do that?"

"Is *he* the Antichrist?" Annie said.

David shook his head. "I still think it's Carpathia."

"But he's really dead, David. I mean really. How long was he in that bag and in that box? I thought he was supposed to come back to life right away."

"Dr. Ben-Judah thought so too," he said. "What do

we know? If we had this stuff figured out, we probably would have figured out the rest and wouldn't have been left behind."

David's secretary buzzed him. "The Supreme Commander would like to see you."

Annie grabbed his hands. "God," she whispered, "protect him on every side."

"Amen," David said.

————————

Buck and Chaim sat shivering in a ditch at the far north end of a deserted and blocked-off road. Only a small stretch remained smooth, and Buck began to wonder whether it was long enough for the Super J. The jet might be able to land and take off without attracting attention, but if T had to circle or take more than one shot at it, who knew?

Worse, the stretch was unlit. T would use his landing lights only as much as he had to, counting on Buck to guide him in by phone. That meant Buck would have to stand at one end of the makeshift runway or the other. He opted for the front end so he could talk T through coming straight over his head, then he could spin and try to keep him straight until he landed. The only danger was T's coming in too low too quickly. Buck would have to leap out of the way. Still, that seemed easier than trying to elude a plane careening toward him at the other end.

"This is a lot of trouble for someone who doesn't want to leave," Chaim said.

"Well, *I* want to leave even if you don't."

Buck's phone rang, and he assumed it was T, though he had not heard the plane yet. It was Rayford.

"We have a situation here," Rayford said, quickly bringing him up to date on Hattie. "The question is whether now is the time to talk."

"It's not," Buck said. "But in a nutshell, what's up?"

"Wouldn't do that to you, Buck. Call us when you're in the air or in Greece. And greet the brothers for us."

"Will do," Buck said, puzzled at Rayford's new tone. It was as if he were talking to his old father-in-law.

"Chloe sends her love and wants to talk with you when you have time."

"Thanks. Me too."

"I love you, Buck."

"Thanks, Ray. I love you too."

David realized how petrified he was when he nearly blundered by heading straight toward the conference room upon reaching the eighteenth floor. "He in there?" he said, trying to mask his anxiety.

"No," Margaret said, clearly puzzled. "He's with Messrs. Hickman and Moon in his office. They're expecting you."

I will not kneel, David vowed. *I will not worship or kiss his hand. Lord, protect me.*

Leon and the other two directors huddled around a TV monitor. Leon still appeared grief stricken. "Once we get His Excellency into the tomb," he said, his voice thick with emotion, "the world can begin approaching some closure. Prosecuting his murderer can only aid in achieving that. Watch this with us, David. Tell me if you see what we see."

David approached the monitor, certain Fortunato could hear his heartbeat and see the flush of his face. He nearly missed the chair, then settled in awkwardly.

Shot from above, the videodisc was crystal clear. At the sound of the gunshot from Carpathia's left, he had turned and run into the wheelchair as Chaim rolled toward him. Chaim grabbed at the metal back support over his left shoulder and quickly produced what appeared to be a two-foot sword. As Nicolae tumbled atop him, Chaim whipped the weapon in front of him, holding it with both hands, point up, sharp edge facing away from the potentate.

Chaim lifted his forearms as Carpathia's body met the blade, and the sword slipped into his neck and straight through the top of his head as easily as a bayonet would slice a watermelon. Carpathia's hands shot to his chin, but David kept his eyes on Chaim, who violently twisted the handle at the base of Nicolae's neck. He let go as Carpathia dropped, then quickly steered stage left and sat with his back to the dying man.

"Well?" Leon said, peering at him. "Is there any doubt?"

David stalled, but all that served was to make the other two glance at him.

"Cameras don't lie," Leon said. "We have our assassin, don't we?"

Much as he wanted to argue, to come up with some other way to interpret what was clear, David would jeopardize his position if he proved illogical. He nodded. "We sure do."

Leon approached him, and David froze. The supreme commander took David's face in his fleshy hands and looked deep into his eyes. David fought the urge to look away, praying all the while that he would do the right thing and hoping that Annie was continuing to pray too. Like Nicolae, here was a man with clear mind control over unbelievers. He felt his pulse in his ears and wondered if Leon could detect his panic through his fingers.

"Director Hassid," Leon said, eyes boring into his. "Rayford Steele shot dead our beloved potentate."

Rayford? Hadn't they watched the same video?

Leon would be suspicious if David agreed too quickly.

"No," David said, "the disc was clear. Dr. Ro—"

"A stroke victim and a great loyal statesman would be incapable of such an act, would he not?"

"But—"

Fortunato's sweaty palms still cupped his cheeks. "The only killing weapon was the Saber in the hands of Rayford Steele, who shall have to pay for his crime."

"Rayford Steele?" David said, his voice cracking like a junior high schooler.

"The assassin."

"The assassin?"

"Look again, David, and tell me what you see."

David was terrified. He had not noticed anyone switching discs, yet this version indeed showed Rayford firing at the stage. David wondered if he was weaker than Buck had been three and a half years before. Was it possible that Leon *could* make him see something that wasn't there? He stared, unblinking. Time seemed to stand still.

Someone had to have changed the disc while he was distracted in Leon's hands. This was no concoction, no mind game. For while this showed the gunshot, it also showed Nicolae falling into Chaim's lap.

"Slow it down," David said, trying to mimic the flat voices he had heard earlier. He believed his ruse was failing miserably, but he had no choice but to play it out.

"Yes, Walter," Leon said. "Show the fatal shot again and slow it down."

David fought for control, determined to watch the lectern, the curtain, the kings. As soon as the flash of fire and the puff of smoke appeared at the end of the Saber, the lectern split, and the pieces hurtled toward the ten kings. The curtain seemed to twist on itself from the middle and shoot into the distance. Chaim appeared to come from behind the falling potentate and steer toward the center of the stage. The angle was wrong for seeing what he had actually done.

To his disgust, David had to submit a second time to Leon's hands on his face. "Well?" Leon said, peering at him. "Is there any doubt?"

This time David could not stall. He was suddenly

aware of Leon's overbearing cologne. How had he missed that before?

"Cameras don't lie," Leon said. "We have our assassin, don't we?"

David nodded, forcing Leon to loosen his grip. "We sure do," he managed. "Steele must pay."

———

"I hate this," Leah said as the three sat inside again. "It's nerve-racking. We shouldn't be out during the day. Too many things can go wrong."

"You shouldn't have gone to the car," Chloe said.

Leah cocked her head and gave Chloe a stare. "*I* shouldn't have gone to the car? I'm not the reason we're here, dear."

"I didn't ask you to come," Chloe said.

"Stop," Rayford said. "This gets us nowhere. Now, Chloe, I'm sorry, but this was a monumentally stupid thing to do."

"Dad! We need to get to the new place."

"And we have to check it out, but we're way past where we can get away with being out one second more than necessary, except at night."

"All right! OK! I'm sorry!"

Leah reached for her hand. "Me too," she said, but Chloe pulled away.

"C'mon, don't do that," Leah said. "I shouldn't have said that, and I'm sorry. We have to be able to work together."

"We need to get out of here," Rayford said. "Those guys think we're just friends in here for a drink. We can't stay till dark."

"We should get closer to Chicago," Chloe said.

"That'll look *more* suspicious," Rayford said, "unless we can find a place where we could leave the cars out of sight and still be able to walk into the city."

"Where the L tracks end now?" Chloe suggested.

"They end everywhere," Leah said. "Totally shut down, right?"

"Well," Chloe said, "the tracks are torn up heading in from the south, and then they're OK in the city, but they're closed."

Rayford looked to the ceiling. "So how about we find a place to hide the cars down that way, coming in from separate directions, then follow the tracks into the city."

Leah nodded. "Good idea."

Chloe said, "That's what I thought."

"If you're where I think you are," T said, "it looks impossible."

"You can see the road?" Buck said. "Why can't I hear you?"

"Wind, maybe, but you'll hear me soon. I'm already lower than I want to be, but I sure hope I'm looking at the wrong road."

"There's only one possibility in this area," Buck said. "If you see any stretch of open road, you're looking at us."

"Buck, do you have any idea how long it takes for one of these to stop? An aircraft carrier would be easier."

"Any options?"

"Yeah! I land at Jerusalem Airport or better yet, Tel Aviv, and we hope for the best."

"It would be more efficient for Chaim to commit suicide right here than to risk that, T. They're looking for him."

"I'm willing to try this, Buck, but it sure seems an uninspired way to become a martyr."

"I hear you."

"Thanks."

"I mean I literally hear you. Flash your landing lights. . . . I see you! You're way to my right!"

"Adjusting."

"More. More! More! There! No, a little left now! Hold."

"I see nothing!"

"Use your lights when you need to. That'll help me too."

"I don't like what I'm not seeing." The landing lights came on and stayed on this time. "Now I don't like what I *am* seeing."

"You seem high. I thought you were too low."

"I was lower than I wanted to be with all those emergency lights off to the left down there. Let's hope they're too busy to look up."

"You still seem high."

"I am. But I still don't see you either."

"If you stay up there, I'm safe. You gonna go 'round again?"

"Negative. I have one shot and I'm going to make it work."

"You'd better start dropping."

"Here I come."

Buck put his phone down and waved, though he couldn't imagine T seeing him from that angle. The plane drifted right, and Buck tried to signal T back to center. With his lights still on, T should have been able to see that for himself.

As the Super J screamed past him, Buck grabbed his phone and shouted, "You straight?"

"Straight as I can get! No way this works! Too steep! Too fast!"

"Abort?"

"Too late!"

Buck shut his eyes as the plane dropped and the hot exhaust swept past him. He covered his ears, knowing that would never block the sound of the impact. But what he heard wasn't a plane crash. He thought he detected the screech of tires over the din of the jets, but that may have been wishful thinking. He peeked through the dust and exhaust to see the plane bounce a couple of feet, the red exhaust flame pointing at him.

The next impact resounded like a rifle shot. White smoke billowed from beneath the craft, and the plane began spinning wildly—the red exhaust, then the landing lights, then the exhaust again. Suddenly the lights went off, but the jets continued to burn. The noise abated except for the whine of the engine, but Buck no longer saw anything. The plane had to be facing him. He had not heard the fuselage break up, as he had feared if T couldn't stop.

He ran toward the plane, amazed to see Chaim beside him, keeping pace.

———————

The New Babylon night was warm and dry. Spotlights from a dozen angles bathed the palace courtyard, nearly bright as day. Nothing would compete with the merciless, cloudless, sun-filled daytime sky, but until then, everyone could clearly see all there was to see.

David and Annie were among the hundreds of employees allowed—or in their case assigned—to file past the bier ahead of the pilgrims from around the globe. The couple waited on the steps while ten pallbearers—four men on each side and one at each end—solemnly carried in the draped Plexiglas box, accompanied by a live orchestra playing a dirge. From behind the barricades an eighth of a mile away, the mourning began. Employees began to wail too. The men gently placed the bier atop the pedestal and carefully positioned it. A technician, with what appeared to be a portable vacuum cleaner tucked under one arm, knelt between one of the end men and a side man and screwed a pressure gauge into the rubber stopper at the foot end. He checked the readout twice, then hooked a hose to the stopper, twisted a dial, and ran the suction machine for two seconds. He checked the pressure once more, removed everything but the stopper, then hurried away.

The eight side men backed smartly away while the two on the ends removed the shroud. Annie seemed to recoil. David was stunned. He had expected Carpathia to appear lifelike. The work of Dr. Eikenberry had been astounding, of course, as there was no evidence of trauma. Yet somehow, even in a dark suit, white shirt, and striped tie, Carpathia appeared more lifeless than any corpse David had ever seen.

The bier itself was shaped like an old-fashioned pine box, the torso area expanding to contain Carpathia's robust physique. The lid was two inches thick and bolted to the sides with huge, stainless steel screws that bit deep into the plastic, pulled the casket gasket tight, and were secured at their undersides by self-locking washers and screws.

The lid was not three inches above Carpathia's face, and as people passed, they could lean over the velvet ropes and see their breath on the top. If this was Carpathia, he would be closer to his people in death than he had ever been in life.

David had listened to the revised autopsy report wherein all references to the sword and its damage were omitted and the bullet trauma was added. At the end of that, Dr. Eikenberry had launched a clinical play-by-play as she secured the eyelids with adhesive and stitched the lips with invisible thread.

David was curious and wanted a closer look. Fortunately, the cluster in front of them paused for more than a minute. David leaned forward and studied the remains, knowing this probably made him look grief stricken. He wondered if this was really Carpathia. The body looked stiff, cold, pale. Could it be a wax figure? Might the resurrection occur in the morgue refrigerator? The vacuum-sealed Plexiglas bier certainly would not be conducive.

Carpathia's hands were more lifelike and convincing. Left was draped over right at the waist, and they looked manicured and only slightly paler than in life. They rested within a quarter inch of the transparent lid. David almost wished the man were worthy of this display.

David was stunned when several ahead of him made religious gestures, from crossing themselves to bowing. A woman nearly toppled as she gave in to tears, and David wondered what the outcry from the public would be like if GC personnel reacted like this.

Three armed guards stood on the other side of the bier. When any mourner touched the glass, the closest guard leaned over and wiped the prints away, polishing, polishing.

Finally the line moved, and David tried to guide Annie for a closer look. She surreptitiously stiffened, and he let her stay outside him as they passed. The man behind David collapsed to his knees upon full view of the body and moaned in a foreign tongue. David turned to see it was Bakar.

Annie left, still looking exhausted, and David moved atop an observation deck that had been fashioned as the second floor of one of the medical tents. He watched as the barricades were pulled away and the crowd slowly began to move toward the bier.

Someone hurrying around the outside of the courtyard distracted David, heading toward where the evidence room had already been dismantled. It was a woman carrying a bulky, paper package. He scampered down and excused himself through the crowd to get to the area from the opposite direction of the woman.

When he arrived he saw her, Dr. Eikenberry, hurrying back the way she had come. Guy Blod stood there with the package. He looked at David and shrugged. "We're going to make dawn," he said. "Thanks to your help."

David didn't want to be pals with Guy. But he did want to know what was in the package. "What've you got there, Minister Blod?"

"Just something she said the Supreme Commander wants in the statue."

"*In* the statue?"

Guy nodded. "Which means it has to go in now, because once we weld this together, the only things that will get inside it will have to be smaller than the eyeballs, nostrils, or mouth. I mean, at four times life-size, they'll be plenty big, but . . ."

"May I?" David said, reaching for the package.

"Whatever," Guy said. "It's going to burn anyway."

"Burn?"

"Or melt. The hollow legs will be an eternal furnace; don't you love it?"

"What's not to love?" David said, peeking through a corner of the paper. In his hands was the real murder weapon.

TWELVE

As RAYFORD followed Leah and Chloe out of the ersatz bar, one of the GC Peacekeepers was coming in. "You wouldn't be Ken Ritz, would you?"

Rayford fought for composure and noticed Leah stiffen and Chloe shoot the man a double take. With a furtive nudge, Rayford urged Chloe to keep moving and hoped Leah would do the same.

"Who's askin'?" Rayford said.

"Just yes or no, pardner," the guard said.

"Then no," Rayford said, brushing past.

"Hold on a second there, pop." Rayford preferred *pardner*. "Let me see some ID."

"I told you I'm not whoever you're looking for."

The guard stood in the doorway with his hand out. Rayford showed his papers.

"So, Mr. Berry, you *know* Ken Ritz?"

"Can't say that I do."

"How about your friends?"

"Guess you'd have to ask them."

"No need to be a smart aleck."

"My apologies, but how would I know about them if I don't know him?"

The guard nodded his dismissal, and as Rayford emerged, he heard him calling out in the bar: "Ken Ritz in here? R-I-T-Z!"

Leah and Chloe waited by the Rover while the other guard had one foot on the bumper of the Suburban. He was on the phone.

Rayford walked nonchalantly to the driver's side of the Rover, and the three climbed in. As he pulled away, Rayford said, "Well, so much for the Suburban."

"Thanks to me," Chloe said. "Go ahead and say it, you two. This is all my fault."

———

Chaim's bravado had finally cracked. Buck thought it might have been due to exhaustion from the running, but for whatever reason, the old man was in a panic. Buck was strangely encouraged. There was little more difficult than rescuing someone who didn't care to be rescued. At least Chaim retained a degree of self-preservation. It was a start.

The Super J sat at a severe angle with a blown tire. The door swung down and T leaned out. "You must be Dr. Rosenzweig," he shouted.

"Yeah, hey, hi, how are ya," Chaim said with a wave. "You know we got people coming, and you've got a flat tire?"

"I was afraid of that," T said. He reached to shake Rosenzweig's hand.

"Save the introductions until the GC shoots us," Chaim said. "We've got to get out of here. Have you taken off in a plane with only one tire?"

"We're not going to outrun anybody on foot. Let's give this a try."

Buck stepped up behind Rosenzweig and tried to guide him up the stairs. He wouldn't be moved. "This is lunacy, Cameron! There's barely enough road here to take off if the plane was healthy."

"You ready to turn yourself in?"

"No!"

"Well, we're leaving. You coming or taking your chances?" Buck pushed past him up the steps. He grabbed the handle and set himself to lift the door. "Last call," he said.

"There's *no* chance on the plane," Rosenzweig whined. "We're all going to die."

"No, Chaim," Buck said. "Our *only* chance is in the air. Have you given up?"

Rosenzweig leaped aboard as T muscled the plane to the end of the road, turned around, and gave it full throttle. Buck and Chaim, listing far to the left, buckled themselves in. Buck prayed. Chaim muttered, "Lunacy, lunacy. No chance. No hope."

With the engines screaming, the plane was suddenly

level, though they weren't moving. Buck didn't know how T was doing it, but he used the propulsion and the brake to feather the craft up onto its one good tire. As he released the brake and maneuvered the controls, the Super J teetered crazily as it shot down the road.

At the other end the pavement had been twisted and tossed up onto its side to form a four- or five-foot barrier. As they hurtled straight toward it, Buck knew T had to find the right combination of speed and runway to pull this off. Buck couldn't tear his eyes from the barrier. Chaim sat with his head between his legs, hands clasped behind his head. He moaned, "Oh, God, oh God, oh God," and Buck had the impression it was a sincere prayer.

It seemed there was no way the J would get enough lift to clear the barrier. T seemed to be doing everything he could to keep the plane level, but the imbalance had to be affecting speed too. At the last instant T seemed to abandon balance and put all his efforts into thrust. The jet lifted off the road, then dropped, and the tire chirped on the pavement before lifting yet again.

Buck grimaced and held his breath as they swept toward the barrier. T must have adjusted one flap to avoid a direct hit, because the plane lurched right, and something underneath slammed the barrier. Now they were in no-man's-land.

"God forgive me!" Chaim shouted as the jet was tossed back to the left, then dipped and nearly crashed as T pulled out all the stops. The tail seemed to drag, and Buck couldn't imagine how it stayed airborne. They headed for a grove of trees, but it was as if T knew he couldn't afford the drag that a turn would require. He seemed to set the jet at the shallowest possible angle to clear the trees and set it at full power. That was their one chance to get airborne, and if successful, the Super J would rocket into the night toward Greece. T would have to worry later about conserving fuel and landing on one tire.

Buck sat with fists clenched, eyes shut, grimacing, fully expecting to hit the trees and crash. He was pressed back against his seat, his head feeling the G forces as the Super J broke into open sky. He allowed his eyes to open, and in his peripheral vision, Chaim remained hunched over, now lamenting in Hebrew.

Buck unstrapped but found himself struggling to step toward the cockpit against the centrifugal force. "You did it, T!"

"Lost what was left of that bad tire, though," T said. "Think we lost the whole wheel assembly. I thought we were going down."

"Me too. That was some takeoff."

"I've got about two hours to decide how to land. I know one-wheel landings can be done, but I'd almost rather pull up the one good wheel and go in belly first."

"Would this thing take it?"

"Not like a big one would. I'd say we're fifty-fifty for success either way."

"That's all?"

T reached for Buck's hand. "I'll see you in heaven, regardless."

"Don't say that."

"I mean it. If I didn't believe that, I'd have taken my chances with the GC back there."

Buck started when Chaim spoke, and he realized the Israeli was standing right behind him. "You see, Cameron? I was right! I should not have come! Now we have a one-in-two chance of surviving, and you two are just fine, knowing where you're going . . ."

"I wouldn't say I'm fine, Chaim," Buck said. "I'll be leaving a wife and son."

"You've already given up?" T said. "I said we've got a fifty-fifty chance of landing successfully. Even a crash landing doesn't have to be fatal."

"Thanks for that cheery word," Buck said, turning to head back to his seat.

"Pray for me," T called after him.

"I will," Buck said.

"So will I," Chaim said, and Buck shot him a look. He didn't appear to be kidding.

After Rosenzweig was buckled in, Buck leaned over and clapped him on the knee. "You don't have to be afraid of death, you know. I mean dying, yeah, I'm afraid of that too, afraid it'll hurt, that I might burn. I hate leaving my family. But you're right. T and I know where we're going."

Chaim looked terrible, worse than Buck had seen him since the night before. He couldn't make it compute. Chaim had seemed almost giddy after escaping the Gala. Then he was suicidal after hearing about Jacov and his family and Stefan. But now he looked grave. So, he was human after all. Despite all the talk of suicide, he was afraid to die.

Buck knew he had to be as forthright with Chaim as he had ever been. "We may meet God tonight, Chaim," he began, but Rosenzweig immediately made a face and waved him off.

"Don't think I wasn't listening all these years, Cameron. There is nothing more you can tell me."

"Still you refuse?"

"I didn't say that. I just said I don't need to be walked through this."

Buck couldn't believe it. Chaim said that as if he were going to do "this" on his own.

"I do have one question, however, Cameron. I know you don't consider yourself an expert like Dr. Ben-Judah, but what is your best guess about how God feels about motives?"

"Motives?"

Chaim looked frustrated, as if he wished Buck caught his drift without Chaim having to explain. He looked away, then back at Buck. "I know God is real," he said, as if confessing a crime. "There has been too much evidence to deny it. I can't explain away any of the prophecies, because they all come true. The evidences for Jesus as Messiah nearly convinced me, and I had never been a Messiah watcher. But if I were to do what you and Tsion have been pleading with me to do for so long, I confess it would be with the wrong motive."

Except for the likelihood that they might be dead within a couple of hours, Buck wished Tsion was with them right then. He wanted to ask Chaim what his motive was, but he sensed he would lose him if he interrupted.

Chaim pressed his lips together and hung his head. When he looked up again, he seemed to fight tears. He shook his head and looked away. "I need to think some more, Cameron."

"Chaim, I've pleaded with you before to not run out of time. Clearly I'm on solid footing to say so now."

Suddenly Rosenzweig leaned over and grabbed Buck's elbow. "That's the very issue! I'm scared to death. I don't want to die. I thought I did, thought it was the only answer to being a murderer, even if I believed I was just in killing the man. But I did it with forethought, with months of forethought. I planned it, fashioned my own weapon, and saw it through. I have no pity, no sympathy for Nicolae Carpathia. I came to believe, as you do, that he was the devil incarnate."

That wasn't quite accurate, but Buck held his tongue. While believers were convinced Carpathia was the Antichrist and deserved to be killed and stay dead, they knew that he would not literally be Satan incarnate until he came back to life. Whether he deserved to live again or not, that was what was prophesied.

"It's hard for me to fathom that I might have been in God's plan from the beginning. If it is true that Carpathia is the enemy of God and that he was supposed to die from a sword wound to the head, I feel like Judas."

Judas? A nonreligious Jew knows the New Testament too?

"Don't look so surprised, Cameron. Everyone understands what a Judas is. Someone was to betray Jesus, and it fell to Judas. Someone was to murder Antichrist, and while I cannot say it actually fell to me, I took the job into my own hands. But say it *was* my destiny. Though apparently God *wanted* it done, it certainly was not legal. And look at what it has cost me already! My freedom. My peace of mind, which, I admit, is only a distant memory. My loved ones.

"But Cameron, can God accept me if my motive is selfish?"

Buck squinted and turned to look out the window. The dim, sparse lights of Israel receded fast. "We all come to faith selfish in some ways, Chaim. How could it be otherwise? We want to be forgiven. We want to be accepted, received, included. We want to go to heaven instead of hell. We want to be able to face death knowing what comes next. *I* was selfish. I didn't want to face the Antichrist without the protection of God in my life."

"But Cameron, I am merely afraid to die! I feel like a coward. Here I did this rash thing, which many would say took courage and even strength of character. At first I took pride in it. Now I know, of course, that God could have used anyone to do it. He could have caused something to pierce Carpathia's head during the earthquake. He could have had a political rival or a crazy man do it. Perhaps he did! Part of it was compulsion, especially perfecting the weapon. But I had motives, Cameron. I hated the man. I hated his lies and his broken promises to my homeland. I hated even what he did to the practicing Jews and their new temple, even though I did not count myself among them.

"I am without excuse! I am guilty. I am a sinner. I am lost. I don't want to die. I don't want to go to hell. But I fear he will cast me out because I squandered so many opportunities, because I resisted for so long, because I suffered even many of the judgments and still was cold and hard. Now, if I come whimpering to God as a child, will he see through me? Will he consider me the little boy who cried wolf? Will he know that down deep I am merely a man who once had a wonderful life and enjoyed what I now see were bountiful gifts from God—a creative mind, a wonderful home and family, precious friends—and became a crazy old fool?

"Cameron, I sit here knowing that all you and Tsion and your dear associates have told me is true. I believe that God loves me and cares about me and wants to forgive me and accept me, and yet my own conscience gets in the way."

Buck was praying as he had not prayed in ages. "Chaim, if you told God what you're telling me, you'd find out the depth of his mercy."

"But, Cameron, I would be doing this only because I'm afraid I'm going to die in this plane! That's all. Do you understand?"

Buck nodded. He understood, but did he know the answer to Chaim's question? People through the ages had all kinds of motives for becoming believers, and surely fear was a common one. He'd heard Bruce Barnes say that people sometimes come to Christ for fire insurance—to stay out of hell—only to later realize all the benefits that come with the policy.

"You said yourself that I don't consider myself an expert," Buck said, "but you also said you knew you were a sinner. That's the real reason we need Jesus. If you weren't a sinner, you'd be perfect and you wouldn't need to worry about forgiveness and salvation."

"But I knew I was a sinner before, and I didn't care!"

"You weren't staring death in the face either. You weren't wondering whether you might end up in hell."

Rosenzweig rubbed his palms together. "I was tempted to do this when I was suffering from the locust attack. I knew that was a prophesied biblical event, but I also knew that becoming a believer would not speed my recovery. You told me that yourself. And relief would have been my only motive then, as I fear it is now. What I should do, intellectually, is wait and see if I survive this landing or this crash or whatever it is we're going to do. If I am not facing imminent death, I won't be so suspicious of my own intentions."

"In other words," Buck said, "'get me out of this and I'll become a believer'?"

Chaim shook his head. "I know better than to bargain with God. He owes me nothing; he need not do one more thing to persuade me. I just want to be honest. If I would not have come to the same conclusion on the ground or in a plane with two good tires, then I should not rush into it now."

Buck cocked his head. "Friend, rushing into this would be the last way I would describe you. My question is, why do you feel in any more danger now than you did on the ground, or than you will feel if we land safely?"

Chaim raised his chin and shut his eyes. "I don't. The GC has already announced my death and is now free to exterminate me without the nuisance of publicity. That's why I found myself running to this plane. I don't need to tell you the dread of living in exile."

"But whatever motive you have now, you will also have if we survive. Nothing changes."

"Maybe I'll lose the urgency," Rosenzweig said, "the sense of imminence."

"But you don't know that. They may have to foam the runway, bring out the emergency vehicles, all that. You can't hide under a blanket or claim to be contagious when we leave the plane. And you can't hide in the lav until the coast is clear. You're going to be as exposed and as vulnerable as ever, safe landing or no."

Chaim held up a hand and slowly closed his eyes. "Give me a minute," he said. "I may have more questions, but just leave me alone a moment."

That was the last thing Buck wanted to do just then, but neither did he want to push Chaim away. He settled back, amazed at how smooth was the ride that might lead them to eternity.

––––––

Kenny Bruce took long afternoon naps, and Tsion looked forward to that. He loved the boy and had had a lot of fun with him for the last fourteen months, even in cramped quarters. He was a good-natured, though normal, kid, and Tsion loved teasing him and playing with him.

Kenny could be wearying, however, especially for one who had not been around infants for nearly twenty years. Tsion needed a nap himself, though he was still desperate not to miss whatever was going to happen in New Babylon.

"Mama?" Kenny asked for the dozenth time, not troubled but curious. It was unusual for her to be gone.

"Bye-bye," Tsion said. "Home soon. Getting sleepy?"

Kenny shook his head, even as he rubbed his eyes and appeared to be trying to keep them open. He yawned and sat with a toy, soon losing interest. He lay on his back, feet flat on the floor, knees up. Staring at the ceiling, he yawned, turned on his side, and was soon motionless. Tsion carried him to the playpen so he wouldn't fuss if he awoke before Tsion did. There were plenty of things to keep him occupied there.

Tsion settled before the TV again and put his feet up. The underground was cool, so he draped a blanket over himself. He tried to keep his eyes open as the GC CNN pool camera remained trained on the transparent coffin and the endless line of the mourning faithful from around the world.

Knowing that young David Hassid and his lady friend Annie Christopher were there, along with who knew how many other believers, he began silently walking through his prayer list. When he closed his eyes to pray for his comrades and his cybercongregation (more than a billion now), he felt himself nodding and his brain longing for sleep.

He peeked at the digital clock on the videodisc player atop the TV. He set the machine to record, just in case he fell asleep and was unable to wake up in time for "the" event. As he settled back in to try to pray, knowing full well he would drift off, the clock showed 12:57 in the afternoon.

Tsion began praying for Chloe, Leah, and Rayford, whom he knew were in the state. Then he prayed for T, Rayford's friend, who was presently unaccounted for. Then Cameron, always in the middle of something and who knew where. As his mind drifted to his old friend and professor, Dr. Rosenzweig, Tsion began feeling a tingle, much like when he had tried to intercede for Rayford.

Was it fatigue, a hallucination? So disconcerting, so real. He forced his eyes open. The clock still read 12:57, but he felt as if he were floating. And when he let his eyes fall shut again, he could still see plain as day. The cramped cellar was cool and musty, the sparse furniture in its place. Kenny slept unmoving in the playpen, blanket still tucked around him.

Tsion saw this from above now, as if in the middle of the room. He saw himself asleep on the couch. He had heard of out-of-body experiences but had never had one, or dreamed one. This didn't seem like a dream, didn't feel like one. He felt weightless, moving higher, wondering if the joists from the flooring above would conk him on the head as he rose and whether that would hurt a floating, hallucinating, dreaming, praying, or sleep-deprived man. He wasn't sure what kind of a man he was right then, but despite his incredible lightness of being, he felt as conscious and aware as he had ever been. Though he knew he was unconscious, he had never been so attuned to his senses. He could see clearly and feel everything from temperature to the air moving over the hair on his arms as he ascended. He heard every noise in the house, from Kenny's breathing to the refrigerator kicking on as he passed it.

Yes, he had drifted through the first floor, but he could still see Kenny and neither worried nor felt guilty about leaving him. For he saw himself too, still on the couch, knowing that if Kenny needed him, he could return as quickly as he had left.

The fall air was crisp above the house, yet he was glad he was in shirtsleeves. It was not uncomfortable, but he was so aware of everything . . . feeling, seeing, hearing—the wind through the dead-leafed trees. He even smelled the decaying leaves on the ground, though no one burned them anymore. No one did anything anymore that used to be mundane. Life was about surviving now, not about incidentals. If a task did not put food on the table or provide shelter, it was ignored.

In an instant Tsion instinctively shot his arms out for balance and felt as if he had returned almost to his sleeping form in the underground. But the house, the half-destroyed village of Mount Prospect, the northwest suburbs, the twisted ribbons that used to be highways and tollways, the whole Chicago area had become minuscule beneath him.

Would he soon grow colder, lose oxygen? How could it be that he was this far from home, now looking at a blue globe that reminded him of the hauntingly beautiful pictures of earth from the moon? Daylight turned to night, but the earth was still illuminated. He felt as if he were in the deep recesses of space, maybe on the moon. Was he on the moon? He looked about him and saw only stars and galaxies. He reached for the earth, because it seemed to recede too quickly. In a strange way, though he could not see it anymore, he sensed he and Kenny still slept in Mount Prospect at the safe house.

He was soon able to see the planets as he drifted, drifted, farther and farther from all that he knew. How fast could he be going? Such physical questions seemed pedestrian, irrelevant. The question was, where was he and where was he going? How long could this go on?

It was so, so strange and wonderful, and for the briefest instant, Tsion wondered if he had died. Was he on his way to heaven? He had never believed heaven was on the same physical plane as the universe, somewhere rocket men could go if they had the resources. And at the same time he had never before felt so thoroughly alive. He was not dead. He was somewhere in his mind, he was convinced.

In an instant, as he seemed to hang weightless in space, it seemed he accelerated yet again. He raced through the vast universe itself, with its numberless galaxies and solar systems. The only sound was his own breathing, and to his amazement, it was rhythmic and deep, as if, as if, as if he were asleep.

But he wondered how so puny a mind could dream

such a vista. And as if a switch had been pulled, the darkness turned to the brightest light, obliterating the utter darkness of space. Just as the stars disappear in the light of the sun, so everything he had passed on his way to this plateau vanished. He hung motionless in soundless, weightless animation, a sense of expectancy coursing through him.

This light, like a burst of burning magnesium so powerful as to chase even a shadow, came from above and behind him. Despite the sense of wonder and anticipation, he feared turning toward it. If this was the Shekinah glory, would he not die in its presence? If this was the very image of God, could he see it and live?

The light seemed to beckon him, to will him to turn. And so he did.

THIRTEEN

RAYFORD drove as close as he could to the Chicago city limits, staying on a rebuilt collar road that had ominous warning signs its entire length, prohibiting traffic beyond its northern line. Patrolling GC cars ignored the sparse traffic, so Rayford looked for a turn that would appear to take him into a local area but which might lead him off-road to the city.

He felt as conspicuous and obvious as he had in a long time, bouncing over dusty lots and through closed forest preserves in the middle of the day. But he detected no tail. He parked the Land Rover beneath a crumbling former L station. He and Chloe and Leah sat in the shade, Rayford beginning to feel the fatigue that had preceded his wonderful sleep in Greece.

"This is my fault," Chloe said. "I was impatient and stupid and selfish. No way we can walk into Chicago until tonight. And how far is it? Twenty miles to the Strong Building? It'll take hours."

Leah shifted in her seat. "If you're looking for someone to argue with you, I can't. I'm not trying to be mean, but we're going to sit here until dark. Then we're going to walk at least five hours to what, check out our next safe house?"

Chloe sat shaking her head.

"We're not walking anywhere," Rayford said. "I know this town like the back of my hand. When it's good and dark, we're going to drive to the building with our lights off. The GC aren't keeping people out of here for fun. They really believe it's contaminated. If we have to turn on the lights now and then to keep from getting swallowed up in a hole and some surveillance plane spots us or some heat detector locates us, at worst they'll warn us to get out. They're not coming in after us."

"No, Dad," Chloe said. "The worst that will happen is that they force us out and figure out who you are."

"They would keep their distance and check us for radiation first."

"And finding none, there goes our whole plan."

"There's enough to think negatively about these days," Rayford said. "Let's think positive. Bad enough I have to give Buck the news about his family soon."

"Let me do that, Dad."

"Are you sure?"

"Absolutely. When he calls, let me talk to him."

But when Buck called, it was clear this was still not the time to give him news like that. Rayford watched as

Chloe seemed to disintegrate on the phone. "Thank you, sweetheart," she said. "Thanks for telling us. We'll be praying. I love you too, and Kenny loves you. Call me as soon as you can. Promise me."

Chloe rang off and quickly brought Rayford and Leah up to speed.

"So that's where T is," Rayford said. "Good thinking on Buck's part. We need to pray for them right now."

"Especially for Chaim," Chloe said. "He sounds close."

"Landing on one wheel is risky," Rayford said, "but it can be done. I think this is T's first time in a Super J, though."

"What kinds of odds would you give them?" Leah said, then appeared to regret asking, realizing Chloe could lose her husband within the next twenty minutes.

"No, I want to know too," Chloe said. "Really, Dad. What are their chances?"

Rayford stalled but saw little value in getting Chloe's hopes up. "About one in two," he said.

Chaim called for Buck, who had joined T in the cockpit. Buck went back and knelt near Chaim's seat. "One more question," Rosenzweig said. "Dare I test God?"

"How?"

"Tell him I want to believe, offer him what's left of my life, and just see if he'll accept me in spite of my selfish motive."

"I can't speak for God," Buck said. "But it seems to me if we're sincere, he'll do what he promised. You already know that this is about more than mere believing, because you believe now. The Bible says the demons believe and tremble. It's a decision, a commitment, a receiving."

"I know."

"We're about fifteen minutes out, Chaim, give or take circling and getting some tower help. Don't stall."

"But you see?" Chaim said. "That just contributes to my problem. I won't be any more just because my time may be running out. I may be even less."

"Let God decide," Buck said.

Chaim nodded miserably. Buck didn't envy his having to work this out while wondering how long he had to live. Chloe and Kenny were at the forefront of Buck's mind, and knowing he would see them again in three and a half years regardless did nothing to abate his desperation not to leave them.

He headed back to the seat next to T. "I've been in touch with the tower at an airport south of Ptolemaïs called Kozani. They agree I might have a better shot trying a belly landing than trying to put down on one wheel. No telling how strong that one is, or how good a pilot I am. If I'm not perfect, we bounce and that's it. Going in flat will allow me to land at the slowest possible speed and hope for the best."

"You've got to really be smooth, don't you?"

"Tell me about it."

"You gonna fly over low first and see if they can get a look at the wheels?"

T pointed to the fuel gauge, buried on empty. "You tell me."

"Well, that could be good news, couldn't it?"

"How so?" T said.

"If we crash, we don't burn."

"If we crash, Buck, you're going to want to burn. You're going to wish we were vaporized."

Tsion felt such a sense of peace and well-being that he didn't want this to end, dream or not. He knew he should be terrified to turn and face the light, but it was the light itself that drew him.

He did not move as if in water or in a vacuum. He didn't have to move his limbs. All he had to do was will himself to turn, and he turned. At first Tsion believed he was looking into a bottomless crevice, the only dark spot in a wall of bright white. But as he backed away from the image, so real he believed he could touch it, other dark spaces of relief came into view. As his eyes adjusted to the light, he pulled back far enough to make out a face. It was as if he dangled between the nose and cheekbone of some heavenly Mount Rushmore image.

But this was neither carved from stone nor made of flesh and bone. Huge and bright and strong, it was also at once translucent, and Tsion was tempted to will himself to pass through it. But as it should have been frightening and was not, he wanted to see the whole. If a head, then a body? He pulled back to see the face ringed with hair massive as prairie grass. It framed a face kindly and yet not soft, loving and yet confident and firm.

Tsion knew beyond doubt he was imagining this, and at the same time it was *the* most sensory-rich experience of his life. It burned into his mind's eye, and he believed he would never forget it nor experience anything like it again as long as he lived.

His voice nearly failed him, but he managed to croak, "Are you Jesus the Christ?"

A rumble, a chuckle, a terrestrial laugh? "No," came a gentle voice that surrounded him and, coming from a mouth that size, should have blown him into oblivion. "No, son of the earth, I am merely one of his princes."

Tsion pulled back farther to take in the scope of this beautiful heavenly being. "Gabriel?" he whispered.

"Gabriel and I are as brothers, child. He announces. I command the heavenly host."

It came to Tsion at once. The great sword long as the Jordan, the breastplate big as the Sinai. "You are Michael! The prince who shall defend my people, the chosen ones of God."

"You have said it."

"Prince of God, have I died?"

"Your time has yet to come."

"May I inquire more?"

"You may, though I prefer righteous warfare to conversation. Gabriel announces. I engage in battle."

242

"A selfish question, sir. Will I remain until the Glorious Appearing?"

"It is appointed unto men once to die, and—"

"But will I die before the—"

"That is not for you to know, created one. It has no bearing on your obligation to serve the Most High God."

Tsion wanted to bow to this being and to the truth he spoke. He could not believe he had interrupted Michael the archangel, one of only two named angels in all of Scripture.

"Why am I here if I am not dead?"

"You have much to learn, teacher."

"Will I learn the identity of Antichrist, the enemy of God?"

Michael seemed to grow stony, if that were possible for an angel. It was as if the mere mention of Antichrist had stoked his bloodlust for battle. He spoke again: "Antichrist shall be revealed in the due time."

"But, sir," Tsion said, feeling like a child, "is not now the due time?"

"We measure past, present, and future with different rods than you, son of earth. The due time is the due time, and to the prudent and watchful ones, the revelation will be clear."

"We'll know for sure the identity of the . . . of the enemy?"

"So I have spoken."

"Teach me all I am here to learn, great prince who stands watch over the sons of Abraham, Isaac, and Jacob."

"Stand silent," the angel said, "observe, and give ear

to the truth of the war in heaven. Since the calling up of the righteous dead and alive, the enemy has competed with the hosts of heaven for the remaining souls of men.

"The evil one, that old serpent, has had access to the throne of the Most High since the beginning of time, until now, the appointed time."

What was he saying? That Tsion was there to witness the end of Satan's access to the throne, where for millennia he had exercised his power to accuse the children of God? Tsion wanted to ask how he earned so great a privilege, but Michael put a finger to his lips and beckoned with his other hand for Tsion to look past him to the very throne room. Tsion immediately fell prostrate in what seemed the midair of the extended universe. He saw only one figure, bigger, brighter, and more beautiful than Michael himself.

Tsion covered his eyes. "Is it the Lamb of God who takes away the sin of the world?"

"Silence, son of earth. This is neither Son nor Father, whom you will not see until *your* due time. Before you is the angel of light, the beautiful star, the great deceiver, your adversary, Lucifer."

Tsion shuddered, repulsed, yet unable to look away. "Is this the present?" he asked.

"Eternity past and future are the present here," Michael said. "Listen and learn."

Suddenly Tsion was able to hear the beautiful angel plead his case before the throne, which was beyond Tsion's view.

"Your so-called children are beneath you, ruler of

heaven," came the persuasive mellifluous tones of the eternal solicitor. "Abandon them to me, who can fashion them for profit. Even after being called by your name, their natures reek with temporal desires. Allow me to surround myself with these enemies of your cause, and I will marshal them into a force unlike any army you have ever assembled."

From the throne came a voice of such power and authority that volume was irrelevant: "Thou shalt not touch my beloved!"

"But with them I shall ascend to a throne higher than yours!"

"No!"

"They are weak and ineffective in your service!"

"No!"

"I can salvage these hopeless wrecks."

"Thou shalt not."

"I beseech you, ruler of heaven and earth—"

"No."

"Grant me these or I will—"

"No."

"I will—"

"No."

"I will destroy them and defeat you! I shall bear the name above all other names! I shall sit high above the heavens, and there shall be no god like me! In *me* there shall be no change, neither shadow of turning."

Suddenly from Tsion's right he saw the flash in the eyes of Michael the archangel, and he spoke with great emotion. "God, the Father Almighty," he shouted, causing the evil one to look his way in disgust, then anger, "I beseech you allow no more blasphemy in the courts of heaven! Grant that I destroy this one and cast him out of your presence!"

Yet Michael apparently neither heard nor sensed the permission of God. Lucifer glared with contempt at Michael, smirking, laughing. He turned back to face the throne.

"Michael, your master shall not assign you an impossible task! He knows I am right about the sons of God. He will eventually concede them to me. You are a fool, weak and unable to face me on your own. You shall lose. I shall win. I shall ascend—"

But as Tsion watched and listened, Lucifer's voice changed. It became high-pitched and whiny, and his persona began to change. As he railed and begged and challenged and blasphemed, the voice from the throne continued to deny him. His bright shining robe lost its luster. His face curled into a hideous mask of scales. His hands and feet disappeared, and his garment fell off, revealing a slimy, writhing, coiling serpent. His eyes sank under deep hoods and his voice became a hiss, then a roar as he seemed to transform himself.

His hands and feet reappeared, but his fingers and toes had turned to great horned appendages. He dropped to all fours. His words had vanished into flaming breaths, and he paced before the throne with such anger that Tsion was glad Michael stood between him and this dragon.

His head grew horns and a crown appeared upon it, and suddenly his whole being turned fiery red. As Tsion watched in horror, the beast grew six more heads with crowns and a total of ten horns. Pacing and growing ever larger with each step, the beast shook itself in rage and threatened the throne and they that sat upon it.

And the voice from the throne said, "No."

With a great roar and stomping and shaking of its heads, the dragon postured threateningly and appeared to want to advance on the throne. Michael stepped that way, and the voice again said, "No."

Michael turned to Tsion. "Behold," he said, pointing behind Tsion.

Tsion turned to see the figure of a woman with clothes as bright as the sun. While Michael's brightness had nearly blinded him and Lucifer proved brighter still, the woman . . . the woman appeared as if clothed in the sun. It seemed she stood on the moon itself, and on her head was a wreath made of twelve stars.

Tsion was transfixed and felt a great kinship with the woman. He wanted to ask Michael who she was. Mary? Israel? The church? But he could not speak, could not turn. He was aware that the hideous seven-headed dragon was behind him but that Michael stood between him and that danger.

The woman was pregnant, her great sun-clothed belly causing her to turn and cry out in labor pains. She grimaced and her body convulsed in contractions, and as she held her abdomen as if about to give birth, the dragon leaped from his place before the throne, clearing Michael and Tsion and pouncing before the woman.

His great tail swept a third of the stars from the heavens, and they plummeted to the earth. And now he crouched before the woman who was ready to give birth, seven mouths open and salivating, tongues darting, ready to devour her child as soon as it was born.

She bore a male child who was caught up to God. The dragon watched in rage as the child was transported to the throne, and when he turned back to the woman, she had fled. He rose up to give chase, and Michael the archangel said, "Behold."

Tsion turned to watch him use both mighty hands to pull the golden sword from its sheath and swing it in a high arc over his head. Immediately he was joined by a heavenly host of warrior angels, who fell in behind him as the dragon's angels also mustered behind him.

Tsion had so many questions, but Michael had led the charge against the dragon. Perhaps Gabriel the announcer was close by. Tsion opened his mouth to ask, but when he said, "Who is the woman?" his words sounded plain to him and he felt enclosed. "Who is the woman?" he repeated, and his words woke him with a start.

He sat up and his blanket slid off. The TV still showed the slow moving line of mourners, bathed in the eerie palace courtyard spotlights. Tsion stood and peered into the playpen where Kenny slept, having not moved. He sat back down and stared unbelieving at the videodisc player clock. It read 12:59.

Movement in the cabin caught Buck's eye. In the darkness he saw Chaim unstrap himself and awkwardly kneel in the aisle, his elbows on the armrest. Buck touched T's arm and nodded back. T looked and glanced at Buck, who raised both fists and bowed his head. He turned sideways so he had one ear facing the cabin. The man who had been so endearing and so stubborn was finally on his knees.

"Oh, God," Chaim began, "I have never before prayed believing that I was actually talking to you. Now I know that you are there and that you want me, and I don't know what to say." He began to weep.

"Forgive me for coming to you only because I am afraid for my life. Only you know the truth about me, whether I am sincere. You know better than I. I know that I am a sinner and need your forgiveness for all my sins, even for murder, regardless that the victim was your archenemy. Thank you for taking the punishment for my sins. Forgive me and receive me into your kingdom. I want to give you all of myself for the rest of my days. Show me what to do. Amen."

Buck looked back to where Chaim remained kneeling, his head buried in his arms. "Cameron?" he called, his voice muffled.

"Yes, Chaim?"

"I prayed, but I'm still scared!"

"So am I!"

"Me too!" T said.

"You tested God?" Buck said.

"I did. I guess I won't know his decision until we crash and I wake up in heaven or hell."

"Oh, the Bible says we can know."

"It does?"

"It says his Spirit bears witness with our spirit that we are children of God. What does your spirit say?"

"My spirit says to land carefully."

Buck laughed in spite of himself. "Chaim, there is a way we can know in advance. Do you want to know?"

"With all my heart."

"T, turn the lights on back there."

———

David stood atop the observation tower again, watching the line. With a couple of hours to go before midnight, the air was cool enough to keep the crowd calm. The next day was expected to be over one hundred degrees, and he worried about health and tempers. The funeral was to begin in twelve hours, but David couldn't imagine the crowds having completely passed by the bier that soon.

From his perch he could see the final touches on the massive, black, hollow, iron and bronze image of the late potentate, made from a postmortem body cast. Guy Blod seemed about to burst, supervising the last welds and the winching of it into place. Guy would stand on a scaffold and do the final sanding and polishing himself, planning to have workmen roll the finished product near the bier sometime before dawn.

Fortunato and his lackeys were making the rounds, and Leon had a couple of folded sheets of paper in his hand and seemed to be taking copious notes. He and his entou-

rage visited the statue-making operation, where Guy
broke long enough to animatedly point out the features
and accept accolades from the Supreme Commander.

The Fortunato juggernaut moved to the middle of the
long line, where many had been waiting for hours. People bowed and knelt and kissed his hands. Often he lifted
them and pointed up to the bier, and they stood nodding
and gesturing.

Leon checked the various concession tents and stands,
none of which would open until daybreak. When he got
to the stand beneath where David stood, David's worst
fears were realized. "Anyone seen Director Hassid?"
Leon said.

While his people were shaking their heads, someone in
the tent said, "He's upstairs, Commander."

"With whom?"

"Alone, I think."

"Gentlemen, wait for me, would you?"

He mounted the steps, and David felt the whole structure sway. David acted as if he was not expecting anyone
and had not heard anyone come up.

"Director Hassid, I presume," Fortunato said.

David turned. "Commander."

"Want to join our little group, David? We're just
greeting the people."

"No, thanks. Long day. I'm about to turn in."

"I understand," Leon said, pulling the pages from his
pocket. "Have time to give me a little input?"

"Sure."

"I'm getting pressure from a few people in Rome for

a memorial service for Pontifex Maximus. Remember him?"

Leon had asked that seriously, as if David wouldn't remember the head of the one-world faith who had died within the week. "Of course," David said.

"Well, he seems to have faded from most people's memories, and I'm inclined to leave it that way."

"Not have the service, you mean?"

"You agree?" Fortunato said.

"I'm just asking."

"Well, I agree with you that we probably shouldn't have it."

That wasn't what David had said, of course, but there was no sense squabbling. Fortunato was likely eliciting the same forced ideas from everyone around him, and he would eventually find himself "acquiescing" to the counsel from his staff.

"I would like spiritual matters centralized here in New Babylon for good, and I believe there is a place for a personal expression of faith better than what that amalgam gave us."

"Everyone seemed to go for that all-faiths-into-one idea, Commander."

"Yes, but with mounting evidence that Potentate Carpathia deserves sainthood, and the possibility that he himself was divine, I believe there's a place for worshiping and even praying to our fallen leader. What do you think?"

"I think you will prevail."

"Well, thank you for that. David, I have found you a

most capable and loyal worker. I want you to know that you can name your role in my regime."

"Your regime?"

"Surely you don't see anyone else in line for Supreme Potentate."

David was tempted to tell him who the potentate would be very soon. "No, I don't suppose."

"I mean, if you do, tell me. I have people watching the three dissident kings closely, and I think Litwala has a lean and hungry look. You know where that's from, Hassid?"

"Shakespeare. *Julius Caesar.*"

"You *are* well read. What role would motivate you?"

"I'm happy where I am, sir."

"*Really?*"

"Yes."

"Well, how would you respond to a healthy raise and a title change, say special assistant to the supreme potentate?"

David knew this would all be moot soon. "I wouldn't oppose it," he said.

"You wouldn't oppose it!" Fortunato laughed. "I like that! Look at this list of people who want to say a few words at the funeral tomorrow." He swore. "Self-serving sons of the devil."

Takes one to know one, David thought.

"You want to say a few words?"

"No."

"Because I could squeeze you in."

"No, thank you."

"It'd be no problem, give you some visibility."

"No."

"Going to get some rest, eh?"

"Yes, sir."

"And you'll be back when?"

"Daybreak, I imagine."

"Hmm."

"Problem, sir?"

"I was looking for someone from our level to be here when the statue is put in place."

"Blod's a minister."

"Yeah, but, you know."

David didn't know, but he nodded nonetheless.

"Could you be there, David?"

"Whatever you say, sir."

"Attaboy."

———————

Buck moved into the cabin as Chaim rose and turned to face him. He looked exhausted and was tearstained. Chaim now had his back to the armrest he had leaned on, and it caught him just above the knee. Buck put a hand on each of Chaim's shoulders, and the old man lurched back and plopped into the seat, his feet on Buck's knees.

"So, you saw it, did you?" Buck said.

"Yes!" Chaim said, rising. "And you can see mine?" He maneuvered until he was directly under a light, and he held a shock of white hair out of the way.

"I sure can, Chaim. You didn't believe us all this time, did you? That we could see each other's marks, I mean."

"Actually, I did believe you," Chaim said. "Not all of you would have lied to me. I was so jealous."

"No more."

"So God knew my heart."

"Apparently."

"That in itself is a miracle."

"Prepare for descent," T hollered.

"I can't say I'm any less scared," Chaim said.

"I'm scared too, friend, but a lot less than I would be if I didn't know my destination."

FOURTEEN

LEAH was tired and bored, despite being fascinated by the change in Rayford and the relationship between him and his daughter. Even with the windows open and a chilly breeze coming through, the Land Rover was cramped and oppressive.

When her phone rang and it was Ming, she was alarmed but glad for the diversion.

"I am going to get to see my parents and my brother again," Ming said.

"That's great. How? Where?"

"At the funeral."

"You're going?"

"And so are they. I called to tell them I had been assigned crowd control and they insisted on coming."

"Well, that's good, isn't it?"

"Leah, I am so worried about my parents. They do not

know about either Chang or me being believers. They were *such* admirers of Carpathia that they are sick with grief. I want to tell them and persuade them, but it would take a miracle."

"It's always a miracle, Ming. We'll pray with you that it will happen."

"You don't know my father."

"I know, but God is bigger than any of that. How are you getting to New Babylon? I heard all flights were full."

"Military transport. I don't know how my family found seats, except that my father has a lot of influence with the GC. His business contributes more than 20 percent of its profits to New Babylon. They are expecting another million people there tomorrow. I'm telling you, Leah, even prisoners here are mourning Carpathia."

"When you're there, look up David Hassid and Annie Christopher."

"Believers?"

"Of course. Keep up the front. Pretend to argue with them. They'll notice your mark and play along to protect you. Introduce your brother. I'll tip them off that your parents don't know. Hey, any more news on Hattie or on Cameron Williams's family?"

A pause.

"You can tell me, Ming."

"Well, it's sort of good news and bad news."

"Shoot."

"The Williamses' home burned and two bodies were

discovered, identified as Cameron Williams's father and brother."

"And?"

"This is unconfirmed, Leah, but there is some evidence that they may have become believers."

"That will be so helpful if Buck could know that for sure."

"I'll see what I can find out without being too obvious, but someone said the murders and the torching had to wait because they were at a church-type meeting."

"Does that mean the GC knows where the church meets?"

"Likely. They know more than most believers want to think."

"We've got to warn that church."

Buck listened to T talk on the radio to the tower at Kozani. "Very low on fuel. I may make one test pass, but I'd better go for it."

"On the downside, Super Juliet, we have no foam and no prospects to get any soon. You might want to jettison remaining fuel before the final attempt."

"Roger that."

"You have friends in high places, Juliet."

"Repeat?"

"You have new equipment coming."

"I'm not following you, tower."

"Man named Albie. Know him?"

"Heard of him. Friend of a friend."

"That's what he said. He's delivering a plane for you, assuming yours is going to need some rehab."

"Roger. What's he bringing?"

"No idea."

"How's he going to get back?"

"I believe he's planning to do the fix on yours and take it in trade."

"He'd better be bringing something pretty nice."

"Just hope yours is worth trading after you scrape our runway."

"Roger."

Buck looked at T. "Do you believe that? Rayford had to set that up."

"Wonder when Albie's expected."

Buck shook his head. "He's got a lot longer flight than we do, and who knows where he's getting the craft?"

"I can't wait to see it."

"I can't wait to see if we survive."

"I believe we will," T said. "We'll take a look at the situation, jettison, and slide her in there nice and smooth."

"I love the confidence in your voice."

"Must be my acting background."

"Don't say that."

"Truth is, Buck, I need both of you strapped in in the very back seats. I'll call out altitude readings. By fifty feet, you should be braced and tucked, but you can get into that position anytime after you hear one hundred feet. Got it?"

Buck nodded.

"We're close. Get Chaim ready."

Buck stood and was moving into the cabin when T said, "Oh, no!"

"What?"

The interior lights went dark. Battery-operated emergency lights eerily illuminated the control board.

"What's happening?" Chaim called out. "Someone talk to me."

"Let's just say we won't have to jettison fuel," T said. "Get strapped in now, back seats, and don't talk to me till we're on the ground."

"I'm ready for heaven!" Chaim said. "But tonight I prefer asphalt to gold, if you don't mind."

"Shut up, Doctor," T said, and he called the tower on batteries. "Mayday, Kozani tower, this is the Super J, and we're out of fuel, repeat, out of fuel. On battery backup, landing lights may not be fully operational."

"Roger, Juliet," came the response, as Buck settled in across the aisle from Chaim. "Landing gear retracted?"

"Roger," T said. "Wheels up. Stand by."

"Repeat? Did we get a wheels-up confirm?"

"Negative."

"Due to power out, or do you think wheels are not up?"

"Didn't feel anything."

"Keep in mind as you come in. You have us in sight?"

"Affirmative."

"All runway lights on."

"Thank you. Landing lights on."

"Roger. Repeat wheels-up procedure."

"Roger."

"Successful?"

"Negative."

"We'll try to see when you come in. It will affect your drag and what you want to do."

"Roger."

"Altitude?"

"A thousand and falling . . . nine hundred . . . eight . . ."

"Dropping too fast, Juliet! You must clear south fence."

"Affirmative. Working on it. Seven . . . six . . . five-fifty."

"Must slow descent, Juliet."

"Worried about airworthiness."

"Roger, but fence must be top priority."

"Roger. Four . . . three . . . two . . ."

Tsion stood and stretched and checked on Kenny. He felt as if he'd been out for hours, yet he was as weary as when he nodded off. While he was determined not to miss anything in New Babylon, he knew he needed sleep. He sat back down and settled in, hoping, praying he would again be transported to the very portals of heaven. He didn't know what to call what had happened to him or how to assess it, but it had been the privilege of a lifetime. He was left with so many questions and so much more to come. But before he slept he again felt compelled to pray for his brothers and sisters on the front lines.

———————

David headed for his quarters, phoning Guy on the way. "I'd like to see the positioning of the statue when you're ready."

"Now?"

"I say, when you're ready. The regular schedule will be fine."

"You're asking permission?"

"I'm just saying I'd like to watch. There a problem with that?"

"I don't need my hand held."

"Believe me, Guy, I don't want to hold your hand."

"Protocol demands that you not refer to me by my first name."

"Sorry, Blood."

"It's Blod, and my last name isn't appropriate either!"

"Oh, I don't think it's that bad."

"Ooh! My title is Minister!"

"Sorry, Reverend Minister. But your supreme commander and mine wants a liaison from administration present when you move naked boy into position."

"How rude and tacky."

"That's sort of what I thought, but I'm surprised you agree."

"David!"

"Ah, Director Hassid to you, Minister Blood. Anyway, he chose me, so don't leave home without me."

"David! *I* am a minister, therefore *I* qualify as a liaison from administration. You just stay in bed until you can be civil."

"Sorry, Minnie, but I have a direct order. If you want to contest it, you may take it up with him."

"Just wait till he hears what you called the potentate."

"Oh, if you tell him that, please clarify that I was referring to your statue. And you might add that you yourself admitted it was—what did you say?—rude and tacky."

"Five A.M., Hayseed, and we're not waiting for you."

"Oh, good. I'd hate to miss that. Have a nice day."

———————

Buck knew he should have his head buried, as Chaim did, but he was too curious. He leaned out into the aisle where he could see through the cockpit. The plane was too steeply nose down, and clearly T was going to try one last maneuver to somehow clear the south fence, which preceded about a hundred yards of grass and then the runway. It struck Buck that most of the tire marks on the runway were at least a quarter mile from the edge of the pavement and only a couple of others showed nearer, none of them really close to the grass. He would not bet T could get the Super J over the fence, let alone into the grass, forget the runway proper.

"Your landing gear is down, Juliet! Repeat, down! Full wheel on right, partial assemblage on left! Lift and good luck!"

"We don't do luck!" Buck shouted, as the fence disappeared from view. "God, do your thing through T!"

"Roger!" T shouted as he yanked on the stick; the plane bucked ever so slightly, clearing the fence, then swept tail first onto the grass.

The impact slammed Buck so deep into his seat that he felt it in every fiber of his being. Chaim had let out a terrific grunt on impact, and it seemed his face was near his shoes. Buck wished he'd been in the same position, because he felt soft tissue give way from his tailbone to his neck, and he was sure both shoulders had nearly been torn from their sockets. He felt it in his feet, ankles, and knees, and the plane was still nose up as the rear tore through the sod.

That meant at least one more impact was to come, but Buck couldn't imagine they would feel it in the back, at least not the way they felt the first one.

The angle and speed T had brought the plane in on somehow carried the craft all the way to the runway on its tail. When the tail hit the edge of the runway, the nose slammed down in a shower of sparks so fast that the front half of the fuselage tore away from the back and the two huge pieces of airplane went sliding and scraping, spinning in opposite directions.

Buck was aware of sky and pavement and lights and hangars and sparks and noise and dizziness, until the G forces were too much and he felt himself losing consciousness. "Lord," he said as blissful darkness invaded his brain, "I can recover from this. Leave me here awhile. Chloe, I love you. Kenny . . ."

Exhausted as he was, David could not sleep. He lay in his quarters, wondering why he got such joy out of tormenting Guy Blod. He couldn't shake from his memory Rayford's story of having tormented Hattie Durham's friend Bo, and how Bo had eventually committed suicide. Sure, Guy was a case, and David enjoyed beating him in a battle of wits and sarcasm. But was he laying groundwork for ever having a positive influence on the man? Guy's becoming a believer seemed remote, but who would have guessed David himself would have ever come to faith? A young Israeli techie with street smarts, he had been a skeptical agnostic his whole life. Could he start over with Guy, or would the man laugh in his face? Regardless, he had to do the right thing.

David tapped out a love message for Annie, telling her that while he agreed they should not even think about children until after the Glorious Appearing, he still wanted to marry her. Her response would determine his next move in the relationship.

He took one last look at messages and E-mail and thought he had an idea where every Trib Force member was. All absent and accounted for, he decided. By now Buck and Chaim ought to be in Greece. He wondered what Chaim was doing for identification.

With a brief prayer for Tsion, who he hoped would get back to his daily Internet studies and commentaries soon, David fell into bed. He asked forgiveness for how he had treated Guy Blod and asked God to give him special compassion for the man. Of course it would not be safe for him to declare himself a believer to a GC insider yet, but he didn't want to shut the door to opportunities once he and Annie had escaped.

Buck's eyes flew open, and he feared he might be going into shock. The night air hit him like a polar blast, though he knew it was not that cold. He could not even see his breath. He sat in the jagged back half of the Super J, staring straight down the runway to the front half, which faced him about half a mile away. He had to get out, get to T, make sure he was OK. T had saved their lives. What a masterful job of flying the lifeless bird!

Chaim! Buck looked to his left to find the old man still curled upon himself, bent all the way forward, the back of his head pressed against the seat in front of him. How could he have not broken his neck? Did Buck dare move him?

"Chaim! Chaim, are you all right?"

Rosenzweig did not move. Buck gently touched Chaim's back and noticed that his own hand quivered like the last leaf on a maple tree. He clasped his hands together to control himself, but his whole body shuddered. Was anything broken, punctured, severed? It didn't appear so, but he would be sore for days. And he must not allow himself to slip into shock.

Worried about Chaim, Buck unstrapped himself and reached for his right wrist, which was by Chaim's foot, his hands tightly wrapped around the ankles. He could not loosen Chaim's grip, so he forced his fingers between Chaim's leg and wrist. Not only did he have a pulse, but it was strong and dangerously fast.

Buck heard footsteps and shouting as three emergency workers appeared, demanding to know if there were any survivors. "I need a blanket," he said. "Freezing. And he needs someone who knows what they're doing to get him out of here and check for neck injuries."

"Blood," one of the men said.

"Where?" Buck said.

"The man's shoes. Look."

Blood dripped from Chaim's face to his shoes.

"Sir!" they called to him. "Sir!" Turning to Buck, one said, "What is his name?"

"Just call him Doctor. He'll hear you."

Someone tossed Buck a blanket, and he saw more workers sprinting down the runway to the other half of the plane. He tried to stand. Everything hurt. His head throbbed. He was dizzy. He pulled the blanket around himself, feeling every muscle and bone, and staggered out the front of the wreckage to solid ground. He stood there, swaying, assuring everyone he was all right. He had to get to T. There was nothing he could do for Chaim. If the worst he had was a racing pulse and facial lacerations, he should be all right. It was too late to tell him not to use his own name.

Buck started toward the other end of the runway, but he moved so slowly and shook so much that he wondered if he could make it. The ground beckoned and almost took him several times. But though he knew he had to look like a drunk, he kept forcing one foot in front of the other. An emergency medical technician ran toward him from the cockpit half and another came from the tail end. As they got close to Buck, he thought they were going to carry him the rest of the way. He would not have resisted.

But they ignored him and shouted to each other. The one from behind him told the other, "Old guy back there looks like the Israeli who died in a house fire last night."

"He gets that a lot," Buck said, realizing that neither heard him.

"How's the pilot?" the first EMT said, but Buck didn't hear the response.

"What'd he say?" he called after the man, who was now running for the cockpit.

"He didn't!"

Buck hadn't seen the man shake his head in response either, but maybe he hadn't been watching carefully enough. At long last he arrived at the front end of the plane. No one was working on T. That could be good or bad. He heard someone call for a body bag.

That couldn't be. If he and Chaim had survived the jolt, surely T had. He was in better shape than either passenger. One of the workers tried to block Buck's way into the plane, but Buck gave him a look and a weak shove, and the man knew there would be no dissuading him. "Please don't touch the body," the man said.

"It's not a body," Buck slurred. They had for sure misread this one, hurriedly misdiagnosed whatever the problem was. "It's a friend, our pilot."

The cockpit portion had come to rest directly under a huge runway lamp, which filled the wreckage with light. Buck saw no blood, no bones, no twisted limbs. He stepped behind T, who was sitting straight up, still strapped in. His left hand lay limp on his lap, his right hung open-palmed in the space between the seats. T's head hung forward, chin on his chest.

"T," Buck said, a hand on his shoulder, "how we doin', pal?"

T felt warm, thick, and muscly. Buck put a finger to the right pressure point in the neck. Nothing. Buck felt the blanket slide from his shoulders. He slumped painfully into the seat across from T and grabbed the lifeless hand in both of his. "Oh, T," he said. "Oh, T."

The rational part of his brain told him there would be more of this. More friends and fellow believers would die. They would reunite within three and a half years. But though he didn't know T the way Rayford had, this one still hurt. Here was a quiet, steady man who had risked his life and freedom more than once for the Tribulation Force. And now he had made the ultimate sacrifice.

"We need to remove the body and the wreckage, sir. I'm sorry. This is an active runway."

Buck stood and bent over T, taking his head in his arms. "I'll see you at the Eastern Gate," he whispered.

Buck dragged his blanket out of the plane but could walk no farther. He tried to sit on the edge of the runway but couldn't catch himself and rolled on his back. A stiff breeze chilled the back of his neck, and he didn't have the energy to protest when he felt a hand in his pocket. "Anyone meeting you here, Mr. Staub?"

"Yeah."

"Who?"

"Miklos."

"Lukas Miklos, the lignite guy?"

"Yeah."

"He's in the terminal. Can you make it?"

"No."

"We'll get a gurney out here."

Buck watched as T's body was lifted out in a bag. "Take care of the old guy back there," Buck managed, pointing the other way.

"We've got the old man," someone said. "Bloody nose and a jittery heart, but he'll make it."

And Buck was out again.

The skies began to darken in Chicago at around seven, but Rayford decided to wait until eight to venture out. He wanted the skies black and no one even looking their direction. The city had been abandoned, condemned, and cordoned off for months, and it wouldn't have surprised him to know that not even a leftover drunk walked those streets. Radiation or not, decaying bodies littered many streets. It might be a safer place to hide out, but it was not going to be a fun place to live.

He pulled slowly from under the L platform with his lights off, hoping to kick up as little dust as possible. There would be no shooting straight into the Loop on the Dan Ryan. Nothing was as it once was.

Between separate bombing raids and the great earthquake, some reconstruction had been attempted, but these were meant to be shortcuts, two-lane roads that cut straight through the city. But only a few were even half finished, so the most direct route anywhere was as straight a line as you could point—over, under, around, and through the natural and man-made obstacles in the best four-wheel-drive vehicle you could find.

Rayford guessed he had between fifteen and twenty miles to drive, his lights off most of the way, traveling at around ten miles an hour. "I hope this is all David says it is," he said.

"Me too," Chloe said. "For my sake. Of course, I watched his little cybertour of the place. If it's half what it looks like, it's going to be as close to ideal as we can find."

Leah was asleep.

———

David showed up at the statue construction site a few minutes after five in the morning, Carpathia Time. Guy started in with something sarcastic about how now they could finish their work. David held up both hands. "Sorry if I held you up. Minister Blod, a word, please?"

Guy seemed so shocked that David had addressed him with proper protocol in front of his staff that he dropped what he was doing and joined him several feet away. David thrust out his hand, and Guy, clearly suspicious, shook it tentatively. "I want to apologize for speaking inappropriately to you, sir. I trust you'll find me helpful and not a hindrance to your work from here on."

"What?"

"I said I want to apologize—"

"I heard you, Hayseed. I'm waiting for the punch line."

"That's all I had to say, sir."

"I'm waiting for the other shoe to drop!" Guy said in a singsong tone.

"That's all, sir. Will you forgive me?"

"I'm sorry?"

"I said, that's all, sir—"

"I heard you; I'm trying to digest this. The supreme commander put you up to this, didn't he? Well, I didn't squeal on you. C'mon, who made you do this?"

David would have loved to have said "God" and blown Guy's mind. "No outside influence, Minister Blod. No ulterior motives. Just want to start over on the right foot."

"Well, count me in, mister!"

"Is that an acceptance of my apology?"

"It's whatever you want it to be, soldier!"

"Thanks. No sense holding up the work any longer."

"I should say not. We're ready to roll in five."

FIFTEEN

BUCK struggled to open his eyes. He had never felt so
beat-up.

The dawn sun peeked through the blinds in a small
infirmary, he wasn't sure where. He had awakened to the
quiet praying of three men who sat holding hands. One
he recognized as Lukas Miklos. The others were a tall,
dark-haired man about his own age and an older,
smaller, Middle Easterner.

"How are you feeling, my friend?" Lukas said,
approaching.

"I've been better, Laslos, but you're a sight. Where are
we, and how is Chaim?"

Lukas stepped closer and whispered. "Chaim will be
all right, but we had to come up with an alias for him.
His nose was severely damaged and his jaw broken. So
he has not spoken, and medical personnel are not suspi-

cious, only curious. He is being operated on right now. Our document forger pulled off the impossible, so . . ."

"And our pilot is gone, right? I wasn't hallucinating."

"That is correct. Praise God he was a believer. His papers identified him as Tyrola Mark Delanty. Was this an alias, or—?"

"Didn't need an alias. He ran a small airport near us and was able to evade suspicious eyes."

Laslos nodded. "The GC will not allow bodies to be transported internationally. Let our church handle the burial."

Buck rolled his shoulders and rotated his head. Pain shot through his neck. "What's your guy going to do about Chaim's picture?"

Lukas looked over his shoulder. "Look what we planted after surgery." He showed Buck an ID with the photograph nearly scraped off, a bit of white hair peeking through the top. "Doesn't that look like it went through the crash? We tried to persuade officials to postpone surgery until the swelling reduced, but they're short staffed here, like everywhere. Meanwhile, he's Tobias Rogoff, a retired librarian from Gaza on his way to North America on a charter flight, the same one you're on."

"Does he know this?"

"We told him a few hours ago. Our story is that the charter insurance company has contracted with Albie Air to guarantee the completion of the trip as soon as you two are airworthy."

"I'm airworthy now," Buck said, looking over Laslos's

shoulder toward the little Middle Easterner. "You must be Albie."

"I am, sir," he said with a thick accent and a slight bow. "Your father-in-law and your friend Mr. McCullum and I go way back. Also Abdullah Smith."

"How well I know. I did not expect to see your mark. Is my father-in-law aware?"

Albie shook his head. "This was very recent, within the week. I tried to contact Rayford, but I found him impossible to connect with. Of course, now I know why."

"And how did you come to faith, sir?"

"Nothing dramatic, I'm afraid. I have always been religious, but Rayford and Mac and Abdullah all urged me to at least consider the writings of Dr. Ben-Judah. Finally I did. You know what reached me? His assessment of the difference between religion and Christianity."

"I know it well," Buck said, "if you're referring to his contention that religion is man's attempt to reach God, while Jesus is God's attempt to reach man."

"The very argument," Albie said. "I spent a couple of days surfing the archives of Dr. Ben-Judah's Web site, saw all his explanations of the prophesied plagues and judgments, then studied the prophecies about the coming Christ. How anyone with a functioning mind could read that and not—"

"Forgive me, Albie," Laslos said, "but we must keep moving. We should tell you, Buck, that Dr. Rosenzweig's eyes danced at the prospect of a new identity. We don't know how long it will be before he can speak, but it's clear he can't wait to playact as someone else."

Buck slid off the side of the bed. "Are we near the airport?"

Laslos shook his head. "We're north of Kozani. Albie has flown the new craft to Ptolemaïs, and when you and, ah, Tobias are healthy, you'll leave from there. Meanwhile, as soon as we can get you out of here, you'll stay with us at the same safe house where we harbored Rayford."

"We have not met," Buck said, reaching past Laslos's hand to shake hands with the tall, willowy one.

"I'm sorry," Laslos said. "Pastor Demeter."

The pastor said, "Mr. Williams, I answered your phone awhile ago and talked to your wife. She and your father-in-law are checking out a new safe house, and she was very relieved to hear that you and Chaim are alive. Naturally, they are distraught over Mr. Delanty, particularly Rayford. Mrs. Williams wants to talk with you as soon as you are able."

"I want to get home soon," Buck said. "Albie, I'll bet you weren't planning on flying that far, were you?"

"I have nothing to return to Al Basrah for, Mr. Williams. Could you use another craft and another pilot?"

"Oh, I think the Trib Force might find room for the best black-market contact in the world."

Demetrius handed Buck his phone. As Buck dialed, Laslos explained that so far they had not seemed to arouse suspicion on the parts of the local GC. "They believe Demetrius works for me and that you are an American come to study the business."

Chloe didn't like the plan. "Get out of there, Buck," she told him. "We've found *the* perfect safe house. Even my curmudgeon father hopes so. Chaim is smart, but this clandestine stuff is not his game. Let us get you two healthy here."

"You may be right, Chlo'," he said. "What time is it there? I've got to call my dad."

She paused. "Buck, it's after eight in the evening and earlier out west, but that was one of the reasons I wanted to talk with you."

He read it in her voice.

"Dad?"

"Yes."

"And—"

"Your brother too, Buck. I'm so sorry."

"How?"

"GC."

"Looking for us?"

"That's what we understand."

"But they didn't know where we are! That's why I never told them!"

"I know, sweetheart. There may be some good news too."

"What?"

"Our source tells us that the first attempt to get information out of them had to be postponed. They were at church."

"Chloe, don't."

"It's true, Buck. Leah found a believer at Buffer who has access to these schemes, and she says that's from a reliable source."

"Why wouldn't Dad have told me?"

"Maybe the timing wasn't right."

"I wish I could know for sure."

"Leah is trying to reach the church so they know what happened and can be on guard. She'll ask for the truth about your dad and brother."

———

Rayford had had to stop driving when news came of T's death. He walked a couple of blocks in the darkness, and when Chloe asked if she could walk with him, he thanked her but added, "I need a few minutes, hon."

Chicago was, naturally, a mess. Buildings in piles, rotting carcasses, vehicles crashed or burned. It seemed an appropriate ambience for Rayford's sojourn.

The hardest thing about living during this period, he decided, was the roller coaster of emotions. He would never get used to the shock of loss and the necessity to telescope mourning into minute slivers so it could be dealt with and yet one could get on with the business at hand.

In the past, with each death of someone close to him, Rayford had rehearsed the ever-growing list in his mind. He didn't do that anymore. He wondered if a person had a limit, some finite reservoir of grief that would eventually peter out and leave him with no tears, no regret, no melancholy. He stopped at what was once a corner and leaned over, hands on his knees. His grief supply was still stocked, and the pain of the loss gushed from him.

Hard as it was, Rayford had to condense the bereavement caused by yet another aching amputation into a few brief hours. He was not allowed to dwell on it, to jot his memories, to console a widow, to break the news to a congregation. There would be no wake, no funeral, not even a memorial service, at the rate they were going. T's church was likely to have one, of course, but there was no way Rayford dared attend. Who knew who might be watching, lying in wait?

Not enough of his comrades in the Tribulation Force really knew T. There would be little reminiscing. He was gone. They would see him in heaven. Now what was next on the crisis docket? It was unfair, unnatural. How was a person supposed to function this way and stay sane?

Rayford was grateful for his own return to what Dr. Ben-Judah liked to call the "first love of Christ," that wonderful season when the plan of salvation and the truth of grace are fresh and new. He was thankful for the counsel of Demetrius Demeter and the refreshing rest and new sense of resolve he enjoyed.

And now this. The thrill ride. He'd had enough ups for twenty-four hours, apparently. He had been due for some downs.

As usual when in a stretch like this, Rayford tried cataloging what he still had to be thankful for. Without fail, every blessing in his life had a name attached: Chloe,

Kenny, Buck, Tsion, Leah, her new friend he hadn't yet met, the two Zekes, Chaim, David and Annie, Mac, Abdullah, Laslos and his wife, Demetrius, Albie. Rayford wondered why Albie had been so eager to help in Greece and what it was he was so eager to tell him, but only in person.

Rayford had to fight the knowledge that while his list might expand, it also had to suffer attrition. He had already lost so many, including two wives. He would not allow himself to think about losing more relatives.

When he returned to the Rover, Leah reported that she had reached the leader of the house church Buck's father and brother had attended. "I told him I'd love it if he could talk directly to Buck and he said he'd be happy to, but I didn't feel right about giving out Buck's number."

"That was wise," Rayford said. "Let Buck decide that. His phone is secure, but this pastor's is likely bugged if they just had a GC cleansing. Try Buck and give him the pastor's number. Let him work out the contact."

A few minutes later Rayford parked near Strong's and they cased the place, only to find it secure. The three of them sat on the sidewalk with their backs to the cold brick, and Rayford pulled out his phone.

———————

Something about the New Babylon predawn David never liked. Maybe Israel was lusher. Both were desert areas, but the hour before daybreak in Israel had always invigorated him, made him look forward to the promise of the day. The dry, windless heat of New Babylon mornings, beautiful as the sunrises could be, David found suffocating.

Watching Guy Blod put the finishing touches on the huge image of Nicolae Carpathia did little to cheer David. Not a hundred feet away, hundreds of thousands of grieving pilgrims from all over the world moved in slow silence, waiting hours for their few seconds before the sarcophagus. It was sad enough that these blind, lost, misled minions clearly worried about their future due to the loss of their beloved leader. But here behind great curtains, Guy and his assistants rhapsodized over the finished product.

"Care to look close?" Guy asked David as he glided down on a motorized scaffold.

Not really, David wanted to say, but how would he explain passing on such a so-called privilege? He shrugged, which Guy interpreted as affirmative, and the sculptor sang out instructions.

"There's only room for one on the scaffold, and you have to run the controls yourself. Be careful! The first time I did it I nearly knocked over one of my own creations!"

Guy showed David the controls, which consisted primarily of a joystick and speed selector. He was tempted to point the thing at the statue's head, shoot up, and knock it over. As David tentatively and jerkily practiced maneuvering the scaffold before rising, Guy hollered his cautions. "Careful of the smoke! The fire is lit under the knees, and the face has the only exhaust."

"Why didn't you wait until it was in place to start the fire?"

"We don't want to distract the crowds. This sort of art is a duet between sculptor and viewer, and my goal is that they participate in the illusion that the statue is alive."

"Twenty-four feet high and made of metal?"

"Trust me, this works. People will love it. But it would spoil everything if they saw us dumping in the stuff for the fire."

"What are you using for fuel?" David asked.

"A form of shale," Guy said. "For kindling, onionskin paper."

"Where'd that come from?"

"Every tribe and nation!" Guy said, and his people laughed. "Seriously, we have an unlimited supply of holy books from all over the world, the last contribution of the late Pontifex Maximus. He shipped from Rome all the holy texts that had been confiscated and donated from the various religions and sects when the one-world faith was established."

David was repulsed, now certain he didn't want the closer look, but he was stuck. "Note the handiwork on the way up!" Guy said. What was there to see but polished black iron? "You can touch, but be careful! It's delicately balanced!"

Nearly two and a half stories up, David could hardly hear Guy anymore. Smoke wafted out the eyes, nostrils, and mouth of the quadruple-size image of Carpathia. It was uncanny. Though from that close the illusion was lost that the eyes were real, the features, having been made from the actual cast of the body, were perfect replicas.

David was high enough to see past the statue to the horizon, where the sun's pinks were just beginning to wash the sky. Suddenly he flinched and backpedaled, hitting the safety bar just above his waist. The whole scaffold shuddered, and he feared it might topple.

"Hey!" one of Guy's assistants hollered.

"What's going on up there?" Guy yelled. "You all right?"

David waved. He didn't want to admit what he'd heard, what had made him jump. He steadied himself and listened. A low rumble, echoing as if from the belly of the image. Muffled and sonorous, it was clearly Carpathia's timbre. What was it saying, and how had they gotten it to do that? A chip? A disc player? A tape?

He felt the vibration again, heard the hum, cocked his head to listen. "I shall shed the blood of saints and prophets."

David whipped the control so the scaffold lurched down about five feet and stopped, swaying again. "How did you do that?" he called down.

"Do what?"

"Get a recording in there!"

Silence.

"Well, how did you? Where's the hardware, and what does the phrase mean?"

Guy was still staring up at him, obviously holding out. "Guy!"

"What?"

"What didn't you hear? Do I have to repeat every-thing?"

"What didn't I hear? I didn't hear anything but you, David. What the devil are you talking about?"

David began his slow descent. "The thing talks. How did you do it? Tape loop? Disc? What? And won't the heat or smoke destroy it?"

Guy rolled his eyes at his people. He whispered, "What are you, serious?"

"You know blamed well I'm serious, Guy."

"So we're back to first names, are we?"

"Can we not get hung up on that right now, Minister-Director-Poten-take-your-choice Blod? The thing speaks. I heard it twice, and I'm not crazy."

"If you're not crazy, you're mistaken."

"Don't tell me I didn't hear what I heard!"

"Then you're hearing things, Director Hassid. This thing hasn't been out of my sight since the shell was delivered. This isn't a theme park. I don't want giant talking action figures. OK? Are we all right now? May I have them start moving my big boy into position?"

David nodded and stepped back to let a monstrous forklift move in behind the statue. His phone chirped, and as soon as he answered he heard a tone indicating another call. "This is Director Hassid, hold please," but as he punched in the other call heard, "Dav—!" and rec-ognized Fortunato's voice.

"This is Director Hassid, hold please," he said again,

switching back to Fortunato. "Sorry, Commander. I'm watching the moving of the statue, and—"

"I'm sure that'll succeed without you, David. I'd appreciate not being put on hold in the future." David knew he should apologize again to keep up appearances, but he was dwelling on how important his getting up before 5:00 A.M. was to Fortunato last night and how incidental it was now. "We've got a situation here," Leon continued. "I need you in the conference room on eighteen as soon as possible."

"Anything I need to bring or be thinking about?"

"No. Well, yes. Captain McCullum's schedule."

"Oh, he's—"

"Tell me when you get here, David. Quickly, please."

David switched to his other call. "That busy that early, huh, kid?" Rayford said.

"Sorry. What's up?" David walked backward as he talked, watching the statue emerge from the preparation room and become visible to the crowds. The murmuring grew louder as people nudged each other and pointed. The statue leaned back against the forks of the truck, and not until it came into the beams of the spotlights did it become apparent to all that it was, as Guy had so delicately put it, *au naturel*.

Oohs and *aahs* rose from the crowd; then they began applauding and soon cheering.

"What in the world is going on there?" Rayford said.

David told him. "I think they've waited so long to see the body that they would worship trading cards if we passed them out." Rayford told David what had happened in Greece. "I'm so sorry, Captain Steele. I only talked to Mr. Delanty a few times by phone, but I know you two were close."

"This is a hard one, David. They don't get any easier. Sometimes I feel like an albatross. The people who get close to me are soon gone."

David told him he was on his way to a mysterious meeting, and they debriefed each other again on what had happened at the Gala. "No matter what they say, sir, it's clear the shooting was accidental and that the bullet totally missed Carpathia."

"That doesn't make me any less of a scapegoat, but—"

"Oh, Captain, wait a second . . ."

"I hear the crowd. What happened?"

"Oh, man, it almost toppled over! They set down the statue, and it rocked forward! People were diving out of the way. The forklift guy moved up to sort of catch it on its way back so it wouldn't fall that way, and that just made it rock forward again! I don't know how it didn't go over. It's settled now, and they're nudging it straight. Oh, man!" He told Rayford of the built-in furnace but said nothing about what he'd heard.

"That jostling must have stoked the fire, because the smoke is really pouring out now. You know they're burning Bibles, among other holy books, in there?"

"No!"

"Sir, I'm heading inside now, and I never asked what you called about."

"I'm at the new safe house, David."

"Yeah? How is it?"

"It looks fabulous, but we have one problem. It must lock automatically in emergencies. We can't get in. Can you unlock it from there?"

David was near the elevator. "I can't talk here, sir, so let me just say yes, I'll get to that as soon as this meeting is over. I wish I could say when that will be."

Tsion took a call from Chloe, informing him it was likely they would be back very late. "Any evidence of GC nosing around?"

"None," he said, but he did not add that he had been 93 million miles from Mount Prospect for at least two minutes.

She spoke briefly to Kenny, who kept wanting to pull the phone from his mouth and "see Mama." Finally he said, "Lub-you-too-see-ya-lader-bye-bye."

"Tsion, I appreciate this more than you know," Chloe said.

"He's easy," he said. "And you know I love him."

She told Tsion what to feed Kenny and to put him to bed at nine. Much as he had enjoyed the baby, that was good news. Kenny often slept through the night.

David had not given himself time to worry what the big meeting was about. He just hoped he would not be in there alone with Fortunato. David was the last to arrive.

A dozen directors and above were there, including television personnel, most yawning and rubbing their eyes.

"Let's get started, people," Leon began. "We have a
crisis. No one is leaving New Babylon. Despite the decimated population in the last three and a half years,
hotels are jammed and people are even agreeing to double up, two whole families in each room. Others are
sleeping in the street, under lean-tos. The airport is
crowded with big jets. They bring in capacity loads for
the viewing, but they're canceling most outbound flights
for lack of interest. You know what's happening, don't
you?"

"The viewing is not meeting their felt needs," a
woman said. David recognized her as Hilda Schnell,
head of Global Community Cable News Network.

"I'm glad it was you who answered, Hilda," Leon
said. "We need your help."

"What can *I* do? I'm staying for the funeral too."

"We were not prepared for this size crowd," Leon
said. "This will be twice as large as the Jerusalem Gala."

Hilda said, "I still don't understand how GC CNN
can help. Even at the Gala we merely—"

"Bear with me," Leon said. "As you know, we already
pushed back the funeral and burial to accommodate the
crowds. We assumed that a million or so people would still
be waiting to view the body by the time we were ready for
the ceremony. With more than three million here already,
another estimated million on their way, and virtually no
one leaving, we have to regroup. Where are the big screens
we used in Jerusalem and do we have more?"

Someone from Event Programming said they were in storage in New Babylon and that there would be enough—supplemented by smaller monitors—to handle the larger crowd. "But," he added, "that will require a lot of man-hours and, of course, a layout scheme. The way the courtyard is cordoned off now will certainly not handle a crowd that size, especially if the ones who have already passed by the bier stay for the funeral, and I can't imagine why they're still in the city if that is not their plan."

"My point exactly," Leon said. "I already have engineers on the new schematic. And let me be clear: laborers are starting to rearrange barricades, chairs, crowd control ropes, and so forth. All this work will go on with no interruption of the viewing process. If the line has to be moved, that should be able to be done in an orderly fashion without stopping the procession.

"My question for you, Ms. Schnell, is whether your equipment can feed that many monitors. Some people, naturally, will be hundreds of yards from the podium."

"We don't worry about that, Commander," Ms. Schnell said. "We concern ourselves with providing the best visual and audio coverage of the event for television and leave it to your event organizers to make it work for their purposes."

Leon stared at her, expressionless. "What I am suggesting, madam, is that you *do* worry about it. We have singers, dancers, speakers, and the like to make this ceremony appropriate, not only to the occasion and the size of the live crowd, but also to the stature of the one we honor."

"Yes, sir."

"Yes, ma'am?"

"Just tell us what you want, sir."

"Thank you."

"Thank you for the privilege."

Now Fortunato was smiling. "That the big screens from Jerusalem are already here, Director Hassid, eliminates my need for one of your pilots to go get them. If we could make use of your entire hangar crew, cargo staff, pilots and all, in crowd control, I would appreciate it. Viv Ivins will be coordinating that, so let her know how many are available and who they are.

"The new times for the ceremony and burial are noon and 2:00 P.M. today respectively. Some dignitaries' speeches may be shortened, but those times are firm and may be announced effective immediately. Ms. Schnell, I'm assuming this event supersedes all other programming so that the entire globe may participate, including those who reach the airport in time to watch on television but too late to be here in person."

She nodded.

David fidgeted, knowing Rayford, Chloe, and Leah were waiting to get into the Strong Building. He wasn't certain he could remotely unlock a door, but he'd rather have been studying that than sitting through a logistics meeting. Fortunato soon left the details in the hands of his engineers, and David hurried out.

On the way to his office, he saw the laborers already

at work refashioning the massive courtyard into a vista that would accommodate the expected flood of humanity. According to the snatches of news reports he caught on the monitors lining the hallways of the palace complex, Leon was right. People of every ethnic background were interviewed at the airport, in line, and on the streets. Nearly every person expressed a desire to attend the funeral, even if they had already passed by the body.

"This was the greatest man who ever lived," a Turkish man said through an interpreter. "The world will never see another like him. It is the worst tragedy we will ever face, and we can only hope that his successor will be able to carry on the ideals he put forth."

"Do you believe Nicolae Carpathia was divine in any sense?" the reporter said.

"In every sense!" the man said. "I believe it's possible that he was the Messiah the Jews longed for all these centuries. And he was murdered in their own nation, just as the Scriptures prophesied."

As David settled in behind his computer in the privacy of his office, he left on the TV monitor hanging from the ceiling in the corner. GC CNN had followed that interview with a live feed from Israel, where thousands were listening to enthusiastic preachers, running forward, falling on their knees, and then shouting of their new allegiance to Jesus the Messiah.

The Jerusalem correspondent had with her a religious expert, who attempted to explain. "In the vacuum created by the deaths of both the head of the One World Faith and the supreme potentate of the Global Community, whom many considered every bit as much a religious as a political figure, spiritually hungry people are rushing to fill the gap. Longing for leadership and bereft of the one man who seemed to fit the bill, they now find attractive this fairly recent craze of ascribing to the historical figure of Jesus the Christ the qualifications of the Messiah Israel has awaited so long.

"This phenomenon existed in small pockets of conservative fundamentalist Christian sects but was fueled shortly after the vanishings by Dr. Tsion Ben-Judah, an Israeli biblical scholar. He had been commissioned by the State of Israel to clarify the prerequisites of the prophesied Messiah for the modern Jew.

"Dr. Ben-Judah created an uproar, particularly among Jews, when at the end of the live, globally televised airing of his views he announced that Jesus the Christ was the only person in history to fulfill all the Messianic prophesies, and that the vanishings were evidence that he had already come."

David was impressed that the "expert," while clearly not agreeing with what was going on, had an accurate handle on the issue. Having studied under Tsion on the Net for so long, David knew that this further outbreak of evangelism in Israel would also spawn many more false christs and second-rate antichrists. Dr. Ben-Judah had often cited Matthew 24:21-24 in urging his followers—now referred to as Judah-ites—to beware:

> For then there will be great tribulation, such as has not been since the beginning of the world until this

time, no, nor ever shall be. And unless those days were shortened, no flesh would be saved; but for the elect's sake those days will be shortened.

Then if anyone says to you, "Look, here is the Christ" or "There!" do not believe it. For false christs and false prophets will rise and show great signs and wonders to deceive, if possible, even the elect.

By now David was deep into the labyrinthine inner workings of the Strong Building. While whirring through the many security pass gates using code breakers of his own design, he had a phone tucked between his cheek and shoulder.

"Captain Steele," he said, "if I can do this, I'm going to get you in through one of the parking garage's inner doors. The gates will be down, but you can walk around those and get to the elevators."

"We were that far," Rayford said. "The glass doors leading to the elevators are the ones we need opened. We could break the glass, but we're afraid that would set off an alarm."

"Who'd hear it?"

"I know, but usually those kinds of alarms are attached to all sorts of interrelated devices. Like at the airport, you force your way through the wrong door, and certain systems automatically shut down."

"Bingo," David said.

"Excuse me?"

"You're in."

"We're not even on that side of the building."

"Well, get there," David said. "I can't wait to hear what you find. Listen, good news: the designers of this building did two very nice things, as if they knew we were coming. First, the electrical panel room and the telephone room, both of which are traditionally on the top floor or even above in some spire, are located on the first floor, one up from where you'll enter. Second, I think I have detected why the structure is so sound below where the bomb damage is. The blueprints show what's called a 'closure for stack effect' every fifteen floors or so. It happens that there is just such a closure one floor beneath where the bomb damage occurred. This closure acts as a new roof for the building. I'm not certain yet, but you may be able to land a helicopter there, if you can deal with the complications of a three-sided opening above that."

"Helicopter?" Rayford said. "We're in the garage, by the way."

"I can see you."

"You can?"

"See the monitor up in the corner to your right?"

The three waved at David and he almost waved back, forgetting this was not a two-way visual feed.

"Yep. I see you. The door directly in front of you should be unlocked. And yes, I said helicopter before."

"Where am I going to get one of those?"

"I don't know," David said. "Know anybody in purchasing anywhere?"

"We also need to start thinking about a new air base,

closer to here. Different anyway. We have no friends at Palwaukee anymore."

"How was Kankakee?"

"Might work. How about we have Albie set up there as a small private transport company, maybe serving Laslos, who's still considered legit by the GC? Then we can come and go as we please out of there with no questions asked. And we can chopper our way up here when we need to."

"I like the way you think, Captain Steele."

"I like the options you provide, David."

"I'll try to keep track of you floor by floor with the various monitors," David said. "But I may have to leave you abruptly too. You know where I am."

Leah and Chloe appeared to be working well together. Though David could hear only Rayford, he could see the women checking out sight angles from various windows.

"Leah wants to talk with you, David. Here she is."

"You're looking at blueprints?"

"On-line," he said, "yeah."

"Am I seeing this right? Are we not visible from the street, at least where we are now?"

"Affirmative."

"And what if we turn on lights?"

"That I wouldn't do."

"What if we spray painted the windows black?"

SIXTEEN

By TEN o'clock Saturday night in Illinois, Tsion had survived two messy operations: feeding and changing Kenny. The boy was now sound asleep in his crib in the other room, and Tsion had turned the sound off on the television. He merely glanced at it occasionally, tired of the endless repetition.

How many times had he seen Rayford's photograph and history and the grave conclusion on the part of Global Community Security and Intelligence forces that he was the lone assassin, the lone gunman? Rayford was also constantly referred to as a committed Judah-ite. Tsion knew, because he knew the Tribulation Force, that Rayford Steele had ceased to exist. He would neither make himself obvious to the public nor leave a trail in his own name. Tsion prayed that would preserve Rayford for as long as possible.

Tsion pored over his Bible texts and commentaries, trying to make sense of the vivid dream. He pleaded with
God for another of the same, but short of that, he wanted
to understand the one he'd had. Scholars were divided on
who the sun-clothed woman was, the one who wore a
garland of stars and used the moon as her footstool.

Clearly she was symbolic, as no woman was that large
or had a child in space. Some believed she represented
womankind as mentioned in Genesis when God told
Satan that the woman would produce a child whose heel
Satan might bruise, but who would crush his head. That
was a prophecy of the Christ child, and of course that
woman turned out to be Mary. Yet further details of this
symbolic woman indicated that she might symbolize
Israel. The Christ came from Israel, and Satan pursued
and persecuted God's chosen people even to the present
day.

As Tsion studied the biblical texts about Lucifer and
his being cast out from heaven, he became convinced
that when he had seen the dragon sweep a third of the
stars from the skies and they fell to earth, he was witness
to eternity past. The Scripture often referred to angels,
righteous or fallen, as stars, so he believed this was a picture of when Lucifer was first cast down due to his sin of
pride.

Yet Tsion also knew that Satan, even up to the halfway point of the Tribulation—where Tsion believed history stood right then—had been granted access to the
throne of God. He was the accuser of believers, yet when
he pursued the woman and her child to devour them,

a great battle was to be waged in heaven and he would be cast out for good.

Tsion was not aware he had fallen asleep again. All he knew was that the trip from the underground safe house into the chilly night air took less getting used to this time. He didn't worry about temporal things. He could see Kenny sleeping in his crib and himself dozing on the couch as clearly as he could see the oceans and continents of the beautiful blue planet. How peaceful it looked from up here, compared to what he knew was happening down there.

When he arrived at the appointed place, the woman had left her footstool. The sun-garment was gone with her, of course, as was the garland of stars. Yet brightness enveloped Tsion again, and he was eager to ask questions before this all faded and he awoke. Though Tsion knew it was a dream, he also knew it was of God, and he rested on the promise of old men dreaming dreams.

Tsion turned to the brightness, marveling again at the size and majesty of the angel. "Michael," he began, "is the woman Mary or—"

"Michael is engaged in battle, as you will soon see. I am Gabriel, the announcer."

"Oh! Forgive me, Prince Gabriel. Can you tell me, who is the woman? Is it Mary, or is it Israel?"

"Yes and yes."

"That was not as helpful as I had hoped."

"When you ponder it, you will find it so."

"And the twelve stars on her head. Do they represent the tribes of Israel?"

"Or . . . ?" Gabriel prodded.

"Or the . . . the apostles?"

"Yes and yes."

"Somehow I knew you were going to—so these things mean whatever we want or need them to mean?"

"No. They mean what they mean."

"Uh-huh."

"Son of earth, did you see what the male child bore in his hand?

"I'm sorry, I did not."

"A rod of iron, with which he shall rule the nations."

"So clearly he is Jesus . . ."

"The Christ, the Messiah, Son of the living God."

Tsion felt unworthy even to hear the description. He felt as if he were in the very presence of God.

"Prince Gabriel, to where has the woman fled?"

"Into the wilderness where God has prepared a place for her, where she will be safe for three and a half years."

"Does this mean God has prepared a place in the wilderness for his chosen people, where they too will be safe during the Great Tribulation?"

"You have said it."

"And what of the dragon?"

"He is enraged."

"And Michael?"

Gabriel gestured behind Tsion. "Behold."

Tsion turned to see a great battle raging. Michael and his angels wielded great double-edged swords against fiery darts from the dragon and his evil angels. The ugly hordes advanced again and again against Michael's mighty forces, but they could not prevail. As his comrades retreated behind him, the dragon fled to the throne. But it was as if a colossal invisible door had been slammed in his face. He fell back and tried to advance again to the place he had enjoyed before the throne. But from the throne came an insistent, "No. There is no longer a place here for you. Be gone!"

The dragon turned, his anger nearly consuming him. With his seven heads grimacing and gnashing their teeth, he gathered his own around him, and they all tumbled toward the earth. And Gabriel announced in a loud voice, "So the great dragon was cast out, that serpent of old, called the Devil and Satan, who deceives the whole world; he was cast to the earth, and his angels were cast out with him." And now louder still, with great joy: "Now salvation, and strength, and the kingdom of our God, and the power of his Christ have come, for the accuser of our brethren, who accused them before our God day and night, has been cast down. And they overcame him by the blood of the Lamb and by the word of their testimony, and they did not love their lives to the death. Therefore rejoice, O heavens, and you who dwell in them! Woe to the inhabitants of the earth and the sea! For the devil has come down to you, having great wrath, because he knows that he has a short time."

"What happens now?" Tsion said.

Gabriel looked at him and folded his arms. "The dragon will persecute the woman who gave birth to the child, but God will protect her. In his wrath the dragon will make war with the rest of her offspring, those who keep the commandments of God and have the testimony of Jesus the Christ."

Michael stood next to Gabriel now, his great sword sheathed, his warriors dispersed. Tsion could not speak. He opened his mouth to form words of gratitude, but he was mute. And he awoke. It was still ten o'clock.

———————

By nine in the morning Carpathia Time, New Babylon was a sea of people. Opportunists had set up shop on every road that led to the palace courtyard. Sellers of chairs, sunblock, umbrellas, bottled water, food, and souvenirs preyed on the pilgrims. Some merchants were run off by GC Peacekeepers, only to set up again a quarter mile away.

It was clear the forecasted one hundred degrees would be surpassed before noon. A canopy was erected behind the bier to protect both it and the armed guards from the relentless sun. Still, mourners and officials dropped right and left and were ferried to medical tents, where they were hydrated and fanned and sometimes doused with water.

David returned to his perch above one of the med tents, though it had been moved more than two hundred yards from the courtyard to make room for the crowds. Barriers, ropes, and makeshift fences forced people to snake back and forth in an agonizingly slow path to the bier. Street entertainers, jugglers, clowns, strippers, and vendors tried to keep people occupied. Here and there scuffles broke out, quickly quelled by the Peacekeepers.

Laborers continued to swarm, finalizing the reconstruction that would allow hundreds of thousands more in the courtyard. The huge screens were in place and operating, as were countless monitors surrounding the palace. When the ceremony was about to begin at noon, the line would be stopped and millions would fan out from the speaker's platform next to the coffin to more than a mile away.

From his spot David heard bands practicing, choirs rehearsing, dance troupes going through their paces. With binoculars he saw Annie manning her station nearly a half mile away. His phone chirped. It was a Peacekeeper at the airport.

"Director Hassid, I have a family here from China looking for their daughter, a GC employee named Ming Toy."

"Yes?"

"They say she told them to contact you or Cargo Chief Christopher if they could not find their daughter. She's come from Buffer in Brussels."

"Do they know where she is positioned here? It's all numbered, you know."

The guard covered the phone and asked them. "No," he said. "They said they thought their daughter was trying to get assigned near Ms. Christopher."

"Ms. Christopher is stationed at marker 53."

"Thank you, sir."

David kept his field glasses trained on Annie and saw

when the red-uniformed Asian approached and they embraced. They engaged in what appeared an animated conversation, and Annie grabbed her phone. David's erupted again. "Hi, babe," he said. "Ming's parents and brother are on their way from the airport and will look for her at your station. Did she get assigned—"

"David!" Annie whispered fiercely. "North American GC has identified the safe house!"

"What?!"

"Ming overheard it. She couldn't let me know before because they gathered everyone's phones for security."

"Call Tsion! I'll call Steele."

Rayford believed the new safe house might be the greatest gift God had bestowed on the Trib Force since the arrival of Tsion Ben-Judah. Several floors had been left virtually unblemished, and all the systems worked. There were more bathrooms than the occupants could ever use, and every service imaginable. It wasn't a home, of course, so beds would have to be brought in or fashioned. But the place could hold hundreds, maybe more. He didn't know how reasonable it was to think a whole lot of people could hide out there undetected, but he dreamed of inviting every dispossessed believer he knew: Leah's friend from Brussels, maybe her brother from China, Albie, maybe the Mikloses one day, all the insiders from New Babylon. A guy could dream.

He and Leah and Chloe were headed back toward

Mount Prospect just after midnight, Central Standard Time, when David called with the news. "Annie's calling Tsion," David said. "He's got to get out of there."

"There are certain things we have to have," Rayford said. "And Tsion doesn't have wheels."

"Captain, he's got to get out of there now."

"We have to go get him, David. Any way you can tell where we might run into GC?"

"Not in time to help you. You might have to take some risks."

"We'll also try to get Tsion on the phone. Who knows where the GC is or when they might strike? Our underground is a pretty good cover."

Tsion thanked Annie and rushed to shut off the power, trying to keep from hyperventilating. He felt his way in the dark and filled two pillowcases with necessities. The TV would stay. He gathered up essential medicines, a few reference works, and all the laptops, baby stuff, a handful of clothes, whatever he could fit into the bulging slipcases. He left enough room at the tops to tie them together and left them at the bottom of the stairs. There was only one way out of the shelter, and that was the way he had come in. Even if he were to throw a blanket over Kenny and lug him and the stuff out into the garage, that would be the second place the GC would look.

His best hope, he knew, was to hear the GC come in

upstairs, pray that they would be stopped by the spoiled food in the phony freezer, find no one, and move on. Then he would be ready to flee as soon as the others arrived.

Chloe called, nearly hysterical. "Tsion," she said, "if the GC gets to the cellar, you have to promise me—"

"I'll protect the baby with my life."

"You have to promise me, Tsion, please! Under my mattress is a syringe with a potassium chloride solution. It'll work quick, but you have to inject it directly into his buttocks. You can do it right through the diaper. It doesn't have to be perfect; it just has to be decisive and sure."

"Chloe! Get hold of yourself! I'm not going to harm Kenny!"

"Tsion," she cried, "please! Don't ever let them have my baby!"

"I won't. But I'll not—"

"Please!"

"No! Now let me do my work! I have to watch and listen. For now, Kenny is down and out. God is with us."

"Tsion!"

"Good-bye, Chloe."

Tsion went to the edge of the underground with the thinnest barrier to the outside and stood listening for engines. Or footsteps. Doors. Windows. So far, nothing. He hated being trapped. He was tempted to lug Kenny and the stuff to the garage, then make a break for it if the GC broke into the house. It was foolishness, he knew. He'd get nowhere on foot. His more-than-lifelike dream had put him on a first-name basis with the archangels of God, yet there he stood, cowering in a corner. He guessed Rayford was, at best, nearly an hour away. And if he happened to arrive when the GC was already there, Rayford would have to disappear.

Tsion prayed the GC had decided to take its time, to come the next day or the next week.

———

Until he sat in a cramped jet for a transatlantic flight, Buck didn't realize how extensive were his injuries. He felt twenty years older, wincing and sometimes yelping when he moved.

A couple of hours after Albie had taken off in a refurbished Jordanian fighter, the type with which Abdullah was most familiar, Buck had gotten word from Leah about the pastor who wanted to speak with him. He told her to give the man his number but to be sure he called from a public phone. The resulting conversation was one bright spot in a harrowing weekend.

"Your brother was the instigator," the pastor told him. "He confronted your father about his stubborn insistence that he was a believer and always had been. Your brother visited our house church by himself the first two or three times, and to hear your father tell it, he finally came just to avoid being alone. Mr. Williams, it took a long time for your father to get the picture."

"It would."

"Your brother less so. It was as if he were ready. But he knew better than to push your father. One of the biggest obstacles was that he knew one day he would have to admit that you were right and he was wrong."

Buck fought tears. "That's Pop all right. But why—"

". . . didn't your brother call? Two reasons. First, he wanted your dad to be the one to share the news. Two, he was scared to death they were going to somehow give you away. He knew well your position and how dangerous it was, or I should say is."

"Only calling from a bugged phone would have caused a problem."

"But he didn't know that. I just want you to know, sir, that your dad and your brother became true believers, and I'm sure they're with God right now. They were so proud of you. And you can tell Dr. Ben-Judah that he has at least one church out here that could lose its pastor and never skip a beat. We all love him."

Buck assured him he would tell Tsion.

They were an hour from Palwaukee when Buck got the call from Chloe about the safe house. While Chaim lay across the backseat, humming in agony over his various ailments, Albie seemed to grow more and more agitated as he realized what was going on.

"How was the safe house compromised?" he said. "Did Miss Durham finally give you up?"

"We don't know, Albie. All we know for sure is that Dr. Ben-Judah and our baby are there without transportation, and we have no idea how far away the GC is or whether Rayford can get there in time."

"And you have a new safe house, somewhere to go if you can get them out of there."

"Yes."

"Grab my bag from behind my seat."

Buck pulled it up, deciding it weighed more than Albie. "What have you got in this thing?"

Albie was all business. "Open, please."

The top layer consisted of Albie's underwear.

"Dig, please. Find side arm and holster."

Buck dug past what looked like a GC uniform. "Is this what I think it is?"

Albie nodded with a pleased look. "See cap. Check rank."

Buck whistled. "Deputy commander? Where did you get this?"

"No questions, no obligations."

"C'mon, did you used to work for the GC?"

"Better not to know."

"But did you?"

"No, but no more questions."

"Just where did you—"

"I have my sources. Sources are my life. Call Rayford. Tell him to meet us at Palwaukee."

"He shouldn't get to the safe house?"

"We need a vehicle. We need it as bad as Rayford needs it."

"How so?"

"Watch and learn. At Palwaukee, where can I change into the uniform?"

"You're going to—?"

"You don't ask. You only answer."

"There's a spot," Buck said. "I can show you."

"Anywhere we can leave Tobias Rogoff?"

"I wouldn't, now that we don't really know anyone there."

"OK. Find my papers. Dig deeper. Between the fake bottom of bag and the real bottom."

Buck found Albie's straight ID, then, right where he said, a worn leather pouch.

"Open, please. How many of us will be in the vehicle, six?"

Buck thought and confirmed that.

"And Mr. Rogoff needs a whole seat to self."

"Maybe not."

"Hope not. Too crowded. Find the papers to go with the clothes."

Buck leafed through until he found documents proving Albie's high-level role with the GC Peacekeeping Force. The picture, in snappy uniform, was of Albie but over a different name.

"Marcus Elbaz?" Buck said.

"Deputy Commander Elbaz to you, citizen," Albie said with such conviction that for a moment Buck thought he was truly upset. Buck saluted and Albie matched him. "Call Steele now."

Rayford was heartsick that Chloe was so determined to kill Kenny rather than see him fall into the hands of the enemy. And yet as a father, he could identify with her passion. It terrified him that she had thought it through to the point where she had an injection prepared.

Rayford had found a way back to a short stretch of unobstructed open road without making it obvious he had emerged from a restricted area. Now he had to find shortcuts and pick his way around debris and craters while careful not to violate any traffic laws. When he was free of other traffic he would make up for lost time and get to the safe house at the highest speed he could muster, his and his passengers' heads banging the roof of the Land Rover or not.

Buck's call was puzzling, and Rayford demanded to talk with Albie.

"What's the deal, friend? What're you up to?"

"Do you trust me, Captain Steele?"

"With my life, and more than once."

"So trust me now. You get to Palwaukee and be waiting for us. Then be prepared to get me to the safe house fast as you can. I'll explain roles as we go. If we're lucky, we beat the GC and we get the rabbi and the baby out. If we engage, everything depends on me."

———

Tsion prayed as he waited, but God did not grant the request to calm his fears. He'd had close calls in his day, but waiting for the enemy was the worst. He tiptoed around, watching, listening. Then he found the TV and bent to turn it on. He would only watch. But it would not come on. *Of course!* He smacked himself in the head. He had turned off the main power.

David hated this more than all the rest that came with working undercover in the enemy camp: knowing all that was happening half a world away, yet being powerless to do anything but warn and open the occasional sky-scraper door.

There was nothing more he or Annie or Ming could do from New Babylon. The players were in their places and the dangers real. All they could do was wait to hear how it turned out.

Ming's parents and brother were reunited with her at marker 53, and David was struck by the formalities. As he watched through binoculars, Ming and Chang embraced enthusiastically and emotionally. Ming kissed her mother lightly on the cheek, and she and her father shook hands. Then came more animated conversation and soon Annie was on the phone again.

"Mr. Wong is insulted that you are not here to greet him."

"Well, I can hardly do anything about th—"

"David, just come. Can you?"

SEVENTEEN

"I TRUST Albie," Rayford said, "but I don't like this."

"What do you think he's up to?" Chloe said.

"I don't know. He's a pretty shrewd guy. The problem is that we have only one vehicle."

"Thanks for reminding me," Chloe said.

"I just wish he'd make arrangements for another car at Palwaukee. I don't like leaving Tsion and Kenny like this."

Leah, strapped in in the backseat, pressed her hands against the ceiling to keep herself from bouncing too high. "How much farther, Daddy?" she said.

Chloe made a face, but Rayford said, "At least one of us is keeping a sense of humor."

———————

"David," Buck said on the phone, "Albie wants to talk with you. What's happening there? I hear the crowd."

"Let's just say I've pulled rank and appropriated an administrative golf cart. I'm on my way to mollify a public relations problem. At least I get to see Annie. Where are you guys?"

"Not sure. I'll let you talk to the pilot."

Buck handed the phone to Albie and listened as he peered out the window.

"David, my friend, good to talk with you again. I'm going to enjoy working with you. . . . We're within forty minutes of Palwaukee. If I represent myself as GC, will they ask for a security code? . . . They will? Is there one I can use?" He covered the phone. "Buck, write this down . . . OK, go ahead . . . zero-nine-two-three-four-nine. Got it. . . . So, anything that starts with zero-nine will be OK in the future and will go back through you for clearance. Good . . . helicopter? Yes, we sure could! You can do that? . . . GC? Perfect! . . . I'll tell the tower it will be delivered when? . . . OK! I know we will meet one day soon."

———————

David was struck by the variety in the crowds that lined the route to the courtyard. People of every ethnic background slowly moved toward the palace—young and old, wealthy and poor, colorfully dressed. Many appeared shell-shocked, as if they truly didn't know what they would do without Nicolae J. Carpathia to lead them through such a tumultuous time.

David called Mac. "Where are you, Captain?"

"Sector 94. Fun work."

"People must love that uniform."

"Yeah, they want to know if I know the supreme commander personally."

"And I'm sure you tell them how thrilled you are that you do."

"What do you want, David?"

"I need you to make a couple of calls for me. Get hold of the tower at Palwaukee and—you got a pencil?—refer to security code zero-nine-two-three-four-nine. Tell 'em they'll be hearing from one of our people who needs to hangar an Egyptian fighter there. Someone will be picking him up along with two passengers, and they must not be detained for clearances and paperwork. We will handle all that from New Babylon. Then call our base in Rantoul."

"Illinois?"

"Right. Tell them we need a chopper in Brookfield, Wisconsin, but all they have to do is get it as far as Palwaukee and we'll take it from there. Tell Palwaukee Tower that too. Can you do that?"

"Gee, I don't know, David. I'm better in the cockpit than on the phone. What's shakin' where you are?"

"Tell ya later. Get on those calls and we'll talk."

David arrived at sector 53, where Annie was keeping the peace and keeping people moving. She answered questions about the times of the ceremony and the burial and also told people how far it was to water, shade, medicine, and the like. In public, of course, she had to be formal with David.

"Welcome, Director Hassid. I would like you to meet our very special guests from China. This is Mr. and Mrs. Wong, their daughter Ming Toy, who works with us in Belgium, and their son, Chang."

David bowed and shook hands all around. Mr. Wong was plainly unhappy. "What language you speak?" he said.

"Primarily English," David said. "Also Hebrew."

"No good," Mr. Wong said. "No Asian language?"

"I'm sorry, no."

"You know German? I know German. English not good."

"No German. I apologize."

"We talk?"

"I'd be honored, sir."

"You forgive bad English?"

"Certainly. Perhaps your daughter can translate."

"No! You understand."

"I'll try."

"You insult no meet me at airport. I tell you through daughter we come."

"I did get that word secondhand, sir, but I was too busy here. I apologize and ask your forgiveness."

"VIP! I VIP because of business. Give lots money to Global Community. Very big patriot. Global patriot."

"You are well known here, sir, and your daughter is highly regarded. Please accept my apologies on behalf of the entire GC management team for our inability to welcome you in the manner you deserve."

"Son work for you someday. Not old enough yet. Only seventeen."

David glanced at Chang and noticed the mark of the believer on his forehead. "I will look forward to having him as a colleague when he's eighteen, sir. More than you can know."

"Whole family so sorry for Nicolae. Great man. Great man."

"I'll pass along your sentiments to the supreme commander."

"I meet supreme commander!"

"Have you?"

"No! I want meet!"

"I'm sorry, but we have been asked not to arrange any more personal meetings for him this week. You understand. Too many requests."

"Special seat! You arrange special seat?"

"Oh, I don't know. That would be diff—"

Mr. Wong shook his head as his wife took his arm as if to calm him. "No meet at airport. No meet supreme commander. Way back in line. You get us up front?"

"I'll see what I can do."

"No! You get special seat for funeral. We want in courtyard."

"I'll see what I can do."

"You see now. Tell us now. Take us now."

David sighed and got on the phone. "Yes, Margaret,

do we have anymore VIP seating at all? . . . I know . . . I know . . . three."

"No! Daughter sit with us too. And you! Five."

"Five, Margaret . . . I know. I'm in a bit of a bind here. I'll owe you . . . just inside the court? That sounds fine, but I'm expected with administrative personnel in the—"

"We sit with you! You can do! Four join you in good seat."

"I'm having trouble appeasing him, Margaret. . . . It's not your problem, no. . . . Yes, it's mine. What's the best you can do? . . . He did? Well, there you go. We can kill two birds, as they say. I owe you. . . . I know. Thanks, Margaret."

David turned back to them. "It seems the sculptor wrongly arranged for his assistants to sit with him in the management section, and the supreme commander's office is going to reverse that."

"I no understand. We sit there?"

"Yes. The sculptor is going to be 'honored' by standing next to the statue and having his assistants with him."

"We sit with you or not?"

"Yes, you sit with me."

"Good! Daughter too?"

"Yes."

"Good! Her new friend here too?" he pressed, pointing at Annie.

"Ah, no. I wish."

"I really can't, Mr. Wong," Annie said. "I must stay here during the ceremony."

"OK, us then."

In the wee hours of Sunday morning, Rayford barreled in to Palwaukee Airport in a cloud of dust. The place was deserted except for a light in the tower. The only lit runway was one that accommodated jets. Rayford laid his head on the steering wheel. "I just pray we're doing the right thing," he said. "To have been so close to the safe house and not check on Tsion and Kenny . . ."

Leah leaned forward. "And yet if the GC nose around there and *don't* discover the underground, we might give our people away by showing up."

"I know," he said, "but I just—"

"No!" Chloe said. "Dad's right. We need to take our chances and get there and get them out. You know what the GC are doing to Judah-ite sympathizers. They killed everybody in Chaim's house and burned it. They killed Buck's dad and brother and burned their place. What happens if they don't find Tsion and Kenny but burn the place anyway, because it's obvious we'd been living there? How would they get out? Tsion would come running right up into a burning house."

"Chloe," Rayford said, "I feel like we should play out Albie's scheme here, whatever it is."

"He can't know our situation."

"Buck has filled him in. And he's right that it makes

no sense for some of us to go to the safe house while others wait here for a ride. This way, if it's obvious the GC haven't been there yet, we need to get what we can and get out of there. That'll make eight of us, including the baby, so we won't have room for much else."

"Surely Tsion will think to bring the computers and necessities."

Rayford nodded.

"I'd better call him one more time," Chloe said. "He may not think to bring the notebooks with the co-op stuff."

"You don't have that on your computer?" Leah said.

Chloe gave her a look. "I always keep hard-copy back-ups."

"But you've got it on disks too, right?"

Chloe sighed and ignored her. And phoned Tsion.

David let the Wong family pile into the two-seat golf cart, first pointing Ming Toy to the front seat next to him and Dad, Mom, and Chang to the back bench. But Mr. Wong wouldn't budge, muttered something about "seat of honor," and Ming joined her mother and brother in the back. Mr. Wong sat straight, chest out, with a solemnly proud look as David carefully steered the cart through the throng toward the palace court-yard.

"They are not seating dignitaries until 11:30," David said. "They'll begin with the ten regional potentates and their entourages, then headquarter management personnel and their guests."

"They seat you right away," Mr. Wong said confidently. "And we with you."

"They'll follow protocol."

"I talk to Supreme Commander Leon Fortunato. He make sure we seat right away."

"He's greeting dignitaries and getting set for the processional now, Mr. Wong. Let's just get to the staging area, and I'm sure they'll accommodate us in due time."

"I want sit now, good view, ready for program." He turned and grabbed his son's knee. "This spectacular, ay? You work here someday, make proud, serve Global Community. Honor memory of Carpathia."

Chang did not respond.

"I know you want to, Son. You not know how say it. Be patriot like me. Duty. Honor. Service."

David pulled up to a corral area where lesser dignitaries were already being led to a line that would eventually fill the VIP area. Manning the gate was Ahmal, a man from David's department.

"We'll take care of the cart," Ahmal said. "You and your guests wait under the canopy by section G."

"Thanks, Ahmal."

"You no introduce! You rude host!"

"My apologies," David said. He introduced the family, emphasizing Mr. Wong's support of the GC.

"An honor, sir," Ahmal said, raising a brow at David.

"We sit now."

"No, sir," Ahmal said. "You're being asked to wait in line at section—"

"Big supporter of Carpathia, Fortunato, GC no wait in line. No one sitting in seats. We sit there now."

"Oh, sir, I'm sorry. There'll be a processional. Very nice. Music. You all file in."

"No! Sit now!"

"Father," Ming said, "it will be better, nicer, to come in all at the same time."

Mrs. Wong reached for her husband's arm, but he wrenched away. "I go sit! You no want sit now, you stay! Where seat?"

Ahmal looked to David, who shook his head.

"Mr. Ahmal! Check sheet! Where I sit?"

"Well, you're going to be in D-three, sir, but no one—"

"I sit," he said, pushing past, daring someone to stop him.

"He's only going to embarrass himself," David said. "Let him go."

Mr. Wong caused a stir in the crowd when he moved up the steps to the permanent amphitheater seating and began looking for his chair. Even people at the viewing platform were distracted and looked to see who was being seated already. Assuming he was someone important, some applauded, causing others to do the same. Soon everyone was aware that an Asian was in the VIP section, and they shaded their eyes to see if they recognized him.

"Must be the Asian States potentate," someone near David said.

Mr. Wong acknowledged the crowd with a nod and a bow.

"He old fool," Mrs. Wong said, and her son and daughter erupted into laughter. "We wait with Mr. Director Hassid."

"I'm afraid I'll have to join you later," David said. "Will you be all right?"

Mrs. Wong looked lost, but Ming took her hand and assured David they would be fine.

David went behind the stage to check progress on the technical aspects. Everything seemed to be in place, though there was a water shortage. The temperature was already 106 and climbing. GC personnel wore damp rags under their caps. Singers, dancers, and instrumentalists moved into place. Banks of monitors kept TV technicians aware of what was happening.

David went up steps that led to the bier from the back, passing armed guards every few feet. He slipped in behind the canopy that kept the coffin and the guards out of the sun, which was directly overhead now. As he squinted out at the courtyard and beyond, the pavement emitted shimmering waves of heat, and the line moved more and more slowly. David saw many looking at their watches and deduced that they were trying to worm their way into up-front positions for the funeral ceremony.

Once mourners were unwillingly urged past the bier, they would not be hurried away. They slowed, lingered, hoping to be stalled for the start of the festivities like some massive game of musical chairs.

David peered past the armed guards to the glass coffin, wondering how it would hold up in this heat. The vacuum seal looked secure and was checked every hour on the hour by the technician. Would the heat soften the box? Build up steam like a pressure cooker? David looked for signs that the heat affected the makeup, wax, or putty Dr. Eikenberry had used. How embarrassing if the real body was cooling in the morgue when the phony one reached its melting point and turned into a pool before the world.

"Stop the line, please!" came the directive from a bullhorn down and behind David's right. Two guards hurried that way and stepped in front of a Dutch couple who had observed the occasion by appearing in native costume. They looked as if they regretted it already, red-faced, sweating, and panting. They seemed pleased, however, at being left first in line some one hundred feet before the stairs. As they waited and the crowd behind them slowly came to a standstill of realization as well, the several dozen mourners ahead of them continued.

When they had passed and started down the stairs on the other side, a wave of silence invaded the entire area. Everyone looked to the courtyard with expectancy, the only movement the last of the mourners, trying to clear the exit stairs. They did not want to leave, but the program would not start until they did.

The stragglers finally reached the bottom and many sat

directly on the pavement. They found it so hot that they began taking off garments to sit on.

With everyone in place and still, the silence of four million plus was eerie. David slipped back down the steps behind the platform and saw that the staging area was full, everyone in place from Fortunato to his ministers and all ten regional potentates with their entourages. After that, high-ranking GC personnel filled the line all the way out of the courtyard.

From David's left, someone with a clipboard and headset signaled the director of the orchestra. With men in tuxedos and tails and women in full-length black dresses, the one hundred members of the orchestra mounted the back steps and made their way out onto the platform at stage left. Sweat poured from their faces, and great dark stains spread under their arms and down their backs. Once seated, they brought instruments into position and waited for their cue.

"Ladies and gentlemen," came the announcement over the massive public-address system, echoing in the courtyard, resounding for nearly a mile, and followed by instant translation into three other major languages. "Global Community Supreme Commander Leon Fortunato and the administration of the one-world government would like to express sincere thanks and appreciation for your presence at the memorial service for former Supreme Potentate Nicolae J. Carpathia. Please honor the occasion by removing head coverings during the performance by the Global Community International

Orchestra of the anthem, "Hail, Carpathia, Loving, Divine, and Strong."

As the orchestra played the dirge, weeping broke out among the crowd until great sobs filled the courtyard. The Global Community vocal band filed in, singing praises to Nicolae. Eventually a troupe of dancers, who seemed to move in slow motion and show remarkable balance, emoted with the music and the mournful groaning of the audience. As they performed, the VIPs filed in to subdued but sustained applause.

David finally made his way to the seat next to Mr. Wong, who gazed beatifically at the stage, tears streaming, both hands clutching his heart. David shaded his eyes and wondered if he himself was prepared to sit in this kind of heat for two hours. They were stage left with a clear view of the podium and coffin, about thirty feet away.

When the music finally ended, orchestra, singers, and dancers moved out and Fortunato and the ten potentates, grim-faced, moved into position one row up and behind the bier. One more joined the three armed guards who had stood behind it, and they moved two to each end of the casket.

The great screens and monitors showed a montage of Carpathia's life, beginning with his fifth birthday party in Romania, hugging his parents at high school graduation while holding some sort of trophy in each hand, being presented an award in college, winning an election in Romania, taking office as president there, speaking at the United Nations three and a half years before, and presiding over various major functions after that. The music that accompanied the visuals was poignant and triumphant, and people began to clap and cheer.

They reached fever pitch when Nicolae was shown announcing the new name of the one-world government, cutting the ribbon on the majestic palace, and welcoming people to the Gala just the week before in Jerusalem. Now fighter jets screamed in from the east and rumbled low over the event as the montage showed Carpathia mocking and challenging the two witnesses at the Wailing Wall. The crowd shouted and screamed with glee as he shot them dead. Of course, the show did not include their resurrections, which had been denounced as a myth.

The crowd fell silent as the jets swept out of earshot and the music again turned melancholy. The screens showed Carpathia back at the Gala, beginning with a long shot that showed much of the devastation from the earthquake. As the camera zoomed in on Nicolae, it changed to slow motion as he responded to the welcome of the crowd, introduced Chaim Rosenzweig, and joked with the potentates. Gasps and moans greeted the super-slow-motion replay of his turning away from a white puff of smoke in the crowd, tumbling over Dr. Rosenzweig, and lying there as the crowds fled.

The montage showed Nicolae being loaded onto a helicopter, GC logo emblazoned on the side, and here artistic license came into play. The screens showed the chopper lifting off from the stage, banking left between scaffolds and past great banks of lights, and almost disappearing into the darkness. The aircraft seemed to fly higher and higher until it pushed past the clouds and into the vastness of space.

Higher and higher it went, to the delight of the largest live crowd ever assembled, until the helicopter itself seemed to fade. Now all they saw on the big screens were space and a large image taking shape. The fighter jets returned, but no one watched. They just listened and watched as the screen morphed into the image of a man wide as the heavens. Standing in midair among the planets in dramatic dark suit, white shirt, and power tie, feet spread, arms folded across his chest, teeth gleaming, eyes flashing and confident, was Nicolae Carpathia, gazing lovingly down on the faithful.

The image froze under Nicolae's benevolent gaze, and the roar from the crowd was deafening. All stood and wildly cheered and clapped and whistled. David had to stand to avoid being conspicuous, and while he clasped his hands in front of him he glanced at Ming and Chang, who stood stone-faced, Chang with a tear rolling. David realized that no one was watching anyone else anyway, so complete was the devotion to Carpathia.

The symbolism could not be lost on anyone. He may have been murdered. He may be dead. But Nicolae Carpathia is alive in our hearts, and he is divine, and he is in heaven watching over us.

When finally the image disappeared and the music faded, Leon Fortunato stood at the lectern, his emotion-gripped face filling the screen. As Leon spread his notes before him, David noticed he was wearing a resplendent dark suit, white shirt, and power tie. It didn't work as well for poor Leon, but he apparently assumed his succession to the throne of the world, and he was giving the look all he had.

"I want to know if it was Hattie who gave us away," Chloe said as the Egyptian jet came into view.

"We can't know that," Rayford said, "unless she tells us. We can't contact her, remember? It's a one-way street right now."

Once the jet touched down, the light in the tower went off and a fat, older man came chugging down the stairs and out the door. Here was a guy with a job to do, and he was going to do it. "You're here to pick up GC personnel, am I right?" he hollered.

"Affirmative," Rayford said.

"Your number match mine? Zero-nine-two-three-four-nine?"

"Absolutely," Rayford said.

"Stay put, please. The airport is officially closed, and I must get the jet hangared and these people accommodated with dispatch."

He hurried off to the edge of the runway and went through a series of gyrations with his clipboard that would have been more effective with a flashlight as he tried to guide Albie toward the hangars.

This amused Rayford, who figured Albie had hangared as many small craft as anyone alive, and he watched as the jet steered a course straight at the tower man. He ran off the runway as the craft whined past and finished his signals with a flourish as if Albie had done precisely what he asked.

As the man ran to be sure the plane got into the hangar, Chloe shot past him. Rayford headed that way too as Leah waited by the car. It didn't take Rayford long to overtake the man, who clearly hadn't run around like this in ages.

The door of the plane, which was parked next to the Gulfstream, popped open, and Albie was the first one off. Rayford couldn't believe it. Albie had a presence, a strut. He looked a foot taller. Carrying his big leather bag, he pointed at the man and said, "You in charge here?"

"Yes, I—"

"Zero-nine-two-three-four-nine, GC, Deputy Commander Marcus Elbaz, requesting service as arranged."

"Yes, sir, Mr., er, Captain, Commander Deputy Commander, sir."

Albie said, "These people are with me. Let them help with my passengers. Refuel the plane overnight, check?"

"Oh, yes, check, sir."

"Now where can I change clothes?"

As the man pointed to a dark office at the end of the hangar, Chloe met Buck coming off the plane. "Careful, babe, careful," he said, as she wrapped her arms around him.

"Let's go, Buck," she said. "We've got to get to Kenny."

"Aliases," he whispered. "Help with Dr. Rogoff. He's had surgery."

Rayford climbed aboard to help with Chaim, who grinned stupidly at everyone and kept pointing to his forehead. "Welcome to the family, Doctor," Rayford said, and Chaim's grin turned to a grimace as he put weight on sore limbs and was helped off the plane.

Rayford noticed that everyone was on edge with the tower man around, but that was quickly taken care of when Albie emerged in uniform. Amazing.

"We're all set then, are we, sir?" Albie said.

"All set. I'll secure the door. We're not expecting any more air traffic tonight. I stay on the grounds, so I'll personally be responsible for the security of your aircraft."

"Both of them. The Gulfstream is ours too."

"Oh, I was unaware of that. No problem."

"Thanks on behalf of the Global Community. Now we have to go."

Leah had driven the Land Rover across the runway and into the hangar. She stayed behind the wheel while Rayford got in behind her and pulled Chaim in from the other side as Albie pushed. Chaim was plainly in agony as he slid across the seat, but once in and supported on both sides, he laid his head back.

Chloe sat next to Leah in the front with Buck on her right. As Leah backed up to pull out of the hangar, Chloe put her arm around her. "Thanks for bringing the car over. And forgive me."

"It's all right, Chloe," Leah said. "Just tell me you

didn't get the potassium chloride idea from any of my texts."

"I did, but right now I'm glad I know Tsion would never hurt Kenny."

Leah sped back the way she had come and headed for the exit. Rayford turned to see the tower man securing the hangar door, and as they reached the road, the runway lights went out.

"OK," Albie said, "we need to get a few things out of the way first. Madam driver?"

"Leah, sir."

"Yes, ma'am, could you turn on the overhead light back here?"

Leah fumbled for it, and Buck reached to flip the switch. Albie took off his uniform cap and turned toward Rayford. "With little time to talk, just look, Captain." Rayford stared and blinked. The mark. "Don't say anything right now," Albie said. "There's too much to do. You can turn the light off. All right, next order of business. Captain Steele, will you surrender command to me, just for tonight?"

"You have a plan?"

"Of course."

"Carry on."

"How far are we from the safe house?"

"Less than half an hour."

"All right. Here's the plan."

EIGHTEEN

DAVID was struck by the fact that Leon, for all his sanctimony, seemed genuinely moved. No doubt he revered Carpathia and was more than the typical sycophant. Clearly he was jockeying for position as new supreme potentate, but here also was a man who grieved the loss of his friend and mentor and champion. And while he did not have the polish, the panache, the charisma of his predecessor, Leon knew how to milk the moment.

"If you'll all be seated, please," he began, his voice so thick with emotion that thousands seemed to involuntarily cover their mouths to contain their own crying. David, his own uniform heavy with sweat, lifted one foot to cross his legs and felt the stickiness on the ground. The heat had made his rubber soles tacky.

Fortunato made a show of collecting himself and

smoothing his notes with meaty hands. "Nicolae Jetty Carpathia," he began in just above a whisper, "excuse me." He wiped a hand across his mouth. "I can do this. I will do this, with your patience. Nicolae Carpathia was born thirty-six years ago, the only child of two only children, in a tiny hospital in the town of Roman, Romania, in the eastern foothills of the Moldavian Carpathian Mountains, a little more than two hundred kilometers north and slightly east of Bucharest."

Fortunato paused again to clear his throat. "The young Nicolae was a precocious and extremely bright child with avid interests in athletics and academics, primarily languages, history, and science. Before the age of twelve he won his first election as president of the Young Humanists. He was a stellar high school student, a celebrated debater and speaker, and valedictorian, repeating that honor at university.

"Mr. Carpathia excelled as an entrepreneur and began public service early, becoming a member of Romania's Lower Parliament before age twenty-five. His devotion to pacifism brought both criticism and praise and became the hallmark of his life's work.

"Mr. Carpathia once told me that he believed the zenith of his career, even after being swept in as president of Romania as a young man at the behest of his predecessor, was his invitation to address the United Nations some three and a half years ago.

"Honored beyond expression, the young head of state worked hard on his presentation, outlining the history of the UN, employing every one of its languages, and memorizing his speech in its entirety. Little did he know that just prior to his appearance at the General Assembly, the earth would suffer its greatest calamity, the tragedy we all know now as the day of the vanishings.

"Stripped of our children and babies—" Fortunato paused again—"and countless friends and relatives and neighbors, the world family grieved as one. We were not aware then of the truth that only a man such as Nicolae Carpathia could bring to light: that the phenomenon that brought such bereavement was preventable, one rooted in our war technology. All we knew when the Romanian president stepped to the podium at the United Nations was that we were terrified to the point of immobility. Despairing of the future, regretting the past, we prayed in our own ways to our own gods for someone to take us by the hand and lead us through the minefields of our own making and into the blessedness of hope.

"How could we have known that our prayers would be answered by one who would prove his own divinity over and over as he humbly, selflessly served, giving of himself even to the point of death to show us the way to healing?"

The crowd could not contain itself and burst into applause. Several times Leon held up a hand, but they would not be silenced. Applause turned to cheering, and then they rose, sector by sector, until again everyone was standing, clapping, cheering, mourning their slain leader.

David was nauseated.

"Give me the rough layout of the safe house," Albie said, "where it stands, what's around it, any other buildings, roads in and out."

"I don't know if you have anything similar in your country, Albie," Rayford said. "But picture a subdivision, a housing development maybe thirty years old that has been tossed into a blender. The roads were ripped up and twisted out of the ground, and so many of the homes and businesses in that area were demolished that after rescue efforts, the area was abandoned. Best we can determine, no one lives within three miles of the place. We took over half of a badly damaged duplex, two homes in one. We expanded a cellar to make an underground hiding place, which we didn't need—at least that we knew of—until now. We rigged our own makeshift well and solar power plant, and took various routes to the place that made it look as if we could have been headed anywhere."

"What else is on the property?"

"About fifty paces from the back door is a barnlike garage that originally served both halves of the duplex. We hid our vehicles in there. We are now down to one, and this is it, so the garage is empty."

"And the other half of the residence?"

"Empty."

"Other dwellings in the area?"

"Pretty much piles of rubble that have never been hauled away."

"What hides you?"

"Besides that no one comes to that area except by mistake, there are mature trees and lots of open fields beyond our place."

"And the usual route from the airstrip takes you into the area from what direction?"

"We use various routes to keep from attracting attention, almost always travel by night, but usually find ourselves coming in from the south."

"Miss Leah," Albie said, "if you find an inconspicuous place to stop, please do." Away from paved roads already, Leah pulled into a shallow gully between two small groves of trees. "Thank you. Now, Captain Steele, your best guess of how the GC would approach the house, if they wanted to surprise."

Rayford searched for a scrap of paper and drew an aerial view of the place. "They'd come through the trees at the north," he said. "Buck, what do you think?"

Buck studied the schematic, then showed it to Chloe and Leah. They all nodded.

"All right, Leah," Albie said. "Come in from the south as usual. As far away from the safe house as you can, drive without lights. Stop about half a kilometer away, ideally where you can see the safe house but someone there would not likely see you."

"Half a kilometer?" Leah said.

"About three-tenths of a mile," Chloe said. "There's a little rise about that far away, isn't there, Dad? Just past where we turn to head toward Des Plaines?"

"Yeah, and we notice it because the rest of the whole area is so flat."

"Let's get there quickly," Albie said. "Lights off as soon as you're confident."

─────────────

As Fortunato held forth, alternately bringing the masses to their feet and making them weep, David surreptitiously pulled his binoculars from a side pocket. Leaning forward, elbows on knees, he trained the glasses on the great crowds seated just past the courtyard. He found the placard that read Sector 53 and carefully panned, looking for Annie. At first he didn't see her but was then intrigued to see a pair of binoculars pointed his direction. Despite hands and glasses covering her face, he could tell it was Annie.

They stared at each other through the lenses, then tentatively waved with just their fingers. David, with his hand still on the binoculars, held up one finger, then four, then three. She mirrored the message, their code for the number of letters in each word: *I love you.*

"I shall have some closing remarks as well," Leon said, winding down. "But I want to give your representatives from every global region the opportunity to express their thoughts before interment in the palace mausoleum. We've requested these be kept brief due to the weather, but we also want these potentates to speak from their hearts. First, from the United Russian States, Dr. Viktor . . ."

———

"Captain Steele," Albie said, "call Tsion and tell him who I am so I may speak to him without his suspicion."

Tsion answered on the first tone. "Tsion, it's me. We're within a half mile of you. Are you OK?"

"So far. Kenny is asleep. I'm packed and ready to go and feeling claustrophobic. I want out of this place."

"Tsion, I'm giving the phone to my dear friend and new believer, Albie. You've heard me mention him before."

"Yes! And he is one of us now?"

"Thanks to your teaching, which we can discuss later. He is using the name Marcus Elbaz and posing as a Global Community Peacekeeping deputy commander."

———

Tsion sat on the steps in the darkness, phone to his ear, the two tied-together packed pillowcases at his feet. All he had to do was grab them in one hand and the baby in the other, and he could be up through the freezer and out the door in seconds. But for now, he had no transportation and no idea whether the GC was waiting to ambush him.

He had heard so much about Rayford's black-market friend, he could hardly believe he was about to speak with him.

"Dr. Ben-Judah?"

"This is Tsion, yes. Albie?"

"Sir, I want to get right to business, but I must tell you, I owe you my soul."

"Thank you, sir. It appears I may soon owe you my life."

"Let's hope so. Tell me, have you heard anyone, anything, that might tell you the GC are nearby?"

"To tell you the truth, I nearly phoned Rayford about half an hour ago. It may have been paranoia, but I heard vehicles."

"Close?"

"Not very, but they were north of here. What frightened me was that they were intermittent."

"Meaning?"

"Starting, stopping, moving. I didn't know what to make of it."

"You don't usually hear any cars or trucks?"

"Right."

"And you've heard nothing since about thirty minutes ago?"

"About that."

"All right, listen carefully. Do you recognize the sound of the Land Rover? I mean, could you confidently distinguish it from, say, a GC Jeep?"

"I believe I could."

"Would you hear it plainly if it came between the house and the garage?"

"Certainly."

"And you can hear garage sounds? Doors opening and closing?"

"Yes, but these aren't typical American garage doors. They are manual and they swing like barn doors."

"All right. Thank you. If in the next fifteen minutes you hear what sounds like the Land Rover, it will be us. Any other noises or sounds, please let us know immediately."

———

Each potentate was greeted by music from his region and wild demonstrations from his people. Some had their people largely together; others saw them spread throughout the crowd. Most of the speakers echoed the sentiments of the potentate of the United Russian States, who listed Carpathia among not only the greatest heads of state and military leaders the world had ever known, but also among the most revered religious leaders and even deities of various faiths and sects.

The Asian leader, the second potentate to speak, said, "I know I speak for every citizen of my great region when I say that my reverence for His Excellency, the supreme potentate, has only increased in his death. I worshiped his leadership, his vision, his policies. And now I worship the man himself. May his fame and legend and glory only grow, now that he is again in heaven from whence he came!"

The potentate of the United Indian States intoned that "while we once believed that a good man comes back at a higher level, and thus that a bright star like Nicolae Carpathia would be guaranteed the role of a Brahman, he himself taught us—with his brilliant vision for a one-world faith—that even such traditional religious views have lost their currency. Even those who have come to believe that when you are dead, you are dead, and there is nothing more, have to admit—and I say this directly to Nicolae Carpathia—you will live for as long as we live. For you will always be alive in our hearts and in our memories."

Though the throng responded enthusiastically, David was intrigued that Fortunato seemed to feel the need to clarify, or at least modify, the effect of that speech. Before introducing the potentate from the United African States, Enoch Litwala, Fortunato took the floor briefly.

"Thank you for those sentiments, Potentate Kononowa. I appreciated the reference to the one-world church, which shall reappear here in New Babylon as an even better expression of a pure, united religion. Ironic, isn't it, that of the two sects most resistant to the ideas of a unified faith, one saw our great leader fall in its own homeland, and the other was responsible for his assassination.

"I do not blame the Israelis, as they are a valued part of the United Carpathian States. They cannot be held responsible for the climate engendered by their stubborn Orthodox Jews, most of whom have resisted to this day the inclusive invitation of the one-world faith. And then the Judah-ites! Espousing such exclusivistic, close-minded doctrines as there being but a single path to God! Should we be surprised that the very assassin of our beloved potentate is a leading member of that cult?"

With that pronouncement and the attendant applause, the great black statue to Leon's left began to smoke profusely, the wisp of black vapor becoming billowing clouds. Leon seemed to take this in stride, quipping, "Even Nicolae the Great has to agree with that.

"But seriously, before our African potentate comes, let me reiterate. Any cult, sect, religion, or individual who professes a single avenue to God or heaven or bliss in the afterlife is the greatest danger to the global community. Such a view engenders divisiveness, hatred, bigotry, condescension, and pride. I say to you with the confidence of one who sat in the presence of greatness every day for the last several years, there are many ways to ensure eternal bliss, if anything is eternal. It is not by walling yourself and your comrades off in a corner claiming you have the inside track to God. It is by being a good and kind human being and helping others.

"Nicolae Carpathia would have been the last person in the world to espouse a one-way religion, and look how he is revered. We will worship him and his memory for as long as we are alive. And that, my friends, will keep him and his ideals alive."

David wondered if the crowd would ever get as sick of itself as he was of the predictable clapping and cheering.

Enoch Litwala cast a pall on the proceedings when his inappropriately brief and lukewarm tribute fell flat. All he said was, "As potentate of the great United African States, it falls to me to express the sentiments of my people. Please accept our sincere condolences to the leadership of the Global Community and to those of you who loved the deceased. The United African States opposes violence and deplores this senseless act by a misguided individual, ignorantly believing what has been spoon-fed him and millions of others who refuse to think for themselves."

With that, Litwala sat, catching even Leon off guard. Two other tributes were lukewarm, which David thought made it obvious who were the loyal and the disloyal among the potentates.

———————

Albie leaned forward and whispered to Rayford, "Come with me. Leah, watch for my signal. If I wave, proceed slowly, lights off. If I call again, stand by for instructions, but be prepared to come fast, lights on, and be sure to stop short of Rayford and me."

"I'm coming with you," Chloe said. "Our baby is in there."

"Just as well," Albie said without hesitation. "Three is better anyway."

They crept from the Rover toward the safe house. Rayford saw Chloe's look in the low light, one of fierce determination that was more than just that of a protective mother. If they were going to engage the enemy, she plainly wanted in on it.

Rayford was aware of the cool air, the sound of his steps in the sparse underbrush, and his own breathing. He felt great melancholy about the safe house as they approached. It had become his base, his home, despite all the places he had been. It had housed his family, his friends, his mentor. And he knew if he had the opportunity to step inside it once again, it would likely be for the last time.

––––––––––––

When the last potentate had spoken, the crowd grew restless. From all over the courtyard and beyond, people stood en masse, ready to once again begin the processional past the bier. But Fortunato was not finished.

"If you'll bear with me a few more minutes," he said, "I have additional remarks I believe you will find inspirational. It should be clear to even the most casual observer that this is more than a funeral for a great leader, that the man who lies before you transcends human existence. Yes, yes, you may applaud. Who could argue such sentiments? I am pleased to report that the image you see to my left, your right, though larger than life, is an exact replica of Nicolae Carpathia, worthy of your reverence, yea, worthy of your worship.

"Should you feel inclined to bow to the image after paying your respects, feel free. Bow, pray, sing, gesture— do whatever you wish to express your heart. And believe. Believe, people, that Nicolae Carpathia is indeed here in spirit and accepts your praise and worship. Many of you know that this so-called man, whom I know to be divine, personally raised me from the dead.

"And now, as your new leader in the absence of the one we all wish were still here, allow me to be forthright.

I am no director, but let me ask the main television camera to move in on my face. Those close enough can look into my eyes. Those remote may look into my eyes on the screen."

David knew what happened to people who allowed themselves to be caught in Fortunato's gaze. He looked left, past the Wongs, who appeared enraptured, and reached to touch Chang and motion with his head to Ming. When they looked at him he shook his head imperceptibly and was grateful they both seemed to understand. They averted their gaze from Fortunato's.

"Today," Fortunato intoned, "I am instituting a new, improved global faith that shall have as its object of worship this image, which represents the very spirit of Nicolae Carpathia. Listen carefully, my people. When I said a moment ago that you may worship this image and Nicolae himself if you felt so inclined, I was merely being polite. Silence, please. With global citizenship comes responsibility, and that responsibility entails subordination to those in authority over you."

There was such deathly silence that David doubted if anyone so much as moved.

"As your new ruler, it is only fair of me to tell you that there is no option as it pertains to worshiping the image and spirit of Nicolae Carpathia. He is not only part of our new religion, but he is also its centerpiece. Indeed, he has become and forever shall *be* our religion. Now, before you break your reverie and bow before the image, let me impress upon your mind the consequences of disobeying such an edict."

Suddenly, from the statue itself—with its great expanses of black smoke now nearly blotting out the sun—came a thundering pronouncement: "I am the lord your god who sits high above the heavens!" People, including Guy Blod and his assistants, shrieked and fell prostrate, peeking at the image. "I am the god above all other gods. There is none like me. Worship or beware!"

Fortunato suddenly spoke softly, fatherly. "Fear not," he said. "Lift your eyes to the heavens." The massive dark clouds dissipated, and the image appeared serene once more. "Nicolae Carpathia loves you and has only your best in mind. Charged with the responsibility of ensuring compliance with the worship of your god, I have also been imbued with power. Please stand."

The masses stood as one, appearing terrified, eyes glued to Leon or to his image on the screens. He gestured grandly behind him, past the glass coffin and the guards, past the ten potentates, three of whom glared stonily. "Let us assume that there may be those here who choose, for one reason or another, to refuse to worship Carpathia. Perhaps they are independent spirits. Perhaps they are rebellious Jews. Perhaps they are secret Judah-ites who still believe 'their man' is the only way to God. Regardless of their justification, they shall surely die."

The crowd recoiled and many gasped.

"Marvel not that I say unto you that some shall surely die. If Carpathia is not god and I am not his chosen one, then I shall be proved wrong. If Carpathia is not *the* only way and *the* only life, then what I say is not *the* only truth and none should fear.

"It is also only fair that I offer proof of my role, in addition to what you have already seen and heard from Nicolae Carpathia's own image. I call on the power of my most high god to prove that he rules from heaven by burning to death with his pure, extinguishing fire those who would oppose me, those who would deny his deity, those who would subvert and plot and scheme to take my rightful place as his spokesman!"

He paused dramatically. Then, "I pray he does this even as I speak!"

Leon turned to face the ten potentates and pointed at the three who opposed him. Great beams of fire burst from the cloudless skies and incinerated the three where they sat. The other seven leaped from their seats to avoid the heat and flames, and even the guards backpedaled.

The crowd shrieked and wailed, but no one moved. No one ran. Every soul seemed paralyzed with fear. And the fire that left the three smoldering in tiny piles of ash disappeared as quickly as it had come.

Fortunato spoke again: "Faithful patriots of the Global Community from the three regions formerly led by men of lying tongues, take heart. Their replacements have already been selected in meetings I have enjoyed with the spirit of Nicolae Carpathia himself. The Global Community shall prevail. We shall reach our goal of utopian living, harmony, love, and tolerance—tolerance of all but those who refuse to worship the image of the man we esteem and glorify today!"

It was clear Fortunato expected applause, but the gathered were so stunned, so filled with terror that they merely stared. "You may express yourselves," Leon said with a smile. Still no one moved. His eyes narrowed. "You may express your agreement," he said, and tentative clapping began.

"You need not fear your lord god," he said, as the applause continued. "What you have witnessed here shall never befall you if you love Nicolae with the love that brought you here to honor his memory. Now before the interment, once everyone has had a chance to pay last respects, I invite you to come and worship. Come and worship. Worship your god, your dead yet living king."

Rayford followed Albie's signal and fanned left while Chloe was sent right. The three, about thirty paces apart, advanced upon the safe house from two hundred yards away. They watched for signs of GC. Had they been there? Were they yet there? Were they coming?

Suddenly Albie dropped into the grass and signaled Rayford and Chloe to do the same. He had taken a call. Then he signaled them to join him.

"Tsion hears the engine noises again," he whispered. "Coming from the north, only steady this time, as if advancing." He spoke as he dialed Leah. "We're going to beat them to the safe house on foot, so be ready to run, and if we encounter GC, stay a step or two behind me. Leah? Give us about ninety seconds, then come fast with lights on. Just be careful not to overtake us. When we stop, you stop as close to the garage as you can. Stay in the vehicle with the lights on and don't worry if you see GC Jeeps coming the other way."

Albie slapped the phone shut, unholstered his side arm, bounced to his feet, and said, "Let's go."

As Rayford loped along in the darkness, wondering how many minutes he might have left on earth, he was impressed that Chloe had no trouble keeping pace. He also wondered at the strange difference in Albie. He'd always been resourceful, but was there something else about him now, besides his new profession of faith?

Rayford wondered, why had he not assured himself of the integrity of Albie's mark? Could he be sure of anything he saw under the dim interior light of the Rover, a wounded old man between him and Albie?

NINETEEN

MR. WONG dropped to his knees next to David, weeping and crying out in his native tongue. His wife sat rocking, fists clenched, eyes closed, appearing more stunned than convinced.

Ming and Chang sat with hands covering their eyes, appearing to pray. To anyone else, it might appear they were praying to the new god of the world, but David knew.

He found it surreal that as Fortunato backed away from the lectern and joined the seven remaining potentates, they seemed to ignore the piles of ashes. They solemnly shook hands with their new leader, appearing to congratulate him on his speech and his display of power.

The security chief instructed his people to remove the barricade from in front of the single-file line. The couple in Dutch garb first refused to move toward the bier, but those behind them began to jostle and push, urging them on. The couple smiled with embarrassment, each clearly wanting the other to go first. They finally locked arms and shuffled along with mincing steps, seeming to want to see Carpathia's body but afraid of not only the gigantic speaking and smoke-belching statue, but also the seats behind the bier, three of which contained only ashes.

Fortunato and the remaining seven stood in front of the row of seats, just far enough behind the coffin to stay out of the guards' way and so that mourners would not be tempted to shake their hands or speak with them. It appeared to David that it suddenly came to Leon why people were shy about approaching. He turned first to one side and then the other and asked the potentates to move away from him.

Then he stepped back and, with a flourish, swept the ashes from each of the three seats, brushing and tidying them with his big hands. This stopped the processional and made anyone close by stare in amazement. With a satisfied look, Leon turned back to face the bier and motioned that the seven should rejoin him. As they did he clapped and rubbed his hands together, and the residue fell away. He and the potentates enjoyed a chuckle.

———————

Three sets of headlights appeared on the horizon, maybe a half mile beyond the safe house. Rayford had feared this day, when the GC would swoop down upon them.

He worried he would be gone or sleeping or unaware. How bizarre to be here and see it happening.

Albie and Chloe had picked up the pace and sprinted now. Rayford tried but found himself suddenly awkward and feeling his age again. "Closer to me now, Captain Steele," Albie called out, then hollered the same to Chloe.

Rayford and Chloe closed ranks, now ten or twelve feet on either side of Albie and about four feet back. Behind them the roaring Land Rover came bouncing over the terrain, projecting eerie shadows on the safe house.

It seemed to Rayford that the three vehicles advancing from the other way had slowed and separated. He and Albie and Chloe stopped between the old garage and the house, and Leah skidded the Land Rover to Chloe's right, next to the garage. "Hold," Albie said quietly. "Hold and maintain positions."

"We're vulnerable, Albie," Rayford said.

"Deputy Commander Elbaz, Mr. Berry," Albie said. "And you have ceded command to me, have you not?"

"Temporarily," Rayford said ruefully. If Albie was legit, he could take it as a joke. If Rayford had stupidly fallen for something and had sacrificed the Tribulation Force to a lapse in judgment, he was saying he would wrest back command and not go down without a fight.

The headlights before them now spread out, the vehicle to Rayford's left heading farther that way, angling toward them and stopping about seventy-five yards away. The one in the middle advanced closer, maybe fifty yards away. And the one to the right mirrored the one on the left.

"Hold," Albie said again. "Hold."

"We're targets here," Rayford said.

"Hold."

"I don't feel good about this," Chloe said.

"Hold. Trust me."

Rayford held his breath. *I wish I could. Lord, tell me I did the right thing.*

Rayford started when he heard someone jump out of the center vehicle, equipment jangling as he hit the ground, and move toward the house. While he could still see all three sets of headlights, Rayford lost behind the house the silhouette of the soldier hurrying their way.

"Hold."

"I'm holding, Alb—Deputy Commander, while they have an armed man on the other side of the house. What if he torches the place? What if the others join him? They have clear shots at us, while they're protected by trees and the house."

"Silence, Mr. Berry," Albie said. "We are outmanned twelve to three."

Rayford felt a deep foreboding. *How would he know that?*

"And unless one of you is packing," Albie added, "we are out-armed twelve to one."

"So, what," Chloe said, "we're surrendering? I'll die first."

"You might if you don't let me handle this."

Rayford had gone from suspicion to fear and now to

full-blown dread. He had walked his charges into the biggest trap imaginable. Wasn't it Albie himself who had once counseled to never trust anyone? They could be dead or in prison within half an hour.

"Global Community squadron leader!" Albie shouted, his voice deep and clear and louder than Rayford had ever heard it. "Show and identify yourself! I am GC Deputy Commander Marcus Elbaz, and that is an order!"

David guessed the temperature at 110 degrees. He couldn't remember being out at midday in New Babylon when it was this hot. He removed his uniform cap and wiped a sleeve across his brow. He was dripping. There was no wind. Just the relentless sun, the body heat of four million people, and the acrid smoke from the imposing statue.

The image began to move as if an earth tremor made it sway and bounce, but nothing else was affected. All eyes turned toward it in terror and word spread quickly throughout the courtyard that something was happening. For a long minute the thing seemed to vibrate in place. Then it rocked, and the smoke began to billow once more.

The image soon glowed red hot, and the smoke poured out so fast that it again formed clouds that darkened the sky. The temperature dropped immediately, but going from daylight to dusk so quickly made many fall to their faces.

The image roared, "Fear not and flee not! Flee not or you shall surely die!"

The blackness covered the sky in the immediate area, but when David sneaked a glance at the horizon, it remained light. At the edges, all the way around as he turned, lightning burst from the low-riding smoke and struck the ground. Seconds later the thunderclaps rolled in, shaking the area.

"Flee not!" the image shouted again. "Defy me at your peril!"

Leon stood with his arms folded, gazing at the statue as the seven potentates dropped to all fours, wide-eyed. The armed guards fell to their knees.

People at the far edges of the crowd turned and ran, only to be struck by lightning as the rest of the throng watched in horror. "You would defy *me?*" the statue roared. "Be silent! Be still! Fear not! Flee not! And behold!"

People froze in place, staring. The smoke stopped rising, yet the sky remained dark. It formed itself into roiling, growing black clouds mixed with deep reds and purples.

David, secure in his faith and believing he knew what was going on, still found himself shaking, shuddering, heart ablaze.

"Gaze not upon me," the statue said, now with no smoke coming from its face. As it cooled it faded from orange to red and back to black. It no longer moved. "Gaze upon your lord god."

It was as if the statue had shrunk, David thought, but it had merely become still, silent, and cold. People slowly rose, and all eyes turned upon the glass coffin where Carpathia, unmolested, remained reposed. Millions stood in the quickly cooled desert, the sky pitch, horrifying clouds churning. The people folded their arms against the sudden chill. Shoulders hunched, they stared at Carpathia's lifeless body.

———————

"I have eleven Peacekeepers with weapons trained on you, sir!" came the reply from the far corner of the safe house. "I'll need to see some identification!"

"Fair enough!" Albie called back. "But be prepared with your own, as I am your superior officer!"

"I suggest we meet on your side of the house with weapons holstered!"

"Agreed!" Albie said, making a show of returning his side arm to its strapped sheath on his belt.

"And your aides?"

"Same as yours, sir," Albie said. "Weapons trained on you."

The squadron leader stepped out from behind the house with his weapon secured, arms away from his body, hands empty. Albie stepped toward him with purpose. "Excellent approach, sir. I'm reaching for my papers now."

"As am I."

The squadron leader pulled a flashlight from behind his belt and they compared documents. "Sorry for the confusion, Deputy Commander," the young man said. "Do I know you?"

"You should, Datillo. I likely taught you. Where did you train?"

"BASALT, sir. Baltimore Area Squadron Leadership Training."

"I only guest lectured there. I was at Chesapeake."

"Yes, sir."

"Squadron Leader Datillo, may I ask what you're doing here?"

Datillo pulled order papers from his pocket. "We were led to believe this was headquarters of a Judah-ite faction, maybe even *the* central safe house. Our orders were to lay siege to it, apprehend any occupants, determine the whereabouts and identities of any others, and destroy the facility."

"Torch it?"

"Affirmative, sir."

Suddenly Albie moved closer to the young squadron leader. "Datillo, where did these orders come from?"

"I assumed New Babylon, sir."

"You assumed. Did you check them with the regional director?"

"No, sir, I—"

"Datillo, do you know what time it is?"

"Sir?"

"Do we not both speak English, Datillo? It's not my mother tongue, but it's yours. Is my accent too thick for you, son?"

"No, sir."

"Do you know what time it is?"

"After 0400 hours, sir. Requesting permission to check my watch."

"Granted."

"It's 0430, sir."

"It's 0430, Datillo. Does that mean anything to you?"

"Mean anything, sir?"

"Listen to me, Squadron Leader. I'm going to tell you this outside the listening range of your subordinates, though you don't deserve it. I'm going to resist the temptation to inform North American States Midwest Regional Director Crawford that you did not check orders through him before proceeding. And I'm even going to give you a pass on your *unbelievable* lack of awareness of the time zone differences between North America and the Carpathian States. I ask you again, Squadron Leader Datillo, what is the significance of 0430 hours?"

"I beg your pardon, Deputy Commander, and I appreciate your lenience on the other matters—particularly not embarrassing me in the presence of my subordinates. But, sir, I am drawing a complete blank on the time issue."

"Honestly," Albie said, "I don't know where they get you kids or what you're doing during basic training. Did you or did you not sit in any of my guest lectures at BASALT?"

"I honestly don't recall, sir."

"Then you didn't, because you wouldn't have forgotten. And you would know what time it is in New Babylon when it's 0430 in your part of the world."

"Well, if you mean do I know the time difference, yes sir, I do."

"You do."

"Yes, sir."

"I'm listening."

"At this time of the year, there's a nine-hour time difference."

"Very good, Datillo. What time does that make it in New Babylon right now?"

"Uh, let's see, they're later than we are, so it's, ah, 1330 hours."

"Do I have to walk you through this, son?"

"I'm sorry, sir. I'm afraid so."

"What is today, Squadron Leader?"

"Saturday, sir."

"You lose. Try again. It's after midnight, officer."

"Oh, yeah, it's Sunday morning already."

"Which makes it what in New Babylon?"

"Sunday afternoon."

"It's Sunday afternoon in New Babylon, Datillo. Ring any bells?"

Datillo's shoulders slumped. "It's the funeral, isn't it, sir?"

"Ding-ding-ding-ding! Datillo hits the jackpot! You're aware of the moratorium on combat-related activity anywhere in the world during the funeral, are you not?"

"Yes, sir."

"And every GC directive requires CPR, correct?"

"Concrete Peacekeeping Reasoning, yes, sir."

"And the CPR behind this directive?"

"Um, that no untoward publicity crowd out the funeral as the top news story."

"There you go. Now, Datillo, I can tell you're an earnest young man. You and your people are going to evacuate this area. You may return at 1000 hours and torch this place, if I leave it standing. My people and I were onto this location long before you were, and we have already apprehended the occupants and evacuated the building. I have a crew here to comb the residence for evidence, and we should be finished by dawn. Do not return until 1000, and if you see smoke on the horizon before that, you'll have no need to come then either. Have I made myself clear?"

"Yes, sir. Any way my people and I can assist, sir?"

"Only by following orders and leaving now. And I'll make a deal with you, son. You don't tell your superiors of the serious mistakes you made this morning, and I won't either."

"I appreciate that, sir."

"I know you do. Now move out."

Datillo saluted and trotted back to the middle Jeep. It popped a U-turn, as did the other two before falling in line behind it. And they raced off in the darkness.

The sky was so black that the lights of the palace courtyard came on automatically. The TV lights were trained on the coffin, and David was sure every eye but his was too. He searched and searched sector 53 for Annie, praying she would stand strong. He couldn't locate her.

David turned back. Heat waves shimmered off the statue in the comparatively chilly air. The potentates appeared paralyzed. Even Fortunato had paled and wasn't moving, his gaze on the casket. A rim of light along the horizon looked like the rim of hair on a bald man. Clouds of ebony and other deep shades, produced by smoke from the statue, hung ominously over the immense gathering. People stood stock-still, riveted. Brilliant lights bathed the platform.

David's eyes were drawn to the body. What was that? Almost imperceptible movement? Or had it been his imagination? He had imagined a corpse's chest rising and falling at a funeral before. But until now, Carpathia's body hadn't given even the illusion of life.

Carpathia's left index finger lifted an inch off his wrist for an instant, then fell again. A few people gasped, but David assumed most had not seen it. Then it rose and fell twice. Next it lifted half an inch, uncurling as if pointing.

One of the potentates apparently saw that and recoiled, trying to back away but falling over a chair. As he scrambled to his feet and tried to exit, lightning struck ten feet from him and knocked him back to where he had been. He stood shakily and brushed himself off, reluctantly looking at Carpathia again.

Now the index finger twitched, and all the potentates stiffened. The guards went into assault position, as if prepared to shoot a dead body. Carpathia's hands separated and rested at his sides. Those close enough began to weep, their faces contorted in terror. It seemed they wanted to escape but could not move.

Those ahead of David edged closer, careful to keep someone between them and the bier. Those in front held their ground or tried to step back, but no one behind them would have that.

Now it was clear that Carpathia's chest did rise and fall. Many fell to their knees, hiding their eyes, crying out.

Nicolae's eyes popped open. David stared, then tore his gaze away to see even Leon and the kings trembling.

The corpse's lips separated, and Nicolae lifted his head until it pressed against the Plexiglas lid. Everyone within a hundred yards of the coffin, including Fortunato, collapsed, covering their faces but, David noticed, most peeking through intertwined fingers.

As if stretching, Carpathia tilted his head back, grimaced, and lifted his knees until they too met the lid of the casket. He straightened his left leg until his heel met the large rubber stopper and forced it free with a loud *thwock!* The plug flew out and knocked the cap off one of the prostrate guards. He dropped his weapon and rubbed his head as the projectile bounced and rolled and finally stopped under a chair.

With the vacuum seal broken, Carpathia slowly brought his hands to his chest, palms up, heels of his hands resting on the underside of the lid. Moans and gasps and shrieks came from the crowd for as far as David could see and hear. Everyone was on the ground now, either peering at the screens or trying to see the platform.

Carpathia lifted his knees again, ripping the massive stainless steel bolts free of the glass. Then he pushed mightily until the top end shattered loose. The lid, more than eighty pounds of Plexiglas, flew away from the coffin, bolts flying, and smashed into the lectern, knocking it over and taking the microphone with it.

Carpathia catapulted himself to a standing position in the narrow end of his own coffin. He turned triumphantly to face the crowd, and David noticed makeup, putty, surgical staples, and stitches in the box where Nicolae's head had lain.

Standing there before now deathly silence, Nicolae looked as if he had just stepped out of his closet where a valet had helped him into a crisp suit. Shoes gleaming, laces taut, socks smooth, suit unwrinkled, tie hanging just so, he stood broad-shouldered, fresh-faced, shaven, hair in place, no pallor. Fortunato and the seven were on their knees, hiding their faces, sobbing aloud.

Nicolae raised his hands to shoulder height and said loudly enough for everyone to hear, without aid of a microphone, "Peace. Be still." With that the clouds ascended and vanished, and the sun reappeared in all its brilliance and heat. People squinted and covered their eyes.

"Peace be unto you," he said. "My peace I give you. Please stand." He paused while everyone rose, eyes still locked on him, bodies rigid with fear. "Let not your hearts be troubled. Believe in me."

Murmuring began. David heard people marveling that he was not using a microphone, but neither was he raising his voice. And yet everyone could hear.

It was as if Carpathia read their minds. "You marvel that I speak directly to your hearts without amplification, yet you saw me raise myself from the dead. Who but the most high god has power over death? Who but god controls the earth and sky?"

Hands still raised, he spoke gently. "Do you still tremble? Are you still sore afraid? Fear not, for I bring you good tidings of great joy. It is I who loves you who stands before you today, wounded unto death but now living . . . for you. For you.

"You need never fear me, for you are my friends. Only my enemies need fear. Why are you fearful, O you of little faith? Come to me, and you will find rest for your souls."

David nearly fainted from nausea. To hear the words of Jesus from this evil man, whom Dr. Ben-Judah taught was now indwelt, Satan incarnate, was almost more than he could take.

"Only he who is not with me is against me," Carpathia continued. "Anyone who speaks a word against me, it will not be forgiven him. But as for you, the faithful, be of good cheer. It is I; do not be afraid."

David searched for Annie again, knowing that no one around him was even aware he was not paying attention to Carpathia. How he wished he could see her, know she was all right, communicate to her that she was not alone, that other believers were here.

"I want to greet you," Carpathia said. "Come to me, touch me, talk to me, worship me. All authority has been given to me in heaven and on earth. I will be with you always, even to the end."

The line that had frozen in place still did not move. Carpathia turned to Fortunato and nodded, gesturing to the guards. "Urge my own to come to me." Slowly the guards rose and began to nudge the people toward the stairs again. "And as you come," Carpathia continued, "let me speak to you about my enemies. . . ."

Tsion had sat praying as vehicles approached the safe house from two directions. "Is this the end, Lord?" he said. "I so long to come to you. But if it is not the due time for my beloved brothers and sisters and me to give our lives for you, give us all strength and wisdom."

The vehicles stopped, and he heard shouting. Tsion moved to the corner of the cellar where he could hear. A Middle Eastern GC commander was calling out a squadron commander. Tsion tried to slow and regulate his breathing so he could hear every word. Was that Albie, the one he had just spoken to, pretending to be GC? Or *was* he GC? He was so convincing, so knowledgeable. How could a man know so much about systems and procedures without being on the inside? Or perhaps he once was and had turned. Tsion could only hope.

Whatever he was, Albie had driven off the squadron commander and his men, and Tsion knew his friends would now come for him. His first order of business? He turned the power back on and fired up the TV. His phone rang.

"Dr. Ben-Judah," Albie said, "are you down there and all right?"

"I am fine and watching the funeral on TV. Come down and see."

"Do you want to come and let us in?"

"Break in! I don't want to miss this, and we're not staying anyway, are we?"

Albie chuckled and the back door was kicked in. Footsteps. The freezer door opened, the rack pulled aside, footsteps on the stairs. Albie entered, followed by Chloe, who raced to pull Kenny from his crib and smother him with kisses. Then Rayford, looking grave even as he embraced Tsion.

"The others are coming," Rayford said.

"Yes, yes, and praise God," Tsion said. "But watch this. A great storm has invaded the palace courtyard, and I am convinced the hour is near."

Buck limped gingerly down the stairs and found Chloe and Kenny. Leah followed, carefully aiding Chaim. Bandaged, mute, and fragile, still he forced a grin when he saw Tsion, and the countrymen embraced. "I praise the Lord for you, my brother," Tsion said. "Now sit and watch."

"We want to get this done before dawn, people," Albie said. "I don't think our young friend will return until ten, but we'd better not test him."

"Are we really going to torch this place once we've got what we want?" Rayford said.

Tsion tried to shush them, but both ignored him. He turned up the TV. "This seems pretty risky," Buck said, emerging from the bedroom with Chloe and Kenny, "partying down here with GC in the area."

"I believe the indwelling is about to occur," Tsion announced.

"Put a videodisc in, Tsion!" Rayford said. "We've got work to do and fast."

"I am confident Albie's ruse was successful," Tsion said. "At least I hope so."

Rayford approached him. "Doctor," he said, "I'm back and I'm in charge, and I need to pull rank, despite my respect for you. Record that and let's get packing."

Tsion read such confidence and also concern in Rayford that he immediately popped in a disc. "Chaim, you can't work in your condition. Monitor this for me until we have to go." He hurried upstairs.

"Bring only what you can carry on your lap," Rayford announced. "Tying stuff atop the car would attract too much attention."

As Tsion busied himself, he worried about Rayford. It was natural for them all to be relieved and yet worried they were not out of the woods yet. Rayford was plainly agitated about something. After Tsion gave his room one last cursory glance for any indispensables, he saw Rayford pull Albie into Buck and Chloe's empty first-floor bedroom.

"You all know me as a forgiving potentate," Carpathia said, as the masses began to queue up once more to file past him. This time they would have the weird experience of touching and chatting with a man who had been dead nearly three days and who still stood in the remains of his own coffin.

"Ironically," he continued, "the person or persons responsible for my demise may no longer be pursued for murder. Attempted murder of a government official is still an international felony, of course. The guilty know who they are, but as for me, I hereby pardon any and all. No official action is to be taken by the government of the Global Community. What steps fellow citizens may take to ensure that such an act never takes place again, I do not know and will not interfere with.

"However, individual would-be assassins aside, there are opponents to the Global Community and to my leadership. Hear me, my people: I need not and will not tolerate opposition. You need not fear because you came here to commemorate my life on the occasion of my death, and you remain to worship me as your divine leader. But to those who believe it is possible to rebel against my authority and survive, beware. I shall soon institute a program of loyalty confirmation that will prove once and for all who is with us and who is against us, and woe to the haughty insurrectionist. He will find no place to hide.

"Now, loyal subjects, come and worship."

TWENTY

RAYFORD pulled Albie into Buck and Chloe's bedroom by his elbow. As he was shutting the door he saw Chaim staggering toward Tsion, gesturing, grunting through his bandages and wired jaw, trying to get Tsion to follow.

Rayford's phone rang. "Stay put," Rayford told Albie. Then, into the phone, "Steele here."

"Rayford, it's Hattie!" She was near hysterics.

"Where are you?" he said.

"The less you know the better, but get your people out of the safe house."

"Why?"

"They're onto you. Don't ask me how I know. And Carpathia has come back from the dead. Did you see?"

"No."

"It's all true, isn't it, Rayford?"

"Of course it is, and you knew that almost as soon as

373

most of us did. I didn't think doubt was why you were holding out."

"It wasn't, totally. But I was still holding out hope that it couldn't all be just the way Dr. Ben-Judah said."

"What're you going to do about it, Hattie? You know how we all feel about it and about you."

"Nothing right now, Rayford. I just wanted to warn you."

"Thanks, but now *I'm* warning *you*. Don't wait any longer."

"I have to go, Rayford."

"Dr. Rosenzweig has made his decision."

"I've really got to—what? He has? He was supposed to be dead. Is he there? May I talk with him?"

"I'll have him call you when he's able."

"I don't want my phone ringing at the wrong time."

"Then call us back tomorrow, Hattie, hear? We'll all be praying you do the right thing."

———

David did not know where Viv Ivins had been sitting. Surely she had been in the VIP section, but he did not notice her until she appeared at Carpathia's side. Fortunato was to her right, so as people swept past they encountered first Leon, then Viv, and finally Carpathia. It was as if this setup was designed to put people at ease. They need not fear a recently dead man who wanted to touch and be touched.

Leon gently pushed them to Viv, who said something

soothing and guided them quickly past Carpathia. He seemed to be looking each one in the eye and cooing something as he grasped his or her hand with both of his. No one was allowed to pause, and all seemed overcome as they floated away. Many swooned and some passed out. David did some quick figuring. If Nicolae gave, say, three million people five or six seconds apiece, it would take more than 200 twenty-four-hour days. Surely those who waited more than a few hours would give up.

"Can this wait, Captain Steele?" Albie said.

Rayford blocked his path. "Why, Albie?"

"Don't *you* want to see what's happening on the news?"

"I'll watch the replay."

"So, you want to see it too."

"Of course," Rayford said. "But I'm starting to wonder if we want to see it for the same reason."

"What are you saying?"

"What is your real name?"

"You know my name, Rayford."

"May I check your mark?"

Albie squinted at him. "In my culture, that is a terrible insult. Especially after everything we have been through."

"Your culture never had the mark before. What's the insult?"

"To not be personally trusted."

"You yourself advised me to trust no one."

"That's a principle, my friend. You think I would fake and lie to you about something I know to be so real to you?"

"I don't know."

"Then you had better check my mark. You could not insult me further."

"Take it as a compliment, Albie. If you're for real, you were so convincing as a GC commander that you made me wonder."

"I must have."

"You did. How did you know we were outmanned twelve to three?"

"I do my homework. It's part of the job. How do you think I outlived the average black marketer by two times? I'm careful. I don't just find a uniform and affect an identity without learning the nuances."

"How did you know three Jeeps carried four Peace-keepers each?"

"That is GC protocol. Night patrols are called squadrons and have a leader, three vehicles, and eleven subordinates. By day they travel in pairs."

"Uh-huh. And BASALT?"

"Never heard of it. I was glad he explained."

"Guest lecturing?"

"Made it up."

"Chesapeake?"

"Guessing. Hoping. I had read something about a GC training facility there. I'm glad I was so convincing,

Rayford, because our lives depended on it. It's what
I do."

"Midwest Regional what-did-you-call-him, Director—"

"Director Crawford, right."

"And you know him from . . . ?"

"A directory I thought it would behoove me to famil-
iarize myself with."

"You've never met him?"

"How would I?"

"You're still a closet hater of Carpathia?"

"Out of the closet soon, I hope. I don't enjoy long-
term playacting. Satisfied?"

"How did you know about the funeral moratorium
and, what did you call it? CPR?"

"I read."

"You read."

"You should know that about me."

"I think I need to know a lot more about you."

Now Albie was mad. "I won't pretend not to be
deeply offended," he said, ripping off his uniform cap
and slamming it to the floor. Rayford was suddenly
aware that they alone remained on the main floor and he
heard no footsteps above. Everyone must have been huddled around the television in the underground shelter.

Albie unstrapped his gun and drew it, Rayford retreat-
ing until the back of his head hit the bedroom door.
Albie turned the weapon around so he was holding the
barrel. He thrust it at Rayford. "Here," he said. "Shoot
me if I am a liar."

Rayford hesitated.

"Go on, take it!"

"I'm not going to shoot you, Albie."

"Even if I'm a phony? Even if I've turned on you, lied to you? Compromised you? Even if I was GC after all? Let me tell you, Captain Steele, if that *were* true about me and I were *you,* I would shoot me without remorse." He stood offering the weapon. "But I will say this. If I *were* GC, this is where and when I would shoot you too. And I would kill every one of your comrades as they rushed from the underground. Then I would secure the place and let Squadron Commander Datillo burn the evidence to the ground. What will it be, Captain Steele? This is a limited offer. Hadn't you better check me to see if you signed the death warrants of all your friends? Or will you risk their lives to keep from insulting me further?"

Rayford would not reach for the gun, so Albie tossed it on the bed. Rayford wished he had taken it, not sure whether he could beat Albie to it now if he had to. Albie took a step closer, making Rayford flinch, but Albie merely stuck his forehead in Rayford's face.

"Touch it, rub it, wash it, put petrol on it. Do whatever you have to do to convince yourself. I already know who I am. If I'm phony, shoot me. If I'm real, assume I have turned command back over to you. Either way, you could not have offended me more."

"I don't mean to offend you, Albie. But I must—"

"Just get on with it! If you are to be the leader, take command!"

David scanned the far reaches of the crowd where carts zigzagged with bullhorns, advising the people that the GC regretted to inform them that "only those already inside the courtyard will be able to greet His Excellency personally. Thanks for understanding, and do feel free to remain for final remarks in an hour or so."

David searched and searched for Annie, finally telling the Wong family he had to go.

Mr. Wong, his face ravaged by tears and exhaustion, said, "No! You get us into receiving line."

"I'm sorry," David said. "They've closed the line."

"But we in courtyard! VIP seat! You make happen."

"No," David said, leaning close. "You're the VIP. You make it happen."

As the older man sputtered, David squeezed Mom's shoulder and embraced both Ming and Chang, whispering in their ears, "*Jesus* is risen."

Both responded under their breath, "He is risen indeed."

"Forgive me, Albie," Rayford said. "Please don't be insulted."

"You have already insulted me, my friend, so you might as well put your mind at ease."

"I'm trying to put *your* mind at ease, Albie."

"That will require more of an apology than you have the time or energy or, I may say, insight to give. Now check the mark, and let's get out of here."

Rayford reached for Albie, who seemed to stiffen. A loud rap on the door made them both jump. Tsion poked his head in. "My apologies, gentlemen, but Carpathia has resurrected! You must come see!"

Rayford retrieved the gun.

"Keep it," Albie said, as they headed downstairs.

"But that would insult you even more."

"I told you, I cannot be more deeply insulted."

Rayford reached back awkwardly, holding the gun out to Albie.

Albie shook his head, grabbed the gun, and slammed it into its holster. As he snapped the strap he said, "The only thing more offensive than not being trusted by an old friend is your simpering style of leadership. Rayford, you and those you are responsible for are entering the most dangerous phase of your existence. Don't blow it with indecision and poor judgment."

Buck held the sleeping baby while Chloe finished packing. He heard Rayford and Albie descending and wondered why they were empty-handed after having been upstairs for so long. Maybe they had already carried stuff to the car.

"Did you see this, Dad?" he said, nodding toward the TV where GC CNN played and replayed the most dramatic moments from New Babylon.

"Better not refer to me informally in front of the rest of the Force," Rayford whispered, as he stared at the TV.

Buck cocked his head. "Whatever you say, Captain Steele."

He limped to where Chloe had gathered their essentials, traded the baby for a bundle, and slowly made his way out to the Land Rover. The coolness of the predawn refreshed him, though he caught himself sniffing the air and listening. The last thing he wanted, after the bizarre story of Albie's ruse, was to hear those GC Jeeps returning. What if the squadron leader was braver than Albie gave him credit for and he risked embarrassment and even reprimand to check out the story? He'd be back with more help, and they could all be imprisoned or killed and the place destroyed.

Buck worried about some of his injuries. He had pain in both legs that felt sharper than soft tissue damage, so he worried about broken bones. He was certain he'd also cracked a rib or two and couldn't imagine that Chaim hadn't as well. They shared whiplash trauma, even though their heads had first been driven forward.

Buck caught a glimpse of himself in the cracked outside rearview mirror of the Rover as he stepped away from the vehicle. Was it possible he was only thirty-three? He felt even worse than he looked, and he looked fifty. A fabric burn on his forehead he hadn't even noticed in the hospital had formed a large, ugly scab that was tender to the touch. That had to have come from the first impact and the forcing of his head into the back of the seat in front of him. Deep lacerations from dropping into a woody bush at the Jerusalem Airport what seemed eons ago had healed as high-ridged scars with crimson centers that covered his chin, cheeks, and forehead.

Worse, his eyes had that world-weary look, a deep fatigue that combined survival desperation, love and concern for his wife and child, and the sheer exhaustion of living as a fugitive and enduring searing personal losses. He took a deep breath that brought stinging pain to his ribs. He wondered where he might next sleep, but he didn't wonder if he would sleep well.

Buck would have returned inside to help, but in his condition he was more help staying put. The others began to straggle out under heavy bundles, except for Tsion who had just two full pillowcases tied together over one shoulder and was supporting Chaim on his other arm.

Albie, the last out, was on the phone. Rayford arranged the seating. He put Chloe, Kenny, Leah, Tsion, and Chaim in the backseat, where they were barely able to close the doors. Buck would ride shotgun in the front with Albie in the middle and Rayford driving. First, however, Rayford and Albie stood between the garage and the house—Albie still on the phone—and Rayford beckoned Buck with a nod.

"The chopper is at Palwaukee," Albie reported. "And the shuttle pilots are on their way back to Rantoul in the trail plane. You want my advice, Captain?"

"You bet."

"I say we go directly to the airstrip and put the wounded and as much of the luggage in the chopper as we can. Then you can fly the chopper to the new safe house, and someone else can drive."

"And you?"

"I should take the fighter to Kankakee. You can pick me up there later in the chopper, and I can fly the Gulfstream into Kankakee."

"How about torching this place?" Rayford said.

"You have materials?"

"Kerosene and gasoline in the garage. Some flares."

"That would do it. Have you left anything incriminating inside?"

"Not that I can think of. You, Buck?"

Buck shook his head. "I'd light 'er up."

"That's me too," Rayford said. "Just in case. Leave 'em nothing to find."

Albie looked at his watch. "I think we're pressing our luck. Let the GC waste time digging through it, and then *they* can cook it. We need to be gone from here as soon as we can."

"You're the expert," Rayford said. "You want a vote, Buck?"

"I'm with you, D—ah, Captain."

At Palwaukee Albie stayed in character and informed the in-residence tower man that the procurement of the chopper and the fuel for the fighter and Gulfstream should all be kept under the same GC order number. Greasy haired and short on sleep, the big man seemed as thrilled as he had been hours before to be doing his duty to the GC and particularly to the deputy commander.

"Did you see the news, sir?" the man said. "The wonderful, wonderful news?"

"Did I ever," Albie said. "Thanks for your kindness. Now we must be off."

"My pleasure, Deputy Commander, sir! A pleasure indeed. If you ever need anything else, don't hes—"

Buck was left to nod to the man. Albie was off to the freshly refueled jet, and Rayford to the chopper.

———————

David searched and searched for Annie, unable to raise her on the phone and not willing to holler for her over the midafternoon crowds. Finally he rushed back to his office, flipped on the TV so he could catch Carpathia's final remarks, and got on his computer to be sure the new safe house was accessible.

He called Rayford, who filled him in on everything since they had last spoken. "I *can* trust Albie, can't I, David?"

"Albie? He was your find, wasn't he? We've been working fairly closely lately. I think he's the best, and you and Mac always said he was. Anyway, he's one of us now, right?"

"Right."

"If you doubt him, check his mark."

"Apparently you don't insult Middle Eastern men that way."

"Hey! Captain! You're talking to one."

"Would someone checking your mark insult you?"

"Well, I suppose if you did, after knowing me so long. I mean, I don't think you ever have."

"If I can't trust you, David, who can I trust?"

"I'd say the same about Albie, but you're the one who needs to feel right about it. We're getting in pretty deep with him, looks like."

"I've decided to take the risk."

"That's good enough for me. Let me know when you get to the Strong Building. You going to try to put down inside the tower?"

"Not with this load. I'll keep the chopper as inconspicuous as I can so it won't be seen from the air."

"The most you'd have to worry about would be satellite shots, because no planes are flying low enough to shoot anything meaningful. But if you get unloaded and can determine before daybreak that the chopper can be housed way up inside there, you'd better do it."

"Roger."

"I'm unlocking everything in the place for you. I'd get in, get settled, and stay quiet and out of sight."

"We need some black spray paint."

"Can do. Where should I ship it?"

"Kankakee, I guess."

"You got it. Rayford? How is Tsion?"

"Chaim and Buck are the banged-up ones."

"But they're going to be all right, right?"

"Looks like it."

"Tsion is the one I worry about. We need him on-line and doing what he does best."

Rayford guessed he was halfway to the safe house.

"I hear that, David. I just hope we can transmit out of the new place like we could out of the old."

"Should be able to. When the day comes for Mac and Smitty and Annie and me to get out of here, we'll come and set up the greatest communications center you can imagine. Hey, you've got your laptop, right?"

"I had left it in Mount Prospect. I'll get back on-line in Chicago."

"Good, because I sent you a list I found, made by a woman named Viv Ivins, Carpathia's oldest confidante. It shows the ten kingdoms with their new names, but it also has a number assigned to each one. There has to be some significance, but I can't decipher it, at least not yet."

"You haven't put one of your fancy computer programs on it by now?"

"Soon, but I don't care what it takes or who figures it out. I just want to know what it means and whether there's any advantage to our knowing it."

"We'll take a shot at it. For now it's going to be great to be back together, all in one place, getting caught up with each other, getting acquainted better with the newcomers, and reestablishing some order."

"I'll know when you get in. I've got my cameras on."

With his computer set, David wanted to return his attention to finding Annie. There were a thousand reasons she might be hard to locate, but he'd rather not consider any of them. He stood and stretched, noticing that the TV picture had changed. The network had switched from a wide shot of the receiving trilogy of Leon, Viv, and Nick and now moved in on Nicolae.

He had stepped down a few rows and looked directly into the camera. In spite of himself, David could see why the man was so riveting. Besides the rugged, European handsomeness, he really sold the care and compassion. David knew he was insidious, but his smarminess didn't show.

The announcer said, "Ladies and gentlemen of the Global Community, your Supreme Potentate, His Excellency Nicolae Carpathia."

Nicolae took one step closer to the camera, forcing it to refocus. He looked directly into the lens.

"My dear subjects," he began. "We have, together, endured quite a week, have we not? I was deeply touched by the millions who made the effort to come to New Babylon for what turned out to be, gratefully, not my funeral. The outpouring of emotion was no less encouraging to me.

"As you know and as I have said, there remain small pockets of resistance to our cause of peace and harmony. There are even those who have made a career of saying the most hurtful, blasphemous, and false statements about me, using terms for me that no person would ever want to be called.

"I believe you will agree that I proved today who I am and who I am not. You will do well to follow your heads and your hearts and continue to follow me. You know what you saw, and your eyes do not lie. I am also eager to welcome into the one-world fold any former devotees of the radical fringe who have become convinced that I am not the enemy. On the contrary, I may be the very object of the devotion of their own religion, and I pray they will not close their minds to that possibility.

"In closing let me speak directly to the opposition. I have always, without rancor or acrimony, allowed divergent views. There are those among you, however, who have referred overtly to me personally as the Antichrist and this period of history as the Tribulation. You may take the following as my personal pledge:

"If you insist on continuing with your subversive attacks on my character and on the world harmony I have worked so hard to engender, the word *tribulation* will not begin to describe what is in store for you. If the last three and a half years are your idea of tribulation, wait until you endure the Great Tribulation."

EPILOGUE

"Woe to the inhabitants of the earth and the sea! For the devil has come down to you, having great wrath, because he knows that he has a short time."
    Revelation 12:12

ABOUT THE AUTHORS

Jerry B. Jenkins (www.jerryjenkins.com) is the writer of the Left Behind series. He is author of more than one hundred books, of which six have reached the *New York Times* best-seller list. Former vice president for publishing for the Moody Bible Institute of Chicago, he also served many years as editor of *Moody* magazine and is now Moody's writer-at-large.

His writing has appeared in publications as varied as *Reader's Digest, Parade,* in-flight magazines, and many Christian periodicals. He has written books in four genres: biography, marriage and family, fiction for children, and fiction for adults.

Jenkins's biographies include books with Hank Aaron, Bill Gaither, Luis Palau, Walter Payton, Orel Hershiser, Nolan Ryan, Brett Butler, and Billy Graham, among many others.

Six of his apocalyptic novels—*Left Behind, Tribulation Force, Nicolae, Soul Harvest, Apollyon,* and *Assassins*—have appeared on the Christian Booksellers Association's best-selling fiction list and the *Publishers Weekly* religion best-seller list. *Left Behind* was nominated for Book of the Year by the Evangelical Christian Publishers Association in 1997, 1998, and 1999.

As a marriage and family author and speaker, Jenkins has been a frequent guest on Dr. James Dobson's *Focus on the Family* radio program.

Jerry is also the writer of the nationally syndicated sports story comic strip *Gil Thorp,* distributed to newspapers across the United States by Tribune Media Services.

Jerry and his wife, Dianna, live in Colorado.

Limited speaking engagement information is available through speaking@jerryjenkins.com.

Dr. Tim LaHaye (www.timlahaye.com), who conceived the idea of fictionalizing an account of the Rapture and the Tribulation, is a noted author, minister, and nationally recognized speaker on Bible prophecy. He is the founder of both Tim LaHaye Ministries and The Pre-Trib Research Center. Presently Dr. LaHaye speaks at many of the major Bible prophecy conferences in the U.S. and Canada, where his nine current prophecy books are very popular.

Dr. LaHaye holds a doctor of ministry degree from Western Theological Seminary and a doctor of literature degree from Liberty University. For twenty-five years he pastored one of the nation's outstanding churches in San Diego, which grew to three locations. It was during that time that he founded two accredited Christian high schools, a Christian school system of ten schools, and Christian Heritage College.

Dr. LaHaye has written over forty books, with over 22 million copies in print in thirty-three languages. He has written books on a wide variety of subjects, such as family life, temperaments, and Bible prophecy. His current fiction works, written with Jerry B. Jenkins—*Left Behind, Tribulation Force, Nicolae, Soul Harvest, Apollyon,* and *Assassins*—have all reached number one on the Christian best-seller charts. Other works by Dr. LaHaye are *Spirit-Controlled Temperament; How to Be Happy Though Married; Revelation Unveiled; Understanding the Last Days; Rapture under Attack; Are We Living in the End Times?* and the youth fiction series Left Behind: The Kids.

He is the father of four grown children and grandfather of nine. Snow skiing, waterskiing, motorcycling, golfing, vacationing with family, and jogging are among his leisure activities.

THE FUTURE IS CLEAR

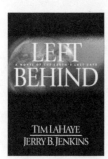

Left Behind
A novel of the earth's last days . . .
In one cataclysmic moment, millions around the world disappear. In the midst of global chaos, airline captain Rayford Steele must search for his family, for answers, for truth. As devastating as the disappearances have been, the darkest days lie ahead.

0-8423-2911-0 Hardcover
0-8423-2912-9 Softcover
0-8423-1675-2 Audio book

Tribulation Force
The continuing drama of those left behind . . .
Rayford Steele, Buck Williams, Bruce Barnes, and Chloe Steele band together to form the Tribulation Force. Their task is clear, and their goal nothing less than to stand and fight the enemies of God during the seven most chaotic years the planet will ever see.

0-8423-2913-7 Hardcover
0-8423-2921-8 Softcover
0-8423-1787-2 Audio book

Nicolae
The rise of Antichrist . . .
The seven-year tribulation period is nearing the end of its first quarter, when prophecy says "the wrath of the Lamb" will be poured out upon the earth. Rayford Steele has become the ears of the tribulation saints in the Carpathia regime. A dramatic all-night rescue run from Israel through the Sinai will hold you breathless to the end.

0-8423-2914-5 Hardcover
0-8423-2924-2 Softcover
0-8423-1788-0 Audio book

Soul Harvest
The world takes sides . . .
As the world hurtles toward the Trumpet Judgments and the great soul harvest prophesied in Scripture, Rayford Steele and Buck Williams begin searching for their loved ones from different corners of the world. *Soul Harvest* takes you from Iraq to America, from six miles in the air to underground shelters, from desert sand to the bottom of the Tigris River, from hope to devastation and back again—all in a quest for truth and life.

0-8423-2915-3 Hardcover
0-8423-2925-0 Softcover
0-8423-5175-2 Audio book

Apollyon
The Destroyer is unleashed . . .
In this acclaimed *New York Times* best-seller, Apollyon, the Destroyer, leads the plague of demon locusts as they torture the unsaved. Meanwhile, despite growing threats from Antichrist, the Tribulation Force gathers in Israel for the Conference of Witnesses.

0-8423-2916-1 Hardcover
0-8423-2926-9 Softcover
0-8423-1933-6 Audio book

Assassins
Assignment: Jerusalem, Target: Antichrist
As a horde of 200 million demonic horsemen slays a third of the world's population, the Tribulation Force prepares for a future as fugitives. History and prophecy collide in Jerusalem for the most explosive episode yet of the continuing drama of those left behind.

0-8423-2920-X Hardcover
0-8423-2927-7 Softcover (available summer 2000)
0-8423-1934-4 Audio book

The Indwelling
The Beast takes possession . . .
It's the midpoint of the seven-year Tribulation. As the world mourns the death of a renowned man, the Tribulation Force faces its most dangerous challenges yet. Time and eternity seem suspended, and the destiny of mankind hangs in the balance.

0-8423-2928-5 Hardcover
0-8423-2929-3 Softcover (available winter 2001)
0-8423-1935-2 Audio book

Watch for book 8 in this best-selling series to arrive fall 2000

Left Behind: The Kids

Four teens are left behind after the Rapture and band together to fight Satan's forces in this series for ten- to fourteen-year-olds.

#1 *The Vanishings* 0-8423-2193-4
#2 *Second Chance* 0-8423-2194-2
#3 *Through the Flames* 0-8423-2195-0
#4 *Facing the Future* 0-8423-2196-9
#5 *Nicolae High* 0-8423-4325-3
#6 *The Underground* 0-8423-4326-1
#7 *Busted!* 0-8423-4327-X
#8 *Death Strike* 0-8423-4328-8

Watch for the next Left Behind: The Kids books, available summer 2000

Have You Been Left Behind?

Based on the video that New Hope Village Church's pastor Vernon Billings created for those left behind after the Rapture. This video explains what happened and what the viewer can do now.

0-8423-5196-5 Video

An Experience in Sound and Drama

Dramatic broadcast performances of the first four books in the best-selling Left Behind series. Original music, sound effects, and professional actors make the action come alive. Experience the heart-stopping action and suspense of the end times for yourself. . . . Twelve half-hour episodes, on four CDs or three cassettes, for each title.

0-8423-5146-9 *Left Behind: An Experience in Sound and Drama* CD
0-8423-5181-7 *Left Behind: An Experience in Sound and Drama* cassette
0-8423-3584-6 *Tribulation Force: An Experience in Sound and Drama* CD
0-8423-3583-8 *Tribulation Force: An Experience in Sound and Drama* cassette
0-8423-3663-X *Nicolae: An Experience in Sound and Drama* CD
0-8423-3662-1 *Nicolae: An Experience in Sound and Drama* cassette
0-8423-3986-8 *Soul Harvest: An Experience in Sound and Drama* CD
       (available fall 2000)
0-8423-3985-X *Soul Harvest: An Experience in Sound and Drama* cassette
       (available fall 2000)

Discover the latest about the Left Behind series
and interact with other readers at **www.leftbehind.com**